The Best
AMERICAN
SHORT
STORIES
1998

GUEST EDITORS OF
THE BEST AMERICAN SHORT STORIES

The Best
AMERICAN
SHORT
STORIES
1998

Selected from
U.S. and Canadian Magazines
by GARRISON KEILLOR
with KATRINA KENISON

With an Introduction by Garrison Keillor

HOUGHTON MIFFLIN COMPANY
BOSTON · NEW YORK   1998

ISSN 0067-6233
ISBN 0-395-87515-3
ISBN 0-395-87514-5 (PBK.)

Printed in the United States of America

QUM 10 9 8 7 6 5 4 3 2 1

"Appetites" by Kathryn Chetkovich. First published in *ZYZZYVA*. Copyright © 1998 by Kathryn Chetkovich. Reprinted by permission of University of Iowa Press.

"The Blue Devils of Blue River Avenue" by Poe Ballantine. First published in *The Sun*. Copyright © 1997 by Poe Ballantine. Reprinted by permission of the author.

"Body Language" by Diane Schoemperlen. First published in *Story*. Copyright © 1998 by Diane Schoemperlen. Reprinted from the collection *Forms of Devotion*, by permission of Viking Penguin, a division of Penguin Putnam Inc., and HarperCollins Publishers Limited.

"Chance" by Edith Pearlman. First published in *The Antioch Review*. Copyright © 1997 by Edith Pearlman. Reprinted by permission of the author.

"Cosmopolitan" by Akhil Sharma. First published in *The Atlantic Monthly*. Copyright © 1997 by Akhil Sharma. Reprinted by permission of the author.

"Elvis Has Left the Building" by Carol Anshaw. First published in *Story*. Copyright © 1997 by Carol Anshaw. Reprinted by permission of the author.

"Every Night for a Thousand Years" by Chris Adrian. First published in *The New Yorker*. Copyright © 1997 by Chris Adrian. Reprinted by permission of the author.

"Flower Children" by Maxine Swann. First published in *Ploughshares*. Copyright © 1997 by Maxine Swann. Reprinted by permission of the author.

"Glory Goes and Gets Some" by Emily Carter. First published in *Open City*. Copyright © 1997 by Emily Carter. Reprinted by permission of the author.

"The Half-Skinned Steer" by Annie Proulx. First published in *The Atlantic Monthly*. Copyright © 1997 by Dead Line Ltd. Reprinted by permission of E. Annie Proulx, President, Dead Line Ltd.

"Morphine" by Doran Larson. First published in *Virginia Quarterly Review*. Copyright © 1997 by Doran Larson. Reprinted by permission of the author.

Contents

Foreword

MY SECOND-GRADE SON, already an avid reader, has been living in Narnia for weeks now. He has one book going on his own; we read chapters from another aloud at bedtime. He is challenged and delighted by C. S. Lewis's language and imagery; for the first time, a flashlight shines from under the bedclothes. But on one recent night *Prince Caspian* was set aside in favor of a storybook we used to read together when he was three. Afterward, he gave a deep, nostalgic sigh. "I remember when we first read that book, a long time ago," he said. "Even though I'm old now, I still like it. It reminds me of being young."

When a story speaks deeply to us, we tend to remember not only the details of the story itself, but also the circumstances in which we first encountered it; the experience is all of a piece — our own time, place, and mood are interwoven somehow with the events and characters of the story. It is a testament to the power of narrative that words on a page can actually affect and color our own experience of the world in a given moment; indeed, they can transport us back to psychological landscapes we wish to revisit. My son, suddenly sensing time passing away — and perhaps even wary of things to come — was carried back to innocence by a story. Of course, it carried me back, too — to the early years of my son's life, and further, all the way to August nights of my own childhood, when my mother had read the very same tattered storybook to me.

In an eloquent essay published last year in the *Georgia Review*, entitled "The Power of Stories," Scott Russell Sanders writes, "Stories create community. They link teller to listeners, and listeners to one another. This is obviously so when speaker and audience share the same space, as humans have done for all but the last few centuries of our million-year history, gathered around fires or huddled in huts; but it is equally if less obviously so in our literate age, when we encounter more of our stories in solitude, on page or screen. When two people discover they have both read *Don Quixote,* they immediately share a piece of history. . . . Strangers who discover their mutual devotion to fairy tales or gangster movies or soap operas or Shakespeare's plays become thereby less strange to one another."

Since the early years of this century, readers and contributors to *The Best American Short Stories* have shared, if not a physical space, then a literary one, in the pages of these volumes. Most of the contributors were first readers of these books; for many, publication in *Best American* is the culmination of a journey that began many years ago, with a volume read and marveled at. And readers are often first introduced in these pages to new writers — writers who more often than not go on to become well-known practitioners of the art. Over time, here, "strangers become less strange to one another."

This year, reading "blind," with the authors' names blacked out on each story, guest editor Garrison Keillor joked that he had no way of knowing whether he was responding "to Saul Bellow or Wally Ballou." In fact, he displayed an uncanny eye for new talent and fresh sensibility. We are grateful to him for the many hours he devoted to the stories of 1997, and for a collection that reflects his sense of humor, his curiosity about the human condition, and his own high standards. Readers who turn to *The Best American Short Stories* to discover new writers just rounding the curve will rejoice in this volume, and in twenty stories that have only diversity and irrefutable quality in common. It is my hunch that this year's "strangers" will become another year's esteemed masters. May these stories forge links between us all, listeners and tellers alike, and may they transport you into other lives, other places, other times — and in so doing, perhaps broaden the horizons of your own.

The stories chosen for this anthology were originally published in magazines issued between January 1997 and January 1998. The qualifications for selection are (1) original publication in nationally distributed American or Canadian periodicals; (2) publication in English by writers who are American or Canadian, or who have made the United States or Canada their home; (3) original publication as short stories (excerpts of novels are not knowingly considered). A list of magazines consulted for this volume appears at the back of the book. Editors who wish their short fiction to be considered for next year's edition should send their publications to Katrina Kenison, c/o The Best American Short Stories, Houghton Mifflin Company, 222 Berkeley Street, Boston, MA 02116.

K.K.

Introduction

I LOVE the stories in this collection, selected from a pile of a hundred and twenty which I read blind, not knowing who wrote them, and judged simply by whether they pulled me through to the end and with what force and pleasure and surprise. These are the stories I read straight through without ever rolling my eyes, without ever saying, *Oh, give me a break,* and when I was done, I wrote *Yes* at the top in ink and set the story aside to read again.

Back when I was an English major, I could read fiction and be thinking up a term paper at the same time ("Updike's verticalization of moral peril parallels the medieval cosmology of mystical painting"), but I don't read for credit anymore, only to amuse myself and for edification and for the companionship, hoping to hear something true about somebody's life. I am a crankier reader than when I was in school, and I get disappointed by stuff in which there's nobody home, just Really Fine Writing about somebody's vague unhappiness and unease. But if a story comes along that succeeds in amazing me, I am incredulous and grateful. Each of these twenty stories surprised and delighted me. Each is a story I'd gladly read out loud to anyone who wanted to be read to. They're about being a child, finding a lover, raising children, and getting old — your basic age-old themes.

It's peculiar to read stories that don't have the name of the author attached. (The names are blacked out to prevent me, a democrat from the prairies, from excluding famous authors, and indeed several big elephants did sneak in here under cover of darkness.) You start reading a story with no clues as to the author's gender or race or age, which is liberating — for one thing, you don't need to think about achieving racial or gender balance — and which strips the story of any prior claims to your loyalty. You simply wade into it, and when a story begins

> Tuesday was about typical. My four daughters — not one of them married, you understand — brought over their kids, one each, and explained to my wife how much fun she was going to have looking after them again. But Tuesday was her day to go to the casino, so guess who got to tend the four babies. My oldest daughter also brought over a bed rail that the end broke off of. She wanted me to weld it. Now, what the hell you can do in a bed that'll cause the end of a iron rail to break off is beyond me . . .

you pay attention to it and don't care if it's by Louis Auchincloss or Louis L'Amour or Louise Erdrich, it's a sweet little tale.

I am a good judge, I don't have anything to prove, and I'll listen to anybody, and when I come on a great line like "She looked like someone whose job, once you're dead, is to introduce you to God," or "He possessed that rare combination of congeniality and the ability to beat you up," it makes me happy. But the crucial question for me, always, is the author's truthfulness, just as it is for any reader.

People love stories, especially truthful ones, and when there's a good one in the paper, people may repeat it to you all day long. Such stories are rare, of course, and most days the paper is full of ephemera and effluvium, pious claptrap and paid flattery and little acorns falling from the sky and the dithering of legislative bodies and the gentle lowing of sacred cows, and when it says "Continued on page 4" you don't bother to make the jump. But then one morning you get a single solid account of a terrible crime, or a story about carryings-on in high places, and you can't put it down. As I write, the American people are in their third month of near-steady enthrallment by the story of the attractive young woman who for a period of time went tripping in and out of the White House, and later, when the door was closed, felt cheated and poured out her grief and anger to a close friend, who happened to be carrying a concealed tape recorder. This story has absorbed the interest of the American people in ways that stories about the federal budget do not. Likewise the old anecdote about Mr. Gingrich's having a snit over not getting a front seat on an airplane, which jibed with his image as a pompous blowhard. The man has struggled to regain his footing ever since.

Overweening pride, lust, natural disaster, sheer avarice, all varieties of personal weirdness, terrible things done by polite and decent people — we will always want to hear about these things. A man once stopped me on the street in Portland, Oregon, grinning, and handed me a newspaper story, "Minnesota Man Denies Having Sex with Cows," which obviously had given the Oregon man a good deal of pleasure. I told him that in Minnesota it's not considered newsworthy if someone denies bestiality but that apparently this was not so in Oregon. "If I'd known it was going to offend you," he said glumly, "I wouldn't have shown it to you."

It was a story about one of those bitter feuds that occur sometimes between neighbors in the country. Sometimes, over the years, people just gradually get on each other's nerves. In this case, a woman had accused her neighbor of unnatural acts involving her cows, and he denied it, though he admitted to having thrown clods of dirt at her dog once. The feud was of many years' standing, and the parties were coy about who started it or what it was about. Reading the story, you just knew that the paper had left out all the best parts and only given you a glimpse of a story, not the story itself.

Newspapers feign innocence about human nature, as in the recent story about a spate of suicides among teenagers in Pierre, South Dakota, in which the reporter expressed incredulity that young people who appeared to be happy and busy could one day go into a room and close the door and blow their brains out.

Fiction has never doubted such things. In "Glory Goes and Gets Some," Glory says, "Everyone is very busy denying the last time they were lonely, but trust me, it happens. It isn't just being a solo act, though that contributes; I know women and men who stand in their back yards, safe in the bosom of their family, at the height of their careers, and stare up into the old reliable silver-maple tree, mentally testing its capacity to hold their weight."

People hope for some truthfulness among their friends. Isn't this why, after dinner, we troop into the living room for coffee and sit and talk? More and more, though, when friends tell stories, they tend to sound like TV talk-show guests or politicians, telling stories as self-justification — What Was Done to Poor Me — which is bor-

ing boring boring. Saint James says in his epistle that we are to
confess our sins to each other, which is the Christian rationale for
storytelling, but mostly people seem to want to spin everything
their way, explain the origins of their bad behavior, show that their
disloyalty and ungenerousness stem from the dirt that was done to
them.

And so people come to the house of fiction, hoping to hear the
truth.

In the early eighteenth century, when the novel was young, people read *Robinson Crusoe* and thought it must be a true account, and
so did I when I read it in 1953. I was eleven. I put my nose into that
book and washed ashore on that island and walked up the beach
and it was all quite real, and therefore truthful. I have landed on a
good many fictional beaches since then, and when I got an inkling
that the author of the island was trifling with me, I jumped right
back in the boat and rowed back to the ship. But when I read "I was
born on the grounds of the Mount Mohonk Hospital for the Insane, where my father was chief of psychiatry, and because of this I
grew accustomed to the sounds of misery before I went to sleep at
night," I trust the story by the very cadence of it, trust it more than
I trust most of what people tell me personally about how they have
never been so completely happy as they are now.

People want stories to be real. Reality is what we crave, as
Thoreau said. If you tell a story and people like it, they don't com-
pliment you on your narrative style, they say, "Is that true?" That is
the highest praise for a writer, that he or she is truthful. People
don't like it if you use a story merely to express your feelings, if you
start out with real Salvation Army furniture in a one-bedroom cin-
derblock apartment overlooking an asphalt parking lot in south
Minneapolis and a Persian cat lying on the Sunday comics spread
out on the table as a snowstorm rages outside and your lover is
stranded in Chicago and Chopin is on the stereo and you suddenly
decide to do a terrible dishonest thing and open your lover's
dresser drawer and take out the shoebox that contains her old
letters and you read one from her previous lover, a single page,
typed, in which he recalls a month with her in northern California,
and your face burns with jealousy — people don't like it if this tale
then turns into an essay and you go to the window and grieve in
some high-falutin literary way about the impossibility of love and

wind up with a set-piece description of the winter landscape. You can publish this story and your friends will tell you they liked it, but anybody who reads it will stop midway and think, *Oh, get out of my face,* and throw it aside.

A story that carries its lesson under its arm is immediately distrusted. Thus we have people who believe, against vast evidence, that the Holocaust is fiction, because it has been told to them as a moral fable. The story of Anne Frank, in contrast, is palpably true for its beautiful ordinariness. We are convinced to believe in it not because Anne thinks luminous thoughts ("In spite of everything, I still believe that people are really good at heart") but because she gets the story down in detail. She sits in her room and thinks about movie stars and royalty and despises the quarrelsome, self-pitying Mrs. Van Daan and daydreams about the thrill of going to the attic with Peter and talking with him and kissing. We read on and on about the ordinary lives of people in desperate circumstances. One October night in 1942, we learn, these Jews in hiding in Amsterdam enjoy the joke "What makes 999 ticks followed by one tock? A millipede with a clubfoot," and a great discovery dawns on us: that the fourteen-year-old Anne Frank is not keeping this diary as a testament against hatred and darkness, that it is simply a writer's notebook; the girl hopes to be a novelist. She writes: "Just imagine how interesting it would be if I were to publish a romance of the 'Secret Annexe.' The title alone would be enough to make people think it was a detective story. But, seriously, it would be quite funny ten years after the war if we Jews were to tell how we lived and what we ate and talked about here."

It was the Nazis who made Anne Frank a martyr and a symbol; she herself would much rather have been a satirist. If only she had survived the prison camp, she might have come out with a novel in 1955 with a passionate love scene between a girl and a boy in an attic full of moonlight, their lips pressed close, her hand on his waist, his hand under her skirt, and in the room below, adult listening for the police at the door and hearing only the lovers' sighs from upstairs. She didn't aim to be a saint; she wanted to write stories in which real people ate the pot roast and boiled potatoes and talked about childhood, lovers, children, loneliness, and old age.

GARRISON KEILLOR

The Best
AMERICAN
SHORT
STORIES
1998

KATHRYN CHETKOVICH

Appetites

FROM ZYZZYVA

I HAD BEEN sleeping on a friend's floor for a week. I was working nights, proofreading at a law firm, so I had the quiet, dusty apartment to myself most of the day. Next door were three children who all seemed to be at the loudest possible age, their voices alive with the sound of killing each other. After I got up, I would wander the empty rooms, looking in the refrigerator, the medicine chest, the mirror. I would put on a CD and not hear a single song. I would turn on the television and walk in the other room.

I sat down on the couch with the free weekly paper and started working my way through the short list of studios. When I satisfied myself there was nothing there I could afford, I moved to the next column over, the depressingly enthusiastic ads for shares.

> *2 wmn seek third for 3-bdrm apt.*
> *Clean, sunny, safe. Hdwd flrs.*

I circled this one.

I got the machine when I called, but halfway into the message a woman broke in with a voice that sounded like an actress playing a normal person on TV. The room had been rented, she told me, but the person who was all lined up to take it had changed her mind and moved in with her boyfriend at the last minute.

I went by that afternoon. I was buzzed in, and when I got to the third floor a door opened to reveal the most attractive woman I had ever seen. She had a look that made you want to take up painting: red hair, green eyes, and incredible pale, freckled skin. She looked like someone whose job, once you're dead, is to introduce you to God.

I would not have thought a woman who looked like that would ever have to advertise for anything, especially not for a roommate.

"Amanda? I'm Faith." She held out her hand. As I took it, I felt myself being pulled out of the leaky lifeboat I had been paddling around in for the last few weeks. I knew that life near this woman, if I could arrange it, would be different and better. I was prepared to give up whatever was asked of me to make that happen.

"Come in, come in," Faith said, with the becoming touch of an eagerness to please. "Let me show you the place."

Carla, the other roommate, appeared from somewhere, and the three of us walked through a series of clean, airy rooms. I hardly looked at them. When we got to the room that would be mine, I tried to show some discriminating interest by taking note of the placement of the outlets.

"Do you have a lot of things to plug in?" Carla asked.

"No, not at all," I said. "But it's nice to have, you know, options."

"Of course it is," Faith said. "Hey, can I get you something to drink? Water? Or I think we may have a beer."

"Water would be great," I said, avoiding the selfish, alcoholic temptation to take the last, possibly nonexistent, beer.

Carla led me back to the living room and motioned me toward one of those big foam couches that you can pick up and carry under one arm. Across from it were a couple of candy-colored director's chairs that sprang like Easter flowers out of the thick green rug. The only piece of furniture in the whole place that could not be moved by a couple of women with a hatchback was a baby grand piano, gleaming like a casket.

Carla saw me looking around. "Do you have a lot of furniture?"

I waved my hand in what I hoped was a pleasantly incomprehensible way. "Oh," I said, "not really. Hardly any, actually. I'm sort of between furniture at the moment."

Faith came in with three tall glasses of water, a slice of lemon floating in each. The ice tinkled cheerfully as she handed the glasses around.

Carla asked if I had a boyfriend or anyone who might be visiting regularly. I had been looking at a print on the wall across from me — three well-dressed men and a naked woman at a picnic — so I said, "Actually, my boyfriend is going to Europe for a while."

"By himself?" Faith said. Her nostrils flexed briefly. She ran a hand up and down her arm.

"He's wanted to go for a long time and I could never afford it, so we kind of compromised," I said. "He's going and I'm moving."

"I've made compromises like that," Carla said, and I took my first real look at her face. We didn't really look alike, but you'd describe us with the same words on a driver's license: brown, brown, corrective lenses.

There was a little more talk about eating habits and schedules and problems we'd had with roommates in the past — the traditional trick question I thought I handled well by saying I'd always had good luck just talking things out.

My eyes kept drifting over to the piano, which seemed to move closer when I looked away.

"That's mine," Carla said finally. "Do you play?"

I thought this might be the bond with her I needed. "Oh, sure," I said. "Well, you know, a little *Für Elise,* a little boogie-woogie. What about you?"

"I was supposed to be a concert pianist," she said. "From the time I was five."

"Parental expectations. Tell me about it." Carla and Faith waited for me to betray some secret to them. "I could never figure out what mine wanted." The inadequacy of this remark hung there while I tried to think of something else. "Boy," I said finally, holding my glass up and rattling the ice cubes, "this water really hits the spot."

Fortunately, Carla seemed willing to let it go at that. She stared at the piano's feet, as though she couldn't bring herself to look it in the keys. "When something's that big a part of your life, it's hard to know who you are without it," she said.

Before I could stop it, a home movie appeared on the screen of my mind. I was pulling up at the emergency-room entrance, and the windshield wipers were slapping the rain back and forth. It was Billy's right arm that I'd broken, so I had to walk around the car, across the path of the headlights, and open the door for him. I helped him out, and then I stood there and watched him move lopsidedly toward the building. When he got close, the big doors swung open like a grocery store and invited him in. For all I knew, he was still in there, though I knew he wasn't.

"Amen to that," I said.

Carla looked at me and nodded.

When I got back from work that night, there was a message from Faith. The room was mine if I wanted it.

I knew, of course, that there were women for whom men did their little dance. But I had never actually seen it up close before Faith. Men were always giving her things — cabs, drinks, their cards. She seemed to know how to move through the world saying yes. She had a job, doing PR for a local television station, but her real vocation seemed to be reminding others what beauty God hath wrought.

In the world I came from, landlords were not people who cared, but now that I was sharing an apartment with Faith our tub was getting recaulked, we had screens on all the windows, we were not expected to just live with that funny gas smell. In my old world, if you told your landlord that you'd seen signs of mice under the sink and heard something skittering across the floor at night, he would have asked what you thought he looked like, an exterminator? But Wayne, our landlord's son, said he wanted to come by and "have a look at the problem."

I saw him out my bedroom window a few days later, walking toward the building. He had a paper bag with him; he folded over the top of it and clamped it between his teeth while he tucked in his shirt.

As I walked over to the door to let him in, I caught sight of myself in the mirror and thought of something my mother used to say: *You have such a pretty face, it seems a shame not to do more with it.*

"Hey," Wayne said when I opened the door.

"Hey."

He took a deep breath that seemed to signal a combination of relief and disappointment that Faith had not answered the door in a black-lace teddy after all.

"I take it you ladies are having rodent problems," he said, making it sound like an embarrassing feminine condition. He was standing just inside the doorway, passing the paper bag from one hand to the other, looking around the room. He had one of those little beards under his lower lip that gave you the impression that the phone must have rung while he was shaving.

"It's nothing we couldn't have handled on our own," I said. "But as long as you're here. Again."

Just then Faith's bedroom door opened and several million pheromones swarmed into the room. "Wayne, hi," she said. She didn't walk over. She just leaned against the door frame, arms crossed. Even from the other side of the room I could make out the jut of her collarbone. Her loose pullover was pitched to one side like a ship in a storm. "I think we must be talking rats here," she said. "I'm not kidding, you should hear these guys."

"Not that we know for sure they're *guys*," I put in, idiotically.

Wayne stood there, nodding.

Faith stepped over and pointed at the bag. "What's in here? Is that for us?" I could still see the half-moon mark of Wayne's teeth along the top of the fold.

He opened the bag and pulled out a box of poison. "We've had a lot of success with this particular product." He cleared his throat. "In our various properties, I mean."

"Oh, are all your various properties rat-infested?" I asked, but my question died without an answer, because as I was reaching for the box, Faith took Wayne's arm just above the elbow and thanked him for coming. I recognized the gesture when I saw it: how to touch a man who has not touched you first.

A few days later, the three of us were in the bathroom together, arguing about the mice. Carla was taking one of what I thought of as her wartime showers — a lukewarm spray with the water pressure turned low enough to talk over.

I was controlling the conversation with the hair dryer. "Poison is mean and slow," I said. "You know how it works, don't you? They die of thirst." I turned the dryer on, then flipped it off to say something else. "It's like death by potato chips."

"I could think of worse ways to go," Faith said. She was wrapped in a towel, standing on one leg with the other one propped in the sink, shaving. Her long pale leg looked new, and so smooth I couldn't tell where her razor — a small, heavy man's model — had already been and where it was headed. I bent over at the waist and aimed for my roots.

By the time I straightened up, the shower had gone silent. "Traps, then," Carla said from behind the curtain. "And since you're the one who's morally opposed to poison, Amanda, you can set them."

Carla was becoming the big sister I was always glad I never had.

"No way," Faith said. "No fucking way am I waking up to a dead rat."

"We don't know they're rats," I said, though I was certainly no fan of the trap approach either.

"We don't know they're not."

"O.K. Poison, then," Carla said. She pulled the curtain aside and our eyes met in the mirror. She was a runner, and she had that runner's body that even naked seems somehow dressed. Her joints were the most prominent thing about her.

"I'm sure there's another alternative," I said. I turned and waved the dryer in her direction. "And if you weren't so gung ho about seeing them eat themselves to death, maybe we could figure out what it is."

Someone had been taking a fork to my peanut butter — the telltale crosshatch of grooves was there whenever I unscrewed the lid — and I was pretty sure it was Carla, whose own refrigerator shelves were dominated by vegetables in plastic bags and fat-free salad dressings.

"Gung ho?" Faith murmured. She shaved like a blind person, following the path of the razor with her free hand, stroking her own leg.

Carla, still naked, put her hands on her hips, daring me. "Amanda, they are not just going to go away."

"I didn't say they would. I said we should consider all our options."

"You don't care," Carla said. "You'll be out of here the minute Billy gets back." This had been Carla's suspicion since I had first arrived, in a cab, all my stuff in grocery bags.

Next to me Faith switched legs, pulling the right one down from the sink and propping the left one in its place. Suddenly her towel slid apart and I caught a glimpse of her obviously manicured pubic hair. It flashed like a rune, a sign of all we didn't know and would not even guess about each other, and then it was gone.

"You know, this Billy thing," I started to say, but saying the words out loud was a little like going all the way in the lake after you've been standing there up to your knees. You thought you were used to it, but you're not.

And then, for the first time, it occurred to me that even though I had told no one, he might have.

"Oh, Mandy," Faith said, "maybe it's time to just forget about him." She ran her hand down my arm and her touch was cool. "What about that new guy downstairs? He's cute."

"What guy?" I said, but I knew she meant Clark, the lawyer who lived under us. We had run into each other at a local café a few days before and had ended up walking home together, talking about jazz and football — subjects I could fake my way through if the trip was short. "You mean the guy downstairs? I don't think so."

"Amanda, when you were little and your dog died, didn't your parents ever take you to the pound to pick out a new one?"

"Faith, Billy's not dead!" Carla pointed out, and for a moment I thought she knew something I didn't.

"He might as well be." Faith swished her razor around in the sink water. "It's not like you've heard from him."

"Since when are you monitoring my mail?"

"Well, *have* you?"

"Never mind," I said.

"Actually," Faith said, "I ran into him the other day and we started talking and I invited him up for dinner sometime."

"You ran into *Billy*?" Of course, I suddenly thought, they would have met, in one of those clubs they both would have gone to. Making conversation at the bar, a fleck of lipstick on her teeth, his arm in a cast.

"How could I run into Billy if he's in Europe somewhere?" Faith gave me a little smile that made me cinch my robe tighter around my waist. "I ran into *Clark*, downstairs by the mailboxes."

"Faith, if you're interested in him, why don't you just *say* so?" I could hear my voice stamping its little foot.

"Say what? God, Mandy, I told you. I was thinking of him for *you*."

"Did it ever occur to you what *he* might be thinking? I doubt it was *Here's an incredibly attractive girl in a short skirt coming on to me, I wonder what her roommate is like.*"

"I was *not* wearing a short skirt."

"Never mind."

"Mandy." Faith waited for me to look at her. Her eyes were the color of moss, of sea-washed glass, of the woods in children's books. "You think being pretty is everything. Believe me, it's not."

Carla, who I had forgotten was even in the room, cleared her throat. "Oh, right," she said.

"What?" Faith said.

"Nothing."

In the mirror I watched Carla oil her arms, touching herself the way a nurse would. I recognized something in her then that I wished I hadn't.

Faith rinsed and dried her leg, then straightened and stretched, her shoulder blades lifting like wings. "Nobody go anywhere," she said, and left the room.

Carla's lotion made the intimate, sucking sound of an animal eating. For a moment it was quiet except for that, and then suddenly a burst of sweet, sad piano music jumped through the floor.

"Listen," Faith called from her room. "Isn't that Chopin he's got on?"

It was a mystery to me how she knew some of the things she knew.

"I've always loved this nocturne," Carla said. She went motionless, a coin of lotion in her upturned hand. She was leaning forward, straining to hear.

I sometimes walked by Carla's room at night and saw her reading sheet music in bed, her fingers quivering as her eyes moved down the page. It reminded me of how my father, after he quit smoking, used to sit at his desk holding an unlit cigar.

Just then Faith appeared in a short black beaded dress that was like a question to which her legs were the answer. She stood in the doorway, the music drifting up around her like smoke.

I wish I could say that the envy I felt was no stronger than what I feel around people who can speak Chinese or understand physics. I wish I could say that any man who would love me for looking like that was not a man I wanted to love.

"How nice!" I said. "Going ice skating?"

"Faith, that is absolutely darling," Carla said. "Can I ask? How much?"

"Oh, I'm not buying it, I'm borrowing it." Until I met Faith, it had never occurred to me that you could actually wear something and then return it. "Think of department stores as huge lending libraries," she said to me once. "Does that make it any easier?"

"So, what the hell," Carla said. She had her towel wrapped around her waist like some old man at a sauna, and her nipples pointed inward in a kind of pigeon-toed stance. "Are we inviting him over for dinner, or what?"

Clark came for dinner that Saturday night. I made spanakopita, Carla assembled a kind of Mondrian salad, everything cut into same-size cubes, and Faith picked up an extravagant cake from the bakery down the street. She had gotten it practically for free, because whoever'd ordered it hadn't picked it up. WAY TO GO, MARIE! was iced in spidery script across the top.

Clark showed up in a tie, carrying a bottle of champagne and a small wire cage. "From what Faith said the other day, I thought you could use one of these," he said. "It's one of those traps that lets you catch the mouse without killing it."

"That is *so* great!" Faith said.

"Then what do we do with it?" I said.

"Then you take it somewhere and release it."

"Clark, we live in the city," I said. "Where are we going to release it?"

Faith put her hand on my shoulder. "Amanda, mice *love* the city. There's plenty of places they can go."

Clark showed Carla how to set the trap. They loaded it with a hunk of my peanut butter and stuck it in the dark pantry off the kitchen. I popped the champagne and began pouring.

Faith led Clark on a quick tour of the apartment, and Carla and I, champagne glasses in hand, tagged along. It felt like parents' night at boarding school. In Faith's room a scarf was draped over a lamp; necklaces hung over the sides of her dresser mirror. Carla's room looked like it had been decorated by nuns.

I still didn't even have a bedspread, but Clark was clearly raised right. "Nice blanket," he said when he stuck his head into my room.

Long after dinner, we were still at the table, peeling the labels off the champagne and wine bottles and playing with the melted candle wax. Clark worked over the wire champagne top with one of the attachments on his complicated pocketknife.

"There," he said, setting a tiny ice-cream-parlor chair on the table.

"Show us how to do that!" Faith cried.

"Only if you show me something."

One of the things I admired about Faith was that she always gave a man only what he actually asked for. "Watch this," she said, and twisted her napkin a few times until a swan appeared, a little triangle of cloth folded over as the head.

"It takes a woman to pull that off," Clark said.

"How about this?" Carla put her fingers to her mouth and let out the clearest, loudest whistle I had ever heard. "Can you do that?"

"Mandy," Faith said, "what can you do?"

I looked at them, the women I lived with, who hardly knew me, and the stranger I wanted to impress. "I was state yo-yo champ when I was a kid," I said. I had no idea where such a lie had come from.

"You never told us that!"

"Oh, the things I haven't told you." And then it occurred to me that I might be able to pass the truth, like a painful kidney stone, through this stream of inconsequential lies. "I can make ink from pyracantha berries. I know the secret to a really excellent pie crust. I could tell you how to get your bearings if you're lost at night."

I felt them looking at me, half smiling, confused. I was almost home. "I sent a man to the hospital once."

"Well," Faith said, "you're my choice for desert island companion."

"Was that by accident?" Carla said. "The man, I mean?"

Aren't most things? I had certainly not intended to find another woman's bracelet on the rug by my side of the bed, and I had not expected to sit on that news until a night when Billy and I had both been drinking.

Billy only made things worse that night — first by lying and then by telling the truth. I didn't mean to do what I did, but I must have known that he would not hit me back. After I punched him, he put out his arm to calm me. I felt no fear. I pushed him away, and when that did not satisfy me, I reached for him. I took his arm and yanked and twisted it as hard as I could.

"More by mistake than by accident," I said.

Carla nodded. My answer seemed enough for her.

Somehow the conversation moved on, and eventually we all ended up in the green playground of the living room with slices of Marie's cake. Whatever her mysterious accomplishment — job or house or husband or baby — we hoped it would revolutionize her life.

Then, for the first time since I had lived there, without warning or announcement, Carla walked over to her piano. As she got near, she put out her hand to stroke it, like someone steadying a nervous horse. Then she sat down and lifted the lid, exposing the keys. For a while she just sat there looking at thcm. "This feels strange," she said. I could see that her fingers were trembling, but also that she had forgotten we were even there.

She began to play, finally, a piece of music I had never heard before. It was an achingly delicate song, not so much music as air, silence outlined by a few notes.

It struck me then that Carla had a gift that had brought her pain simply because it was not a bigger gift, and in my woozy, naked state I felt I had found a key — a key I have found again and lost, found and lost, a hundred times since.

We sat there listening to Carla play. In the pantry I heard a trap door fall. A mouse had been caught, alive. It would be our task to find a safe, hospitable place to let it go.

The Blue Devils
of Blue River Avenue

FROM THE SUN

Every Night and every Morn
Some to Misery are Born;
Every Morn and every Night,
Some are born to Sweet Delight;
Some are born to Sweet Delight,
Some are born to Endless Night.

— WILLIAM BLAKE

OUR FIRST HOUSE, in the autumn of 1963, was a small, mustard-colored tract home in the older working-class suburbs of northeast San Diego. Before that we'd rented. My father had been a mailman, but now he was a schoolteacher. There was nothing on the other side of our street but a mountain and a few cows. Around the corner was a Jack-in-the-Box, where you could talk to the clown and get a hamburger for fifteen cents. They got rid of the clown eventually. For a while you could get deep-fried jumbo shrimp in tissue paper with fries; fried chicken, too, almond brown with miles of crust. It was years before I figured out the secret sauce on the hamburgers was Thousand Island dressing. Behind the Jack-in-the-Box was a Thriftimart with a colossal red neon *T* that burned in the sky twenty-four hours a day. It was like a crucifix, a giant symbol of grocery-store truth flaming against the mountain. People who came to visit my parents would be guided by the giant red neon *T.* About ten years later, Safeway bought the store and took down the *T,* but the Jack-in-the-Box is still there. The cows are all gone: we ordered them through the clown and ate them with Thousand Island dressing.

Our house had yellow cupboard doors and a leaky fireplace and a thin brown carpet. The living room was all windows with a sliding glass door at the back, like a giant glass bakery case with people instead of pastries inside. We had long white curtains, like bridal veils, over all the windows. The yellow and pink rosebushes climbed all the way to the tops of the little triangular windows under the eaves and gobbled at the sunlight. There were three lemon trees and the spirit of a long-dead dog and the grave of a pet chicken out back. There was a hedge that was a pain in the ass to clip. The neighbors had a kumquat tree that grew over our fence, and we would pick the fruit. The seeds were shiny, smooth, and brown as walnut, and fit perfectly in your nostrils. You could put one up each nostril and squeeze them out in front of people and tell them your *brains* were falling out.

My parents were Adlai Stevenson Democrats, which meant they felt sorry for people who were less fortunate than we were. It meant that they read *Time* magazine. It meant that they admired John Steinbeck. It meant that they watched *The Dick Van Dyke Show*. It meant that we had roast beef with baked potatoes every Sunday evening at six.

In the mornings we had eggs sunny or pancakes, French toast or cornmeal mush, waffles or cold cereal, cream of wheat or oatmeal. Sometimes we had bacon or sausage. We always had toast and orange juice. My parents drank coffee. We used whole milk, butter, mayonnaise, white flour, and eggs. Sometimes we poured real cream on strawberries, and my mom put it in her coffee. My father always drank his coffee black. He smoked Pall Mall Reds for thirty years and coughed like gurgling red death in the morning. My mother was a housewife who later became a court reporter. My sister was four years younger than me and didn't like mushrooms or green vegetables or oatmeal or anything that appeared to have raisins in it. She gripped her spoon in her fist and boycotted liver and anything else that looked strange — especially strange meat and casseroles that might have raisins sneaked into them. Mom ladled up the hot cereal and fried the bacon, standing in the holy, twisting bars of sun and steam. My father held the paper up before his face. The sunlight came down through the triangular windows, soaked through the curtains, spread across the table. My father lit a Pall Mall Red. The smoke twirled in slow blue columns through the air. He rattled the paper. The news was important. I remember headlines: "Earth Turns in Flames of Eternal Desire." The sun turned the paper yellow before my eyes.

I had to stand around the neighborhood for a while and look stupid before anyone would be my friend. Roland Sambeaux was the first. We were something like instant friends, no need for introductions or background checks. Roland was skinny and dark with a little cap of oily brown hair. He had an older brother named Langston and a younger stepbrother and three younger stepsisters. His eyes were like crystal balls filled with olive oil, and his face was lean and wrinkled in a fine, cracked way, like brown eggshell. Sometimes he had a black eye, once a broken arm, another time a tooth knocked out. He would say that he had fallen off the roof, or stepped in a bucket, or slipped in the bathtub, or tripped into the dining room table. On the odd days he went to school, we walked together, and he stayed at my left shoulder, like the moon at night. When he came over to my house, we played mumblety-peg or heaved guava berries or played Chinese checkers. We drank lemonade or root beer, and ate kumquats and stuffed the seeds up our noses. On Saturday afternoons, we watched horror movies on *Science Fiction Theater.* Once, I accidentally hit Roland with a baseball bat and gave him a concussion and two black eyes. He was in bed for three days. I took him over a Wheel-O and a get-well card. His eyes were a pale green, and when they looked at you, you couldn't help but feel sorry for him.

My mother didn't like my going over to the Sambeauxs'. There was something mysterious and menacing about that house: a blood-curdling scream, a silhouette of a knife in the window, a wolf on its hind legs with a leather tail scuffling along behind the juniper trees. Out front were statues of undressed women holding up grapes or baskets and showing their armpits. A cactus garden grew against the living room window: prickly pear, barrel, agave. Handmade birdhouses swung from the branches of a big yellow poplar. Mr. Sambeaux was an upholsterer. You caught only rare glimpses of him — drinking from a tumbler, or getting into his car to head down to the liquor store, or coming out of the bathroom, his pudgy, scarred, Babe Ruth face shining as red as the Thriftimart *T.* The sight of him invariably induced immediate, inexplicable terror. He spent most of his days in the dimness of his leather-and-machine-oil-smelling garage, amid the stacked slabs of moldering foam rubber and great, rolled-up bolts of fabric and spools of vinyl and leather. At the back of the garage crouched an industrial sewing machine with a chrome ring the size of a steering wheel; the long, thick needle thumped and slugged like a jackhammer. Often, you could not see Mr. Sambeaux running it; there was only the sound of the heavy needle thumping in the darkness.

Inside the Sambeaux house the walls were upholstered like car seats, red plush with brass studs. Coal-red lanterns hung from the ceiling and a big, gold, ceramic Buddha sat in a lotus on the hearth. Potted Venus's-flytraps thrived in the cool green shade of the enclosed patio. If Roland caught a fly he might drop it in for you with a pair of tweezers, so you could watch the hairy, gooey pod fold around it, like a slow and obscene birth sequence in reverse. In the back yard, below shelves of waterfall granite, was a mossy pool with plump, tattered, red-mottled goldfish flicking along its bottom. Against the fence next to the house were stacked crates of empty wine and whiskey bottles; we set them in cardboard-box shooting galleries and blasted them to pieces with BB guns. Roland's brother Langston, who at twelve was already going bald and sprouting blackheads in the grease on his high forehead, shot the bottles with a vengeance, shot them with glee. Langston would rough me up, get me in wrestling holds, pin my arm against my back, make me say uncle. It got to where I would say uncle before he even touched me. I came to think of him as Uncle Langston. Roland and Langston both had kind of tricky, troubled, hair-trigger tempers.

Stories about the Sambeaux house circulated for miles. Kids from blocks away would come to stare at it as if it were a house on fire or a house that had burned down or the house of Red Riding Hood's granny with the wolf still inside — the handmade birdhouses swaying in the yellow poplar tree, the naked women holding up their baskets, the sound of a sewing needle pounding up and down.

The Carrs lived next door to us in a falling-down purple house. There were five kids in that house. Queenie Carr, the youngest, was a dumpling runt who would change into a glittering sex princess in high school. Her brother Whitey was a year older than me and used to beat me up just about every Sunday. Like me, he suffered from asthma, and he would often come over a couple of hours after he beat me up to borrow my prescriptions. He was a nine-year-old Lucky Strike smoker. His father was a giant with leukemia, and his mother had died when he was six. In a few years his oldest brother would go to Vietnam and lose his mind. Whitey had long, straggly white hair and a bluish tint to his lips and eyelids, and hard little fists. He hooked his arms when he fought, as if hugging a telephone pole, his eyes glinting sadistically as he laid the hard little punches on.

Out behind our drab pink elementary school was a series of neglected arroyos and small canyons and brushy vacant lots where people would dump their junk: tires and mattresses and refrigerators and old cars. We'd wander down into these sunken otherworlds, these Roman ruins of junk, and look around, sit behind the wheels of rusted cars, lie on mattresses and watch the clouds sail over, catch scorpions and put them in jars. Whitey Carr would talk dirty and smoke cigarettes with Snooks Miller. Snooks always carried around a tube of Crest to cover her breath; she'd smear the blue-green paste on her tongue. We would practice talking like adults ("Goddammit, I forgot my cigarettes"), holding adult subjects up like mysterious glass balls for consideration. Snooks had a brother my age named Fubsy, a fat kid who was always practicing his pseudojudo on me. The only reason I went down to their house at all was because Snooks, though she acted like a boy, liked me in a way I didn't understand. She often told me she was horny, which I thought meant she needed skin lotion. (She did, especially on her legs.) Snooks's father drove the ferryboat to Coronado and didn't live at home anymore. Her mother was a barmaid. They had a clock in their house that said, "No Drinking Till After Five," and all the numbers on the clock were fives.

Every time we went to the End Store, Roland or Langston had to steal something. We called it the End Store because it was the last in a row of shops. The man who ran it was from another country and spoke very little English. Where he came from, children probably did not steal the way they did here in America. America is all about freedom; we have an idea in America that things should be as free as possible. This was Roland and Langston's idea, too. They would walk into the End Store, load up, and come out looking like lumpy scarecrows, their sleeves and socks and underwear jammed with Paydays and Abba-Zabas and Neccos and Red-Hots. Roland would fill the saddlebag on the back of his bicycle, stuff it until he could barely get the flap over. Then we would go back to their house and sit in their room and gorge. In a trunk under the bed they kept nudist magazines and old *Playboys* that their father had given them. Uncle Langston would light a cigarette and blow the smoke in yellow streams out the louvered windows. Once, when Mr. and Mrs. Sambeaux were gone, we put away the magazines and played Twister with Roland and Langston's three sisters in the living room. The sisters all had skinny legs and big, yearning eyes, like stained glass windows in French cathedrals. Bizzy was the prettiest and, at seven, the eldest of the three. Langston asked me if I "wanted" Bizzy. He had the most curious look on his face. The question made no sense to me. Everyone laughed when I blushed and said no. I went home, jaded and jumpy from sugar and nudity and crime. I ate poorly, thinking of bushy-looking adults playing volleyball or shuffleboard in the nude. My mother cut sharp glances at me. She had the kind of vision that went right through you and saw into your future. She saw me taking LSD, or driving drunk off a cliff, or marrying a Filipino go-go dancer with a long scar across her abdomen. She saw weeds coming up in the garden of my innocence, and wormy, wild apples waving in the wind.

The Millers had a pinup calendar in their garage — you peeled up the cellophane and the girl's bathing suit came with it. Fubsy claimed to know all about sex firsthand: he had been with the baby sitter, who was fifteen. I didn't believe him. He said he'd tasted mother's milk. So had I, I told him, but I'd forgotten what it was like. Snooks rubbed up against me and talked in the language she heard through the walls after her mother came home from the bar. Once, I went over to spend the night and watch *Lost in Space* and giggle in Fubsy's bunk bed. The barmaid mother was rarely home. Snooks kept up her edgy patter and periodically went out on the patio for a smoke.

Whether I was at the Sambeauxs' or the Millers' or the Carrs', or just out in the street with my little buddies, it was always the same. They were like hothouse tomatoes pushing hard for what they thought was the light. We would hide in a bush, or cluster in the treehouse, or lean back among the interstices of the towering, ragged, catwalk hedge, and the topic would invariably arise, spelled out in red letters above our heads: S-E-X. And if Langston or Roland was there, someone might say, Go get your sisters. I kept my ears up, listened sharply, but at the same time I kept a hand on the door handle, looking back at the receding point of innocence. If you knew too much, you ended up a drooling, bug-eyed hermit living in a cave with people's fermenting decapitated heads all around. My mother's voice rang out across the neighborhood, the diamond-mother vibration of salvation, calling me in earlier than anyone else. I was scrubbed and in bed and staring at the ceiling with the burble of the Dodger game on the living room radio before the red letters disappeared.

One day, my mother told me I couldn't go to the Sambeaux house anymore. She thought Mr. Sambeaux was a bad man. I didn't think he could be all bad: he laughed and told us jokes; he had a salty, bowlegged fraternity about him; he gave his children spending money and let them stay up as late as they wanted; he never made them go to the dentist or the doctor or school; he gave them booze now and then, and handed down his nudist magazines; whenever he went down to Mexico, where the liquor was cheap, he brought back firecrackers — black cats and ladyfingers, quarter sticks and cherry bombs, triangles and M-8os. Anybody who did all that couldn't be *entirely* bad. My mother, however, thought it best that I not associate with the Sambeauxs. She had a way of announcing things with her jaw cocked slightly, which meant there would be no discussion about it. I didn't doubt my mother's wisdom, but she was beginning to make my life difficult. Already I was not allowed to watch *Rat Patrol*, could have only one soft drink a day, and had to go to bed every night at 8:30 sharp. Play with the Rose children, she said. Play with the Bendonellis; the Bendonellis are very nice. I did my best to stay simultaneously together with and away from the Sambeauxs. I still walked to and from school with Roland when he went, which was about every other day. Whenever he said, Whyncha come on over to my house? I would say I had homework to do, a book to read. He'd look at me with disbelief and disdain. I couldn't tell him the truth: that my *mother* controlled my life.

At Christmastime 1966, the Ashmonts, a navy family from Illi-

nois, moved in next door to the Millers. The Ashmonts looked like
Illinois people to me: all big teeth and dimples. Homer Ashmont,
the oldest child, drifted down to the Sambeaux house on his second or third day in the neighborhood. It was the natural course to
take when you were new on the block, like a sailor strolling down to
the red-light district, or a tourist looking for the Museum of Modern Man. The Sambeaux house glowed with the kind of desperate energy children give off when slowly broiling in a vodka base
with frequent tenderizing chops to the jowls. Homer wore his red
ball cap cockeyed. He was tall and careless and let his long arms
swing as he walked up the street. He had a big chest and enormous
lungs, and could swim or run forever. He was a baseball player — a
pitcher, to be exact. He could throw a curve that raped the air with
its seams and whistled as it sank for a strike into the dusty catcher's
mitt behind you. His hair was short and fair, and he had the polite
and unassuming stride of a farm boy. From a distance, the Sambeaux house must have appeared to him to be the place to make
friends. There were children everywhere: peeping from windows,
lounging against cars, hanging lemurlike from trees, barelegged,
barefoot, the spirit of Peter Pan and Tobacco Road. There were
paper clouds above the Sambeaux roof, pink pastel streaks painted
across the sky, devils on the rooftop, monkeys on wires. A big cardboard vulture squealed over. Homer knocked on the door. Roland
and Langston ushered him in.

After that, Homer was at the Sambeaux house every day, doing
the things I had once done. He was more popular than any other
kid I had ever seen. He possessed that rare combination of congeniality and the ability to beat you up. He traveled with the Sambeauxs, and I knew everything that was happening — the shoplift-
ing, the porno, the BB guns, the firecrackers, the cigarettes. Whitey
was there, too, along with half the other kids on the block, even the
Roses and the Bendonellis. The Sambeauxs invited me over, too,
but I pretended I had better things to do, like sitting by myself on
the curb whittling a dumb piece of wood with the cold clouds
blowing overhead. It was my mother's fault. She wanted me to be a
sissy. Well, that was all right with me. I would be a sissy and have no
friends. It would serve her right. I would grow up to be the boy of
my mother's dreams.

In the wintertime in San Diego it rains, and when you are a deprived and oppressed child it rains every day. You stay inside with the swollen, bleating television at your back, the eye of your prison-warden mom permanently stitched to your right shoulder, the patches of fog on the windows that you can draw a face into with your fingertip, the smell of mushroom soup and cinnamon toast and frying onions and hamburger meat. The rain streams silver off the eaves like strips of Christmas tinsel. You have about six thousand games stacked up in the closet, but what good are any of them with only one player? All the children across the street are having the child-orgy time of their lives. Your father pulls into the driveway, wipers going, a dark car with black windows. He gets out with his briefcase, stoops his way around the slatted fence and in the door, shedding sparkling drops. He is tired, he says, and gets himself a drink. You don't wonder about what he's been doing all day; he just goes round and round from home to work like a hand on the round clock face of the gray days. You have the dreariest family on earth: a father who is always tired; a sister who bawls if you touch her arm; a mother with nothing better to do than manage every waking moment of your life. You are all prisoners in a rainy glass case called home.

One winter morning my mother went out to get the paper and found Bizzy Sambeaux sitting dazed in the mist on our front lawn. We were having bacon and eggs sunny with toasted, buttered English muffins and orange juice. My mother hurried back in with a wild look and took my father's arm. No one would tell me anything, except to go to my room. My father called the police. My mother went back outside. I watched from the window as two patrol cars glided in from either direction. The neighbors had gathered in their driveways. Bizzy had birdlike legs with baseball knees. She hugged them to her, shivering in her thin green nightgown. There was a brown, egg-shaped blotch, like dried blood, on the front of the gown. Her big green eyes did not blink. I watched her get into one of the cars. The neighbors jabbered and nodded their heads. The patrol car parted gently from the curb and took her away.

The mist did not lift for a long time. Some days it was so thick you couldn't see the hands on your watch. It was clammy and smelled of mushrooms and bandages and Styrofoam cups. It spun and drifted with a lime tint on its edges, and did not stop at your eyes but trickled and pooled in creepy lagoons all the way down to the bottom of your brain. I walked to school by myself in the chilly green mushroom mist with the bare trees like bleached arms and fingers groping for the sky. The mist made me tired and slow. It squashed and muffled time and snickered dankly, like witch voices urging me to dash out in front of a car.

Then one day Homer Ashmont was there walking next to me. He was about six inches taller than I was, wore his cockeyed red ball cap with the white script *L* on the front, and carried a lunch bag in his hand: salami sandwiches — I could smell the peppercorns through the mist. He put out his hand. "I'm Homer," he said.

"Hi," I said, shaking his hand. "I know."

"How come you walk to school by yourself all the time?"

"I don't know."

"My mom said you weren't allowed to go over to the Sambeaux house."

"That's right."

"I can't go over there anymore either. Did you hear about what happened?"

"Yeah."

"I never heard of nothing like that before. Hey, do you like beef stroganoff?"

"I guess."

"We're having it tonight. Do you want to come over to my house for dinner?"

A big shaft of sunlight broke through the cloud canopy and fell across the housetops.

"O.K."

That night, at Homer's house, we had beef stroganoff that was pink. That was his mother's specialty: pink stroganoff. She made it with sour cream and real mushrooms, not canned, and red wine, not white — that was what made it pink. Mr. Ashmont was a taller version of Homer, a big, cool hound dog with deep creases in his cheeks. He shoveled up the stroganoff and made jokes no one understood. He was a lieutenant commander in the navy, and went from here to there in a battleship. Homer's mom was the tallest one: all teeth and long, stringy brown arms. The daughters looked like Homer, too, girlish Homers. The whole family had a rich, square-jawed, dimply, big-toothed vitality. They were swimmers and ballplayers, horseback riders and golfers. They put their napkins in their laps. They treated me as if I were twenty-six years old. They took a keen, warm interest in the dullest details of my life. They were Catholics. (I had never known any Catholics before.) I scooped up a little pink stroganoff and took a taste off the tip of my spoon, expecting raspberry, but it was beef, creamy beef with wine and melted onions. I had to restrain myself from eating too fast.

The Ashmonts were the only people on the block who owned a color TV. Other than that, their house was just like my house — a clean house with clean air in it, not hot, hairy, vegetable-soup-smelling air, like at the Carrs' or the Sambeauxs'. The Ashmonts' air smelled like aftershave from the 1940s. *These are Illinois people,* I kept telling myself. In my mind, Illinois was another country: cornstalks rustling in the breeze; old men sitting on a bench in front of the post office; kids racing their Flexies down the hill in the weightless thickness of twilight; friendly drunks with bottles of red wine who give you a dollar; a guy with a handlebar mustache polishing the chrome spigots at the soda fountain. There was a sort of unaccountable, cottony religion of humanity about them. *This is how people are supposed to be!* I thought. My head began to spin with the subtle intoxication of wholesomeness. It was a shock to my system, like Shangri-La to the downed American war pilot.

We had ice cream with hot fudge sauce for dessert, and after dinner Homer took me down to his room and we played two games of Stratego and one of Battleship. We didn't speak once about adult temptations, not a word about unspeakable desire. When Homer swore, he said *shoot,* or *nuts.* Our only talk about growing up was about the major leagues. He would pitch for a good club. They would call him the Cobra, on account of the fantastic way his curve ball broke.

I did not know, when I walked out of my mustard-colored house now, whether it was I or the world that had changed. Somewhere, a war was on that I was only dimly aware of. In our town, a trial was on that I was only dimly aware of, even though my mother was a principal witness, and the children across the street — my friends — were the unwilling plaintiffs. Sometime in that year of 1967, the first kiddie-consumptive, recreational drugs began to appear on our street. They came with the war. They were anesthesia for the war. They were packed like candy; they even looked like candy, and had edible, colorful names: greenies and blue devils and yellow sunshine. They were in the songs on the radio, and in the magic feeling of being young and blossoming in a changing world. Many of the children did not resist their siren call, the Carrs and the Sambeauxs especially. Homer was not in the least tempted. He knew what devils were. The devil comes around just to mess you up; he doesn't want you to pitch in the major leagues. I envied the logic and cleanliness of his mind. I tried to think of myself as an Illinois farm boy with the Virgin Mary watching over me.

When I saw them on the street, my old pals were quivering like little electric beasts. They stood out under the threatening sky like lightning rods for adulthood. Queenie Carr, ten years old, already had green eyelids and a slinky walk and a bleary lipstick grin and tacky, thrilling, hussy perfume and a rack of whites for a dollar in her purse. She would sidle up to me and dabble her fingers along my ribs. Meet me later, big boy, she'd say; ten o'clock, out by the gas meter. They gathered in little crowds on the sidewalk like old men around trash fires, their movements jagged or slow, shattered or dreamy, wrong-eyed, puppet-wired, bamboozled. They watched me with bitter cigarette scowls as I walked down to Homer's house. He was going to be a ballplayer, and to be a ballplayer you had to live clean. Sex might take some of the bite off your curve ball, and you certainly didn't eat speed or drink malt liquor. He and I got some money from our parents and went to the grocery store and bought packages of Carl Buddig smoked meats. We came back and Homer built a fire in the fireplace. There was a movie on that night: *Hush, Hush, Sweet Charlotte*. We got out the plates, pickles, cocktail peanuts, cream soda. The sparks from the chimney whirled up into stars.

The Sambeaux trial dragged on. At first, the children tried to protect their father. Opinions varied as to the degree of his guilt and what should be done with him afterward. My mother came home every day from the trial with reports, and rendered careful, Victorian scenes. My playmates painted cruder portraits. Neighbors volunteered scraps and morsels. Rumors and suspicions abounded. I reconstructed the entire chilling tale in my head.

Every weekend, Homer and I went to the matinee at the Helix Theater. Then we rode our bicycles four miles to the great blue-green vat of urine and chlorine called La Mesa Public Pool. Our moms drove us to the beach, and we learned how to surf on ten-foot boards. We tried to stay off the street as much as possible. The street was the enemy.

Mr. Sambeaux was sent away to a work camp for two years to sharpen up his Ping-Pong and metallurgy skills. (He was originally sentenced to a mental facility, but since this man who covered up things for a living would never admit to any wrongdoing, they were unable to treat him.) My mother, who had a new interest in the law, began to attend court-reporting school. The Sambeaux house was strangely quiet now. Bizzy went away for a while. Langston left, too, to live with an uncle in Florida. The remaining Sambeaux children had crumpled shoulders and bewildered, ruined expressions and smoldering eyes, like snuffed-out candles.

When eighth grade started, Homer and I tried to get into the same classes. We walked to school together every day, and Roland came with us once or twice a week, whenever he got organized enough to go. He followed along glumly, walking most of the way in the gutter, head down, kicking scraps. He carried a pack of cigarettes to school in his jacket — tricked up in his sleeve, slipped into the lining somehow — and he'd light one on the way, smoking it sullenly, cupping it in his palm. Homer and I were antismoking; it was the same as being antideath. Roland was tough, though. He didn't care if he died. He had once considered Homer his best friend.

The next fall, when Roland found out he'd flunked eighth grade, he was so shocked he couldn't speak. He hadn't imagined that he could flunk. You went to school and they passed you along. It happened to everyone. All you had to do was go through the motions. It was the first day of ninth grade. We'd gone in to get our schedules, and they'd told Roland he'd have to do eighth grade over again. Now we stood outside under the clouds, and he looked at us and blinked in disbelief. Then his face shrank into a wrinkle, his big green eyes disappeared, and he began to bawl. He wept freely without covering his face, the water pouring down his cheeks. Homer and I patted his shoulder and said that it was probably some kind of mistake. But we walked home from ninth grade by ourselves that afternoon. And the next morning it was the same, and I hardly ever saw Roland after that. He watched me from the shadows, a slow, bitter shadow himself. I had taken his luck and his best friend — I might as well have taken his life.

Much later, Roland and I got to be something like friends again, though it was never the same. There would always be that wound of resentment, those long months of insurmountable shame. And even when he was married and I was his best man and he was happy for a few days and thanked me for being someone who had never turned on him, it didn't change. I was simply too lucky to be forgiven.

DIANE SCHOEMPERLEN

Body Language

FROM STORY

ON A GOOD DAY (a good day being one on which they have not argued at breakfast, she has kissed him goodbye on the mouth at the door before they make their separate ways to work, they have plans for the evening that involve good friends, fancy clothes, white wine, and red meat) his throat goes loose with happiness. His tongue is nimble and lithe. The words flow out of him, clever, witty, and remarkably intelligent. He smiles at strangers on his way to the subway station and laughs aloud with delight at the watery gurgling of a fat baby in a blue stroller. He is confident, fluent, and affable. He could talk all day long to anyone about anything.

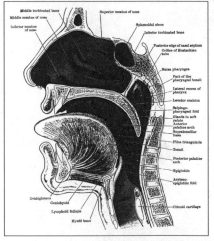

On a bad day (a bad day being one on which she has cursed him because the coffee is cold, the toast is burnt, the sun is not shining; and she cannot look him in the eye when they leave for work, she says she won't be home till late, she's not sure how late) his throat freezes into formality. He is articulate but icy. His language is laden with precision and good grammar. To his coworkers he says, "Perhaps I shall . . . we intend . . . I assume . . . I spoke with you previously regarding this issue." His sentences are weighted with pompous pauses. His chest is puffed out with what looks like self-importance but is in fact injury. His spine is stiff with offense.

All day long (on a bad day) there is a knot in his stomach, a sour bow of anxiety that tightens and loosens and tightens again as the hours slowly pass. Sometimes it shakes itself free and flows upward to his chest so he cannot fill his lungs with breath, or downward to his intestines, which creak and whistle dangerously. His coworkers ask him to join them for lunch. He declines in a whisper of melancholy martyrdom. They know better than to ask what's wrong. He will say, "Nothing!" in an accusing voice, affronted by their curiosity.

By the end of the day, his stomach is a tight hot drum of gray worry and black bile. It appears slightly distended and he carries it before him like a volatile barrel of toxic waste.

He closes up his office and walks the four blocks to the subway station. He takes no notice of the weather. It could be sunny, it could be raining, it could be a hurricane for all he cares. He pushes past an old lady walking too slowly, elbows his way around a young mother consoling a crying toddler at the curb. He keeps his head down and trudges through the traffic, glaring at the ground. His legs are a pair of aching stumps. His knees alternately threaten to give out or seize up. He stands and waits. He studies his shoes. They are ugly.

He takes a seat on the train and crosses his numb legs primly. A woman sits down beside him but shrinks into her side of the seat and looks away. Perhaps he is muttering to himself. Perhaps he is moaning softly as he clutches his knees with both hands.

The house when he gets there is empty. Although he has expected this, still he goes from room to room searching. The kitchen is ominously immaculate, as if it will never be used again. Every surface shines, as if even the fingerprints have been wiped clean. The living room is a well-appointed museum, entirely free of clutter, dust, and oxygen. He goes upstairs. Only the bedroom is in disarray, the sheets and blankets in a rumpled pile, three of her silk blouses tossed among them, her white nightgown discarded in a puddle on the floor, her earrings scattered sparkling across the black dresser. In the bathroom he faces himself in the mirror. He

opens his eyes as wide as he can
and still he cannot see her.

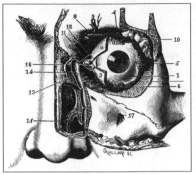

On a good day she would have
been home before him. If they
have planned to have dinner
out, she is already getting
dressed when he arrives. She
asks his opinion on her outfit.
She suggests other possibilities,
holding each up against herself
and sashaying through the bedroom. He tells her they are all perfect, the shimmering expensive dresses that cling to her slim body,
sliding over her like water when she moves. They are all perfect:
how can he ever decide? Downstairs in the living room they have
drinks and discuss the day. They put on some music and sometimes
they dance. Once she places her little feet on top of his and holds
tight to his neck while he waltzes her round the room like a child at
a wedding. Even on a bad day, he will always remember this: her
little hands, her little feet upon him.

Or (on a good day) she would have been in the kitchen starting
supper with the radio on, humming and chopping and stirring. He
puts down his briefcase and takes off his shoes (which are not so
ugly on a good day). He hangs his suit jacket carefully in the front
closet next to hers. In the kitchen he gratefully discovers that she is
making his favorite pasta. In the kitchen he joyfully discovers that
she has already changed out of her work clothes and is wearing her
black silk kimono with the red dragon on the back. She greets him
with a kiss. He slides both arms inside her kimono to where her
alarming flesh awaits.

   On a good day she lets him.

On a bad day she doesn't exactly push him away but turns, gracefully, out of his embrace, like a ring once stuck on a finger magically
removed with soap. Both her skin and her kimono are slippery and
he cannot hold on. He is left with his arms hanging empty at his
sides, then braced hard against the kitchen counter to keep himself
from grabbing her, begging her, forcing himself upon her. He tries

to console himself with the thought that all relationships have their ups and downs.

But on a good day the black kimono slips from her shoulders and then she puts her tongue in his mouth.

He doesn't exactly want to make love. What he wants is comfort. What he wants is to lay his head between her breasts, plump breasts, marvelously heavy breasts on such a small body. He wants to close his eyes and press his lips against them. He wants to bury his nose in them and suffocate with pleasure. He wants to hold his ear against them one by one and listen to her heart beating, her blood flowing, like the ocean inside a seashell. But he is afraid to tell her this. Perhaps she would think he is weak. Perhaps she already thinks he is weak. Perhaps he *is* weak.

They make love. Then they eat pasta with clam sauce. They drink red wine, toasting themselves liberally. They make small talk and are happy.

On a bad day, when the house is empty, he hangs up her blouses and her nightgown. He puts her earrings back in the jewelry box. He makes the bed, moving woodenly around it, as quietly as if she were sleeping and he must not wake her. He removes his clothes and lies down naked on the bed. He presses his ear to the pillow. He will wait here until she arrives and then he will ask her where

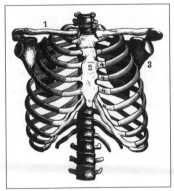

she's been. Yes, he will ask her. Finally he will ask her. And she will answer.

Finally she will answer, and finally the flute-edged silence that surrounds them will be filled with the truth.

For now the only sound is that of his own blood throbbing in his ear.

He doesn't mean to fall asleep but he does, and quickly, exhausted by anxiety. He does not dream. He does not move a muscle. He awakens instantly at the sound of the front door opening. Is it her or is it an intruder? Either way his heart is pounding and his ribs are aching as if he had been thoroughly kicked by a horse or a pair of steel-toed boots.

He thinks of the Bible story, God causing Adam to fall into a deep sleep, then removing one of his ribs and closing his body up again. No mention of which rib, which side, or whether Adam missed it. Then God created Eve from Adam's rib: Eve, bone of his bone, flesh of his flesh. *And the man and his wife were both naked, and were not ashamed.*

He hears her humming as she takes off her jacket. She calls his name. She sounds happy, excited, girlish. He is relieved, even though her good mood likely has nothing to do with him. She calls his name again. Somehow it does not occur to him to answer. He looks at the bedside clock and finds he has only been asleep for forty-five minutes. She is hardly late at all. He hears her coming up the stairs.

If she is surprised to find him naked on the bed at this early hour, she does not say so. She lies down beside him and slips her

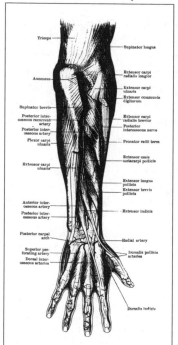

hands between his legs. Her hands are cool and very small. Her diamond rings catch lightly in his pubic hair. He sighs. Her fingers are like the stems of young flowers. His hands upon her are clumsy and large. His thick gold wedding band shines.

The tradition of wearing the wedding ring on the third finger of the left hand began with the early Romans. The reason was that when the human body was cut open, it was discovered that a single nerve led from that finger up the arm to the shoulder and then straight down to the heart.

He doesn't mean to respond. He means to be cool, logical, mature, rational, and philosophical if necessary — none of which are states of mind that may, generally speaking, be achieved or sustained while making love. He means to remain in control of the situation. He means to speak to her as he spoke to his coworkers earlier: "Perhaps I shall . . . we must . . . I presume . . . I intended to consult with you earlier regarding this important issue." Her breath all over him is sweet and fermented, as if she has been recently sipping expensive liqueurs. He means to ask her about that, too. He means to speak to her. He means to make her speak to him.

But slowly, slowly his penis grows hard under her little hands, her little tongue, her hard little teeth. Slowly, slowly his large body betrays him and he cannot help but enter her.

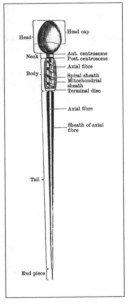

Each sperm cell has a long tail called a *flagellum*. This tail whips back and forth, causing the sperm to move as if swimming. Fully developed testes produce 300 million functional sperm every day. They have not had sex for two weeks.

Afterwards she goes back downstairs and continues her supper preparations. He has a shower and gets dressed.

If she has a lover (he is pretty sure she has a lover, but he has not asked her, will not ask her, at least not today), then maybe he should get one too: thrust and parry, tit for tat, an eye for an eye, and all of that. There is a woman at work who flirts with him all the time: at the Xerox machine, at the water cooler, in the parking lot where he could kiss her and no one would know. In the shower he thinks about how eager this woman is, how easy it would be to have her. But he is afraid that if he sleeps with this woman, he will discover that between her legs she is exactly like his wife. Or nothing like her at all. Either way he could not bear it. Either way he would be humiliated and his body would turn away from her, stunned and soft.

*

Getting dressed, he imagines his wife in the kitchen below. He pictures her as he always does, one perceptible part at a time. Ankle, elbow, that small round bone protruding at the wrist, cheekbone, jawbone, left temple with one blue vein showing, the nape of her neck, her collarbone like a turkey wishbone, her hands in her lap, silent. He has to admit that he cannot imagine who she is when he's not with her, who she is when she's alone. He has no idea what resides within that small body, all of these parts joined seamlessly together to produce *her:* this one woman, a mystery without precedent or duplicate, entirely singular: *her.* When he tries to understand her, she escapes him entirely. The heart of the matter is no longer visible to his naked eye.

He can feel it in his bones: her restlessness, her silence, her moodiness, her guilt, and sometimes her fear. He does not know if she still loves him. If not, he does not know when she stopped. He wonders what you do with love when you're done with it — where do you put it, where does it go, how do you make sure it stays there?

He can feel it in his bones. They wake him up in the night, the long strong bones of his legs, not exactly aching or cramping, but shrinking, sinking, dissolving, and draining away.

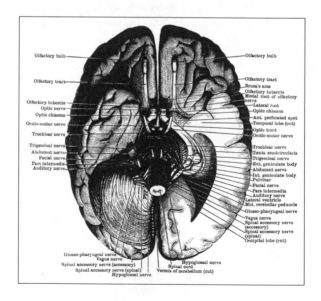

He can feel it in his bones: the future. Eventually he will have to get it through his head.

The human brain weighs an average of three pounds in a man and two pounds, twelve ounces in a woman. It is the size of two clenched fists held tightly together.

The capacity of the human brain has been expressed as the number one followed by 6.5 million miles of zeros — a number so large that it would stretch from the earth to the moon and back again more than thirteen times.

For now, as long as nobody says the words out loud, he can concentrate instead upon the language of her ankles, elbows, that small round bone protruding at the wrist. Eventually he will have to get it through his head. But for now, he need listen only to her body, near him, humming. For now they will make small talk and be happy.

EDITH PEARLMAN

Chance

FROM THE ANTIOCH REVIEW

WHEN OUR SYNAGOGUE was at last selected to become the new home of a Torah from Czechoslovakia — a Torah whose old village had been obliterated — the Committee of the Scroll issued an announcement, green letters on ivory, very dignified. Our presence was requested, the card said, at a Ceremony of Acceptance at two in the afternoon on Sunday the sixteenth of November, nineteen hundred and seventy-five.

Nothing in the invitation suggested that the Committee of the Scroll had chafed under the dictatorship of its chairwoman, the cantor's wife. But my parents and I heard all about it from our neighbor Sam, a committee member. Sam said that the cantor's wife wanted the Ceremony of Acceptance to take place on a Friday night or a Saturday morning — not on the pale Sabbath of the Gentiles. The group united against her. Here in America's heartland Sunday was the proper day for special ceremonies, they said. Also we'd get better attendance — faculty from the university, interested non-Jews, maybe even the mayor. Then the sexton expressed dismay that the Torah would enter the premises three weeks before the date of the ceremony. It would lie in the basement — a corpse! he cried — because the Leibovich-Sutton nuptials were scheduled for the first Sunday after its arrival and the Lehrman-Grossman ones for the second. But what could anyone do? — weddings must never be postponed. So Sam and the sexton cleared out a little room off the social hall directly under the sanctuary, and the rabbi blessed the room; and they fitted its door with a lock. The congregation continued its busy life.

Lots of activities went on weekly in our synagogue. The Talmud class met on Monday nights. Hebrew for Adults was taught on Tuesdays. Wednesdays belonged to committees. On Thursdays from six to eight a university professor conducted a seminar on Hasidic thought. Friday nights and Saturday mornings were devoted to worship, and on Sundays children straggled into the hateful old school building next to the new sanctuary. Parents had to pay for Sunday school (some also paid their kids); the other courses were free, and open to anyone.

On a Monday morning the Czech Torah arrived by plane. The cantor, the rabbi, the sexton, and Sam laid it reverently in the little cleared-out room. They locked the room. And there it remained, its presence unsuspected by the Talmud class, the Hebrew students, the scholars of Hasidism, and the committees. Perhaps the sexton visited it sometimes. The Torah study group left it entirely alone.

The Torah study group was *not* open to anyone. It met on Sunday nights in private homes, usually at our house but sometimes at the cantor's apartment. His flat had a formal dining room, my father told me: panels, and dark wallpaper, and a weak chandelier. When the Torah study group assembled at the cantor's long mahogany table, no one sat at the head or the foot. The men huddled near the center, three to a side. The cantor's wife insisted on protecting the table with a lace cloth. The complicated geometry of the cloth was distracting, even more distracting than my mother's habit of dealing in a singsong voice when the Torah study group met at our house.

"Why is the cantor's wife so stern?" I asked my parents.

"She's from Brussels," was my father's reply.

"They have no children," my mother explained.

"Or maybe Antwerp," sighed my father. "The chips snag on the goddamn lace."

The round Formica table in the breakfast area of our kitchen didn't require a cloth. It seated eight easily. At my fourteenth birthday party in September, some dozen girls had squeezed around it to eat pizza and make voodoo gourds under the supervision of Azinta, a sophomore at the university, our then live-in.

For the Torah study group our table was usually adorned with a single bowl of pretzels. But on the Sunday evening after the

Lehrman-Grossman wedding it wore a centerpiece of Persian lilies and freesia. My parents had attended the wedding and its luncheon. My mother found a paper daisy under her plate, signifying that she had won the flowers.

I was fiddling with the blossoms. "Dede o savalou!" I sang. I was still partial to voodoo, despite Azinta's having left us.

"Oh, shut up," said my mother, though agreeably. "Help me with this food."

I joined her at the counter that separated the kitchen from the breakfast area. Halloween had passed. Outside the window our back yard was covered with leaves. A pumpkin was softly decaying on the windowsill.

My mother sliced the beef to be served later to the group. She sliced the cheese and the tomatoes and the rye. I arranged the food in horizontal rows on a long platter. I laid pickles here and there, vertically, like notes. She slid the platter into the refrigerator.

I turned on the hanging lamp over the table. Its brilliant cone would soon illuminate not only the Lehrman-Grossman flowers but seven glasses of beer or cider. (The cantor's wife provided only ginger ale.) Later in the evening the light would fall upon the sandwich materials. (The cantor's wife left a plate of hard pastries on the sideboard.) In the hours of play the lamp would light up the faces of the six learned men and the one woman.

It was seven-thirty. My father emerged from his study and stretched. The doorbell rang.

The cantor and the rabbi came in, one immediately after the other. These two spent a lot of time as a pair. They got together not only to conduct services and prepare bat mitzvahs and report to the officers; they also went skating in winter and took bicycle rides out to the farm area in spring. I had seen them on their bikes. The cantor's buttocks lapped over his seat like mail pouches. The rabbi's curls stuck up on either side of his cap like the horns of a ram. Sometimes the cantor's wife went biking too. She maintained her strict posture even on a ten-speed.

"Hello, hello," said the cantor to us all, remembering not to pinch my cheek.

"Hi," said the rabbi to my father and me.

My friend Margie's father arrived next, along with her grandfather. Margie's father was treasurer of the synagogue. Also he ran a successful finance business. Margie referred to him as the usurer.

After his wife's death he had invited his own father to live with him and Margie. Margie called *him* the patriarch. The patriarch's moist mouth protruded from a ruche of a beard. His son kept him supplied with white silk shirts embossed with further white, and shawl-collared sweaters.

The usurer's walk had a dancer's grace. He greeted my mother with a friendly hug. He greeted me with an imperfect kiss, lips not quite touching my skin. The patriarch raised his hand in a general blessing.

Sam, who had to trot over from only next door, came last. I let him in. The others were already seated at the round table in the kitchen. My mother had transferred the Lehrman-Grossman flowers to the counter.

Sam just reached my shoulder. He was in his fifties and worn out. "Hello, darling," he said glumly.

I followed Sam into the kitchen. He took the empty seat next to my mother. I placed my own chair at a little remove, behind my mother's right shoulder. But I didn't plan to remain seated. I would soon stand and begin to move around the group, pausing above one person and then another, looking at the fan of cards each held. I was allowed this freedom on the promise of silence and impassivity. The tiniest flare of a nostril, my father warned, might reveal to some other player the nature of the hand I was peeking at. So I kept my face wooden. Eventually I'd settle on a high stool next to the counter and hook my heels on the stool's upper rungs and let my clasped hands slide between my denim thighs. Hunched like that, I'd watch the rest of the game.

Now, though, I sat behind my mother's silk shoulder. She was wearing the same ruby-colored dress she'd worn to the wedding. I could see just the tip of her impudent nose. My mother was a devoted convert, but she could not convert her transcendental profile. Even in the harsh glow of the lamp she was, in the words of my nasty Great-Aunt Hannah, a thing of beauty and a goy forever.

Two of the men — the slate-haired cantor and the young rabbi — were also handsome enough to withstand the spotlight. The patriarch was elderly enough to be ennobled by it.

The usurer had a reputation for handsomeness. Margie told me he was pursued by women, not all of them single. At the table he warmly accepted the cards dealt him as if his love for each was infinite. When he folded — turned cards down, withdrawing from a game — he did it with an air of fatherly regret. The overhead lamp greased his hair and darkened his lips.

Sam, our neighbor, was less than handsome. His small curved nose was embellished with a few hideous hairs. His upper lip often rose above his yellow teeth, and sometimes stayed there, on the ledge of his gum, twitching. His upper body twitched a lot too. "Maybe he a duppy," Azinta had suggested one September day, looking through our broad kitchen window at Sam raking leaves in the next back yard. "Cannot lie properly in he grave. Tormented by need to venge self."

Azinta — christened Ann — was the daughter of two Detroit dentists who were extremely irritated by her adoption of island speech. They became even more irritated when she left us in October to share quarters with Ives Nielson, the owner of a natural food shop called, more or less eponymously, the Red Beard. My mother spent a long evening on the telephone with Azinta's mother, trying to reassure her. I eavesdropped on the extension in my bedroom.

"A phase, I'm certain," said my mother. "Azinta, Ann I mean, wasn't happy with the philosophy department."

"She could have switched to premed instead of to that Swede."

"A short-lived rebellion," predicted my mother.

"Like yours?" said the dentist.

Duppy or not, tonight Sam was suffering from all his tics. His shoulders moved up and down in defeated shrugs.

My father was not handsome either. I had recently and suddenly become aware of his lack of looks, as if a snake had hissed the secret in my ear. I was ashamed of my awareness. His bald head shone grossly back at the lamp. His big pocky nose gleamed too. His cigar glowed. Only his voice revealed his soul — the velvet voice of a scholar. He was a professor of political theory. His smile was broad, and there was a space between his two front teeth. He used that space to good effect at the lake in the summer. Lying on his back in the water, he could spout like a whale.

Whatever I know about poker I learned from watching the Torah study group. I learned that a royal straight flush was the best possible hand. This made sense — what could be grander than king, queen, and offspring, with a ten as steward, all under the tepee of an ace? Four cards of the same denomination were next best, and extremely likely to win the pot; then three of one value and two of another — that was called a full house; then five of the same suit, a flush; and so on down to a pair. Sometimes nobody had a pair, and the highest card won all the money.

I learned that whoever was dealing chose the form of the game. The deal passed from player to player in a clockwise direction. Betting within each round followed the same clockwise rule. Some games were called draw; in those each player held his cards in his hand, not revealing them to anyone. He had to guess other players' holdings from their behavior and their betting and how many cards they drew. Other games were stud; each player's cards lay overlapping on the table, forming a wiggly spoke toward the center, some cards face up and some face down. The down cards were called the hole. A player could look in his own hole but not in anybody else's.

During my twenties I kept brief company with a fellow who played in a big-money weekly, and I discovered from him that my parents' pastime had been poker in name only. "Two winners?" he laughed. (In my parents' stud games, the best hand usually divided the money with the worst.) "What's Chicago?" he wondered. The lowest spade in the hole split the pot with the high hand, I diffidently told him. "Racist nomenclature, wouldn't you say?" he remarked.

"Oh dear."

"I'm sure the gatherings were pleasant," he quickly added.

White chips stood for nickels, red for dimes, blue for quarters. My mother was forbidden to deal her frivolous inventions like Mittelschmerz, where the most middling hand won, and Servitude, where you had to match the pot if you wanted to fold. The ante was a dime in draw and a nickel in stud. You couldn't bet a dime in stud until a pair was showing, and the amount of the raise could be no greater than the initial bet, and there were only three raises each round. In short: very small sums were redistributed among these friends. Even between them my parents rarely recovered the price of the sandwiches.

And yet everybody — or at least every man — played with ardor, as if something of great value were at stake — a fortune, a reputation, a king's daughter.

The patriarch dealt first that evening. "Five-card draw," he announced. "Ante a dime."

He dealt five cards to everybody. From my chair I could see only

Sam's cards and my mother's. Sam had a jack/ten and I knew he'd draw to it. My mother had a low pair and I knew she'd draw to *it*.

The patriarch turned to his left. "If you please."

"Ten cents," responded the cantor, and tossed in a red chip.

"Raise," said the rabbi. Two red chips.

He was sitting to the left of the cantor and to the right of Sam. I couldn't see Sam's face, only his crummy cards. Of the rabbi I could see only a portion of his curls.

"Call," said Sam, matching the rabbi's bet. He put in two red chips.

"Raise," said my mother, on her silly pair of fives.

The usurer smiled and called. Dad passed a hand over his brow and called. The patriarch folded. Everybody else called.

The draw began. The cantor drew one card, the rabbi two, Sam three. My mother drew two. She picked up the five of clubs, and a queen. The usurer drew one and seemed to welcome the new-comer. My father drew one and frowned, but that message too could have been false.

The next round of betting began with my mother. She bet ten cents. The usurer folded. Dad folded. The cantor folded. The rabbi tossed in a red chip. Sam folded, his shoulder shuddering.

The rabbi and my mother laid their cards on the table. He had three nines to her three fives.

Did it happen exactly that way? A deck of cards has fifty-two factorial permutations — fifty-three factorial times two if you use jokers. (The Torah study group didn't play with jokers, though my mother had made a plea for their inclusion.) Fifty-two factorial is an enormous number. Roughly that many angels dance on any pin. Furthermore, two decades have passed since the night the rabbi's three nines (missing the spade) beat my mother's three fives (missing the diamond) in the first game of the weekly group. I would be wise to distrust my memory.

Yet I can see the moment as if it were happening now. The two of them inspect each other's cards. My mother then smiles at the rabbi, looking up at his eyes. The rabbi smiles at my mother, looking down at the pile of chips.

"I was dealt two pairs," says my father's thrilling voice. "But I didn't improve."

"I was dealt one pair," says my mother.

"You raised on a pair?" says my father. "God help me."

"I improved!"

"Insufficiently," smiles the usurer.

The rabbi leans forward and sweeps the pile of chips toward him. A white one rolls onto the floor. I pick it up and idly stow it in the front pocket of my jeans.

At the Torah study group I learned the *politesse* of dealing, at least as it was practiced there. In stud games, though everyone could see all the up cards, it was the custom for the dealer to name them as they appeared. Also he commented on the developing hands. "Another heart, flushing," the cantor might have said in the second game, dealing to the rabbi. "Possible straight," he said as a nine followed an eight in front of Sam. "Good low," as a four followed a six in my mother's display. "No visible help," he sympathized when the usurer's jack of diamonds took on an eight of spades like a bad debt. "Who knows?" he would shrug sooner or later, and then, reverting to the Yiddish of his ancestors, "Vehr vaist?" *Vehr vaist?* was the standard interpretation of some unpaired, unstraightening, unflushing, medium-value hodgepodge. If the player behind this mess didn't fold when he received yet another unworthy card, the dealer's "Vehr vaist?" became ominous, reminding us that there were cards we couldn't see, things we couldn't know.

On Sunday nights it was my job to refill the drinks, and to tell people on the telephone that my parents were out. This work kept me pretty busy. One of the calls was always from Margie.

"What's he wearing?" she inquired by way of hello.

"A cassock."

"Stop that! Torturer —"

"Gray pants, gray striped shirt, tan sweater."

"Thanks. I'm absolutely devouring 'Rebecca at the Well,' next week's portion. Are you going to the ceremony for the Czech scroll?" And without waiting for an answer, "What are you wearing?" And without waiting for that answer either, "I'm wearing an exceedingly biblical outfit. How old do you guess Rebecca was when she watered the stranger's camel?"

"Thirty."

"Thirteen!"

I went back to the game. The deal had gone around to the cantor again, or so I think I remember. Seven-card stud. Now I stood behind the patriarch. My mother was wiping her glasses with a handkerchief. She wore glasses over her Wedgewood eyes to deflect admiration, my father had told me. His great-grandmother had achieved the same thing with a matron's wig.

"The pair of queens bets," said the cantor, nodding to the patriarch.

"Ten cents," said the patriarch.

"I call," said the cantor, making the cadence sound like the beginning of a declaration of love. Some thirty years earlier, just out of high school, he had fought on the beaches of Anzio. I figured he had picked up his rich tenor on the march north. He had met his wife in Paris, after the liberation.

Sam did not conceal his disappointment in the cards he was being dealt. But disappointment was different from misery. He became noticeably miserable when the game ended and he had to go home. Sam had two sons, but both had escaped from his gloomy house. One was a physiotherapist in New York and the other was something unspeakable on the West Coast — at any rate, Sam wouldn't speak of him.

As far as I was concerned, Sam's wife was as dead as Margie's poor mother. She was just a pale face seen briefly at the kitchen window or an arm pulling down a second-floor shade. One rainy morning, when I was home from school with a cold, she ran down her front path after the mailman in order to give him a letter — perhaps one she'd forgotten to post, perhaps one that had been wrongly delivered. The mailman took the letter. Mrs. Sam turned and walked slowly back up the path. The wind further unsettled her scant red hair and her pink wrapper was coming undone and the rain lashed her squirrel face.

"Why is Mrs. Sam so strange?" I'd asked my mother.

"She drinks." My mother knew about drinking. She worked in a family service agency.

At ten-thirty, right after the patriarch had taken an entire pot by winning both high and low, Mother pushed back her chair. "Count me out."

"Already?" moaned Sam.

The men continued to play. My mother took the platter from the refrigerator and plugged in the coffee while I removed the empty beer glasses from the table and cut a defrosted carrot cake into eight slices. My mother loaded the glasses into the dishwasher, and I resumed my perch on the high stool and at last allowed myself to observe the rabbi. I did this at Margie's behest. I myself was in love with our chemistry teacher.

The rabbi was about thirty. He had a doctorate in sociology as well as a certificate of ordination, and he knew how to play the guitar. He was haltingly eloquent. Since his arrival two years ago, attendance at Saturday morning services had swollen. Every Friday night Margie washed her hair with shampoo and then with flea soap, which added body. On Saturday mornings she put on a velvet skirt and a blouse with romantic sleeves. She walked to the synagogue. After services she descended to the social hall and drank the sweet wine and ate the seed cookies the sisterhood provided. Sooner or later she edged toward the rabbi. The women behind the refreshments stiffened. Poor motherless vamp! Margie said something about the Torah portion. The interpretation was borrowed from the Herz Commentaries but the vivacity was all her own. The rabbi gave her a kindly reply. She moved away.

The game now being dealt was seven-card stud. The rabbi unabashedly peeked twice at his hole cards. His eyes were as black as calligrapher's ink. There were faint smudges under them. His hair made my fingers tingle. All at once I became unable to reconstruct the chemistry teacher's face in my mind. The white chip I had picked up earlier scorched my groin. I was no longer peeking at the rabbi for Margie's sake; now I was feasting my eyes on him for myself. I noticed that he had stopped checking on his pair. Through the medium of the darkened kitchen window, he was feasting *his* eyes on my mother.

That chilly replica of our kitchen in the window was like a photograph that a son of mine might one day look at; he'd cautiously name me and my parents and wonder about the identity of the other five figures — the theatrical man with the gray hair, the bearded old fellow, the Latin lover, the shrimp, the young man burning up inside. I thought of my inquisitive descendant, not yet born, and then I thought of the Czech Torah, alone in its locked room, waiting to be born again. I shivered and shook myself — not like a dog, I hoped, again eyeing the rabbi. Maybe like a water nymph?

The rabbi lost to the patriarch, as I recall. It was now the last game. Dad announced Pot Limit, an unbuckled end to the evening. Pot Limit was five-card draw: any number of raises allowed, and you could bet the amount that was already on the table.

My father dealt. Chips hit the table immediately. Dad's was the only hand I could see. He wisely folded a jack/ten when it was his turn, but everybody else stayed in for three raises. At the draw everybody took two cards except for the rabbi, who took none.

There was a hoarse murmuring at this display of strength or nerve.

"Check," said the patriarch.

"Check," said the cantor.

The rabbi bet the pot. It amounted by then to five dollars or so.

"Too rich for me," said Sam, and folded.

But the usurer, smiling his tolerant smile, raised back. The patriarch and the cantor folded.

And then the rabbi raised again. I stepped down from my stool and slid behind the patriarch. I heard a squish: the pumpkin on the windowsill had imploded. I passed the cantor and stopped behind the rabbi. He held four spades to the king, and the nine of clubs.

Shocked by this four-flush that our man of God was so recklessly promoting, I nonetheless managed to obey my father's directions. I did not snicker, did not gasp, did not smile, did not frown, did not incline my head further or change the angle of my shoulders or grip the back of the rabbi's chair any tighter than I was already gripping it. But my forehead felt as if a flame had been brought very near, and I wouldn't have been surprised to learn that my hair was on fire.

The usurer glanced up in order to evaluate the rabbi's face. He could not have avoided seeing mine, too. Who could fault him for misinterpreting my close-wrapped excitement? — I must be looking down on a royal straight flush, he'd have thought, or at least four of a kind.

"The pot's yours," said the usurer graciously to the rabbi. He showed his straight, which he was not obliged to do. The rabbi collapsed his own fan of cards with one hand and collected the discards with the other and merged his nothing with the other nothings. He was under no obligation to show what he'd held. I knew that good poker strategy recommended allowing yourself sometimes to be caught in a failed bluff. But a successful bluff is best not proclaimed, particularly one that you guess has been aided by the kibitzer behind your back. My father told me later that my face resembled a tomato.

Though the ceremony to receive the Czech Torah was scheduled to begin at two o'clock, the entire congregation and a host of other people had assembled by a quarter before the hour. We crowded into the pews of the sanctuary — an octagonal room paneled in light oak, its broad windows unmediated by stained glass. The room glowed in the radiant afternoon.

My parents and I had arrived at half past one. I entered between them, as if this were my wedding, but they let me take the seat on the aisle. I watched people come in. Mrs. Sam leaned noticeably against her husband. His body adopted a matching slant, and he seemed to be doing the walking for them both. I saw Margie swish down the aisle on her grandfather's arm. She was wearing an outfit that Azinta must have helped her assemble — an orange caftan, an orange turban, and silver earrings the size of kiddush cups. The mayor nodded to several acquaintances. The university provost nodded to no one. Other Christians looked stiffly appreciative, as if they were at a concert. Azinta held hands with her Viking lover. She wore a pioneer's high-necked dress in a brown shade that just matched her skin. I wondered if she was now speaking with a Scandinavian accent.

At exactly two o'clock Mrs. Cantor marched across the bima to the lectern. In a manly voice she welcomed us. "This is a momentous occasion," she boomed. "It is the culmination of the efforts of many people." Her speech was brief. Perhaps it was not meant to be brief, but by the time she had reached the fifth or sixth sentence, our attention had been diverted to the rear of the sanctuary.

The cantor stood in the open double portal. He was wearing the white robe of the Days of Awe. His arms were wrapped around the Czech Torah, not confidently, as when he carried our Law on Shabbat, but awkwardly, as if he held something fragile. The scroll, swaddled in yellowing silk, might have been an ailing child.

The cantor moved forward. His footfalls were silent on the thick carpet of the aisle. There was no organ, no choir. There was no sound at all. Behind the cantor walked the rabbi, also enrobed. His eyes were fixed on the spindles of the Torah that poked above the cantor's white shoulder. Behind the rabbi marched the officers of the temple, tallises over their business suits. The usurer's tango glide was restrained.

The little crowd of tallises followed the two white robes down the middle aisle and across the front aisle and up the three stairs to the bima and across the bima toward the lectern. The cantor stopped short of the lectern, though, and turned to face the members of the congregation. The rabbi turned too. The elders, unrehearsed, bumped into their priests, and there was some shuffling on the platform, and one old man almost fell. Soon everyone was still. The cantor's wife had disappeared. But I saw her green shoulder bulking in the front row. Then I lost sight of it as the congregation, without any signal, rose.

"Oh God of our Fathers," began the cantor. His plummy voice broke. "God," he began again, and this time he kept talking, though his face glistened like glass. "We of Congregation Beth Shalom accept this sacred scroll, the only remnant of Your worshipers of the village of Slavkov, whose every inhabitant perished in Maidanek. Whenever we read from this Torah we will think of our vanished brothers and sisters and their dear children. God, may we be worthy of this inheritance."

He began a Hebrew prayer, which I might have followed, but I was thinking of what I'd learned in confirmation class about the village of Slavkov. Its Jews were artisans and peddlers and moneylenders. Some of them read holy books all day long in the House of Study. Then I thought about things I only guessed: some of them drank too much and others coveted their neighbors' silver and one or two of them lay with peasant women. A few little boys plotted to set their *cheder* on fire. On Sunday nights a group of men gathered in a storefront, putting troubles aside for a few hours, consulting the wise numeracy of a pack of cards.

The cantor ended his prayer. He handed the scroll to the rabbi. The rabbi held it vertically in his arms. He turned toward the Ark. The president of the congregation opened the Ark. The rabbi placed the Czech Torah beside our everyday one.

The congregation sobbed. I sobbed too, weeping over a confu-

sion of disconnected things, *vehr vaist:* Margie who missed her
mother, and the rabbi who lived alone; childless Mrs. Cantor and
forsaken Mrs. Sam; the sons and daughters of the Jews of Slavkov,
who had dreamed of love and were ashes now. My cheeks flamed. I
gripped the pew in front of me, looked at my knuckles, looked up,
and met the usurer's rueful gaze.

AKHIL SHARMA

Cosmopolitan

FROM THE ATLANTIC MONTHLY

A LITTLE AFTER ten in the morning Mrs. Shaw walked across
Gopal Maurya's lawn to his house. It was Saturday, and Gopal was
asleep on the couch. The house was dark. When he first heard the
doorbell, the ringing became part of a dream. Only he had been in
the house during the four months since his wife had followed his
daughter out of his life, and the sound of the bell joined somehow
with his dream to make him feel ridiculous. Mrs. Shaw rang the bell
again. Gopal woke confused and anxious, the state he was in most
mornings. He was wearing only underwear and socks, but his blanket was cold from sweat.

He stood up and hurried to the door. He looked through the
peephole. The sky was bright and clear. Mrs. Shaw was standing
sideways about a foot from the door, and appeared to be staring out
over his lawn at her house. She was short and red-haired and wore a
pink sweatshirt and gray jogging pants.

"Hold on! Hold on, Mrs. Shaw!" he shouted, and ran back into
the living room to search for a pair of pants and a shirt. The light
was dim, and he had difficulty finding them. As he groped under
and behind the couch and looked among the clothes crumpled on
the floor, he worried that Mrs. Shaw would not wait and was already
walking down the steps. He wondered if he had time to turn on the
light to make his search easier. This was typical of the details that
could baffle him in the morning.

Mrs. Shaw and Gopal had been neighbors for about two years,
but Gopal had met her only three or four times in passing. From his
wife he had learned that Mrs. Shaw was a guidance counselor at the

high school his daughter had attended. He also learned that she had been divorced for a decade. Her husband, a successful orthodontist, had left her. Since then Mrs. Shaw had moved five or six times, though rarely more than a few miles from where she had last lived. She had bought the small mustard-colored house next to Gopal's as part of this restlessness. Although he did not dislike Mrs. Shaw, Gopal was irritated by the peeling paint on her house and the weeds sprouting out of her broken asphalt driveway, as if by association his house were becoming shabbier. The various cars that left her house late at night made him see her as dissolute. But all this Gopal was willing to forget that morning, in exchange for even a minor friendship.

Gopal found the pants and shirt and tugged them on as he returned to open the door. The light and cold air swept in, reminding him of what he must look like. Gopal was a small man, with delicate high cheekbones and long eyelashes. He had always been proud of his looks and had dressed well. Now he feared that the gray stubble and long hair made him appear bereft.

"Hello, Mr. Maurya," Mrs. Shaw said, looking at him and through him into the darkened house and then again at him. The sun shone behind her. The sky was blue dissolving into white. "How are you?" she asked gently.

"Oh, Mrs. Shaw," Gopal said, his voice pitted and rough, "some bad things have happened to me." He had not meant to speak so directly. He stepped out of the doorway.

The front door opened into a vestibule, and one had a clear view from there of the living room and the couch where Gopal slept. He switched on the lights. To the right was the kitchen. The round Formica table and the counters were dusty. Mrs. Shaw appeared startled by this detail. After a moment she said, "I heard." She paused and then quickly added, "I am sorry, Mr. Maurya. It must be hard. You must not feel ashamed; it's no fault of yours."

"Please, sit," Gopal said, motioning to a chair next to the kitchen table. He wanted to tangle her in conversation and keep her there for hours. He wanted to tell her how the loneliness had made him fantasize about calling an ambulance so that he could be touched and prodded, or how for a while he had begun loitering at the Indian grocery store like the old men who have not learned English. What a pretty, good woman, he thought.

Mrs. Shaw stood in the center of the room and looked around her. She was slightly overweight, and her nostrils appeared to be perfect circles, but her small white Reebok sneakers made Gopal see her as fleet with youth and innocence. "I've been thinking of coming over. I'm sorry I didn't."

"That's fine, Mrs. Shaw," Gopal said, standing near the phone on the kitchen wall. "What could anyone do? I am glad, though, that you are visiting." He searched for something else to say. To extend their time together, Gopal walked to the refrigerator and asked her if she wanted anything to drink.

"No, thank you," she said.

"Orange juice, apple juice, or grape, pineapple, guava. I also have some tropical punch," he continued, opening the refrigerator door wide, as if to show he was not lying.

"That's all right," Mrs. Shaw said, and they both became quiet. The sunlight pressed through windows that were laminated with dirt. "You must remember, everybody plays a part in these things, not just the one who is left," she said, and then they were silent again. "Do you need anything?"

"No. Thank you." They stared at each other. "Did you come for something?" Gopal asked, although he did not want to imply that he was trying to end the conversation.

"I wanted to borrow your lawn mower."

"Already?" April was just starting, and the dew did not evaporate until midday.

"Spring fever," she said.

Gopal's mind refused to provide a response to this. "Let me get you the mower."

They went to the garage. The warm sun on the back of his neck made Gopal hopeful. He believed that something would soon be said or done to delay Mrs. Shaw's departure, for certainly God could not leave him alone again. The garage smelled of must and gasoline. The lawn mower was in a shadowy corner with an aluminum ladder resting on it. "I haven't used it in a while," Gopal said, placing the ladder on the ground and smiling at Mrs. Shaw beside him. "But it should be fine." As he stood up, he suddenly felt aroused by Mrs. Shaw's large breasts, boy's haircut, and little-girl sneakers. Even her nostrils suggested a frank sexuality. Gopal wanted to put his hands on her waist and pull her toward him. And then he realized that he had.

"No. No," Mrs. Shaw said, laughing and putting her palms flat against his chest. "Not now." She pushed him away gently.

Gopal did not try kissing her again, but he was excited. *Not now,* he thought. He carefully poured gasoline into the lawn mower, wanting to appear calm, as if the two of them had already made some commitment and there was no need for nervousness. He pushed the lawn mower out onto the gravel driveway and jerked the cord to test the engine. *Not now, not now,* he thought each time he tugged. He let the engine run for a minute. Mrs. Shaw stood silent beside him. Gopal felt like smiling, but wanted to make everything appear casual. "You can have it for as long as you need," he said.

"Thank you," Mrs. Shaw replied, and smiled. They looked at each other for a moment without saying anything. Then she rolled the lawn mower down the driveway and onto the road. She stopped, turned to look at him, and said, "I'll call."

"Good," Gopal answered, and watched her push the lawn mower down the road and up her driveway into the tin shack that huddled at its end. The driveway was separated from her ranch-style house by ten or fifteen feet of grass, and they were connected by a trampled path. Before she entered her house, Mrs. Shaw turned and looked at him as he stood at the top of his driveway. She smiled and waved.

When he went back into his house, Gopal was too excited to sleep. Before Mrs. Shaw, the only woman he had ever embraced was his wife, and a part of him assumed that it was now only a matter of time before he and Mrs. Shaw fell in love and his life resumed its normalcy. Oh, to live again as he had for nearly thirty years! Gopal thought, with such force that he shocked himself. Unable to sit, unable even to think coherently, he walked around his house.

His daughter's departure had made Gopal sick at heart for two or three weeks, but then she sank so completely from his thoughts that he questioned whether his pain had been hurt pride rather than grief. Gitu had been a graduate student and spent only a few weeks with them each year, so it was understandable that he would not miss her for long. But the swiftness with which the dense absence on the other side of his bed unknotted and evaporated made him wonder whether he had ever loved his wife. It made him think that his wife's abrupt decision never to return from her visit to India was as much his fault as God's. Anita, he thought, must have decided upon seeing Gitu leave that there was no more reason to stay, and that perhaps after all it was not too late to start again. Anita had gone to India at the end of November — a month after Gitu got on a Lufthansa flight to go live with her boyfriend in Germany — and a week later, over an echoing phone line, she told him of the guru and her enlightenment.

Perhaps if Gopal had not retired early from AT&T, he could have worked long hours and his wife's and daughter's slipping from his thoughts might have been mistaken for healing. But he had nothing to do. Most of his acquaintances had come by way of his wife, and when she left, Gopal did not call them, both because they had always been more Anita's friends than his and because he felt ashamed, as if his wife's departure revealed his inability to love her. At one point, around Christmas, he went to a dinner party, but he did not enjoy it. He found that he was not curious about other people's lives and did not want to talk about his own.

A month after Anita's departure a letter from her arrived — a blue aerogram, telling of the ashram, and of sweeping the courtyard, and of the daily prayers. Gopal responded immediately, but she never wrote again. His pride prevented him from trying to continue the correspondence, though he read her one letter so many times that he inadvertently memorized the Pune address. His brothers sent a flurry of long missives from India, on paper so thin that it was almost translucent, but his contact with them over the decades had been minimal, and the tragedy pushed them apart instead of pulling them closer.

Gitu sent a picture of herself wearing a yellow-and-blue ski jacket in the Swiss Alps. Gopal wrote her back in a stiff, formal way, and she responded with a breezy postcard to which he replied only after a long wait.

Other than this, Gopal had had little personal contact with the world. He was accustomed to getting up early and going to bed late, but now, since he had no work and no friends, after he spent the morning reading the *New York Times* and the *Home News & Tribune* front to back, Gopal felt adrift through the afternoon and evening. For a few weeks he tried to fill his days by showering and shaving twice daily, brushing his teeth after every snack and meal. But the purposelessness of this made him despair, and he stopped bathing altogether and instead began sleeping more and more, sometimes sixteen hours a day. He slept in the living room, long and narrow with high rectangular windows blocked by trees. At some point, in a burst of self-hate, Gopal moved his clothes from the bedroom closet to a corner of the living room, wanting to avoid comforting himself with any illusions that his life was normal.

But he yearned for his old life, the life of a clean kitchen, of a bedroom, of going out into the sun, and on a half-conscious level that morning Gopal decided to use the excitement of clasping Mrs. Shaw to change himself back to the man he had been. She might be spending time at his house, he thought, so he mopped the kitchen floor, moved back into his bedroom, vacuumed and dusted all the rooms. He spent most of the afternoon doing this, aware always of his humming lawn mower in the background. He had only to focus on it to make his heart race. Every now and then he would stop working and go to his bedroom window, where, from behind the curtains, he would stare at Mrs. Shaw. She had a red bandanna tied around her forehead, and he somehow found this appealing. That night he made himself an elaborate dinner with three dishes and a mango shake. For the first time in months Gopal watched the eleven o'clock news. He had the lights off and his feet up on a low table. Lebanon was being bombed again, and Gopal kept bursting into giggles for no reason. He tried to think of what he would do tomorrow. Gopal knew that he was happy and that to avoid depression he must keep himself busy until Mrs. Shaw called. He suddenly realized that he did not know Mrs. Shaw's first name. He padded into the darkened kitchen and looked at the phone diary. "Helen Shaw" was written in the big, loopy handwriting of his wife. Having his wife help him in this way did not bother him at all, and then he felt ashamed that it didn't.

The next day was Sunday, and Gopal anticipated it cheerfully, for the Sunday *Times* was frequently so thick that he could spend the whole day reading it. But this time he did not read it all the way through. He left the book review and the other features sections to fill time over the next few days. After eating a large breakfast — the idea of preparing elaborate meals had begun to appeal to him — he went for a haircut. Gopal had not left his house in several days. He rolled down the window of his blue Honda Civic and took the long way, past the lake, to the mall. Instead of going to his usual barber, he went to a hair stylist, where a woman with long nails and large, contented breasts shampooed his hair before cutting it. Then Gopal wandered around the mall, savoring its buttered-popcorn smell and enjoying the sight of the girls with their sometimes odd-colored hair. He went into some of the small shops and looked at clothes, and considered buying a half-pound of cocoa amaretto coffee beans, although he had never cared much for coffee. After walking for nearly two hours, Gopal sat on a bench and ate an ice cream cone while reading an article in *Cosmopolitan* about what makes a good lover. He had seen the magazine in CVS and, noting the article mentioned on the cover, had been reminded how easily one can learn anything in America. Because Mrs. Shaw was an American, Gopal thought, he needed to do research into what might be expected of him. Although the article was about what makes a woman a good lover, it offered clues for men as well. Gopal felt confident that given time, Mrs. Shaw would love him. The article made attachment appear effortless. All you had to do was listen closely and speak honestly.

He returned home around five, and Mrs. Shaw called soon after. "If you want, you can come over now."

"All right," Gopal answered. He was calm. He showered and put on a blue cotton shirt and khaki slacks. When he stepped outside, the sky was turning pink and the air smelled of wet earth. He felt young, as if he had just arrived in America and the huge scale of things had made him a giant as well.

But when he rang Mrs. Shaw's doorbell, Gopal became nervous. He turned around and looked at the white clouds against the enormous sky. He heard footsteps and then the door swishing open and Mrs. Shaw's voice. "You look handsome," she said. Gopal faced her, smiling and uncomfortable. She wore a different sweatshirt but still had on yesterday's jogging pants. She was barefoot. A yellow light shone behind her.

"Thank you," Gopal said, and then nervously added "Helen," to confirm their new relationship. "You look nice too." She did look pretty to him. Mrs. Shaw stepped aside to let him in. They were in a large room. In the center were two pale couches forming an L, with a television in front of them. Off to the side was a kitchenette — a stove, a refrigerator, and some cabinets over a sink and counter.

Seeing Gopal looking around, Mrs. Shaw said, "There are two

bedrooms in the back, and a bathroom. Would you like anything to drink? I have juice, if you want." She walked to the kitchen.

"What are you going to have?" Gopal asked, following her. "If you have something, I'll have something." Then he felt embarrassed. Mrs. Shaw had not dressed up; obviously, "Not now" had been a polite rebuff.

"I was going to have a gin and tonic," she said, opening the refrigerator and standing before it with one hand on her hip.

"I would like that too." Gopal went close to her and with a dart kissed her on the lips. She did not resist, but neither did she respond. Her lips were chapped. Gopal pulled away and let her make the drinks. He had hoped the kiss would tell him something of what to expect.

They sat side by side on a couch and sipped their drinks. A table lamp cast a diffused light over them.

"Thank you for letting me borrow the lawn mower."

"It's nothing." There was a long pause. Gopal could not think of anything to say. *Cosmopolitan* had suggested trying to learn as much as possible about your lover, so he asked, "What's your favorite color?"

"Why?"

"I want to know everything about you."

"That's sweet," Mrs. Shaw said, and patted his hand. Gopal felt embarrassed and looked down. He did not know whether he should have spoken so frankly, but part of his intention had been to flatter her with his interest. "I don't have one," she said. She kept her hand on his.

Gopal suddenly thought that they might make love tonight, and he felt his heart kick. "Tell me about yourself," he said with a voice full of feeling. "Where were you born?"

"I was born in Jersey City on May fifth, but I won't tell you the year." Gopal tried to grin gamely and memorize the date. A part of him was disturbed that she did not feel comfortable enough with him to reveal her age.

"Did you grow up there?" he asked, taking a sip of the gin and tonic. Gopal drank slowly, because he knew that he could not hold his alcohol. He saw that Mrs. Shaw's toes were painted bright red. Anita had never used nail polish, and Gopal wondered what a woman who would paint her toenails might do.

"I moved to Newark when I was three. My parents ran a news-paper and candy shop. We sold greeting cards, stamps." Mrs. Shaw had nearly finished her drink. "They opened at eight in the morn-ing and closed at seven-thirty at night. Six days a week." When she paused between swallows, she rested the glass on her knee.

Gopal had never known anyone who worked in such a shop, and he became genuinely interested in what she was saying. He remem-bered his lack of interest at the Christmas party and wondered whether it was the possibility of sex that made him fascinated with Mrs. Shaw's story. "Were you a happy child?" he asked, grinning broadly and then bringing the grin to a quick end, because he did not want to appear ironic. The half-glass that Gopal had drunk had already begun to make him feel lightheaded and gay.

"Oh, pretty happy," she said, "although I liked to think of myself as serious. I would look at the evening sky and think that no one else had felt what I was feeling." Mrs. Shaw's understanding of her own feelings disconcerted Gopal and made him momentarily think that he wasn't learning anything important, or that she was in some way independent of her past and thus incapable of the sentimental attachments through which he expected her love for him to grow.

Cosmopolitan had recommended that both partners reveal them-selves, so Gopal decided to tell a story about himself. He did not believe that being honest about himself would actually change him. Rather, he thought the deliberateness of telling the story would rob it of the power to make him vulnerable. He started to say some-thing, but the words twisted in his mouth, and he said, "You know, I don't really drink much." Gopal felt embarrassed by the non sequi-tur. He thought he sounded foolish, though he had hoped that the story he would tell would make him appear sensitive.

"I kind of guessed that from the juices," she said, smiling. Gopal laughed.

He tried to say what he had wanted to confess earlier. "I associate drinking with being American, and I haven't been able to truly Americanize. On my daughter's nineteenth birthday we took her to dinner and a movie, but we didn't talk much, and the dinner finished earlier than we had expected it would. The restaurant was in a mall, and we had nothing to do until the movie started, so we wandered around Foodtown." Gopal thought he sounded pathetic, so he tried to shift the story. "After all my years in America, I am still astonished by those huge grocery stores and enjoy walking in them. But my daughter is an American, so our wandering around in Foodtown must have been very strange for her. She doesn't know Hindi, and her parents must seem very strange." Gopal noticed that his heart was racing. He wondered if he was sadder than he knew.

"That's sweet," Mrs. Shaw said. The brevity of her response made Gopal nervous.

Mrs. Shaw kissed his cheek. Her lips were dry, Gopal noticed. He turned slightly so that their lips could touch. They kissed again. Mrs. Shaw opened her lips and closed her eyes. They kissed for a long time. When they pulled apart, they continued their conversation calmly, as if they were accustomed to each other. "I didn't go into a big grocery store until I was in college," she said. "We always went to the small shops around us. When I first saw those long aisles, I wondered what happens to the food if no one buys it. I was living then with a man who was seven or eight years older than I, and when I told him, he laughed at me, and I felt so young." She stopped and then added, "I ended up leaving him because he always made me feel young." Her face was only an inch or two from Gopal's. "Now I'd marry someone who could make me feel that way." Gopal felt his romantic feelings drain away at the idea of how many men she had slept with. But the fact that Mrs. Shaw and he had experienced something removed some of the loneliness he was feeling, and Mrs. Shaw had large breasts. They began kissing again. Soon they were tussling and groping on the floor.

Her bed was large and low to the ground. Behind it was a window, and although the shade was drawn, the lights of passing cars cast patterns on the opposing wall. Gopal lay next to Mrs. Shaw and watched the shadows change. He felt his head and found that his hair was standing up on either side like horns. The shock of seeing a new naked body, so different in its amplitude from his wife's, had been exciting. A part of him was giddy with this, as if he had checked his bank balance and discovered that he had thousands more than he expected. "You are very beautiful," he said, for *Cosmopolitan* had advised saying this after making love. Mrs. Shaw rolled over and kissed his shoulder.

"No, I'm not. I'm kind of fat, and my nose is strange. But thank you," she said. Gopal looked at her and saw that even when her mouth was slack, the lines around it were deep. "You look like you've been rolled around in a dryer," she said, and laughed. Her laughter was sudden and confident. He had not noticed it before, and it made him laugh as well.

They became silent and lay quietly for several minutes, and when Gopal began feeling self-conscious, he said, "Describe the first house you lived in."

Mrs. Shaw sat up. Her stomach bulged, and her breasts drooped. She saw him looking and pulled her knees to her chest. "You're very thoughtful," she said.

Gopal felt flattered. "Oh, it's not thoughtfulness."

"I guess if it weren't for your accent, the questions would sound artificial," she said. Gopal felt his stomach clench. "I lived in a block of small houses that the army built for returning GIs. They were all drab, and the lawns ran into each other. They were near Newark airport. I liked to sit at my window and watch the planes land. That was when Newark was a local airport."

"Your house was two stories?"

"Yes. And my room was on the second floor. Tell me about yourself."

"I am the third of five brothers. We grew up in a small, poor village. I got my first pair of shoes when I left high school." As Gopal was telling her the story, he remembered how he used to make Gitu feel lazy with stories of his childhood, and his voice fell. "Everybody was like us, so I never thought of myself as poor."

They talked this way for half an hour, with Gopal asking most of the questions and trying to discover where Mrs. Shaw was vulnerable and how this vulnerability made him attractive to her. Although she answered his questions candidly, Gopal could not find the unhappy childhood or the trauma of an abandoned wife that might explain the urgency of this moment in bed. "I was planning to leave my husband," she explained casually. "He was crazy. Almost literally. He thought he was going to be a captain of industry or a senator. He wasn't registered to vote. He knew nothing about business. Once, he invested almost everything we had in a hydroponic farm in Southampton. With him I was always scared of being poor. He used to spend two hundred dollars a week on lottery tickets, and he would save the old tickets in shoeboxes in the garage." Gopal did not personally know any Indian who was divorced, and he had never been intimate enough with an American to learn what a divorce was like, but he had expected something more painful — tears and recriminations. The details she gave made the story sound practiced, and he began to think that he would never have a hold over Mrs. Shaw.

Around eight Mrs. Shaw said, "I am going to do my bills tonight." Gopal had been wondering whether she wanted him to have dinner with her and spend the night. He would have liked to, but he did not protest.

As she closed the door behind him, Mrs. Shaw said, "The lawn mower's in the back. If you want it." Night had come, and the stars were out. As Gopal pushed the lawn mower down the road, he wished that he loved Mrs. Shaw and that she loved him.

He had left the kitchen light on by mistake, and its glow was comforting. "Come, come, cheer up," he said aloud, pacing in the kitchen. "You have a lover." He tried to smile and grimaced instead. "You can make love as often as you want. Be happy." He started preparing dinner. He fried okra and steam-cooked lentils. He made both rice and bread.

As he ate, Gopal watched a television movie about a woman who had been in a coma for twenty years and suddenly woke up one day; adding to her confusion, she was pregnant. After washing the dishes he finished the article in *Cosmopolitan* that he had begun reading in the mall. The article was the second of two parts, and it mentioned that when leaving after making love for the first time, one should always arrange the next meeting. Gopal had not done this, and he phoned Mrs. Shaw.

He used the phone in the kitchen, and as he waited for her to pick up, he wondered whether he should introduce himself or assume that she would recognize his voice. "Hi, Helen," he blurted out as soon as she said "Hello." "I was just thinking of you and thought I'd call." He felt more nervous now than he had while he was with her.

"That's sweet," she said, with what Gopal thought was tenderness. "How are you?"

"I just had dinner. Did you eat?" He imagined her sitting on the floor between the couches with a pile of receipts before her. She would have a small pencil in her hand.

"I'm not hungry. I normally make myself an omelet for dinner, but I didn't want to tonight. I'm having another drink." Then, self-conscious, she added, "Otherwise I grind my teeth. I started after my divorce and I didn't have health insurance or enough money to go to a dentist." Gopal wanted to ask if she still ground her teeth, but he did not want to imply anything.

"Would you like to have dinner tomorrow? I'll cook." They agreed to meet at six. The conversation continued for a few minutes longer, and when Gopal hung up, he was pleased at how well he had handled things.

While lying in bed, waiting for sleep, Gopal read another article in *Cosmopolitan,* about job pressure's effects on one's sex life. He had enjoyed both articles and was happy with himself for his efforts at understanding Mrs. Shaw. He fell asleep smiling.

The next day, after reading the papers, Gopal went to the library to read the first part of the *Cosmopolitan* article. He ended up reading articles from *Elle, Redbook, Glamour, Mademoiselle,* and *Family Circle,* and one from *Reader's Digest* — "How to Tell If Your Marriage Is on the Rocks." He tried to memorize jokes from the "Laughter Is the Best Medicine" section, so that he would never be at a loss for conversation.

Gopal arrived at home by four and began cooking. Dinner was pleasant, though they ate in the kitchen, which was lit with buzzing fluorescent tubes. Gopal worried that yesterday's lovemaking might have been a fluke. Soon after they finished the meal, however, they were on the couch, struggling with each other's clothing.

Gopal wanted Mrs. Shaw to spend the night, but she refused, saying that she had not slept a full night with anyone since her divorce. At first Gopal was touched by this. They lay on his bed in the dark. The alarm clock on the lampstand said 9:12 in big red figures. "Why?" Gopal asked, rolling over and resting his cheek on her cool shoulder. He wanted to reassure her that he was eager to listen.

"I think I'm a serial monogamist and I don't want to make things too complicated." She twisted a lock of his hair around her middle finger. "It isn't because of you, sweetie. It's with every man."

"Oh," Gopal said, hurt by the idea of other men and disillusioned about her motives. He continued believing, however, that now that they were lovers, the power of his concern would make her love him back. One of the articles he had read that day had suggested that people become dependent in spite of themselves when they are constantly cared for. So he made himself relax and act understanding.

Gopal went to bed an hour after Mrs. Shaw left. Before going to sleep he called her and wished her goodnight. He began calling her frequently after that, two or three times a day. Over the next few weeks Gopal found himself becoming coy and playful with her. When Mrs. Shaw picked up the phone, he made panting noises, and she laughed at him. She liked his being childlike with her. Sometimes she would point to a spot on his chest, and he would look down, even though he knew nothing was there, so that she could tap his nose. When they made love, she was thoughtful about asking what pleased him, and Gopal learned from this and began asking her the same. They saw each other nearly every day, though sometimes only briefly, for a few minutes in the evening or at night. But Gopal continued to feel nervous around her, as if he were somehow imposing. If she phoned him and invited him over, he was always flattered. As Gopal learned more about Mrs. Shaw, he began thinking she was very smart. She read constantly, primarily history and economics. He was always surprised, therefore, when she became moody and sentimental and talked about how loneliness is incurable. Gopal liked Mrs. Shaw in this mood, because it made him feel needed, but he felt ashamed that he was so insecure. When she did not laugh at a joke, Gopal doubted that she would ever love him. When they were in bed together and he thought she might be looking at him, he kept his stomach sucked in.

This sense of precariousness made Gopal try developing other supports for himself. One morning early in his involvement with Mrs. Shaw he phoned an Indian engineer with whom he had worked on a project about corrosion of copper wires and who had also taken early retirement from AT&T. They had met briefly several times since then and had agreed each time to get together again, but neither had made the effort. Gopal waited until eleven before calling, because he felt that any earlier would make him sound needy. A woman picked up the phone. She told him to wait a minute as she called for Rishi. Gopal felt vaguely deceitful, as if he were trying to pass himself off as just like everyone else, although his wife and child had left him.

"I haven't been doing much," he confessed immediately to Rishi.

"I read a lot." When Rishi asked what, Gopal answered, "Magazines," with embarrassment. They were silent then. Gopal did not want to ask Rishi immediately if he would like to meet for dinner, so he hunted desperately for a conversational opening. He was sitting in the kitchen. He looked at the sunlight on the newspaper before him and remembered that he could ask Rishi questions. "How are *you* doing?"

"It isn't like India," Rishi responded, complaining. "In India, the older you are, the closer you are to the center of attention. Here, you have to keep going. Your children are away and you have nothing to do. I would go back, but Ratha doesn't want to. America is much better for women."

Gopal felt a rush of relief that Rishi had spoken so much. "Are you just at home or are you doing something part-time?"

"I am the president of the Indian Cultural Association," Rishi said boastfully.

"That's wonderful," Gopal said, and with a leap added, "I want to get involved in that more, now that I have time."

"We always need help. We are going to have a fair," Rishi said. "It's on the twenty-fourth, next month. We need help coordinating things, arranging food, putting up flyers."

"I can help," Gopal said. They decided that he should go to Rishi's house on Wednesday, two days later.

Gopal was about to hang up when Rishi added, "I heard about your family." Gopal felt as if he had been caught in a lie. "I am sorry," Rishi said.

Gopal was quiet for a moment and then said, "Thank you." He did not know whether he should pretend to be sad. "It takes some getting used to," he said, "but you can go on from nearly anything."

Gopal went to see Rishi that Wednesday, and on Sunday he attended a board meeting to plan for the fair. He told jokes about a nearsighted snake and a water hose, and about a golf instructor and God. One of the men he met there invited him to dinner.

Mrs. Shaw, however, continued to dominate his thoughts. The more they made love, the more absorbed Gopal became in the texture of her nipples in his mouth and the heft of her hips in his hands. He thought of this in the shower, while driving, while stirring his cereal. Two or three times over the next month Gopal picked her up during her lunch hour and they hurried home to make love. They would make love and then talk. Mrs. Shaw had once worked at a dry cleaner's, and Gopal found this fascinating. He had met only one person in his life before Mrs. Shaw who had worked in a dry-cleaning business, and that was different, because it was in India, where dry cleaning still had the glamour of advancing technology. Being the lover of someone who had worked in a dry-cleaning business made Gopal feel strange. It made him think that the world was huge beyond comprehension, and to spend his time trying to control his own small world was inefficient. Gopal began thinking that he loved Mrs. Shaw. He started listening to the golden-oldies station in the car, so that he could hear what she had heard in her youth.

Mrs. Shaw would ask about his life, and Gopal tried to tell her everything she wanted to know in as much detail as possible. Once he told her of how he had begun worrying when his daughter was finishing high school that she was going to slip from his life. To show that he loved her, he had arbitrarily forbidden her to ski, claiming that skiing was dangerous. He had hoped that she would find this quaintly immigrant, but she was just angry. At first the words twisted in his mouth, and he spoke to Mrs. Shaw about skiing in general. Only with an effort could he tell her about his fight with Gitu. Mrs. Shaw did not say anything at first. Then she said, "It's all right if you were that way once, as long as you aren't that way now." Listening to her, Gopal suddenly felt angry.

"Why do you talk like this?" he asked.

"What?"

"When you talk about how your breasts fall or how your behind is too wide, I always say that's not true. I always see you with eyes that make you beautiful."

"Because I want the truth," she said, also angry.

Gopal became quiet. Her desire for honesty appeared to refute all his delicate and constant manipulations. Was he actually in love with her, he wondered, or was this love just a way to avoid loneliness? And did it matter that so much of what he did was conscious?

He questioned his love more and more as the day of the Indian festival approached and Gopal realized that he was delaying asking Mrs. Shaw to go with him. She knew about the fair but had not mentioned her feelings. Gopal told himself that she would feel uncomfortable among so many Indians, but he knew that he hadn't asked her because taking her would make him feel awkward. For some reason he was nervous that word of Mrs. Shaw might get to his wife and daughter. He was also anxious about what the Indians with whom he had recently become friendly would think. He had met mixed couples at Indian parties before, and they were always treated with the deference usually reserved for cripples. If Mrs. Shaw had been of any sort of marginalized ethnic group — a first-generation immigrant, for instance — then things might have been easier.

The festival was held in the Edison First Aid Squad's square blue-and-white building. A children's dance troupe performed in red dresses so stiff with gold thread that the girls appeared to hobble as they moved about the center of the concrete floor. A balding comedian in oxblood shoes and a white suit performed. Light folding tables along one wall were precariously laden with large pots, pans, and trays of food. Gopal stood in a corner with several men who had retired from AT&T and, slightly drunk, improvised on jokes he had read in *1,001 Polish Jokes*. The Poles became Sikhs, but he kept most of the rest. He was laughing and feeling proud that he could so easily become the center of attention, but he felt lonely at the thought that when the food was served, the men at his side would drift away to join their families and he would stand alone in line. After listening to talk of someone's marriage, he began thinking about Mrs. Shaw. The men were clustered together, and the women conversed separately. They will go home and make love and not talk, Gopal thought. Then he felt sad and frightened. To make amends for his guilt at not bringing Mrs. Shaw along, he told a bearded man with yellow teeth, "These Sikhs aren't so bad. They are the smartest ones in India, and no one can match a Sikh for courage." Then Gopal felt dazed and ready to leave.

When Gopal pulled into his driveway, it was late afternoon. His head felt odd still, as it always did when alcohol started wearing off, but Gopal knew that he was drunk enough to do something foolish. He parked and walked down the road to Mrs. Shaw's. He wondered if she would be in. Pale tulips bloomed in a thin, uneven row in front of her house. The sight of them made him hopeful.

Mrs. Shaw opened the door before he could knock. For a moment Gopal did not say anything. She was wearing a denim skirt and a sleeveless white shirt. She smiled at him. Gopal spoke solemnly and from far off. "I love you," he said to her for the first time. "I am sorry I didn't invite you to the fair." He waited a moment for his statement to sink in and for her to respond with a similar endearment. When she did not, he repeated, "I love you."

Then she said, "Thank you," and told him not to worry about the fair. She invited him in. Gopal was confused and flustered by her reticence. He began feeling awkward about his confession. They kissed briefly, and then Gopal went home.

The next night, as they sat together watching TV in his living room, Mrs. Shaw suddenly turned to Gopal and said, "You really do love me, don't you?" Although Gopal had expected the question, he was momentarily disconcerted by it, because it made him wonder what love was and whether he was capable of it. But he did not think that this was the time to quibble over semantics. After being silent long enough to suggest that he was struggling with his vulnerability, Gopal said yes and waited for Mrs. Shaw's response. Again she did not confess her love. She kissed his forehead tenderly. This show of sentiment made Gopal angry, but he said nothing. He was glad, though, when Mrs. Shaw left that night.

The next day Gopal waited for Mrs. Shaw to return home from work. He had decided that the time had come for the next step in their relationship. As soon as he saw her struggle through her doorway, hugging sacks of groceries, Gopal phoned. He stood on the steps to his house, with the extension cord trailing over one shoulder, and looked at her house and at her rusted and exhausted-looking station wagon, which he had begun to associate strongly and warmly with the broad sweep of Mrs. Shaw's life. Gopal nearly said, "I missed you" when she picked up the phone, but he became embarrassed and asked, "How was your day?"

"Fine," she said, and Gopal imagined her moving about the kitchen, putting away whatever she had bought, placing the teakettle on the stove, and sorting her mail on the kitchen table. This image of domesticity and independence moved him deeply. "There's a guidance counselor who is dying of cancer," she said, "and his friends are having a party for him, and they put up a sign saying 'RSVP with your money now! Henry can't wait for the party!'" Gopal and Mrs. Shaw laughed.

"Let's do something," he said.

"What?"

Gopal had not thought this part out. He wanted to do something romantic that would last until bedtime, so that he could pressure her to spend the night. "Would you like to have dinner?"

"Sure," she said. Gopal was pleased. He had gone to a liquor store a few days earlier and bought wine, just in case he had an opportunity to get Mrs. Shaw drunk and get her to fall asleep beside him.

Gopal plied Mrs. Shaw with wine as they ate the linguine he had cooked. They sat in the kitchen, but he had turned off the fluorescent lights and lit a candle. By the third glass Gopal was feeling very brave; he placed his hand on her inner thigh.

"My mother and father," Mrs. Shaw said halfway through the meal, pointing at him with her fork and speaking with the deliberateness of the drunk, "convinced me that people are not meant to live together for long periods of time." She was speaking in response to Gopal's hint earlier that only over time and through living together could people get to know each other properly. "If you know someone that well, you are bound to be disappointed."

"Maybe that's because you haven't met the right person," Gopal answered, feeling awkward for saying something that could be considered arrogant when he was trying to appear vulnerable.

"I don't think there is a right person. Not for me. To fall in love I think you need a certain suspension of disbelief, which I don't think I am capable of."

Gopal wondered whether Mrs. Shaw believed what she was saying or was trying not to hurt his feelings by revealing that she couldn't love him. He stopped eating.

Mrs. Shaw stared at him. She put her fork down and said, "I love you. I love how you care for me and how gentle you are."

Gopal smiled. Perhaps, he thought, the first part of her statement had been a preface to a confession that he mattered so much that she was willing to make an exception for him. "I love you too," Gopal said. "I love how funny and smart and honest you are. You are very beautiful." He leaned over slightly to suggest that he wanted to kiss her, but Mrs. Shaw did not respond.

Her face was stiff. "I love you," she said again, and Gopal became nervous. "But I am not *in* love with you." She stopped and stared at Gopal.

Gopal felt confused. "What's the difference?"

"When you are *in* love, you never think about yourself, because you love the other person so completely. I've lived too long to think anyone is that perfect." Gopal still didn't understand the distinction, but he was too embarrassed to ask more. It was only fair, a part of him thought, that God would punish him this way for driving away his wife and child. How could anyone love him?

Mrs. Shaw took his hands in hers. "I think we should take a little break from each other, so we don't get confused. Being with you, I'm getting confused too. We should see other people."

"Oh." Gopal's chest hurt despite his understanding of the justice of what was happening.

"I don't want to hide anything. I love you. I truly love you. You are the kindest lover I've ever had."

"Oh."

For a week after this Gopal observed that Mrs. Shaw did not bring another man to her house. He went to the Sunday board meeting of the cultural association, where he regaled the members with jokes from *Reader's Digest*. He taught his first Hindi class to children at the temple. He took his car to be serviced. Gopal did all these things. He ate. He slept. He even made love to Mrs. Shaw once, and until she asked him to leave, he thought everything was all right again.

Then one night Gopal was awakened at a little after three by a car pulling out of Mrs. Shaw's driveway. It is just a friend, he thought, standing by his bedroom window and watching the Toyota move down the road. Gopal tried falling asleep again, but he could not, though he was not thinking of anything in particular. His mind was blank, but sleep did not come.

I will not call her, Gopal thought in the morning. And as he was dialing her, he thought he would hang up before all the numbers had been pressed. He heard the receiver being lifted on the other side and Mrs. Shaw saying "Hello." He did not say anything. "Don't do this, Gopal," she said softly. "Don't hurt me."

"Hi," Gopal whispered, wanting very much to hurt her. He leaned his head against the kitchen wall. His face twitched as he whispered, "I'm sorry."

"Don't be that way. I love you. I didn't want to hurt you. That's why I told you."

"I know."

"All right?"

"Yes." They were silent for a long time. Then Gopal hung up. He wondered if she would call back. He waited, and when she didn't, he began jumping up and down in place.

For the next few weeks Gopal tried to spend as little time as possible in his house. He read the morning papers in the library and then had lunch at a diner and then went back to the library. On Sundays he spent all day at the mall. His anger at Mrs. Shaw soon disappeared, because he thought that the blame for her leaving lay with him. Gopal continued, however, to avoid home, because he did not want to experience the jealousy that would keep him awake all night. Only if he arrived late enough and tired enough could he fall asleep. In the evening Gopal either went to the temple and helped at the seven o'clock service or visited one of his new acquaintances. But over the weeks he exhausted the kindheartedness of his acquaintances and had a disagreement with one man's wife, and he was forced to return home.

The first few evenings he spent at home Gopal thought he would have to flee his house in despair. He slept awkwardly, waking at the barest rustle outside his window, thinking that a car was pulling out of Mrs. Shaw's driveway. The days were easier than the nights, especially when Mrs. Shaw was away at work. Gopal would sleep a few hours at night and then nap during the day, but this left him exhausted and dizzy. In the afternoon he liked to sit on the steps and read the paper, pausing occasionally to look at her house. He liked the sun sliding up its walls. Sometimes he was sitting outside when she drove home from work. Mrs. Shaw waved to him once or twice, but he did not respond, not because he was angry but because he felt himself become so still at the sight of her that he could neither wave nor smile.

A month and a half after they separated, Gopal still could not sleep at night if he thought there were two cars in Mrs. Shaw's driveway. Once, after a series of sleepless nights, he was up until three watching a dark shape behind Mrs. Shaw's station wagon. He waited by his bedroom window, paralyzed with fear and hope, for a car to pass in front of her house and strike the shape with its headlights. After a long time in which no car went by, Gopal decided to check for himself.

He started across his lawn crouched over and running. The air was warm and smelled of jasmine, and Gopal was so tired that he thought he might spill to the ground. After a few steps he stopped and straightened up. The sky was clear, and there were so many stars that Gopal felt as if he were in his village in India. The houses along the street were dark and drawn in on themselves. Even in India, he thought, late at night the houses look like sleeping faces. He remembered how surprised he had been by the pitched roofs of American houses when he had first come here, and how this had made him yearn to return to India, where he could sleep on the roof. He started across the lawn again. Gopal walked slowly, and he felt as if he were crossing a great distance.

The station wagon stood battered and alone, smelling faintly of gasoline and the day's heat. Gopal leaned against its hood. The station wagon was so old that the odometer had gone all the way around. Like me, he thought, and like Helen, too. This is who we are, he thought — dusty, corroded, and dented from our voyages, with our unflagging hearts rattling on inside. We are made who we are by the dust and corrosion and dents and unflagging hearts. Why should we need anything else to fall in love? he wondered. We learn and change and get better. He leaned against the car for a minute or two. Fireflies swung flickering in the breeze. Then he walked home.

Gopal woke early and showered and shaved and made breakfast. He brushed his teeth after eating and felt his cheeks to see whether he should shave again, this time against the grain. At nine he crossed his lawn and rang Mrs. Shaw's doorbell. He had to ring it several times before he heard her footsteps. When she opened the door and saw him, Mrs. Shaw drew back as if she were afraid. Gopal felt sad that she could think he might hurt her. "May I come in?" he asked. She stared at him. He saw mascara stains beneath her eyes and silver strands mingled with her red hair. He thought he had never seen a woman as beautiful or as gallant.

CAROL ANSHAW

Elvis Has Left the Building

FROM STORY

"I'M JUST WONDERING. Would it be okay if I came by?"

"Tonight?" Jean says, pulling the fatigued cord of the wall phone across the kitchen, crooking the receiver between cheek and shoulder as she stretches a skin of plastic wrap across a burrito left from dinner. It's nine-thirty. She was just about to fold up her tents, take a little soak with Mr. Bubble.

"You're busy," Alice says from the vast beyond of the night outside. "Forget it. I'm a tyrant of self-absorption."

Jean can hear Gloria Gaynor in the background, belting out "I Will Survive," and so guesses Alice is having a terrible moment in a terrible bar. She starts toting up how much friendship tonight will require. It will probably take Alice half an hour to find her car and get over here. When she does, she'll be looped and maudlin. She'll go into some riff parodying herself and the underlying hilarity of her tragedy. The last time she was over, she wound up lip-synching "Tears of a Clown" along with the radio. What Jean wants to say is No, don't come. It's too late.

"Sure," she says. "Come. It's not that late. We can have tea. Tom's sleeping over tonight. He's out for the count with this flu. But he'll be just as miserable whether you're here or not. So come. Maybe he'll even rally and you can match miseries."

Alice's malady is a broken heart, one of the staples — along with breaking them herself — of her emotional life, which is dramatic in Sophoclean proportions. This time, she let herself be taken to Italy by a wealthy architect she's been wild about for months. The actual breakage took place in the middle of what Alice thought was a romantic dinner overlooking the sea in Sorrento.

"We have to face it," was what the architect — Roxanne — said. "The pieces don't fit. It's simply not happening between us," she told Alice, who had just been thinking how everything was happening quite wonderfully, the pieces fitting tongue and groove.

This, according to Alice, was the worst part. The second worst part was that she couldn't tear out of the restaurant and run back to her apartment to lick her wounds, it being quite late at night, her apartment being thousands of miles away. All the money she had with her, which is to say all the money she had, period, was $150.

". . . and a supersaver ticket for a flight that was still six days off. So there I was — left to bleed in front of the very person who'd stabbed me."

"But you didn't. You were cool," Jean had told her, cheerleading. "I can just see you."

"Oh no. I totally lost it. I followed her back to the stupefyingly expensive hotel room and just collapsed on the floor. But what a floor. It was covered, layered kind of, in these opulent Persian carpets. The moonlight was pouring in through the French doors, like sun almost. You could see Vesuvius in the distance. I felt like Maria Callas. I cried for hours. Finally Roxanne collapsed next to me and started crying, too. I'm not sure why. Maybe I just made it seem like the thing to do. Maybe it made her feel like an okay person as opposed to the kind of person who would do something that rotten to someone. And then, of course — well, you know, we started having big sex down on those stupid rugs.

"Pretty soon the people next door turned their TV on real loud. There they were, paying zillions of lire a night for a room — probably the trip of a lifetime — and they had to drown out their lousy neighbors. We were like those rock bands they won't ever let back into the Chateau Marmont."

Jean has been talking Alice through this — listening her through, really — in pretty much daily installments. Over the phone mostly, but in person whenever Alice feels she's becoming one with her sofa and needs to brood in a fresh location. She has come to look at Alice's broken hearts as her charitable activity. Their friendship has enough mileage to absorb her pitying Alice, even to absorb Alice knowing she's being pitied.

They have been friends since they lived in the same commune in Wisconsin in the seventies. They are women who dropped acid together, tie-dyed T-shirts in a washtub. They were even lovers for about ten minutes early on, those being more fluid times, before everyone settled on one or another gender as their dating pool.

"Interesting cut," she says when Alice is pulling herself by the banister up the final half-flight of stairs to the apartment, looking about ten pounds thinner than the last time Jean saw her, a week or so ago, and with half as much hair on her head.

"Yeah?" Alice says, patting her hair, which is short on the sides, long on top, with the front falling in a hoody wave over her forehead. She gets these cuts at a beauty school — one of the million pieces she has assembled into a life lived on almost no money. (Alice is a painter — both kinds, houses and canvases.) Each cut is dramatically different from the one before, but the same in being another desperate interpretation of high style by one or another cosmetology student. Alice always seems indifferent to these hairdos, as if they are about someone else.

"I'm dying. Call a priest! I need extreme unction," Tom shouts down the hall from the back bedroom in a bogus stage voice.

"He's not that sick, but he wants me to call Dr. Fletcher anyway," Jean says in a low voice.

"The old guy?" Alice says. "The quackologist?"

"Herbalist."

"Right. The one who thought your ear infection was a broken jaw."

"Well, but he's nice, and he'll come by in a pinch. To rattle beads or something. Tom thinks he needs a poultice on his chest. To draw out the toxins."

Alice rolls her eyes, then pulls them back into place as she rounds the corner into the bedroom.

"How's it going, Al?" Tom says in a weak voice, like a hand puppet. He pats a spot next to him for her to sit down. "Jean told me about your travel disaster. You know what they used to say in the guys' locker room, though. Girls are like buses. Wait ten minutes and another one'll be along."

"I don't want another bus," Alice tells him.

A little while later, Tom's in the john, coughing and blowing his nose.

"Boy, he sounds like he's got something worse than just flu — something they could maybe name after him," Alice says, leaning back against the counter while Jean shuts down the flame under the whistling blue enamel kettle.

"I went to see an astrologer," Alice says as Jean shuffles through a high cabinet until she comes up with a box of Ceylon tea, scalds the inside of the pot, then sprinkles a small, sight-measured pile of cut leaves into the bottom. "She says the whole thing with me and Roxanne was doomed from the start. I'm supposed to meet someone new. Someone from a culture very different from my own. Brilliant and creative. I may meet her while at sea. Honestly, I don't think I'm up to it. Even just the going out to sea part."

"What astrologer? Now there's an astrologer in the mix?" Jean says, picking up the tray with the pot and cups on it, nodding Alice toward the living room. At least Alice is consulting a human. The last time Alice went through something like this, she was going solely on the advice of fortune cookies.

"She was really comforting about the whole thing. It was a good experience. Like tossing pillows into the abyss. Making it a homier place."

"I called her," Alice confesses when they've assembled themselves on the rag rug, on opposite sides of the coffee table. This is the one thing she has sworn she wouldn't do. She has Post-its stuck on both her phones. They say DON'T CALL, in capital letters with exclamation points. Now she drops her head and looks intently into her tea. "Last night around two-thirty. She wasn't home. Or wasn't picking up. I listened to her tape a few times. She has a new message. Do you think that means anything?"

Through Alice, Jean now knows more about Roxanne, a woman she has only met a few times in superficial social settings, than she does about most of the people in her own life. At first, listening to this recitation of Roxanne's emotional limitations, possible mo-

tives, secret pathologies, sexual penchants, and (presumed) cur-
rent state of regret was interesting, then boring, then oddly mes-
merizing, in the way litanies are.

"How about some music?" Jean says now, not sure what else she
can offer.

"Oh yes. A good idea. Do you think you could play some Sylvie?"

Sylvie Artaud is an obscure singer whom Jean produces and records, an ancient *chanteuse réaliste* she discovered in a tourist trap in
Montmartre, playing piano, backed by a Mr. Drum, singing "C'est
Si Bon" and "Hi Lili, Hi Lo" at the request of Americans killing time
waiting for their buses to the Moulin Rouge.

Jean fears that Sylvie's problem, in terms of being commercial, is
that she's too good at what she does. Her own songs — about crippled streetwalkers and women whose lovers are killed as they bring
flowers, the hurtling truck obscured from view by the bouquet —
are so sad that hardly anyone can bear to listen to them. Only the
heartbroken, really. The very souls to whom they are the most
devastating. Sylvie's records are mostly bought by the same handful
of devotees — multiply divorced women and older gay guys — who
live in some far reach of romantic nihilism. In this place, Sylvie's
songs hold a kind of liturgical value. Jean has taken Sylvie's most
dangerous album, *Crise de coeur,* away from Alice for the time being,
but of course it's precisely this Alice wants to hear, and Jean reluc-
tantly obliges, snapping the disk out of its plastic case and setting it
in the player, allowing Alice to steep like a tea bag in her misery.

Tom is asleep by the time Alice leaves. Jean goes in and takes away
the worst of his sickroom debris and refills the vaporizer. She slides
his glasses off. They have become bleached out with age; a whitish
film coats the tortoiseshell.

When she met him years ago, he was singing down at the Earl of
Old Town, Wise Fools, Orphans — the Chicago folk circuit. Opening for Bonnie Koloc and John Prine. Singing twenty-four-verse
songs about sweatshop fires and mine cave-ins. Now he's a lawyer
working for a firm that tries to get in the way of union busting.
When the papers do articles on what happened to the radicals of
the seventies, to show the irony of how many of them are now
selling junk bonds, they often include Tom by way of balance.

He has a wife and five kids. When Jean started up with him, he
had a wife and two kids.

"He took being Irish seriously" is how she deflects friends who are curious about his situation and, by implication, hers.

He's in his late forties now, and although he hasn't really put on weight, he's softer somehow. His features and voice have thickened along with the lenses in his glasses. Maybe because of this stuff, but probably, Jean thinks, because of some weave of familiarity and loss of expectation, she is no longer attracted to him in a sexual way. He may no longer be attracted to her. They have little context for talking about these matters. Their connection has always been tacit. In its initial passion, there wasn't a need for talk, and since then their circumstances have required them to sidestep discussion. And so he continues to make elaborate deceptive arrangements in order to steal a night here and there to spend in Jean's bed, where they are sleepy and affectionate, good companions. Still, they've been some version of together for more than twenty years, and she can't imagine a future without him. A blank that would have to be filled in with an astrologer's calculations.

He wakes up a little. His eyes are red-rimmed, his nose is chapped. Jean would feel worse for him if he didn't enjoy this quite so much. Ten years ago, she would have been happy to play nurse to him. But she's been worn down by his hypochondria. In addition to his herbalist, Tom also has standing appointments with both a naprapath and a shiatsu massage therapist. He has a subscription to *Prevention* magazine.

The small failures of his body and his fascination with them are only one aspect of his seeming to have succumbed to the gravity of living. His work (both in its day-to-day, and in the long run of losing ground against musclebound corporations), his kids and their problems (always shifting, but also always overwhelming), and his wife's need for his attention (a reasonable demand, even Jean admits) have combined to bring him closer and closer to the ground he walks on, stooped over with the weight of his good intentions.

"I really don't mind being sick in a way," he understates now, rolling onto his back and pushing himself up the steep bank of pillows behind him. "Not advanced brain cancer, of course. Or anal fissures. But a little flu, a little fever. I don't have to go down to the firm. When they call, they say I sound terrible. I don't have to worry about doing something worthwhile with this stretch of time. I don't have to finally get down to reading *Ulysses*. My brain cells can just seek their own level, which at the moment seems to be the level of daytime dramas."

He suddenly looks stricken, jerks into a sitting position, and makes three or four frantic grabs for Kleenexes from the box in the middle of the bed, just in time to sneeze wildly into them. There's a bit of follow-up honking before he continues.

"I wish Al had stayed longer. I have so much good advice to give her. Half the characters on my new favorite shows have broken hearts or are in unrequited love. I'm getting to be a pretty big expert on the subject."

"You think her situation is funny," Jean says. "Not truly grave. And I suppose it is just one more go-round. But still. I can't stand to see how hard this one is on her. I want to go over and slap this Rox-anne's smug face." She flips her hand to illustrate. "Kkhh-kkhh. I'd like to trip her and watch her fall. Dunk her in a lake."

"You're a good friend."

"Oh, I know it. It's one of the best things about me."

A few days later, Alice is so quiet coming into the recording booth that Jean doesn't see her until she looks up when the session is over, the musicians and singers folding up their music and leaving.

The studio — E-Z Corp. — is Jean's bread and butter. Here she homogenizes popular songs of a few seasons past into calming gray noise for people captured in small places or unpleasant situations. Elevators, dental offices, phones on hold.

She funnels most of the profits from this into producing Sylvie and another obscure artist she's devoted to — Big Tiny Raymond, a five-hundred-pound blues singer who lives in Cleveland, but more specifically lives in his bathtub, where the water gives him a break of buoyancy. Jean flies to Ohio to record him. She rents a van and picks him up at his house and takes him to a small studio where they have a couch ready — no chair can hold Big Tiny — where he sits and plays an old guitar and sings his songs about troubles with women. Alice thinks all of Big Tiny's songs sound the same, and says she has trouble imagining him involved in any of the innuen-doed activities he sings about. Jean admits you'd want to be on top with Big Tiny.

"I thought maybe we could have breakfast," Alice says, although it's four-thirty in the afternoon.

"Sure," Jean says and flips a few switches along one of the mixing boards, gets up to go. "You look a little better," she tells Alice as they come out of the studio into the hard light of the street. "More upbeat."

"I'm not. I just went to a tanning parlor. A vampire could look pretty good coming out of there."

They go to the Friendly Café across the street, squeezing through a break in the line of hulking Harleys angled in front. They sit across from each other in a booth patched together with duct tape, wait while the waitress pours them coffee. Alice tamps three sugar packets on the worn-down Formica tabletop, rips them open with one tear, tips them halfway, so the sugar sifts down into her coffee, like a drug.

When Alice was just back from Italy, bruised and off balance, Jean was only going through the standard friend paces: being there, bucking up, putting the best possible construction on everything, running through the clichés of comfort. For a while this seemed enough, that it was the ritual that counted anyway. That this was something women naturally do together, something ancient, like keening, or putting the overturned cup on the chest of the plague victim to draw off evil spirits.

But more recently she has begun to really *think* about this broken heart of Alice's, both in how it's particular to her and in how it is really all the broken hearts in the world. Which leads her to think of all the heartbreak she has avoided by not allowing herself to experience it. She sometimes feels an imposter as an adviser to Alice; better she should just give her Sylvie Artaud's phone number. Actually, by now, Alice might be her own best adviser. She has copious knowledge on the subject, has been reading up.

"Dorothy Parker," she will say in the middle of talking about something else. "Some guy wouldn't return her calls. She drank a bottle of shoe polish."

Today, before their eggs arrive, she says, "It's getting worse. You know. Instead of better."

"Maybe the dust is just settling," Jean says. "At first it's just impact. She's left. Boom. It's event. You can tell everyone, crack open those fortune cookies, go see the astrologer. It's almost as though the relationship is still going on, even though Roxanne is not there. Then with time, the worse truth settles in. It's no longer an event;

it's a permanent state of omission. It's like what they used to put out over the loudspeaker to get everybody chilled and resigned after concerts. You know — 'Elvis has left the building.'"

Alice seems to hear this, but then says, "Here's the scene I play over and over. We were on the ferry to Capri. And she drew this little line sloping in the air — the falling graph of her affection for me. Like this." She dips her finger through the air above their mugs of coffee.

Jean can imagine this vividly — the watery sunshine, the saline spray clinging to the light hair on Alice's forearms, her abandoned hopes for the holiday. Worse, her dread of coming back home to what she had expected to be a cushy time of snapshots, dinners with friends who'd listen to them run an anecdotal highlighter over the trip. Now all of this was being revised downward. Jean can feel exactly what it was like to be Alice in the moment when it sank in that what she was going back to now was the vacuum created by Roxanne no longer loving her.

Some days later, Alice calls to say she's been getting mystery calls. The person on the other end just waits until Alice says "hello," then "hello" again, then clicks off.

"I know it's her. I can feel her there on the other end."

Jean says she supposes this might really be happening, but then again it could just be the usual phone vapors. She herself has a number that ends in 999, which must be easy and fun to punch because she gets an amazing number of calls from babies.

"The thing is," Alice presses on, undaunted by information, "I'm coming to see that silence has shape, just like conversation. Only a little more oblique. In different lights, this silence between Roxanne and me looks like different things. Sometimes it's angry. Sometimes it just looks like a pause, like she's drawing a breath before speaking again."

Jean listens nervously. The silence isn't quite so oblique to her. Two days ago she saw Roxanne coming out of Provisions, a ridiculously expensive food emporium. Roxanne was being fed a bite of smoked mink nipple, or hummingbird tongue, or whatever, from a plastic fork held by a woman Jean didn't recognize. The woman and Roxanne had the damp, scrubbed look of two people just out of the same shower, hydroplaning on the light air of fresh start.

*

"What do you think I should do?" Jean asks Tom. He has recovered from his flu, has his appetite back with a vengeance, is chopping onions and black olives and tomatoes for his specialty — Tom's Taco Bar.

"I don't know, I guess you should probably tell her, but I wouldn't want anyone telling *me*. I'd want to sit there nice and cozy with my delusions for a while. She doesn't look as though she's up to bad news yet. She looks like someone having a hard time staying away from her drug of choice. Except for the tan. The tan's great."

Alice's sexuality has quite a bit of range. No matter that she's scrawny and plainspoken and wears outer-spacey haircuts. There are nonetheless emanations of heat around her, like the wavy air above a radiator. Maybe, Jean thinks, it's the way she seems always to be operating as though the stakes are high and time is running out, trying to rush a stack of chips onto the felt as the croupier reaches to spin the wheel. Because the concept of passion is so abstract, it has to get interpreted as something, and that something is usually sex. And then, from time to time, there's the added element of her spectacular sadness. Jean herself feels a little bit of the grade-school crush she had on Joan of Arc, just from staring at her holy card, a gold-edged, pastel death at the stake.

"Do you envy her her broken heart?" Tom asks now, still holding the cleaver suspended over the tiny pile of onion bits.

"Nah," Jean says. "You could still break my heart," she adds so he'll go back to chopping. "Honestly."

"Not like that," he says. "And not in Sorrento."

They have gone away together a few times, when Tom had business that could be puffed out to include a weekend. Since his clients are unions, his travel is not to quaint and charming destinations. Once they went to someplace in West Virginia amid miles and miles of strip-mined hills. Another time they stayed in a bed-and-breakfast, but in Pittsburgh.

When Alice doesn't call for a while, Jean doesn't notice, or pretends not to. She is bogged down for a couple of long days with Harold Lasky, her partner in E-Z Corp. They're putting together a test market demo for a line of tapes a little more hip than the ones they privately refer to as "dental-zak." The new line would feature lite versions of Billie Holiday, Joan Armatrading, Pachelbel. For subscription sale to restaurants with pale decors and pinpoint spots on the table flowers.

By the time they're finished with the tape, it's Labor Day, a long-stretch weekend Jean doesn't particularly want invaded by anyone. Tom will be in Wisconsin with his two youngest boys at an Indian Guides sleepover camp. She likes knowing where he is, even though it's of no real use. She can never call him, and so he is either with her or unavailable to her. They can be together only in planned moments, which often exclude the times when lovers are most necessary to each other. She couldn't call him for his extra set of keys the time she locked herself out of her apartment. Couldn't visit him in the hospital after he'd gotten his head bashed in during a picket-line fracas. If he won the Nobel Prize, she couldn't tag along to Stockholm. If he died, she'd have to sit in a back pew along with the small group of fans from his singing days. More and more lately she has been questioning the wisdom of having chosen this detoured avenue of love.

This weekend, though, she doesn't mind that he's gone. She has solitary pursuits in mind. She's going to colorfoam her hair. Go to her yoga class, which she has skipped the past two Saturdays.

By Sunday afternoon, though, she falls into her deepest reserves of gloom. She leaves a message on Alice's machine. When she doesn't hear back by seven, she gets in the car and drives down to Pilsen to see what's up. Alice lives in a rough loft on 18th Street. She answers the door with a heavy thumb on the release buzzer and seems happy and not at all surprised to see Jean. She takes her into the living space at the front of the studio. The first floor of the building is fronted by a Mexican stand that sells snow cones with breathtakingly lurid syrups. Chartreuse and ultraviolet and blood orange. The scents, which in a weird way match the colors, drift sweetly up through the gray air of the long summer dusk.

The loft is huge and hot, but breezy from a ceiling fan. Jean collapses onto an old maroon velvet sofa. She remembers making out with Tom on this sofa in the late stages of a bicentennial party back in 1976, when she and Alice and the sofa were still in the commune and everyone was smoking joints of some stupefying dope called Monkey Paw.

Alice comes back from the kitchen with her fingers curled around the necks of a couple of bottles of Rolling Rock. They talk about everything and nothing — *rien et tout,* as Sylvie would say — and after a little while, Jean notices that Alice is saying everything brightly, that she is also looking bright, eyes glossy like someone with a tropical fever. She's even tanner than before, which Jean now takes as a bad sign. Her conversation seems to be alighting on preselected "topics." A certain architecturally oriented person is not being mentioned. Jean falls in something like love with Alice in this moment, her heart stung by how game Alice is trying to be through her wet-eyed, skinny, lousy-haircutted misery.

Then, when they're into their third pair of beers, as a non sequitur to whatever Jean has just said, Alice loses her tenuous hold on courage and starts silently sobbing, terrible little convulsions around the shoulders and tears falling down her face, but no sound. Jean responds by erasing the space between them on the sofa.

"Maybe I'll just stay over," she says after a while, making it sound as though what she has in mind is something along the lines of a high school slumber party, even though their fingers have already started looking for buttons, tugging off each other's shirts, and Alice, even as she is still sniffling, is also tracing Jean's ear with the tip of her tongue.

A few days pass during which Jean catches herself wishing Alice would call. And then, when she finds herself wandering into Arcadia, stopping in front of the display of blank cards with photos designed to articulate oblique emotions, she feels ridiculous, and then a little exhilarated, then once again ridiculous.

The first real occasion she finds to call Alice is a week or so later, and on account of troubles of her own.

"Big Tiny got himself arrested last night. Beating up Eunice. The neighbors called the cops. He phoned me for bail. I sent it, but I'm going to quit producing him. I mean, how can I call myself a feminist if I don't? You work years with someone, and then . . . I don't know. I'm losing confidence a lot lately, in the choices I made when I was younger. In the people I was so certain would be durable."

"What do you think he's sitting on? In the jail cell?"

"They brought in a sofa. I asked. Are you okay?"

"Oh. Yes," Alice says, and laughs.

Jean doesn't like the sound of this. She has been caught off-guard. Here she is, still dancing dreamily to the four-four beat of Alice's suffering while Alice, she can tell from her tone, has moved into a little cha-cha.

"What's going on?"

When Alice can't say, after having been able to say everything else, Jean makes a guess.

"She called."

Alice's silence lets Jean know.

"You've seen her." Jean is doodling on a scratch pad — a lightning bolt, one of the small repertoire of things she can draw. She goes over the jagged lines many times, wearing deep grooves in the paper.

"It's not really like before," Alice says, the lie in her mouth like three sticks of gum, making her trip over her words a little. "She's in hypnotherapy. She's seeing a past-life regression therapist. He takes her way back, to her earliest self."

Jean floods with a rush of lightly murderous impulses. "I don't think Roxanne needs to know what she was doing in 5 B.C. I think she needs to think about why she behaves so badly on late-twentieth-century vacations."

"There was someone else," Alice says. "I sort of knew. But she says that's all over, and I believe her."

Jean immediately assumes Roxanne got dumped.

"I'd like for us all to get together. I could make a little supper maybe," Alice says, giving Jean her discharge papers. "I think if you two just got to know each other better . . ."

Jean tears off the top sheet of the scratch pad and rubs the side of the pencil lead back and forth across the new sheet, bringing the lightning into relief.

"Yes," she says. "Soon."

CHRIS ADRIAN

Every Night for a Thousand Years

FROM THE NEW YORKER

HE DREAMED his brother's death at Fredericksburg. General Burnside appeared as an angel at the foot of his bed to announce the tragedy: "The Army regrets to inform you that your brother George Washington Whitman was shot in the head by a lewd fellow from Charleston." The General alit on the bedpost and drew his dark wings close about him, as if to console himself. Moonlight limned his strange whiskers and his hair. His voice shook as he went on. "Such a beautiful boy. I held him in my arms while his life bled out. See? His blood made this spot." He pointed at his breast, where a dark stain in the shape of a bird lay on the blue wool. "I am so very sorry," he said, choking and weeping. Tears fell in streams from his eyes, ran over the bed and out the window, where they joined the Rappahannock, which had somehow come north to flow through Brooklyn, bearing the bodies of all the battle's dead.

In the morning he read the wounded list in the *Herald*. There it was: "First Lieutenant G. W. Whitmore." He knew from George's letters that there was nobody named Whitmore in the company. He went to his mother's house. "I'll go find him," he told her and his sister and his brothers.

So he went. Washington, he quickly discovered, was a city of hospitals. He looked in half of them before a cadaverous-looking clerk told him he'd be better off looking at Falmouth, where most of the Fredericksburg wounded still lay in field hospitals. In Falmouth he wandered outside the hospital tents, afraid to go in and find his mangled brother. He stood before a pile of amputated limbs, arms and legs of varying length, all black and blue and rotten in the chill. A thin layer of snow covered some of them. He circled the heap, thinking he must recognize his brother's hand if he saw it. He closed his eyes and considered the amputation: his brother screaming when he woke from the chloroform, his brother's future contracting to something bitter and small.

But George had only got a hole in his cheek. A piece of shell pierced his wispy beard and scraped a tooth. He spit blood and hot metal into his hand, put the shrapnel in his pocket, and later showed it to his worried brother, who burst into tears and clutched him in a bear hug when they were reunited in Captain Francis's tent, where George sat with his feet propped on a trunk and a cigar stuck in his bandaged face.

"You shouldn't fret," said George. But he could not help fretting, even now that he knew his brother was alive and well. A great fretting buzz had started up in his head, inspired by the pile of limbs and the smell of blood in the air and ruined Fredericksburg across the river, all broken chimneys and crumbling walls. He stayed in George's tent and, watching him sleep, felt a deep satisfaction. He wandered around the camp, sat by fires with sentries who told him hideous stories about the death of friends.

Ten days later he still couldn't leave Falmouth. Even after his brother moved out with the healthy troops on Christmas Day, he stayed and made himself useful, changing dressings, fetching for the nurses, and just sitting with the wounded boys, with the same satisfaction on him as when he watched George sleep. In Brooklyn a deep and sinister melancholy had settled over him. For the past six months he had wandered the streets, feeling as if all his vital capacities were sputtering, about to die. In the hospital that melancholy was gone, scared off, perhaps, by all the misery, and replaced by something infinitely more serious and real.

He finally went back to Washington in charge of a transport. With every jolt and shake of the train a chorus of horrible groans wafted through the cars. He thought it would drive him insane. What saved him was the singing of a boy with a leg wound. The whole trip he sang in a rough voice indicative of tone-deafness. His name was Henry Smith. He'd come all the way from divided Missouri, and said he had a gaggle of cousins fighting under General Beauregard. He sang "Oh! Susanna" over and over again, and no one told him to be quiet.

All the worst cases went to Union Square Hospital, because it was closest to the train station. He went with them, and kept up the service he'd begun at Falmouth — visiting, talking, reading, fetching and helping. Months passed.

He went to other hospitals. There were certainly enough of them to keep him busy — Finley, Campbell, Carver, Harewood, Mount Pleasant, Judiciary Square. And then there were the churches and public buildings, also stuffed with wounded. Even the Patent Office held them: boys on cots set up on the marble floor of the model room. He brought horehound candy to an eighteen-year-old from Iowa, who lay with a missing arm and a sore throat in front of a glass case that held Ben Franklin's printing press. Two boys from Brooklyn had beds in front of General Washington's camp equipment. He read to them from a copy of the *Eagle* his mother sent down, every now and then looking up at the General's tents rolled neatly around their posts, his folded chairs and mess kit, sword and cane, washstand, his surveyor's compass, and, a few feet down, in a special case all to itself, the Declaration of Independence. Other boys lay in front of pieces of the Atlantic cable, ingenious toys, rattraps, the razor of Captain Cook.

He could not visit every place all in a day, though he tried at first. Eventually he picked a few and stuck with those. But mostly he was at Union Square, where Hank Smith was.

"I had my daddy's pistol with me," said Hank Smith. "That's why I got my leg still." It wasn't the first time he'd been told how Hank had saved his own leg from the "chopping butchers" in the field hospital. But he didn't mind hearing the story again. It was spring. The leg was still bad, though not as bad as it had been. At least that was the impression that Hank gave. He never complained about his leg. He'd come down with typhoid, too, a gift from the hospital. "I want my pistol back."

"I'll see what I can do." Walt always said that, but they both knew no one was going to give Hank back the pistol with which he threatened to blow out the brains of the surgeon who had tried to take his leg. They had left him alone then, and later another doctor said there wasn't any need to amputate. They would watch the wound. "Meanwhile, have an orange." Walt pulled the fruit out of his coat pocket and peeled it. Soldiers' heads began to turn in their beds as the smell washed over the ward. Some asked if he had any for them.

"Course he does," said Hank. In fact, he had a coatful of them. He had bought them at Center Market, then walked through the misty, wet morning, over the brackish canal and across the filthy Mall. The lowing of cattle drifted toward him from the unfinished monument as he walked along, wanting an orange but afraid to eat one lest he be short when he got to the hospital. He had money for oranges, sweets, books, tobacco from sponsors in Brooklyn and New York and elsewhere. And he had a little money for himself from a job, three hours a day as a copyist in the paymaster's office. From his desk he had a spectacular view of Georgetown and the river, and the three stones that were said to mark the watery graves of three Indian sisters. They had cursed the spot: anyone who tried to cross there must drown. He would sit and stare at the rocks, imagining himself shedding his shirt and shoes by the riverside, trying to swim across. He imagined drowning, the great weight of water pressing down on him. Inevitably his reverie was broken by the clump-clump of one-legged soldiers on their crutches, coming up the stairs to the office, located perversely on the top floor of the building.

Union Square was under the command of a brilliant drunk named Canning Woodhull. Over whiskey he explained his radical policies, which included washing hands and instruments, throwing out sponges, swabbing everything in sight with bitter-smelling Labarraque's solution, and an absolute lack of faith in laudable pus.

"Nothing laudable about it," he said. "White or green, pus is pus, and either way it's bad for the boys. There are creatures in the wounds — elements of evil. They are the emissaries of Hell, sent earthward to increase our suffering, to increase death and increase grief. You can't see them except by their actions." They knocked glasses and drank, and Walt made a face because the whiskey was medicinal, laced with quinine. It did not seem to bother Woodhull.

"I have the information from my wife, who has great and secret knowledge," Woodhull said. "She talks to spirits. Most of what she hears is garbage, of course. But this is true." Maybe it was. His hospital got the worst cases and kept them alive better than any other hospital in the city, even ones that got casualties only half as severe. Woodhull stayed in charge despite a reputation as a wastrel and a drunk and an off-and-on lunatic. Once he was removed by a coalition of his colleagues, only to be reinstated by Dr. Letterman, the medical director of the Army of the Potomac, who had been personally impressed by many visits to Union Square. "General Grant is a drunk, too," he would say in response to a charge against Dr. Woodhull.

"They are vulnerable to prayer and bromine, and whiskey and Labarraque's. Lucky for us." He downed another glass. "You know, some of the nurses are complaining. Just last Tuesday I was in Ward E with the redoubtable Mrs. Hawley. We saw you come in at the end of the aisle and she said, 'Here comes that odious Walt Whitman to talk evil and unbelief to my boys. I think I would rather see the Evil One himself — at least if he had horns and hoofs — in my ward. I shall get him out as soon as possible!' And she rushed off to do just that. She failed, of course." He poured again.

"Shall I stop coming, then?"

"Heavens, no. As long as old Horse-Face Hawley is complaining, I'll know you're doing good. God keep some dried-up old shrew from driving you away."

Two surgeons came into Woodhull's makeshift office, a corner of Ward F sectioned off by three regimental flags.

"*Assistant* Surgeon Walker is determined to kill Captain Carter," said Dr. Bliss, a dour black-eyed man from Baltimore. "She has given him opium for his diarrhea and, very foolishly, in my opinion, withheld ipecac and calomel." Dr. Mary Walker stood next to him, looking calm, her arms folded across her chest. She held the same rank as George did. Their uniforms had the same gold stripes, the same gold braid on the hat.

"Dr. Walker is doing as I have asked her," said Woodhull. "Ipecac and calomel are to be withheld in all cases of flux and diarrhea."

"For God's sake, why?" asked Dr. Bliss, his face reddening. He was new in Union Square. Earlier the same day, Woodhull had castigated him for not cleaning a suppurating chest wound.

"Because it is for the best," said Woodhull. "Because if you do it that way, a boy will not die. Because if you do it that way, some mother's heart will not be broken."

Dr. Bliss turned redder, then paled, as if his rage had broken and ebbed. He scowled at Dr. Walker, turned sharply on his heel, and left. Dr. Walker sat down.

"Buffoon," she said. Woodhull poured whiskey for her. It was an open secret in the hospital that they were lovers.

"Dr. Walker," said Woodhull, "why don't you tell Mr. Whitman about your recent arrest?" She sipped her whiskey and told how she'd been arrested outside her boarding house for masquerading as a man. Walt only half listened to her talk. He was thinking about diarrhea. It was just about the worst thing, he had decided. He'd seen it kill more boys than all the mines and shrapnel, and typhoid and pneumonia — than all the other afflictions combined. He'd written to his mother, "I think we ought to stop this war, however we can. Just stop it. War is nine hundred and ninety-nine parts diarrhea to one part glory. Those who like wars ought to be made to fight in them."

"I did my best to resist them," said Dr. Walker. "I shouted out, 'Congress has bestowed on me the right to wear trousers!' It was to no avail." She was silent for a moment, and then all three of them burst out laughing.

In the summer he saw the President almost every day, because he lived on the route the President took to and from his summer residence north of the city. Walking down the street, soon after leaving his rooms in the morning, he'd hear the approach of the party. Always he stopped and waited for them to pass. Mr. Lincoln, dressed in plain black, rode a gray horse, surrounded by twenty-five or thirty cavalry with their sabers drawn and held up over their shoulders. They got so they would exchange bows, he and the President, he tipping his broad, floppy felt hat, Lincoln tipping his high stiff black one and bending a little in the saddle. And every time they did this the same thought bloomed large in Walt's mind: A sad man.

With the coming of the hot weather Dr. Woodhull redoubled his efforts to eradicate the noxious effluvia. They threw open the windows and burned eucalyptus leaves in small bronze censers set in the four corners of each ward. The eucalyptus, combined with the omnipresent reek of Labarraque's solution, gave some of the boys aching heads. Dr. Woodhull prescribed whiskey.

"I want a bird," Hank Smith said one day late in July. The weather was hot and dry. Hank had been fighting a bad fever for a week. Walt helped him change out of his soaked shirt, then wiped him down with a cool wet towel. The wet shirt he took to the window, where he wrung out the sweat, watching it fall and dapple the dirt. He lay the shirt to dry on the sill and considered his wet, salty

hands. In the distance he could see the Capitol, gleaming mag-
nificently in the late-afternoon sun.

"I want a bird," Hank said again. "When I was small, my sister got
me a bird. I named it for her — Olivia. Would you help me get
one?" Walt left the window and sat on a stool by the bed. The sun lit
up the hair on Hank's chest and made Walt think of shining fields
of wheat.

"I could get you a bird," he said. "I don't know where, but I will
get you a bird."

"I know where," said Hank, as Walt helped him into a new shirt.
With a jerk of his head he indicated the window. "There's plenty of
birds out in the yard. You just get a rock and some string. Then we'll
get a bird."

He came back the next day with rock and string, and they set a
trap of bread crumbs on the windowsill. Walt crouched beneath the
window and grabbed at whatever came for the crumbs. He missed
two jays and a blackbird, but caught a beautiful cardinal by its leg. It
chirped frantically and pecked at his hand; the fluttering of its
wings against his wrists made him think of the odd buzz that still
thrilled his soul when he was in the wards. He took the bird to
Hank, who tied the string to its leg and the rock to the string, then
set the rock down by his bed. The cardinal tried to fly for the
window but only stuck in midair, its desperate wings striking up a
small breeze that Walt, kneeling near it, could feel against his face.
Hank clapped and laughed.

They called the bird Olivia. She became the ward's pet. Other
boys would insist on having her near their beds. It did not take her
long to become domesticated. Soon she was eating from Hank's
hand and sleeping at night beneath his cot. They kept her secret
from the nurses and doctors, until one morning Hank was careless.
He fell asleep having left her out in the middle of the aisle while
Woodhull was making his rounds. Walt had just walked into the
ward, his arms full of candy and fruit and novels.

"Who let this dirty bird into my hospital?" Woodhull asked. He
very swiftly bent down and picked up the stone, then tossed it out
the window. Olivia trailed helplessly behind it. Walt dropped his
packages and rushed outside, where he found the bird in the dirt,
struggling with a broken wing. He put her in his shirt and took her
back to his room, where she died three days later, murdered by his

landlady's cat. He told Hank she flew away. "A person can't have anything," Hank said, and stayed angry about it for a week.

At Christmas, Mrs. Hawley and her cronies trimmed the wards; evergreen wreaths were hung on every pillar and garlands strung across the hall. At the foot of every bed hung a tiny stocking, hand-knitted by Washington society ladies. Walt went around stuffing them with walnuts and lemons and licorice. Hank's leg got better and worse, better and worse. Walt cornered Dr. Woodhull and said he had a bad feeling about Hank's health. Woodhull insisted he was going to be fine; Walt's fretting was pointless.

Hank's fevers waxed and waned, too. Once Walt came in from a blustery snowstorm, his beard full of snow. Hank insisted on pressing his face into it, saying it made him feel so much better than any medicine had, except maybe paregoric, which he found delicious, and said made him feel like he was flying in his bed.

Walt read to him from the New Testament, the bit about there being no room at the inn.

"Are you a religious man?" Hank asked him.

"Probably not, my dear, in the way that you mean." Though he did make a point of dropping by the Union Square chapel whenever he was there. It was a little building, with a quaint onion-shaped steeple. He would sit in the back and listen to the services for boys whom he'd been visiting almost every day. He wrote their names down in a small leatherbound notebook that he kept in one of his pockets. By Christmas he had pages and pages of them. Sometimes at night he would sit in his room and read the names softly aloud by the light of a single candle.

Dr. Walker came by and asked to borrow his Bible. She said she had news from the War Department.

"What's the news?" he asked her.

"Nothing good," she said. "It is dark, dark everywhere." She wanted to read some Job, to cheer herself.

Sometimes when he could not sleep, which was often, he would walk around the city, past the serene mansions on Lafayette Square, past the President's house, where he would pause and wonder if a light in the window meant Mr. Lincoln was awake and agonizing. Once he saw a figure in a long, trailing black crepe veil move, lamp in hand, past a series of windows, and he imagined it must be Mrs. Lincoln, searching forlornly for her little boy, who had died two winters ago. He walked past the empty market stalls, along the ever-stinking canal. He would pause by it, looking down into the dirty water, and see all manner of things float by. Boots and bonnets, half-eaten vegetables, animals. Once there was a dead cat drifting on a little floe of ice.

Walking on, he would pass into Murder Bay, where the whores hooted at him, but he was otherwise left alone. From a distance he was large and imposing, not an easy target, and up close he looked so innocent and sweet that even the most heartless criminal would not raise a hand against him. He would peek into alleys that housed whole families of "contraband." Sometimes a dirty child would rush out of a dank shanty and ask him a riddle. He got to keeping candy in his pockets for the children. He would cut back along the canal, then across, sometimes watching the moon shine on the towers of the Smithsonian castle and on the white roofs of Union Square. He would walk among the shrubs and trees of the Mall, sometimes getting lost on a footpath that went nowhere, but eventually he would cross the canal again and walk up to the Capitol. The great statue of General Washington was there, the one that everyone ridiculed because he was dressed in a toga. It was said that his sword was raised in a threat to do harm to the country if his clothes were not returned.

He liked the statue. He would crawl up into its lap and sprawl out, Pietà-like, or else put his arms around the thick marble neck and have a good wrenching cry. At dawn he would stand outside the Capitol, writing his name in the snow with his foot, and he could smell the bread baking in the basement. He had a friend in the bakery, who loaded him down with countless hot loaves. He'd walk back to Union Square, warmed by the bread in his coat, and sometimes he'd have enough so that every full-diet boy in a ward would wake with a still-warm loaf on his chest.

"They want to take my leg," Hank told him. It was early May, and still cold. "I ain't going to let them. You've got to get me a gun."

"Hush," said Walt. "They won't take your leg." Though in fact it looked as if they would have to. Just when he had seemed on the verge of good health, just when he had beaten off the typhoid, the leg flared up again and deteriorated rapidly. Dr. Woodhull cleaned the wound, prayed over it, swabbed it with whiskey, all to no avail. A hideous, stinking infection had taken root and was growing.

He went looking for Dr. Woodhull, to discuss Hank's case. He did not find him in his office. There was a pall of silence and gloom over all the wards. News of the horrible casualties accrued by General Grant in his Wilderness campaign had reached the hospital. Dr. Bliss and Mrs. Hawley were having a loud discussion as she changed dressings. "Trust a drunk not to give a fig for our boys' lives," said Dr. Bliss. "This war is an enterprise dominated by inebriates, charlatans, and fools." He gave Walt a mean look. Walt asked if either of them had seen Woodhull. Neither of them replied, but the young man whose dressings were being changed told him he had gone out to the deadhouse.

Walt found him there, among the bodies. There were only a few, just the dead from the past few days. He was weeping over a shrouded form. Dr. Walker stood beside him, her hand on his shoulder.

"Canning," she said, "you've got to come back now. We've got boys coming from Spotsylvania."

"Oh, darling," said Woodhull, "I just can't stand it." He was leaning over the shrouded body, dropping tears onto the face. As the fabric became wet, Walt could make out the boy's features. He had a thin mustache and a mole on his cheek. "There's such an awful lot of blood. You'd think they could do something with all that blood. A great work. Oughtn't something great to be coming?"

Dr. Walker noticed him standing by the door. "Mr. Whitman," she said. "If you would assist me?" He put his arm around Dr. Woodhull and bore him up, away from the body and out of the deadhouse. They put him on an empty cot in a half-empty ward.

"Oh, darling," said Woodhull, "I don't even want to think about it." He turned over on his side and began to breathe deeply and evenly. The odor of urine began to rise from him.

Dr. Walker took a watch from her pocket and looked at it. "We got a wire," she said. "They're moving a thousand boys from the field hospitals." Then she leaned down close to Woodhull's snoring face and said, "You had better be well and awake in five hours, sir."

"I will do whatever I can," said Whitman.

"I am glad to hear it." She adjusted her hat on her head and uttered an explosive sigh. "General Stuart has died," she said. "Did you know that? Shot by a lowly infantryman. I had a dream once that he came for me on his horse, with garish feathers in his hat. 'Come along with me, Mary,' he said. 'We'll ride away from it all.' 'Not by your red beard, General Satan,' said I. 'Get thee behind me.' Do you suppose I did the right thing? Would you have gone with him?"

Walt thought about it. He pictured himself riding west with General Stuart to a place where the war could not touch them. He imagined the tickly feeling General Stuart's feathers would make in his nose as they rode to the extreme end of the continent. And he thought of the two of them riding shirtless through sunny California and of reaching out their hands to pick fat grapes.

"I've got to get out," said Hank. A week had passed, and Union Square was stuffed to the gills with new patients. Hank's leg was scheduled to come off in two days. In the deadhouse there was a pile of limbs as high as Walt's head.

"Settle down," said Walt. "There's no cause for alarm."

"I won't let them have it. You've got to help me get out. I won't make it if they take my leg. I know I won't." He had a raging fever and had been acting a little delirious.

"Dr. Walker is said to wield the fastest knife in the Army. You'll be asleep. You won't feel it."

"Ha!" said Hank. He gave Walt a long, wild look. "Ha!" He put his face in his pillow and wouldn't talk anymore. Walt walked around the wards, meeting the new boys. He went to the chapel. The limbs piled higher in the deadhouse, many of them joined there soon by their former proprietors.

That night, unable to sleep, he made his usual tour of the city, stopping for a long time outside Union Square. He found himself outside Hank's window, and then inside, next to his bed. Hank was sleeping, his arm thrown up above his head, his sheet thrown off, and his shirt riding up his belly. Walt reached out and touched his shoulder.

"All right," Walt said. "Let's go." It was not a difficult escape. The hardest part was getting Hank's pants on. It was very painful for him to bend his knee, and he was feverish, disoriented. They saw no one on their way out; the night attendants were in another ward.

They stole a crutch for Hank. He fell on the Mall, and the crutch broke under him. He wept softly with his mouth in the grass. Walt picked him up and carried him on his back, toward the canal and over it, then into Murder Bay. Hank cried to be put down. They rested on a trash heap teeming with small crawly things that were unidentifiable in the dark.

"I think I want to sleep," said Hank. "I'm so tired."

"Go ahead, my dear," said Walt. "I shall take care of you."

"I would like to go home." He put his head against Walt's shoulder. "Take me back to Hollow Vale. I want to see my sister." He slowly fell asleep, still mumbling under his breath. They sat there for a little while. Some people passed them but did not disturb them. If this heap were a horse, thought Walt, we could ride to California. "Never mind General Stuart," he said aloud, taking Hank's wet hand in his own. "In California there is no sickness. Neither is there death. On their fifth birthday, every child is made a gift of a pony." He looked at Hank's drawn face glowing eerily in the moonlight and said, "In California, if you plant a dead boy under an oak tree, in just one day's time a living hand will emerge from the soil. If you grasp that hand and pull with the heart of a true friend, a living body will come out of the earth. Thus in California death never separates true friends." He looked for a while longer into Hank's face. His eyes were darting wildly under the lids. Walt said, "Well, if we are to get there soon, we had best be going now." But when he picked him up he took him back to the hospital.

"You will wash that beard before you come into my surgery," said Dr. Woodhull. Walt stank of garbage. He went to a basin, and Dr. Walker helped him scrub his beard with creosote, potassium permanganate, and Labarraque's solution. Walt held a sponge soaked with chloroform under Hank's nose, even though he hadn't woken since falling asleep on the heap. He kept his hand on Hank's head the whole time, though he could not watch as Dr. Walker cut in and Dr. Woodhull tied up the arteries. He looked down and saw blood seeping across the floor, into mounds of sawdust. Looking up, he fixed his attention on a lithograph on the far wall. It had been torn from some book of antiquities, a depiction of reclining sick under the care of the priests of Asclepius, whose statue dominated the temple. There was a snake-entwined staff in his hand and a big friendly-looking stone dog at his feet. A large caption beneath the picture read, "Every night for a thousand years the sick sought refuge and dreams in the Temple of Asclepius." He closed his eyes and heard the saw squeak against Hank's bones.

Hank woke briefly before he died. "They got my leg," he said. "You let them take it."

"No," said Walt. "I've got it right here." In fact, he did. It lay in his lap, bundled in two clean white sheets. It could have been anything. He would not let them take it to the deadhouse. He put it in the bed. Hank hugged it tight against his chest.

"I don't want to die," he said.

He packed his bag and sat on it, waiting at the station for the train that would take him back to Brooklyn. The train came and went; he stayed sitting on his bag. Then he got up and went back to Union Square. It was night. Hank's bed was still empty. He sat down on it and rummaged for a pen and paper. When he had them, he wrote in the dark:

Dear Friends,

I thought it would be soothing to you to have a few lines about the last days of your son, Henry Smith — I write in haste, but I have no doubt anything about Hank will be welcome.

From the time he came — there was hardly a day but I was with him a portion of the time — if not in the day then at night — (I am merely a friend visiting the wounded and sick soldiers). From almost the first I felt somehow that Hank was in danger, or at least was much worse than they supposed in the hospital. As he made no complaint they thought him nothing so bad. I told the doctor of the ward over and over again he was a very sick boy, but he took it lightly and said he would certainly recover; he said, "I know more about these fever cases than you do — he looks very sick to you, but I shall bring him out all right — " Probably the doctor did his best — at any rate about a week before Hank died he got really alarmed, and after that he and all the other doctors tried to help him but it was too late. Very possibly it would not have made any difference.

I used to sit by the side of his bed generally silent, he was opprest for breath and with the heat, and I would fan him — occasionally he would want a drink — some days he dozed a great deal — sometimes when I would come in he woke up and I would lean down and kiss him, he would reach out his hand and pat my hair and beard as I sat on the bed and leaned over him — it was painful to see the working in his throat to breathe.

Some nights I sat by his cot far into the night, the lights would be put out and I sat there silently hour after hour — he seemed to like to have me sit there — I shall never forget those nights in the dark hospital, it was a curious and solemn scene, the sick and the wounded lying around and this dear young man close by me, lying on what proved to be his death-bed. I did not know his past life; but what I saw and know of he behaved like a noble boy — Farewell, deary boy, it was my opportunity to be with you in your last days. I had no chance to do much for you; nothing could be done — only you did not lie there among strangers without having one near who loved you dearly, and to whom you gave your dying kiss.

Mr. and Mrs. Smith, I have thus written rapidly whatever came up about Hank, and must now close. Though we are strangers and shall probably never see each other, I send you and all Hank's brothers and sisters my love. I live when at home in Brooklyn, New York, in Portland Avenue, fourth floor, north of Myrtle.

He folded up the letter and put it in his shirt, then lay down on his side on the bed. In a while a nurse came by with fresh sheets. She thought she might scold him and tell him to leave, but when she looked in his face she turned and hurried off. He watched the moon come up in the window, listening to the wounded and sick stirring in the beds around him. It seemed to him, as he watched the moon shine down on the dome of the Capitol, that the war would never end. He thought, In the morning I will rise and leave this place. And then he thought, I will never leave this place. He slept briefly and had a dream of reaching into Hank Smith's dark grave, hoping and fearing that somebody would take his groping hand. He woke with the moon still shining in his face. Somewhere down the ward a boy began to weep.

MAXINE SWANN

Flower Children

FROM PLOUGHSHARES

THEY'RE FREE to run anywhere they like whenever they like, so they do. The land falls away from their small house on the hill along a prickly path; there's a dirt road, a pasture where the steers are kept, swamps, a gully, groves of fruit trees, and then the creek from whose far bank a wooded mountain surges — they climb it. At the top, they step out to catch their breath in the light. The mountain gives way to fields as far as their eyes can see — alfalfa, soybean, corn, wheat. They aren't sure where their own land stops and someone else's begins, but it doesn't matter, they're told. It doesn't matter! Go where you please!

They spend their whole lives in trees, young apple trees and old tired ones, red oaks, walnuts, the dogwood when it flowers in May. They hold leaves up to the light and peer through them. They close their eyes and press their faces into showers of leaves and wait for that feeling of darkness to come and make their whole bodies stir. They discover locust shells, tree frogs, a gypsy moth's cocoon. Now they know what that sound is in the night when the tree frogs sing out at the tops of their lungs. In the fields, they collect groundhog bones. They make desert piles and bless them with flowers and leaves. They wish they could be plants and lie very still near the ground all night and in the morning be covered with tears of dew. They wish they could be Robin Hood, Indians. In the summer, they rub mud all over their bodies and sit out in the sun to let it dry. When it dries, they stand up slowly like old men and women with wrinkled skin and walk stiff-limbed through the trees toward the creek.

Their parents don't care what they do. They're the luckiest children alive! They run out naked in storms. They go riding on ponies with the boys up the road who're on perpetual suspension from school. They take baths with their father, five bodies in one tub. In the pasture, they stretch out flat on their backs and wait for the buzzards to come. When the buzzards start circling, they lie very still, breathless with fear, and imagine what it would be like to be eaten alive. That one's diving! they say, and they leap to their feet. No, we're alive! We're alive!

The children all sleep in one room. Their parents built the house themselves, four rooms and four stories high, one small room on top of the next. With their first child, a girl, they lived out in a tent in the yard beneath the apple trees. In the children's room, there are three beds. The girls sleep together and the youngest boy in a wooden crib that their mother made. A toilet stands out in the open near the stairwell. Their parents sleep on the highest floor, underneath the eaves, in a room with skylights and silver-papered walls. In the living room, a swing hangs in the center from the ceiling. There's a woodstove to one side with a bathtub beside it; both the bathtub and the stove stand on lion's feet. There are bookshelves all along the walls and an atlas too, which the children pore through, and a set of encyclopedias from which they copy fish. The kitchen, the lowest room, is built into a hill. The floor is made of dirt and gravel, and the stone walls are damp. Blacksnakes come in sometimes to shed their skins. When the children aren't outside, they spend most of their time here; they play with the stones on the floor, making pyramids or round piles and then knocking them down. There's a showerhouse outside, down a steep, narrow path, and a round stone well in the woods behind.

There's nowhere to hide in the house, no cellars or closets, so the children go outside to do that too. They spend hours standing waist-high in the creek. They watch the crayfish have battles and tear off each other's claws. They catch the weak ones later, off-guard and from behind, as they crouch in the dark under shelves of stone. And they catch minnows too, and salamanders with the soft skin of frogs, and they try to catch snakes, although they're never quite sure that they really want to. It maddens them how the water changes things before their eyes, turning the minnows into darting chips of green light and making the dirty stones on the bottom

shine. Once they found a snapping turtle frozen in the ice, and
their father cut it out with an axe to make soup. The children dunk
their heads under and breathe out bubbles. They keep their heads
down as long as they can. They like how their hair looks underneath the water, the way it spreads out around their faces in wavering fans. And their voices sound different too, like the voices of
strange people from a foreign place. They put their heads down
and carry on conversations, they scream and laugh, testing out
these strange voices that bloom from their mouths and then swell
outwards, endlessly, like no other sound they have ever heard.

The children get stung by nettles, ants, poison ivy, poison oak,
and bees. They go out into the swamp and come back, their whole
heads crawling with ticks and burrs. They pick each other's scalps
outside the house, then lay the ticks on a ledge and grind their
bodies to dust with a pointed stone.

They watch the pigs get butchered and the chickens killed. They
learn that people have teeth inside their heads. One evening their
father takes his shirt off and lies out on the kitchen table to show
them where their organs are. He moves his hand over the freckled
skin, cupping different places — heart, stomach, lung, lung, kidneys, gall bladder, liver here. And suddenly they want to know
what's inside everything, so they tear apart everything they find,
flowers, pods, bugs, shells, seeds, they shred up the whole yard in
search of something; and they want to know about everything they
see or can't see, frost and earthworms, and who will decide when it
rains, and are there ghosts and are there fairies, and how many
drops and how many stars, and although they kill things themselves, they want to know why anything dies and where the dead go
and where they were waiting before they were born. In the hazelnut
grove? Behind the goathouse? And how did they know when it was
time to come?

Their parents are delighted by the snowlady they build with huge
breasts and a penis and rock-necklace hair. Their parents are delighted by these children in every way, these children who will be
like no children ever were. In this house with their children, they'll
create a new world — which has no relation to the world they have
known — in which nothing is lied about, whispered about, and
nothing is ever concealed. There will be no petty lessons for these
children about how a fork is held or a hand shaken or what is best

to be said and what shouldn't be spoken of or seen. Nor will these children's minds be restricted to sets and subsets of rules, rules for children, about when to be quiet or go to bed, the causes and effects of various punishments which increase in gravity on a gradated scale. No, not these children! These children will be different. They'll learn only the large things. Here in this house, the world will be revealed in a fresh, new light, and this light will fall over everything. Even those shady forbidden zones through which they themselves wandered as children, panicked and alone, these too will be illuminated — their children will walk through with torches held high! Yes, everything should be spoken of in this house, everything, and everything seen.

Their father holds them on his lap when he's going to the bathroom, he lights his farts with matches on the stairs, he likes to talk about shit and examine each shit he takes, its texture and smell, and the children's shits too, he has theories about shit that unwind for hours — he has theories about everything. He has a study in the toolshed near the house, where he sits for hours and is visited regularly by ideas, which he comes in to explain to their mother and the children. When their mother's busy or not listening, he explains them to the children or to only one child in a language that they don't understand, but certain words or combinations of words bore themselves into their brains, where they will remain, but the children don't know this yet, ringing in their ears for the rest of their lives — repression, Nixon, wind power, nuclear power, Vietnam, fecal patterns, sea thermal energy, civil rights. And one day these words will bear all sorts of meaning, but now they mean nothing to the children — they live the lives of ghosts, outlines with no form, wandering inside their minds. The children listen attentively. They nod, nod, nod.

   Their parents grow pot in the garden, which they keep under the kitchen sink in a large tin. When the baby sitter comes, their mother shows her where it is. The baby sitter plays with the children, a game where you turn the music up very loud, Waylon Jennings, "The Outlaws," and run around the living room leaping from the couch to the chairs to the swing, trying never to touch the floor. She shows them the tattoo between her legs, a bright rose with thorns, and then she calls up all her friends. When the children come down later to get juice in the kitchen, they see ten naked bodies through a cloud of smoke sitting around the table, playing cards. The children are invited, but they'd rather not play.

Their parents take them to protests in different cities and to concerts sometimes. The children wear T-shirts and hold posters and then the whole crowd lets off balloons. Their parents have peach parties and invite all their friends. There's music, dancing, skinny-dipping in the creek. Everyone takes off their clothes and rubs peach flesh all over each other's skin. The children are free to join in, but they don't feel like it. They sit in a row on the hill in all their clothes. But they memorize the sizes of the breasts and the shapes of the penises of all their parents' friends and discuss this later amongst themselves.

One day, at the end of winter, a woman begins to come to their house. She has gray eyes and a huge mound of wheat-colored hair. She laughs quickly, showing small white teeth. From certain angles she looks ugly, but from others she seems very nice. She comes in the mornings and picks things in the garden. She's there again at dinner, at birthdays. She brings presents. She arrives dressed as a rabbit for Easter in a bright yellow pajama suit. She's very kind to their mother and chatters to her for hours in the kitchen as they cook. Their father goes away on weekends with her; he spends the night at her house. Sometimes he takes the children with him to see her. She lives in a gray house by the river that's much larger than the children's house. She has six Siamese cats. She has a piano and many records and piles of soft clay for the children to play with, but they don't want to. They go outside and stand by the concrete frog pond near the road. Algae covers it like a hairy green blanket. They stare down, trying to spot frogs. They chuck rocks in, candy, pennies, or whatever else they can find.

In the gray spring mornings, there's a man either coming or going from their mother's room. He leaves the door open. Did you hear them? I heard them. Did you see them? Yes. But they don't talk about it. They no longer talk about things amongst themselves. But they answer their father's questions when he asks.

And here again they nod. When their father has gone away for good and then comes back to visit or takes them out on trips in his car and tells them about the women he's been with, how they make love, what he prefers or doesn't like, gestures or movements of the arms, neck, or legs described in the most detailed terms — And what do they think? And what would they suggest? When a woman stands with a cigarette between her breasts at the end of the bed and you suddenly lose all hope — And he talks about their mother too, the way she makes love. He'd much rather talk to them than to anyone else. These children, they're amazing! They rise to all occasions, stoop carefully to any sorrow — and their minds! Their minds are wide open and flow with no stops, like damless streams. And the children nod also when one of their mother's boyfriends comes by to see her — she's not there — they're often heartbroken, occasionally drunk, they want to talk about her. The children stand with them underneath the trees. They can't see for the sun in their eyes, but they look up anyway and nod, smile politely, nod.

The children play with their mother's boyfriends out in the snow. They go to school. They're sure they'll never learn to read. They stare at the letters. They lose all hope. They worry that they don't know the Lord's Prayer. They realize that they don't know God or anything about him, so they ask the other children shy questions in the schoolyard and receive answers that baffle them, and then God fills their minds like a guest who's moved in, but keeps his distance and worries them to distraction at night when they're alone. They imagine they hear his movements through the house, his footsteps and the rustling of his clothes. They grow frightened for their parents, who seem to have learned nothing about God's laws. They feel that they should warn them, but they don't know how. They become convinced one night that their mother is a robber. They hear her creeping through the house alone, lifting and rattling things.

At school, they learn to read and spell. They learn penmanship and multiplication. They're surprised at first by all the rules, but then they learn them too quickly and observe them all carefully. They learn not to swear. They get prizes for obedience, for following the rules down to the last detail. They're delighted by these rules, these arbitrary lines that regulate behavior and mark off forbidden things, and they examine them closely and exhaust their teachers with questions about the mechanical functioning and the hidden intricacies of these beings, the rules: If at naptime you're very quiet, with your eyes shut tight and your arms and legs so still you barely breathe, but really you're not sleeping, underneath your

arms and beneath your eyelids you're wide awake and thinking
very hard about how to be still, but you get the prize anyway for
sleeping because you were the stillest child in the room, but actually that's wrong, you shouldn't get the prize or should you, because the prize is really for sleeping and not being still, or is it also
for being still. . . ?

When the other children in the schoolyard are whispering themselves into wild confusion about their bodies and sex and babies
being born, these children stay quiet and stand to one side. They're
mortified by what they know and have seen. They're sure that if
they mention one word, the other children will go home and tell
their parents who will tell their teachers who will be horrified and
disgusted and push them away. But they also think they should be
punished. They should be shaken, beaten, for what they've seen.
These children don't touch themselves. They grow hesitant with
worry. At home, they wander out into the yard alone and stand
there at a terrible loss. One day when the teacher calls on them,
they're no longer able to speak. But then they speak again a few
days later, although now and then they'll have periods in their lives
when their voices disappear utterly or else become very thin and
quavering like ghosts or old people lost in their throats.

But the children love to read. They suddenly discover the use of
all these books in the house and turn the living room into a lending
library. Each book has a card and a due date and is stamped when
it's borrowed or returned. They play card games and backgammon.
They go over to friends' houses and learn about junk food and how
to watch TV. But mostly they read. They read about anything, love
stories, the lives of inventors and famous Indians, blights that affect
hybrid plants. They try to read books they can't read at all and skip
words and whole paragraphs and sit like this for hours, lost in a
stunning blur.

They take violin lessons at school and piano lessons and then
stop one day when their hands begin to shake so badly they can no
longer hold to the keys. What is wrong? Nothing! They get dressed
up in costumes and put on plays. They're kings and queens.
They're witches. They put on a whole production of *The Wizard of
Oz*. They play detectives with identity cards and go searching for the
kittens who have just been born in some dark, hidden place on
their land. They store away money to give to their father when he

comes. They spend whole afternoons at the edge of the yard waiting for him to come. They don't understand why their father behaves so strangely now, why he sleeps in their mother's bed when she's gone in the afternoon and then gets up and slinks around the house like a criminal, chuckling, especially when she's angry and has told him to leave. They don't know why their father seems laughed at now and unloved, why he needs money from them to drive home in his car, why he seems to need something from them that they cannot give him — everything — but they'll try to give him — everything — whatever it is he needs, they'll try to do this as hard as they can.

Their father comes and waits for their mother in the house. He comes and takes them away on trips in his car. They go to quarries, where they line up and leap off cliffs. They go looking for caves up in the hills in Virginia. There are bears here, he tells them, but if you ever come face to face with one, just swear your heart out and he'll run. He takes them to dances in the city where only old people go. Don't they know how to foxtrot? Don't they know how to waltz? They sit at tables and order sodas, waiting for their turn to be picked up and whirled around by him. Or they watch him going around to other tables, greeting husbands and inviting their wives, women much older than his mother, to dance. These women have blue or white hair. They either get up laughing or refuse. He comes back to the children to report how they were — like dancing with milk, he says, or water, or molasses. He takes them to see the pro wrestling championship match. He takes them up north for a week to meditate inside a hotel with a guru from Bombay. He takes them running down the up escalators in stores and up Totem Mountain at night in a storm. He talks his head off. He gets speeding tickets left and right. He holds them on his lap when he's driving and between his legs when they ski. When he begins to fall asleep at the wheel, they rack their brains trying to think of ways to keep him awake. They rub his shoulders and pull his hair. They sing rounds. They ask him questions to try to make him talk. They do interviews in the back seat, saying things they know will amuse him. And when their efforts are exhausted, he tells them that the only way he'll ever stay awake is if they insult him in the cruelest way they can. He says their mother is the only person who can do this really well. He tells them that they have to say mean things about her, about her boyfriends and lovers and what they do, or about how much she hates him, thinks he's stupid, an asshole, a failure, how much she doesn't want him around. And so they do. They force themselves to invent insults or say things that are terrible but true. And as they speak, they feel their mouths turn chalky and their stomachs begin to harden, as if with each word they had swallowed a stone. But he seems delighted. He laughs and encourages them, turning around in his seat to look at their faces, his eyes now completely off the road.

He wants them to meet everyone he knows. They show up on people's doorsteps with him in the middle of the day or late at night. He can hardly contain himself. These are my kids! he says. They're smarter than anyone I know, and ten times smarter than me! Do you have any idea what it's like when your kids turn out smarter than you?! He teaches them how to play bridge and to ski backwards. At dinner with him, you have to eat with your eyes closed. When you go through a stoplight, you have to hold on to your balls. But the girls? Oh yes, the girls — well, just improvise! He's experiencing flatulence, withdrawal from wheat. He's on a new diet that will ruthlessly clean out his bowels. There are turkeys and assholes everywhere in the world. Do they know this? Do they know? But he himself is probably the biggest asshole here. Still, women find him handsome — they do! They actually do! And funny. But he *is* funny, he actually is, not witty but funny, they don't realize this because they see him all the time, they're used to it, but other people — like that waitress! Did they see that waitress? She was laughing so hard she could barely see straight! Do they know how you get to be a waitress? Big breasts. But he himself is not a breast man. Think of Mom — he calls their mother Mom — she has no breasts at all! But her taste in men is mind-boggling. Don't they think? Mind-boggling! Think about it too long and you'll lose your mind. Why do they think she picks these guys? What is it? And why are women almost always so much smarter than men? And more dignified? Dignity for men is a completely lost cause! And why does anyone have kids, anyway? Come on, why?! Because they like you? Because they laugh at you? No! Because they're fun! Exactly! They're fun!

Around the house there are briar patches with berries and thorns. There are gnarled apple trees with puckered gray skins. The windows are all open — the wasps are flying in. The clothes on the line

are jumping like children with no heads but hysterical limbs. Who
will drown the fresh new kitties? Who will chain-saw the trees and
cut the firewood in winter and haul that firewood in? Who will do
away with all these animals, or tend them, or sell them, kill them
one by one? Who will say to her in the evening that it all means
nothing, that tomorrow will be different, that the heart gets tired
after all? And where are the children? When will they come home?
She has burned all her diaries. She has told the man in the barn to
go away. Who will remind her again that the heart has its own
misunderstandings? And the heart often loses its way and can be
found hours later wandering down passageways with unexplained
bruises on its skin. On the roof, there was a child standing one day
years ago, his arms waving free, but one foot turned inward, weakly
— When will it be evening? When will it be night? The tree frogs
are beginning to sing. She has seen the way their toes clutch at the
bark. Some of them are spotted, and their hearts beat madly against
the skin of their throats. There may be a storm. It may rain. That
cloud there looks dark — but no, it's a wisp of burned paper, too
thin. In the woods above, there's a house that burned down to the
ground, but then a grove of lilac bushes burst up from the char. A
wind is coming up. There are dark purple clouds now. There are
red-coned sumacs hovering along the edge of the drive. Poisonous
raw, but fine for tea. The leaves on the apple trees are all turning
blue. The sunflowers in the garden are quivering, heads bowed —
empty of seed now. And the heart gets watered and recovers itself.
There is hope, everywhere there's hope. Light approaches from
the back. Between the dry, gnarled branches, it's impossible to see.
There are the first few drops. There are the oak trees shuddering.
There's a flicker of bright gray, the underside of one leaf. There was
once a child standing at the edge of the yard at a terrible loss. Did
she know this? Yes. The children! (They have her arms, his ears, his
voice, his smell, her soft features, her movements of the hand and
head, her stiffness, his confusion, his humor, her ambition, his
daring, his eyelids, their failure, their hope, their freckled skin —)

EMILY CARTER

Glory Goes and Gets Some

FROM OPEN CITY

HELLO CAMPERS, it's me, little Gloria Bronski, Campfire girl manqué, and your guide through the twisted streets of Glorytown, coming to you live on W-M-E-E. Me, oh Glorious Me, if you want to know where I'm coming from. Tune me out and rest in silence, because I sing no garden variety song of myself. I sing you too, even though it might at first seem somewhat otherwise.

Everyone is very busy denying the last time they were lonely, but trust me, it happens. It isn't just being a solo act, although that contributes; I know women and men who stand in their back yards, safe in the bosom of their family, at the height of their careers, and stare up into the old reliable silver maple tree, mentally testing its capacity to hold their weight. There is that loneliness that other people can't alleviate. And then there's that loneliness that they can, which is what I was dealing with when I put the ad in the personals.

I hate the word *horny*, redolent as it is of yellowed calluses and pizza-crust bunions, but there you go. Sober for eighteen months, I'd been giving up my will to God and practicing the three *m*'s — meetings, meditation, masturbation. But no matter the electronic reinforcement, it gets old mashing the little pink button all by your lonesome, night after night. Now here's the dilemma I'm staring at: "I AM HIV POSITIVE, WHO WILL HAVE SEX WITH ME?" If I was a guy it might be different, but carrying around the eve of destruction between my creamy white thighs doesn't exactly make me feel like a sex goddess. But I can't possibly be the only positive heterosexual recovering drug addict on huge amounts of Prozac in the universe. And of course, as it turned out, I wasn't. As they tell you in

Treatment, don't wear yourself out with Terminal Uniqueness. Another kitchy-coo catchphrase that turns out, finally, to have the
distinctly unsamplerlike ring of truth.

The problem was the research. I hate doing it, I hate thinking
about doing it, I hate, with every fiber of my being, the process of
going to libraries, making phone calls, looking things up, writing
them down. Especially on this particular topic, which I'd rather not
think about to begin with. But there you go, no stick, no carrot, if
you get my drift. I found what I was looking for with very little
trouble, as a matter of fact, a magazine called *Positive People,* and I
put in my ad: Female, 35, hetero. Permanent graduate student.
Red hair, green eyes. You: neither sociopath nor systems analyst.
Will consider anything in between.

My first meeting was for coffee with a blue-eyed lanky man who told
me that being HIV+ was a small entrance fee to pay to be granted
admission into the bosom of Christ. I could see he meant it, because his gaze was flashing out a beam that went all the way into the
golden distance of the Final Judgment. He had come through his
trials with one gleaming jewel of truth, and that was all he needed,
except maybe a partner to walk through the pearly gates with. "Life
is a long joke," he told me. "Heaven is when you finally get it." He
was smiling, beaming with happiness, bursting out every now and
then into relieved laughter, as if he'd just been missed by a truck.
"You're sure about that," I asked him, and he, laughing, held out
his hand over the table, as if he was inviting me to run across a
meadow toward the horizon. I gave it a friendly squeeze and never
called the number he left with me, because I know very well what
happens when you run toward the horizon; you get smaller and
smaller until you vanish. Was I discouraged? Of course I was discouraged, I was born somewhat discouraged, but in terms of action
that's neither here nor there. "Pray as if everything depended on
God, act as if everything depended on you" goes the slogan I picked
up either at an AA meeting or in one of the many pamphlets I'm
always being offered by the well-meaning souls who infest the Twin
City area.

The next call I got was from a man named Jake and he was witty
to the point of glibness on the phone, so I thought I'd give him a
shot. Over lunch he began to tell me a little bit about himself.
While he himself was not HIV+, he had no trouble understanding

it — the lifestyle he had once lived, he said, it was a miracle he wasn't. He had picked up *Positive People* because he was looking for a woman who had explored alternative lifestyles and was comfortable enough with herself to be open about it. He had always, he said, loved my type — brainy girls, maybe Jewish, with wild hair and full lips and notions of freedom. Of course he was married, so we couldn't actually have sexual intercourse, but he would love to come all over my beautiful red hair and round breasts. As long as I had a reasonable sense of perspective. He so clearly meant to humiliate and degrade me that it was all I could do not to fall head over heels in love with him, but my vitamin regimen made me strong, and I left him there midsentence.

There followed an interlude with an AIDS activist named Garrett, a self-proclaimed Professional Person with AIDS. He was always zipping back and forth to Washington, at great cost, he said, to his energy level and serenity. He tried to get me involved in a suit against the NIH for excluding women from early drug studies. And here's me just wanting a simple, frivolous fuck.

It began to seem to me as if there was simply no hope of finding a little comfort in the world outside my apartment, but just when I had turned my attention elsewhere I stumbled on an uncut jewel, a pretty boy who liked girls, had green eyes, and could spell *phlegm* if he had to. Recovering Like Me. Answered the ad with great trepidation, feelings of overwhelming shame and geekiness overridden by the normal human imperatives. But here I am to tell you I definitely made it worth his while. His name is Stefan, and I myself love that name. Not that it changes much in my life to be, as someone said, getting it regular, but avenues are opening that I thought I'd have to detour. Apparently Stefan feels the same because after our second night together, he told me he had never thought this was going to be a part of his life again, and he'd answered my ad out of sheer desperation, which of all human motivations is the only one you can absolutely trust, as far as I'm concerned.

Spring is coming, even to this frozen town, and people here are warming up. This morning on my way home from his house I got out of the car and looked down at the Mississippi River. The sunlight hit it so it sparkled royal blue and diamond-flecked. All winter long it had been the color of frozen iron and here it was now, just like me, babbling away merrily in the sunshine of early spring.

ANNIE PROULX

The Half-Skinned Steer

FROM THE ATLANTIC MONTHLY

IN THE LONG UNFURLING of his life, from tight-wound kid hustler in a wool suit riding the train out of Cheyenne to geriatric limper in this spooled-out year, Mero had kicked down thoughts of the place where he began, a so-called ranch on strange ground at the south hinge of the Big Horns. He'd got himself out of there in 1936, had gone to a war and come back, married and married again (and again), made money in boilers and air-duct cleaning and smart investments, retired, got into local politics and out again without scandal, never circled back to see the old man and Rollo, bankrupt and ruined, because he knew they were.

They called it a ranch and it had been, but one day the old man said cows couldn't be run in such tough country, where they fell off cliffs, disappeared into sinkholes, gave up large numbers of calves to marauding lions; where hay couldn't grow but leafy spurge and Canada thistle throve, and the wind packed enough sand to scour windshields opaque. The old man wangled a job delivering mail, but looked guilty fumbling bills into his neighbors' mailboxes.

Mero and Rollo saw the mail route as a defection from the work of the ranch, work that consequently fell on them. The breeding herd was down to eighty-two, and a cow wasn't worth more than fifteen dollars, but they kept mending fence, whittling ears and scorching hides, hauling cows out of mudholes, and hunting lions in the hope that sooner or later the old man would move to Ten Sleep with his woman and his bottle and they could, as had their grandmother Olive when Jacob Corn disappointed her, pull the place taut. That bird didn't fly, and Mero wound up sixty years later as an octogenarian vegetarian widower pumping an Exercycle in the living room of a colonial house in Woolfoot, Massachusetts.

One of those damp mornings the nail-driving telephone voice of a woman said she was Louise, Tick's wife, and summoned him back to Wyoming. He didn't know who she was, who Tick was, until she said, Tick Corn, your brother Rollo's son, and that Rollo had passed on, killed by a waspy emu, though prostate cancer was waiting its chance. Yes, she said, you bet Rollo still owned the ranch. Half of it anyway. Me and Tick, she said, we been pretty much running it the past ten years.

An emu? Did he hear right?

Yes, she said. Well, of course you didn't know. You heard of Wyoming Down Under?

He had not. And thought, What kind of name is Tick? He recalled the bloated gray insects pulled off the dogs. This tick probably thought he was going to get the whole damn ranch and bloat up on it. He said, What the hell is this about an emu? Were they all crazy out there?

That's what the ranch is called now, she said. Wyoming Down Under. Rollo'd sold the place way back when to the Girl Scouts, but one of the girls was dragged off by a lion, and the GSA sold out to the Banner ranch, next door, which ran cattle on it for a few years and then unloaded it on a rich Australian businessman, who started Wyoming Down Under, but it was too much long-distance work and he'd had bad luck with his manager, a feller from Idaho with a pawnshop rodeo buckle, so he'd looked up Rollo and offered to swap him a half interest if he'd run the place. That was back in 1978. The place had done real well. Course we're not open now, she said. It's winter and there's no tourists. Poor Rollo was helping Tick move the emus to another building when one of them turned on a dime and come right for him with its big razor claws. Emus is bad for claws.

I know, he said. He watched the nature programs on television.

She shouted, as though the telephone lines were down all across the country, Tick got your number off the computer. Rollo always said he was going to get in touch. He wanted you to see how things turned out. He tried to fight it off with his cane, but it laid him open from belly to breakfast.

Maybe, he thought, things hadn't finished turning out. Impatient with this game, he said he would be at the funeral. No point talking about flights and meeting him at the airport, he told her; he didn't fly, a bad experience years ago with hail, the plane had looked like a waffle iron when it landed. He intended to drive. Of course he knew how far it was. Had a damn fine car, Cadillac, always drove Cadillacs, Gislaved tires, interstate highways, excellent driver, never had an accident in his life, knock on wood. Four days; he would be there by Saturday afternoon. He heard the amazement in her voice, knew she was plotting his age, figuring he had to be eighty-three, a year or so older than Rollo, figuring he must be dotting around on a cane too, drooling the tiny days away — she was probably touching her own faded hair. He flexed his muscular arms, bent his knees, thought he could dodge an emu. He would see his brother dropped in a red Wyoming hole. That event could jerk him back; the dazzled rope of lightning against the cloud is not the downward bolt but the compelled upstroke through the heated ether.

He had pulled away at the sudden point when the old man's girl-friend — now he couldn't remember her name — seemed to have jumped the track, Rollo goggling at her bloody bitten fingers, nails chewed to the quick, neck veins like wires, the outer forearms shaded with hairs, and the cigarette glowing, smoke curling up, making her wink her bulging mustang eyes, a teller of tales of hard deeds and mayhem. The old man's hair was falling out, Mero was twenty-three and Rollo twenty, and she played them all like a deck of cards. If you admired horses, you'd go for her with her arched neck and horsy buttocks, so high and haunchy you'd want to clap her on the rear. The wind bellowed around the house, driving crystals of snow through the cracks of the warped log door, and all of them in the kitchen seemed charged with some intensity of purpose. She'd balanced that broad butt on the edge of the dog-food chest, looking at the old man and Rollo, now and then rolling her glossy eyes over at Mero, square teeth nipping a rim of nail, sucking the welling blood, drawing on her cigarette.

The old man drank his Everclear stirred with a peeled willow stick for the bitter taste. The image of him came sharp in Mero's mind as he stood at the hall closet contemplating his hats. Should he take one for the funeral? The old man had had the damnedest curl to his hat brim, a tight roll on the right where his doffing or

donning hand gripped it, and a wavering downslope on the left like
a shed roof. You could recognize him two miles away. He wore it at
the table listening to the woman's stories about Tin Head, steadily
emptying his glass until he was nine times nine drunk, his gangstery
face loosening, the crushed rodeo nose and scar-crossed eyebrows,
the stub ear, dissolving as he drank. Now he must be dead fifty years
or more, buried in the mailman sweater.

The girlfriend started a story, Yeah, there was this guy named Tin
Head down around Dubois when my dad was a kid. Had a little
ranch, some horses, cows, kids, a wife. But there was something
funny about him. He had a metal plate in his head from falling
down some cement steps.

   Plenty of guys has them, Rollo said in a challenging way.

   She shook her head. Not like his. His was made out of galvy, and
it eat at his brain.

   The old man held up the bottle of Everclear, raised his eyebrows
at her: Well, darlin'?

   She nodded, took the glass from him, and knocked it back in one
swallow. Oh, that's not gonna slow *me* down, she said.

   Mero expected her to neigh.

   So what then, Rollo said, picking at the horse manure under his
boot heel. What about Tin Head and his galvanized skull plate?

   I heard it this way, she said. She held out the glass for another
shot of Everclear, and the old man poured it, and she went on.

Mero had thrashed all that ancient night, dreamed of horse breeding or hoarse breathing, whether the act of sex or bloody, cutthroat
gasps he didn't know. The next morning he woke up drenched in
stinking sweat, looked at the ceiling, and said aloud, It could go on
like this for some time. He meant cows and weather as much as
anything, and what might be his chances two or three states over in
any direction. In Woolfoot, riding the Exercycle, he thought the
truth was somewhat different: he'd wanted a woman of his own, not
the old man's leftovers.

   What he wanted to know now, tires spanking the tar-filled road
cracks and potholes, funeral homburg sliding on the back seat, was
if Rollo had got the girlfriend away from the old man, thrown a
saddle on her, and ridden off into the sunset.

                                    *

The interstate, crippled by orange cones, forced traffic into single lanes, broke his expectation of making good time. His Cadillac, boxed between semis with hissing air brakes, showed snuffling huge rear tires in the windshield, framed a looming Peterbilt in the back window. His thoughts clogged as if a comb working through his mind had stuck against a snarl. When the traffic eased and he tried to cover some ground, the highway patrol pulled him over. The cop, a pimpled, mustached specimen with mismatched eyes, asked his name, where he was going. For the minute he couldn't think what he was doing there. The cop's tongue dapped at the scraggy mustache while he scribbled.

Funeral, he said suddenly. Going to my brother's funeral.

Well, you take it easy, gramps, or they'll be doing one for you.

You're a little polecat, aren't you? he said, staring at the ticket, at the pathetic handwriting, but the mustache was a mile gone, peeling through the traffic as Mero had peeled out of the ranch road that long time ago, squinting through the abraded windshield. He might have made a more graceful exit, but urgency had struck him as a blow on the humerus sends a ringing jolt up the arm. He believed it was the horse-haunched woman leaning against the chest and Rollo fixed on her, the old man swilling Everclear and not noticing or, if noticing, not caring, that had worked in him like a key in an ignition. She had long, gray-streaked braids; Rollo could use them for reins.

Yeah, she said, in her low and convincing liar's voice. I'll tell you, on Tin Head's ranch things went wrong. Chickens changed color overnight, calves was born with three legs, his kids was piebald, and his wife always crying for blue dishes. Tin Head never finished nothing he started, quit halfway through a job every time. Even his pants was half buttoned, so his weenie hung out. He was a mess with the galvy plate eating at his brain, and his ranch and his family was a mess. But, she said, they had to eat, didn't they, just like anybody else?

I hope they eat pies better than the ones you make, said Rollo, who didn't like the mouthful of pits that came with the choke-cherries.

His interest in women had begun a few days after the old man had said, Take this guy up and show him them Ind'an drawrings, jerking his head at the stranger. Mero had been eleven or twelve at the time, no older. They rode along the creek and put up a pair of mallards who flew downstream and then suddenly reappeared, pursued by a goshawk who struck the drake with a sound like a handclap. The duck tumbled through the trees and into deadfall trash, and the hawk shot away as swiftly as it had come.

They climbed through the stony landscape, limestone beds eroded by wind into fantastic furniture, stale gnawed bread crusts, tumbled bones, stacks of dirty folded blankets, bleached crab claws and dog teeth. He tethered the horses in the shade of a stand of limber pine and led the anthropologist up through the stiffbranched mountain mahogany to the overhang. Above them reared corroded cliffs brilliant with orange lichen, pitted with holes, ridged with ledges darkened by millennia of raptor feces.

The anthropologist moved back and forth scrutinizing the stone gallery of red and black drawings: bison skulls, a line of mountain sheep, warriors carrying lances, a turkey stepping into a snare, a stick man upside-down dead and falling, red-ocher hands, violent figures with rakes on their heads that he said were feather headdresses, a great red bear dancing forward on its hind legs, concentric circles and crosses and latticework. He copied the drawings in his notebook, saying Rubba-dubba a few times.

That's the sun, said the anthropologist, who resembled an unfinished drawing himself, pointing at an archery target, ramming his pencil into the air as though tapping gnats. That's an atlatl, and that's a dragonfly. There we go. You know what this is, and he touched a cloven oval, rubbing the cleft with his dusty fingers. He got down on his hands and knees and pointed out more, a few dozen.

A horseshoe?

A horseshoe! The anthropologist laughed. No, boy, it's a vulva. That's what all of these are. You don't know what this is, do you? You go to school on Monday and look it up in the dictionary.

It's a symbol, he said. You know what a symbol is?

Yes, said Mero, who had seen them clapped together in the high school marching band. The anthropologist laughed and told him he had a great future, gave him a dollar for showing him the place. Listen, kid, the Indians did it just like anybody else, he said.

He had looked the word up in the school dictionary, slammed the book closed in embarrassment, but the image was fixed for him (with the brassy background sound of a military march), blunt ocher tracing on stone, and no fleshly examples ever conquered his belief in the subterranean stony structure of female genitalia, the pubic bone a proof, except for the old man's girlfriend, whom he imagined down on all fours, entered from behind and whinnying like a mare, a thing not of geology but of flesh.

Thursday night, balked by detours and construction, he was on the outskirts of Des Moines. In the cinder-block motel room he set the alarm, but his own stertorous breathing woke him before it rang. He was up at five-fifteen, eyes aflame, peering through the vinyl drapes at his snow-hazed car flashing blue under the motel sign, SLEEP SLEEP. In the bathroom he mixed the packet of instant motel coffee and drank it black, without ersatz sugar or chemical cream. He wanted the caffeine. The roots of his mind felt withered and punky.

A cold morning, light snow slanting down: he unlocked the Cadillac, started it, and curved into the vein of traffic, all semis, double and triple trailers. In the headlights' glare he missed the westbound ramp and got into torn-up muddy streets, swung right and right again, using the motel's SLEEP sign as a landmark, but he was on the wrong side of the interstate, and the sign belonged to a different motel.

Another mudholed lane took him into a traffic circle of commuters sucking coffee from insulated cups, pastries sliding on dashboards. Half around the hoop he spied the interstate entrance ramp, veered for it, collided with a panel truck emblazoned STOP SMOKING! HYPNOSIS THAT WORKS!, was rammed from behind by a stretch limo, the limo in its turn rear-ended by a yawning hydroblast operator in a company pickup.

He saw little of this, pressed into his seat by the airbag, his mouth full of a rubbery, dusty taste, eyeglasses cutting into his nose. His first thought was to blame Iowa and those who lived in it. There were a few round spots of blood on his shirt cuff.

A star-spangled Band-Aid over his nose, he watched his crumpled car, pouring dark fluids onto the highway, towed away behind a wrecker. When the police were through with him, a taxi took him, his suitcase, the homburg funeral hat, in the other direction, to Posse Motors, where lax salesmen drifted like disorbited satellites and where he bought a secondhand Cadillac, black like the wreck but three years older and the upholstery not cream leather but sun-faded velour. He had the good tires from the wreck brought over and mounted. He could do that if he liked, buy cars like packs of cigarettes and smoke them up. He didn't care for the way the Caddy handled out on the highway, throwing itself abruptly aside when he twitched the wheel, and he guessed it might have a bent frame. Damn. He'd buy another for the return trip. He could do what he wanted.

He was half an hour past Kearney, Nebraska, when the full moon rose, an absurd visage balanced in his rearview mirror, above it a curled wig of a cloud, filamented edges like platinum hairs. He felt his swollen nose, palped his chin, tender from the stun of the airbag. Before he slept that night, he swallowed a glass of hot tap water enlivened with whiskey, crawled into the damp bed. He had eaten nothing all day, but his stomach coiled at the thought of road food.

He dreamed that he was in the ranch house but all the furniture had been removed from the rooms and in the yard troops in dirty white uniforms fought. The concussive reports of huge guns were breaking the window glass and forcing the floorboards apart, so that he had to walk on the joists. Below the disintegrating floors he saw galvanized tubs filled with dark, coagulated fluid.

On Saturday morning, with four hundred miles in front of him, he swallowed a few bites of scorched eggs, potatoes painted with canned salsa verde, a cup of yellow coffee, left no tip, got on the road. The food was not what he wanted. His breakfast habit was two glasses of mineral water, six cloves of garlic, a pear. The sky to the west hulked sullen; behind him were smears of tinselly orange shot through with blinding streaks. The thick rim of sun bulged against the horizon.

He crossed the state line, hit Cheyenne for the second time in sixty years. He saw neon, traffic, and concrete, but he knew the place, a railroad town that had been up and down. That other time he had been painfully hungry, had gone into the restaurant in the Union Pacific station although he was not used to restaurants, and had ordered a steak. When the woman brought it and he cut into the meat, the blood spread across the white plate and he couldn't help it, he saw the beast, mouth agape in mute bawling, saw the comic aspects of his revulsion as well, a cattleman gone wrong.

Now he parked in front of a phone booth, locked the car although he stood only seven feet away, and telephoned the number Tick's wife had given him. The ruined car had had a phone. Her voice roared out of the earpiece.

We didn't hear so we wondered if you changed your mind.

No, he said, I'll be there late this afternoon. I'm in Cheyenne now.

The wind's blowing pretty hard. They're saying it could maybe snow. In the mountains. Her voice sounded doubtful.

I'll keep an eye on it, he said.

He was out of town and running north in a few minutes.

The country poured open on each side, reduced the Cadillac to a finger snap. Nothing had changed, not a goddamn thing, the empty pale place and its roaring wind, the distant antelope as tiny as mice, landforms shaped true to the past. He felt himself slip back; the calm of eighty-three years sheeted off him like water, replaced by a young man's scalding anger at a fool world and the fools in it. What a damn hard time it had been to hit the road. You don't know what it was like, he had told his wives, until they said they did know, he'd pounded it into their ears two hundred times, the poor youth on the street holding up a sign asking for work, the job with the furnace man, *yatata yatata ya.* Thirty miles out of Cheyenne he saw the first billboard: WYOMING DOWN UNDER, Western Fun the Other Way, over a blown-up photograph of kangaroos hopping through the sagebrush and a blond child grinning in a manic imitation of pleasure. A diagonal banner warned, Open May 31.

So what, Rollo had said to the old man's girlfriend, what about that Mr. Tin Head? Looking at her, not just her face but up and down, eyes moving over her like an iron over a shirt and the old man in his mailman's sweater and lopsided hat tasting his Everclear and not noticing or not caring, getting up every now and then to lurch onto the porch and water the weeds. When he left the room, the tension ebbed and they were only ordinary people to whom nothing happened. Rollo looked away from the woman, leaned down to scratch the dog's ears, saying Snarleyow Snapper, and the woman took a dish to the sink and ran water on it, yawning. When the old man came back to his chair, the Everclear like sweet oil in his glass, glances resharpened and inflections of voice again carried complex messages.

Well, well, she said, tossing her braids back, every year Tin Head butchers one of his steers, and that's what they'd eat all winter long, boiled, fried, smoked, fricasseed, burned, and raw. So one time he's out there by the barn, and he hits the steer a good one with the ax, and it drops stun down. He ties up the back legs, hoists it up and sticks it, shoves the tub under to catch the blood. When it's bled out pretty good, he lets it down and starts skinning it, starts with the head, cuts back of the poll down past the eye to the nose, peels the hide back. He don't cut the head off but keeps on skinning, dewclaws to hock, up the inside of the thigh and then to the cod and down the middle of the belly to brisket. Now he's ready to start siding, working that tough old skin off. But siding is hard work (the old man nodded) and he gets the hide off about halfway and starts thinking about dinner. So he leaves the steer half-skinned there on the ground and he goes into the kitchen, but first he cuts out the tongue, which is his favorite dish all cooked up and eat cold with Mrs. Tin Head's mustard in a forget-me-not teacup. Sets it on the ground and goes in to dinner. Dinner is chicken and dumplins, one of them changed-color chickens started out white and ended up blue, yessir, blue as your old daddy's eyes.

She was a total liar. The old man's eyes were murk brown.

Onto the high plains sifted the fine snow, delicately clouding the air, a rare dust, beautiful, he thought, silk gauze, but there was muscle in the wind rocking the heavy car, a great pulsing artery of the jet stream swooping down from the sky to touch the earth. Plumes of smoke rose hundreds of feet into the air, elegant fountains and twisting snow devils, shapes of veiled Arab women and ghost riders dissolving in white fume. The snow snakes writhing across the asphalt straightened into rods. He was driving in a rushing river of cold whiteout foam. He could see nothing; he trod on the brake, the wind buffeting the car, a bitter, hard-flung dust hissing over metal and glass. The car shuddered. And as suddenly as it had risen, the wind dropped and the road was clear; he could see a long, empty mile.

How do you know when there's enough of anything? What trips the lever that snaps up the stop sign? What electrical currents fizz and crackle in the brain to shape the decision to quit a place? He had listened to her damn story and the dice had rolled. For years he believed he had left without hard reason and suffered for it. But he'd learned from television nature programs that it had been time for him to find his own territory and his own woman. How many women were out there! He had married three of them and sampled plenty.

With the lapping subtlety of an incoming tide the shape of the ranch began to gather in his mind; he could recall sharply the fences he'd made, taut wire and perfect corners, the draws and rock outcrops, the watercourse valley steepening, cliffs like bones with shreds of meat on them rising and rising, and the stream plunging suddenly underground, disappearing into a subterranean darkness of blind fish, shooting out of the mountain ten miles west on a neighbor's place but leaving their ranch some badland red country as dry as a cracker, steep canyons with high caves suited to lions. He and Rollo had shot two early in that winter, close to the overhang with the painted vulvas. There were good caves up there from a lion's point of view.

He traveled against curdled sky. In the last sixty miles the snow began again. He climbed out of Buffalo. Pallid flakes as distant from one another as galaxies flew past, then more, and in ten minutes he was crawling at twenty miles an hour, the windshield wipers thumping like a stick dragged down the stairs.

The light was falling out of the day when he reached the pass, the blunt mountains lost in snow, the greasy hairpin turns ahead. He drove slowly and steadily in a low gear; he had not forgotten how to drive a winter mountain. But the wind was up again, rocking and slapping the car, blotting out all but whipping snow, and he was sweating with the anxiety of keeping to the road, dizzy with the altitude. Twelve more miles, sliding and buffeted, before he reached Ten Sleep, where streetlights glowed in revolving circles like Van Gogh's sun. There had not been electricity when he left the place. In those days there were seventeen black, lightless miles between the town and the ranch, and now the long arch of years compressed into that distance. His headlights picked up a sign: 20 MILES TO WYOMING DOWN UNDER. Emus and bison leered above the letters.

He turned onto the snowy road, marked with a single set of tracks, faint but still discernible, the heater fan whirring, the radio silent, all beyond the headlights blurred. Yet everything was as it had been, the shape of the road achingly familiar, sentinel rocks looming as they had in his youth. There was an eerie dream quality in seeing the deserted Farrier place leaning east as it had leaned sixty years ago, and the Banner ranch gate, where the companionable tracks he had been following turned off, the gate ghostly in the snow but still flying its wrought-iron flag, unmarked by the injuries of weather, and the taut five-strand fences and dim shifting forms of cattle. Next would come the road to their ranch, a left-hand turn just over the crest of a rise. He was running now on the unmarked road through great darkness.

Winking at Rollo, the girlfriend had said, Yes, she had said, Yes, sir, Tin Head eats half his dinner and then he has to take a little nap. After a while he wakes up again and goes outside, stretching his arms and yawning, says, Guess I'll finish skinning out that steer. But the steer ain't there. It's gone. Only the tongue, laying on the ground all covered with dirt and straw, and the tub of blood and the dog licking at it.

It was her voice that drew you in, that low, twangy voice, wouldn't matter if she was saying the alphabet, what you heard was the rustle of hay. She could make you smell the smoke from an imagined fire.

How could he not recognize the turnoff to the ranch? It was so clear and sharp in his mind: the dusty crimp of the corner, the low section where the snow drifted, the run where willows slapped the side of the truck. He went a mile, watching for it, but the turn didn't come up; then he watched for the Bob Kitchen place, two miles beyond, but the distance unrolled and there was nothing. He made a three-point turn and backtracked. Rollo must have given up the old entrance road, for it wasn't there. The Kitchen place was gone to fire or wind. If he didn't find the turn, it was no great loss; back to Ten Sleep and scout a motel. But he hated to quit when he was close enough to spit, hated to retrace black miles on a bad night when he was maybe twenty minutes away from the ranch.

He drove very slowly, following his tracks, and the ranch entrance appeared on the right, although the gate was gone and the sign down. That was why he'd missed it, that and a clump of sagebrush that obscured the gap.

He turned in, feeling a little triumph. But the road under the snow was rough and got rougher, until he was bucking along over boulders and slanted rock and knew wherever he was, it was not right.

He couldn't turn around on the narrow track and began backing gingerly, the window down, craning his stiff neck, staring into the redness cast by the taillights. The car's right rear tire rolled up over a boulder, slid, and sank into a quaggy hole. The tires spun in the snow, but he got no purchase.

I'll sit here, he said aloud. I'll sit here until it's light and then walk down to the Banner place and ask for a cup of coffee. I'll be cold but I won't freeze to death. It played like a joke the way he imagined it, with Bob Banner opening the door and saying, Why, it's Mero, come on in and have some java and a hot biscuit, before he remembered that Bob Banner would have to be 120 years old to fill that role. He was maybe three miles from Banner's gate, and the Banner ranch house was another seven miles beyond the gate. Say a ten-mile hike at altitude in a snowstorm. On the other hand, he had half a tank of gas. He could run the car for a while, turn it off, start it again, all through the night. It was bad luck, but that's all. The trick was patience.

He dozed half an hour in the wind-rocked car, woke shivering and cramped. He wanted to lie down. He thought perhaps he could put a flat rock under the goddamn tire. Never say die, he said, feeling around the passenger-side floor for the flashlight in his emergency bag, and then remembering the wrecked car towed away, the flares and car phone and AAA card and flashlight and matches and candle and power bars and bottle of water still in it, and probably now in the damn tow driver's damn wife's car. He might get a good enough look anyway in the snow-reflected light. He put on his gloves and buttoned his coat, got out and locked the car, sidled around to the rear, bent down. The taillights lit the snow beneath the rear of the car like a fresh bloodstain. There was a cradle-sized depression eaten out by the spinning tire. Two or three flat ones might get him out, or small round ones — he was not going to insist on the perfect stone. The wind tore at

him; the snow was certainly drifting up. He began to shuffle on
the road, feeling with his feet for rocks he could move, the car's
even throbbing promising motion and escape. The wind was sharp
and his ears ached. His wool cap was in the damn emergency bag.

My Lord, she continued, Tin Head is just startled to pieces when he
don't see that steer. He thinks somebody, some neighbor, don't like
him, plenty of them, come and stole it. He looks around for tire
marks or footprints but he don't see nothing except old cow tracks.
He puts his hand up to his eyes and stares away. Nothing in the
north, the south, the east, but way over there in the west, on the
side of the mountain, he sees something moving stiff and slow,
stumbling along. It looks raw and it's got something bunchy and
wet hanging down over its hindquarters. Yeah, it was the steer,
never making no sound. And just then it stops and it looks back.
And all that distance Tin Head can see the raw meat of the head
and the shoulder muscles and the empty mouth without no tongue
open wide and its red eyes glaring at him, pure teetotal hate like
arrows coming at him, and he knows he is done for and all of his
kids and their kids is done for, and that his wife is done for and that
every one of her blue dishes has got to break, and the dog that
licked the blood is done for, and the house where they lived has to
blow away or burn up and every fly or mouse in it.
    There was a silence and she added, That's it. And it all went
against him too.
    That's it? Rollo said in a greedy, hot way.

Yet he knew he was on the ranch, he felt it, and he knew this road
too. It was not the main ranch road but some lower entrance he
could not quite recollect that cut in below the river. Now he remembered that the main entrance gate was on a side road that
branched off well before the Banner place. He found another good
stone, another, wondering which track this could be; the map of the
ranch in his memory was not as bright now, but scuffed and obliterated as though trodden. The remembered gates collapsed, fences
wavered, while the badland features swelled into massive promi-
nence. The cliffs bulged into the sky, lions snarled, the river cork-
screwed through a stone hole at a tremendous rate, and boulders
cascaded from the heights. Beyond the barbwire something moved.
    He grasped the car-door handle. It was locked. Inside, by the

dashboard glow, he could see the gleam of the keys in the ignition where he'd left them to keep the car running. The situation was almost comic. He picked up a big two-hand rock, smashed it on the driver's-side window, and slipped his arm in through the hole, into the delicious warmth of the car, a contortionist's reach, twisting behind the steering wheel and down, and had he not kept limber with exercise and nut cutlets and green leafy vegetables he could never have reached the keys. His fingers grazed and then grasped, and he had them. This is how they sort out the men from the boys, he said aloud. As his fingers closed on the keys, he glanced at the passenger door. The lock button stood high. And even had it been locked as well, why had he strained to reach the keys when he had only to lift the lock button on the driver's side? Cursing, he pulled out the rubber floor mats and arranged them over the stones, stumbled around the car once more. He was dizzy, tremendously thirsty and hungry, opened his mouth to snowflakes. He had eaten nothing for two days but the burned eggs that morning. He could eat a dozen burned eggs now.

The snow roared through the broken window. He put the car in reverse and slowly trod the gas. The car lurched and steadied in the track, and once more he was twisting his neck, backing in the red glare, twenty feet, thirty, but slipping and spinning; the snow was too deep. He was backing up an incline that had seemed level on the way in but now showed itself as a remorselessly long hill, studded with rocks and deep in snow. His incoming tracks twisted like rope. He forced out another twenty feet, spinning the tires until they smoked, and then the rear wheels slued sideways off the track and into a two-foot ditch, the engine died, and that was it. He was almost relieved to have reached this point where the celestial fingernails were poised to nip his thread. He dismissed the ten-mile distance to the Banner place: it might not be that far, or maybe they had pulled the ranch closer to the main road. A truck might come by. Shoes slipping, coat buttoned awry, he might find the mythical Grand Hotel in the sagebrush.

On the main road his tire tracks showed as a faint pattern in the pearly apricot light from the risen moon, winking behind roiling clouds of snow. His blurred shadow strengthened whenever the wind eased. Then the violent country showed itself, the cliffs rear-ing at the moon, the snow rising off the prairie like steam, the white flank of the ranch slashed with fence cuts, the sagebrush glittering, and along the creek black tangles of willow, bunched like dead hair. Cattle were in the field beside the road, their plumed breath catching the moony glow like comic-strip dialogue balloons.

His shoes filled with snow, he walked against the wind, feeling as easy to tear as a man cut from paper. As he walked, he noticed that one from the herd inside the fence was keeping pace with him. He walked more slowly, and the animal lagged. He stopped and turned. It stopped as well, huffing vapor, regarding him, a strip of snow on its back like a linen runner. It tossed its head, and in the howling, wintry light he saw he'd been wrong again, that the half-skinned steer's red eye had been watching for him all this time.

DORAN LARSON

Morphine

FROM VIRGINIA QUARTERLY REVIEW

DESPITE tests and retests — her mammogram dittoed across clinic walls like some sick Warhol print — Sarah had not understood her disease until she'd sketched the body it was quickly dismantling. Yet facets of dying remain welcome. There is the peculiar silence. No one can understand what she is going through. No one is fool enough to try. They are much too busy, and satisfied, fidgeting with her body. Death, it occurs to her now, watching Philip fold and stack towels on the bed near her feet, it's like a soundproof booth in an old quiz show. Through the glass the audience can express commiseration, but words simply do not penetrate. And as she arcs her hand, softening a detail on her sketchpad, it occurs to her, that too is what she once loved about her art — the exclusivity, the surprise even in making copies, recreating the original as one's own.

Inside the glass booth, she decides, dying is a pantomime, a performance art without rehearsal; always finale, always debut: each day a fresh nuance in the languorous touch of a glass, a wistful grin, the daily papers growing heavy with old news, the laughter of children in the adjacent yard, the tea strainers and folding of warm clean towels . . . death is a kind of duty which the grief of others makes sure — mimicking sorrow, gesturing false hope behind the glass plate — that you perform.

"I washed the ones you were using already," he says to her, "since the nap is less stiff. Your skin has been so sensitive lately." (She smiles.) "How's the cocktail?"

To counter the burning in her lungs and liver, the gnawing

through her bones, she is allowed to give herself morphine. She floats now upon her bed, anchored to earth by the drip bag and sheathed in sunlight from a southern window. And death's grip, like that of a fairy-tale giant, remains paralyzed by the magic spell. She rolls her head from side to side in the strange mix of heavy and light the drug brings, as though her soul were leaden while her body fades. She's tempted to laugh. "I'm okay. Maybe, a little less."

He turns the plastic dial down one number. She reaches out, her elbow bulbous inside her skin, to touch his leg. What can she say to this man she must abandon? She kisses his brow as he leans awkwardly down. She whispers, "You wonderful, sweet . . ." He whispers, "You're high."

There had been bad moments, of course. The shock following the initial report. Her breasts carved away and sealed up in specimen jars — things no one could imagine. And he is so good-natured; it had thus taken time to appreciate how it all weighed upon Philip.

Without colleagues of his own, here in a Midwest that had never been part of their plans, his research had slowed to a halt while her career took off. And when he announced he was turning his dissertation on the English Civil War into a book, she'd been unsure whether to be encouraged or detect a fiction it would require years to dispel. She'd felt his resentment at department parties, whenever called upon to play faculty spouse. She saw his bitter pleasure in being the perfect host, even in other people's houses.

It was his capacity for self-punishment that had kept her quiet after she'd winced, finding the tiny node, lying on the beach in the Caribbean three springs ago. (Face-down on the sand, her top undone, she thought a knot in the strap had been trapped beneath her.) But once the diagnosis was sure and she did suspect his panic, she became a better patient.

"I made shortbread this morning. I'll set you up before I go to the library."

"Yes." Her mind is clearing but her mouth is still loose. "Will you be long?" He says no, bringing corners together.

To show him she wanted to get well, she bought books and read articles. She even attended a support group. Women in pastel warm-up suits, sitting on big pillows, talked of husbands and children left alone. They wept for eating too much fat or smoking cigarettes . . . Such good little soldiers, such diligent students of where they went wrong, so impeccably blameworthy.

She could not tell Philip she'd quit the group. The diagnosis had brought silence like a deafening fog into the house — shutting cupboards gently, catching the kettle before it screamed — as though a loud noise might break the unraveling thread of life. And into that quiet, like a flat white stone into dark water, sank the sounds of real joy — wavering, flashing in unexpected currents, while her body withered and shared laughter fell from sight. Except when she left for her group. Except when his stoic grin brightened toward something deeper.

So she would leave, to bury herself in a corner of the medical-school library, among subterranean graduate students, reading histories. At home she pretended to continue her work on seventeenth-century royal portraits. She talked of tenure here or their getting jobs together at some private college back east. But in the library she pored over medieval and Renaissance anatomies. Bearded, austere men standing over corpses (why so often women?) ripped open to the world. Even more fascinating, a whole genre of live bodies with viscera exposed. For more than an hour once, unconsciously touching her own belly, she gazed at a sixteenth-century German print: a woman sitting on a squat stone block, her smooth legs spread, hair wrapped up in braids except one hank in sexy disarray, her abdomen peeled and each organ — liver, kidneys, bladder, and womb — hovering in a black vacuum. Like a whore on an auction block, moonlighting as a butcher's display.

This was the first plate she copied. She had only a blue ballpoint and an envelope, yet she had to feel the image translated through her own hand. She had not drawn in years. It was as painful as stretching a cramped limb. She glanced up, self-conscious, to see an Asian woman bent over molecular diagrams. She tried again.

Her raw talent had survived, but the training from high school and her first year in college skittered away just ahead of her fingers in each too-heavy shade and line. In her enormous early ambitions, she'd studied Dürer in detail and shading, Monet in her use of color, the epic lighting in Delacroix . . . So when she turned away, she'd turned completely. She had not so much as sketched in more than ten years, since breaking herself from studio art to art history, avoiding the creation of images obsessively — even giving directions in neat verbal instructions rather than drawing a map. At first she'd told herself she could work in off hours. But the moment she tried, like an addict, she would miss classes and sleep as a painting teased mercilessly to express a real vision.

Yet once the anatomy was done (her hand sweating, her stomach in a knot) she noted that she'd kept the hair trim and had made the legs heavier. And in comparing the copy to the original, her stress was transformed. Perhaps because she felt her death so near, and searched for no other promise, she saw only what was good and true, and felt a strange elation. In the following weeks, she sustained this feeling by drawing similar plates, eventually taking the work home. To spare Philip worry that she'd grown morbid, when he was in the house she copied classical sculpture — the Farnese Hercules, Laocoön, the Barberini Faun — ignoring heads and limbs to focus on torsos. Philip seemed encouraged at her new work. But she sensed too, settling at the bottom of his smile, a silt of envy.

"The shading is wonderful," he'd said once, sitting on the edge of the bed, just in from shopping. "You haven't lost your hand."

"Yes. But it's the eye that's gone. All I can see is history and precursors. I have trouble finding the body on the paper."

"You could try this," and he'd lifted his shirt, exposing, as a joke, his own pale ribs and chest, and she'd wondered if he weren't jealous, as though she were being unfaithful in drawing the bodies of masculine gods. She still does not know why she had reached out with her pen and — while he remained uncannily still, as though they had agreed — drew the outlines of heavy pectoral and abdominal muscles across his skin. He watched her hand as though observing his own painless dissection. Then he'd finished it by posing, flexing his arms, pushing up his biceps. And they had laughed again; across ambivalence and unspoken concern, they had laughed the most raucous forced notes to wander those rooms in weeks. Yet she listened to how long he took in the shower, the rush of water unvarying as he scrubbed away her joke. There was no sequel, because she could not show him the other sketches; she could not explain how the riddled abdomens, the precipitous laterals of sculpted male bodies bore the shading and texture and complexity, the heroic sacrifice women's bodies could offer only in being cut open.

Philip stands to stretch his back. In the gray flannel shirt he wears

to do housework, its tails bearded with loose threads, it strikes her
to the heart — a vision of him as an old man, and how her own
death will age him. She tries to continue her drawing of a mirrored
corner of the room. But as Philip begins folding sheets, despite the
thinning of the drug, her thoughts wander to Dr. Michaels's cool
fingers outlining the tumor in the first X-rays.

She recalls the chill in her breast while his hands ran over the
image and she'd remembered their drive south to New Orleans,
the summer before she started her job, only weeks after moving
from the East Coast. She recalled the road as blurred trees behind
Philip's profile singing "Rocky Raccoon," and cornfields wheeling
away while she made sandwiches in her lap. But only days later, in a
French Quarter café, she'd gazed at a heat-sensitive photo of the
entire Mississippi Valley: patches of blood-red hot, cooler yellows,
and suddenly their own experience of that landscape was made
irretrievably distant. As though they had been blind to the larger
truth and authority in the photograph. In Michaels's office, she'd
crossed her arms over her breasts as his hand traced their X-rayed
interiors, and in every word, every translation of technical into lay
language (subtly flexing his own well-muscled body, excited because her tumor was "classic," a textbook case), in every poke of his
silver pen, her breasts were already being taken, as incomprehensible as geography, except to radiation. And once they were gone —
right, then left — Michaels himself became repulsive. This man
whose hands had been inside her, his muscles working to find what
was of interest beneath her surface (a beardless son of the men in
the plates, towering over eviscerated bodies), she'd felt how he
seemed to relax only when his hands were on her body as he mentioned showing her early X-rays to his students, aching for her to
die and complete the smooth curve of her pathology. Though she
could explain it to no one, his touch became terrifying, and she
insisted on a new doctor.

Was that why she'd drawn these women set up like anatomical
tarts? Taking the power role, tracing these women's organs as
Michaels had fondled hers?

This thought had upset her. Recalling it now, she tears her mind
away from Michaels and raises her head slightly, letting cool air
beneath her neck, and tries to sketch. Her hand is hers again as the
drug weakens, but it is like drawing in bad light, her fingers be-

neath the morphine's shadow. She wonders, how many hours had she sat cross-legged, her hips numb in cold stone museums, re-creating the strokes of Degas and da Vinci, and always perfectly — her hell to be the brilliant copyist. Yet now she was not hoping to reproduce a style. She was attempting to reclaim the very bodies dissected in words by Michaels and his students. Still, she'd felt a kind of trespass. The saving grace of the plates was that faces and bodies were generic, mere masculine ideals of sex, ransacked for their contents. But the idiosyncracies of her own hand granted these women personalities, stripping away their anonymity in the very gestures by which she grasped after her own body. She did not stop, but she felt as though indulging in a practice less morbid than traitorous.

"Would you like some tea?" he asks her, stacking the towels on one arm. With a nod back, he flips the thick brown hair from his eyes, a habit that has always touched her. She feels a rush of thanks washing through her bones and blood and scraping pain from the fog of sensation — thanks that he is not one of them, not a Michaels or . . . the thought sinks. The drug's farewell is like waking from a pleasant dream, her body resuming weight and density sufficient for pain. She twists her head back toward the window. It is a bright day, luxuriant with dry summer.

She winces. Gravity has reached up and gripped her spine. He sees, and spilling the towels — "Here" — darts to turn up the drip two numbers. She closes her eyes tight, then opens them, riding above the pain by focusing on the sun through the lace curtains as it veils him in delicate shadows, like a shifting tattoo over face and arms. His hands open. And because there really is nothing he can do, he offers again to make tea. She says yes. But he asks, "Or would you rather sleep?" Despite his thin chest, he has strong hands, like his father the cabinetmaker. "No" — she forces calm into her voice — "But tea . . . tea would be lovely."

The pain softens. She breathes. Her body begins to rise again, again grows light. "Thank you" — hands like her grandfather's, though his memory reaches only to her eleventh year, when he was himself (her mind totters upon the gently rising curve of the drug) just fifty-five, a craftsman of expensive carved picture frames. (Philip sees her relax, and strokes her hand.) As a girl she felt fully herself only in his workshop, set back thirty yards behind her grand-

mother's rambling Montreal house through the garden of endive
and dill and cabbage, the stone wall hoary with mold and lichen,
set so far because *grandmère* could not stand the smells of paint and
lacquer; *"Comme la cuisine du diable!"* her grandmother cried whenever the wind shifted, though it was the smells that had seduced
Sarah first. (As Philip turns, her body rising above the bed and
sensation, she feels drawn after him in the mild draft of air.) The
bite of rubbing oil and varnish in the ramshackle building, the
dusty dry loft of warm cherry and cool maple, poplar for turning
on the old peddled lathe, the workbench cut and gouged by tools,
blistered with dripping glue — like a low landscape; the smudged
windows that radiated a strangely opaque light in the even twenty-
three degrees centigrade — the brass thermometer her Titi had
brought from his home near Rouen before the First World War he
said, exhaling smoke, and she could watch the wood — oak and
cedar and mahogany — sculpted into reliefs of branch and leaf and
claw like the creation of new life; for a time she'd dreamed of de-
signing interiors, imagining for each picture frame its proper room
though she was not even allowed to be in the shop, for her grandmother feared an accident, her mother how her clothes smelled of
her grandfather's rank French cigarettes . . . (Philip's hands continue refolding towels while her fingers rest on the sketchpad, the
corner of the room reflected in the mirror; she can feel the charcoal and paper, sees the three reflected planes but these sensations
drift wide apart) . . . the scraps of birch and walnut her Titi would
give her to cut and sand, making a relief of the whole family with
Titi in dark cherry holding a cigarette of maple, and Whisk the cat
in pine, while he pressed delicate gold leaf to intricate wood foli-
age, singing *"Plaisir d'amour ne dure qu'un moment/Chagrin d'amour
dure toute la vie,"* singing to her in the sweetly grumbling sad voice
he gave to no one else and he turns, lifting his thick cap to wink at
her until her mother rings the brass ship's bell on the back porch
and it was he who had made her want to be an artist — his mischie-
vous green eyes, the left always so wickedly lazy as though the very
diable were peeking encouragement. And after they'd returned
from the cemetery Sarah ran out through yellow sunshine, down
the path through the garden, dill plants whipping her legs as she
sobbed into the shop where she felt like hunger the absence of
his bent shadow on the dusty floor, his smoking wink, his voice
singing for her as she folded sandpaper the way he'd shown her,

like the point of a tiny trowel, to reach inside delicate filigree as her mother came in — stern and teary — plucked the cigarette away and slapped Sarah hard, twice across the mouth. She smeared her own face with red walnut stain ("Sarah-Sarah, burnt in the Sahara!"), pungent, penetrating, it would not come off for weeks though her mother never really tried, shame a better punishment than the scrub brush my young thing; on the playground they called her wetback and pushed her into the circle of little Mexican and Puerto Rican girls ("Sarah-Sarah, burnt in . . .") but she just sat silently at the edge of the yard for she knew now. She knew.

She was an artist. She was an artist and whatever that meant (at eleven she only dimly suspected, though it was surely romantic and grand), her grandfather's faith would sustain her in this secret part of herself, inside her marked skin.

The bathroom cupboard, muffled by the towels and blankets inside, thumps shut. She opens her eyes. Her body reconverges from the corner and paper and pillow. His shoes squeak, turning on the tile. She breathes deep. Raw air brings her back to the surface of the bed.

She regrips the charcoal, then gently shifts her body to reorient the extremities into a whole. She focuses. Where the walls and ceiling meet in the upper corner, in the mirror's upper curve, there are speckled flaws in the glass's tain. It is a hard detail to keep upon the plane of glass and free of the walls. She tries and erases, and feathers with the edge of her palm as she tried in the mirror of her room after her Titi's death when she felt so alone. When she was not drawing, she read about artists — Van Gogh and Claudel and Kahlo — anyone who had burned brightly, dying young or insane or unappreciated. And soon it was this rich fantasy life that she inhabited. For seven years, amid acrylics and oils, charcoal and graphite and watercolor, she was convinced that like magic potions, the scents and odors would transport her physically into that world — until the second year of college, when it became clear: she lacked brilliance, the talent, one instructor commented, residing entirely in a workmanlike hand rather than in her eye. And in her forced exile, in every glowing response to her term papers on Renaissance perspective or graduate essays on restoration techniques, she felt her Titi wink to say, We only frame what others have created, but we get along, *plaisir d'amour ne dure* . . .

She listens to Philip stacking sheets in a drawer. She breathes deep again, rests the charcoal, crosses her arms loosely over the flat of her chest.

The day she drew her death, tracing in pencil her own ruined body, she did not think, If only I'd eaten less fat, or not smoked at parties, or avoided solvents and cadmium paint. What keeps coming back is the thought, If I had only been brilliant. From the first days of her diagnosis, despite the horror, she had been subtly unnerved that she did not want more life. She only wished that her life, what she'd already been granted, had blazed.

Stretched across the yellow wall, she watches the shadow of her lamp veiled in lace. She looks long enough to see the sun move. Her life had not blazed. And all of her fear of falling and falling into endless mimicry at the end of that long leap, scared down the valley path of research and teaching, this is all made flesh in a single problem as he comes from the bathroom wearing his wan smile, poised to ask if there is anything she needs to ease the anguish infusing her body as she had once hoped it might be filled with art — the problem of helping Philip survive.

And yet there are moments (he suggests a bit of cinnamon in her tea, then vanishes into a mild clatter of cups and kettle), moments when she wonders if he will do so badly without her. She remembers the vacation when she first detected the lump. Her third year in the department, she'd grown slightly mad with worry over her book project. Still, they enjoyed the long flight, drinking too much, taking pictures through the window like crass tourists. They were only to be away for a week. But once they were checked into their bright room, she could not relax; she forced herself to swim with him, and explore throughout the day, finding craft shops of brightly painted wood, eating fried goat and plantains at open-air stands . . . yet a part of her mind awaited night, while he slept, when she could write and read in the tiny bathroom. Then, the third morning, before she woke, he posted her research materials to her office back home.

Equatorial sunlight pushed through the window slats, striping him side to side and giving him unnatural width. She still could not believe what he'd told her. She saw his flexed fist, and a simmering anger. Sitting up under the sheets, her thin legs were draped in linen like a Giotto Christ.

"Everything? I have nothing to work on?" His jaw rippled. "Can you have grown this resentful of my work?"

"You haven't slept decently in weeks. What was the point of coming? We're only *here* for five more days."

"If you had anything of your own . . . Don't talk to me about *my* sake. I could have given you a chapter to work on. If you can't get your own research together, you could help me. Somebody has to feed us while you do your groundbreaking work."

Her bitterness shocked them both. Then he yelled. Though a gentle man, he pulled her from the bed and held her before the mirror, forcing her to look at her wasting limbs.

And this, she sees now, this was his strongest act of their life together. Later, when she felt the lump, lying on a remote beach, she had made love with him as though she could share her fear, and so defeat it. She'd climbed atop him there in the clean air and warm sun, feeling his cock gripped in her lips, rocking it up and down to milk the weakness from him. But that night, alone in the bathroom before they went to dinner, she held her hands over her small breasts, pressing them out of existence. Her look had always been boyish, with her thin frame, short red hair, and muscular jaw. And behind the glass, it seemed not so great a change. It was when she crowned her hands over her brow (she did not *know* she was ill, she told herself, let alone that she would need treatment), obliterating her hairline, her childhood romance with a young death ran into the cool marble of fear.

At home she put off the test, still plagued by the thought that it was an image, a romantic idea that would kill her. But while she watched herself again missing meals and sleeping too little, she also saw Philip fail to intervene. And she saw too how his intellectual life in fact had become her own. Critiquing her articles rather than doing his own work, or allowing whole days to slip into replacing a porch step or turning earth for the garden while his dissertation grew old. She remembers now, hearing the kettle start to sing, a comment of English friends during their year in Brussels, after the birth of the couple's first child: "Our relationship is on a back burner. We've become Danny Inc." That was what had happened to her and Philip, even before her illness. Like some fifties housewife, his life — she hears it as he moves around the kitchen — was becoming absorbed, and erased, in hers. Sarah Inc.

The morning that phrase occurred to her, she went into the bedroom where he was reading her chapter on Velásquez. She dropped the shoulder of her nightgown. She had already sensed, staring into the back yard, watching spring mellow into summer, his deep loneliness. She did not know how else to get him back, except to show him that she too could be weak.

What had she felt as he stood on his bare feet, his hand rounding her breast, deftly searching? As their eyes locked, she had imagined herself breaking down, but of course they only said the inevitable things: it was probably nothing, a cyst, though he made an appointment and she was encouraged when he became angry the second time she put it off, coaxing him toward the rage he'd expressed in the Caribbean, the rage that might place them on an even footing once again.

But what she did not feel as his hand explored her, what she could not have suspected was the sense of isolation once the malignancy was confirmed and parts of her body, hair, breasts, muscle, were taken away; no one could share that — no one could prepare you. Least of all could anyone have imagined her relief, that after telling herself her early dreams had been sheer romance — that she didn't want what was eating her soul to live without — no one could have prepared her for the conviction that it was better to die soon, of a thing mapped and tested, than later of a lingering question.

And no one could have said to her, You will wake from your first surgery with a mysterious sense of integrity, you will feel an ironic wholeness once your body looks the fragment you have felt inside for so long.

She remembers waking, the film she had to blink away, machine bleeps, a scuffled chair, her own gasp around the tube shoved through her nose. And then the absence. The feeling — in this ammonia-smelling world — the sense of nothing atop her right ribs . . . Philip's hand finding hers between the bedrails and tubes . . . the nurse's saccharine smile. And then the chiseled words, as though spoken by someone in the room: This is the world after. This is the real you. A part. A remainder. Yet it was not until she'd drawn it, a week after the final surgery, that she fully understood.

He turns the radio on low while the tea steeps. Voices joust, a talk show, discussing some issue that will be played out after she is gone. It was at her last clinic appointment, before the first surgery that she insisted on keeping one X-ray. The exposure — her breast flattened from the side — was too light to be useful: a sky-gray traversed by small lines like a river delta skirting the malignant white island. Dr. Michaels was suspicious when she asked, as though she'd demanded his tie pin. Philip did not comment on the string-tied envelope, in the waiting room or on the drive home.

The first moment he was away from the house, she held it to the bedroom window. It was then late fall, and the sun poured in low from the south. The lines in the exposure were projected onto the front of her blouse. She looked down and saw her lethal breast, stenciled sideways like a cubist detail across the white linen covering her flesh. She pulled the shade on the other window, then found tape and newspaper.

She taped the paper around the borders of the exposure, covering the southern window until the only light in the room was what filtered through the X-ray. Then she took off her clothes.

Like the death-beam in some cheap movie, the X-ray breast was projected over her own. She touched the brightest spot on her pale skin — the trace of her tumor. She was trained to read images, yet she could decipher neither what was being revealed nor her own motives. It was as though she had proved Michaels right, that it was presumptuous to claim to know her own body better than he, and she felt ridiculous. She stripped the windows and threw the envelope and exposure to the back of her closet. And when Philip came home she made love with him for the first time since the diagnosis. Perhaps the last time, they both knew, with her whole.

Once the surgery was done, and done again a few months later (the second was welcome; the asymmetry as repulsive as the absence), she entered into a brief remission. It was the morning she woke to feel the liquid returned to her lungs that she again darkened the room and taped up the X-ray.

Fall had become a mild winter warming toward spring. The sun was at nearly the same angle as before. But now the image of her breast, in profile, was cast beyond her flattened body, onto the wall beside the door. She tore a sheet from her sketchpad and taped it to the spot. With her bedside lamp on its low setting, by playing with angles, she finally managed to project her silhouette onto the paper without washing away the thin projection of her missing breast. With a pencil, at arm's length, she outlined the profile of her body, reunited to the machine's memory of her breast.

When it was done, she sat on the edge of the bed with the sketch on her knees, her fists tucked tight in her armpits. This was the drawing that made her feel death in her heart and gut — death's work, death's image . . . She forced her mind to the words, remaining there dangerously long as she heard Philip drive in. But there was some secret the proper title would unlock, as though in the ordering of letters lay the combination. It came to her in a semiconscious dream.

Her own torso — headless, armless, the breasts cracked away — was twisted at a painful angle, a classical fragment, set up in a niche in a slowly curving corridor. There were other niches but they were shadowed. She came close and saw her scars — like seams waiting to be filled — and understood that the corridor had been created for her alone; and then she saw them receding toward a vanishing point: repeated versions of her own body, neck to waist, covering the history of her life. Infant, child, a delicate pubescent torso, young woman, and adult. Two breasts. One breast. None.

She'd woken with a start. She called to Philip but there was no answer. She stood before the bureau mirror, stripped off her T-shirt, and held her arms tight behind her back to approximate the image in the dream. She stared at the scars where her breasts had been, her ribs visible through the abject nakedness of missing flesh. And she knew immediately what the dream and drawing had tried to tell.

If her art had not filled her life, in turning away, her own body had become this single work, recording the hours in her grandfather's shop breathing paint and lacquer, the paling years in libraries, her disappointment, her love for Philip . . . and the theft, at the hands of radiologists and surgeons. She took the sketch of the X-ray from the back of her closet. It was this image, a classic of its type, that had made them cut — that had justified their desire to slash and sculpt her; this image, as surely as the scalpel, that had carved her away.

She sat on the edge of the bed, pressing her eyes shut with her fists. She recalled Camille, Vincent, Frida, and felt with them an intimacy in her very blood. She wept briefly. Then a strange sense came to her — the strangest of all.

The day was blustering; shadows sprang across the mattress as the sun found a break, then vanished. And beneath this show she felt it.

She was happy.

She could not say why. But something was unspeakably good in this moment. And happiness — she embraced Philip as he came through the back door juggling books and groceries, drunk with the smell of him and bread and brown paper — happiness allowed her to give up. Her condition degenerated quickly, for she refused all treatment. Her hair started to grow back and she smiled at her restored image in the mirror. It was then too that she stopped sketching anatomies.

Instead she drew interiors. Rooms with tall, fully draped windows, complicated doorways, designs from her early imagination of the rich houses where her Titi's picture frames would hang. And then she began drawing this room: curtains and bureau, rumpled sheets, window frames. Her own gallery. Her exhibition space. And she remembered.

Before she learned to regulate the flow of morphine, one day shortening into two or three with the softening of the pain in her joints and spine, she had a fantastic mix of dream and memory, of the torso Belvedere twisting itself straight and impatiently, limblessly straining to serve her coffee and tart. Then their meddling landlady, Mrs. Matheson, the time they came home from a department party to find her dog clawing the couch (she heard Mrs. Matheson's voice, from the kitchen? talking at Philip). And her sister's tantrum when she was six and Sarah sixteen, because Susan could not drive the gargoyle Philip had bought for the house before she showed him, rising up on its stone wings and crashing through the window into the sky above his parents' home, his brother Frank grabbing her on the laundry porch and her feeling offended yet excited, Frank's way of getting even because Philip was the beloved son. Frank the first, where you make your mistakes, like her own parents had done she told Philip arguing over his brother and the things they had in common, his father a wood craftsman like her Titi, though they never talked about these things at first — so caught up with each other, with the mass and touch of their bodies, as though newly discovered that sophomore year in college, the year she abandoned her art and the attention he gave her, almost filling that absence, still fresh all through graduate school, and in their Brussels apartment, on Lambermont overlooking the park somehow a thrill to be fucking in a foreign country.

While in other moments, she thinks: I will not be so badly remembered, or die like King Hamlet with my sins upon my head, they will remember kindly that Fourth of July picnic after my first year, the one I put on to return the rounds of invitations — every couple in the department, never suspecting I was being recruited to sides in old rivalries, I have always been a little naive about these things, not because I can't be suspicious Philip jokes I'm a cynic I always liked to say the things no one should dare with Susan's rages and my father's Lutheran guilts; and Mother's life a running denial of her mother's aching Catholicism yet so intent on confessions and penance writing five hundred times "I will not hit my little sister" and playing with her bracelets like a rosary after we'd been to the Met and I became so enamored of Ingres's *Le Bain turc* with the women draped upon each other; from a library book I sketched outlines on tracing paper, Titi said you must practice and be precise and shy from nothing but the way she found me my God, the poor woman, sprawled across my bed drawing nipples and vulvae and, yes, it felt good on the old Flintstones bedspread because it was naughty she thought I'd been spying on her how else could I know it was the Polaroids snuck in odd minutes from her night table never thinking my father had taken them and the shame she must have felt at his ogling flashbulbs damning her to hell she nearly choked not understanding how I felt about Titi's things Father leaving the paint and oils open like salt flats and finally wrapped in bloody butcher paper for the trash I just laughed, ashamed for her and scared as though we did not share the same body parts (orgasm a rumor started by bad girls to make you sin) and yet how strange just a week later when I started to bleed, my panties like the bloody paper with its swipes from the pork roast to celebrate Father's one drunken promotion to branch manager I screamed at her to show me they never explained in class and my father pounding the bathroom door with Susan toddling in the dry tub and she pulled the curtain, my poor mother, the poor thing, Titi needed a son and Grandmother honestly dreaded a daughter after her sister in Paris with her tough old lesbian lover overlooking Trocadero, Gran living like a widow long before he died coming from the shop only to eat and sleep, it seemed like the center of the world I felt that erotic relation with all the paraphernalia of art though God knows I was never highly sexed as they used to say, yet Rodin's *Age of Brass* or a Bernini just running my eyes over them . . . in some cold museum

Donatello's David comes to life — a recurrent dream in college — all dark burnished bronze and shining in his lovely girlish flowered hat like we used to get for Easter his body lithe and slender and so suggestively androgynous come from waging war at a garden party and we walk out of the museum along a streambank, the sunlight blazing from his surfaces the water and sky and trees and richly scented flowers — peonies and gardenia — reflect and flow across him like a passing mirror even when we lie down the images keep flowing he is a slender river of landscape and we kiss like children just the edges of lips yet all the heat in him, the fires to melt brass and copper enter into me and I am burning with sex and when we make love — I am a girl dressed in clean white butcher paper, breastless, he tears gently and neatly — and I am entered by the sky and white peonies and lazy, gentle stream that rolls across his body tenderly insisting between my tender lips and I wake in my cold room and warm blankets, alone in my young skin, then with Philip at my side and the sticky dampness and I cry.

Her eyes open. Her heart rises seeing Philip come into the room bearing the last of the lilacs from the yard, on the tray with mugs of tea and shortbread.

As he sets the tray on the floor and carefully shifts her legs so he can sit, she manages to reach over and turn the drip back down. Then his perfect concern makes her heart tighten and she clutches his arm. Seeing her eyes, he says, "Somebody been spiking your morphine?" but she will not be put off.

"You remember — when I showed you, the first time. I came in here."

"Yes."

But she is still drugged and cannot finish. He is accustomed to her lapses. He will not insist. He starts to hand her a mug. She wants to say, when she came to him, to let him feel, she had wanted to share it; she had known already for months but if she explains he will see why she'd delayed — to spare him, because he is not strong.

"Here. Drink."

"Please —"

"Here."

The morning she let him feel the spot inside her breast, she'd been standing in the kitchen for nearly an hour before he awoke. It had rained during the past week. Philip had talked about trimming the trees to bring more sun to the grass where it was drowning near the back of the house. That is what she so loves in him. He is a caretaker, a good-looking man, competent in the kitchen, meticulous with the laundry or reglazing a window. She wanted to show him the lump in order to say how she relied upon him, that whatever success she'd had in her career, she could not have done it without him. It was for him she'd come into the bedroom and dropped the shoulder of her gown. And when he touched her, carefully, she realized his sensual appeal: the depth of the attention he could give, a comprehensiveness, like the Donatello, as though his body made flesh of the surrender to vision, of the tender elegance of a landscape.

She remembers, when their eyes met that morning, as his hand cupped and pressed, exploring the shallow rise, the brown nipple's sudden stiffness, she remembers feeling both saddened and aroused; conscious of the pea-sized spot, internally turning away from the knowledge that this could be the last time his touch would speak both sex and concern, his worry filling the very air between them, the hands of the lover becoming those of the tender nurse. And she remembers how, even at that early moment, she'd felt her breasts wither. So she had insisted on making love, after they had talked, after he'd made the initial appointment. And in the following weeks, before the test and diagnosis, she would wake in the night and fuck him strenuously to steal away the lover she knew was becoming trapped inside his good heart.

She takes the mug but sets it on the night table. She pushes her sketchpad away and makes him lie beside her. He knows these moods, and because he believes they bespeak her fear of the end, he turns his face down as she holds him, stroking his back. She looks at the wall, where the sketch sheet was once taped. She decides she will find a moment to destroy that page, to spare him confusion and hurt when he must go through her things. And what will he do with them? Even he could not speak for the man he will be then. Through his shirt, she traces the riddled path of his spine. This sense of loss, that in dying she will take something of him too and he will become another man, stronger but harder, this fills her with a desire simply to continue to be here, for him to care for.

"You have to promise me something," she says into his hair. He nods. "You have to promise me . . ." but the morphine, or fatigue, her thought dissolves, into the empty longing to have the thought back. He does not ask again. He only turns his face to her and she kisses his brow, his nose, his mouth. Their tongues delicately touch and suddenly she feels his warmth as she does the sunlight flooding the room, igniting the scent of lilacs, making her skin and blood translucent to his concern, to the movement of his heart.

"I want you to . . ."

"Yes."

"I want . . ." to tell him it is here she feels triumph over the years of self-doubt; here is her masterwork; absorbing his mild gaze, her genius simple as sensing his hand carefully avoid the plastic tubing to her wrist and surround her weightless flesh — surrounding the silver pool of absence spreading from the center of her awareness — pulling the remains of her body close to his.

Mr. Sweetly Indecent

FROM PLOUGHSHARES

I MEET MY FATHER in a restaurant. He knows why I have asked to meet him, but he swaggers in anyway. It's a place near his office, and he hands out hellos all around as he makes his way over to my table. "My daughter," he explains to the men who have begun to grin, and he can't resist a wink just to keep them guessing. "Daddy," I say; his arms are around me. He squeezes a beat too long, and I'm afraid I might cry. He kisses me on both cheeks, my forehead and chin. "Saying my prayers," he has called these kisses ever since he used to tuck me into bed each night. They started as a joke on my mother, who is French and a practicing Catholic. Because my mother always kept her relationship with God to herself, the only prayer I knew is one my father taught me.

> Now I lay me down to sleep.
> I pray the Lord my soul to keep.
> If I should cry before I wake,
> I pray the Lord a cake to bake.

I only realized years later that he had changed the words of the real prayer so I wouldn't be scared by it.

My father orders a bottle of expensive red wine. He's had this wine here before. When it arrives, he insists that I taste it. He tells the waiter that I'm a connoisseur of wines. The truth is that I worked one summer as a hostess in a French restaurant, where I attended some wine-tasting classes. We learned that a wine must be tasted even if it's from a well-known vineyard and made in a good year because there could be some bad bottles. I could never tell the good wines from the bad ones, but I picked up some of the vocabulary.

I make a big fuss, sniffing the cork, sloshing the wine around in my mouth. "Fruity. Ripe," I say.

The waiter and my father smile at my approval. I smack my lips after the waiter leaves. "But no staying power. Immature, overall."

My father gets a sour look on his face. He's taken a big sip so that his cheeks are puffed out with the liquid. After he gulps it down, he says, "It's fine." And then he adds, "You know, it's all right for you to like it. It costs forty dollars."

"I'll drink it, but I don't really like it."

He looks ready to argue with me and then thinks better of it, glancing instead around the restaurant to see if anyone else he knows has come in.

We don't say anything for a bit. I'm hesitating. I sip the wine, survey the room myself. I've recently begun to realize that my father's life exists outside the one in which I have a place. Rather than viewing this outside life as an extension of the part that I know, I choose to see it instead as a distant land. Some of its inhabitants are here. Mostly men, they chuckle over martini glasses; one raises his eyebrow. They all look as if they have learned something that I have yet to discover.

Finally I put my glass down and smooth some wrinkles in the tablecloth. "Dad, what are we going to do?" I ask without looking up.

He takes my hand. "We don't need to do anything. We should just put it behind us. We can pretend that it didn't even happen, if that's what you want."

"That's what you want," I say. I'd caught him, after all, kissing a woman on the street outside his apartment.

As long as I can remember, my father has kept an apartment in this city where he works and I now live. In his profession, he needs to stay in touch, he has always said. That has meant spending every Monday night in the city having dinner with his associates. Occasionally it had occurred to me that his apartment might be used for reasons other than a place to sleep after late business dinners. Then one night, while I still lived at home, my mother confided that a friend of my father's contributed $100 a month toward the rent to use it once in a while. I remember that my mother and I were eating cheese fondue for dinner. On those nights my father was away, my mother made special meals that he didn't like. She ripped off a piece of French bread from the loaf we were sharing and dipped it in the gooey mixture. "This friend brings his mistress there," she explained. "I hate that your father must be the one to supply him with a place to carry out his affair." I didn't say anything, my suspicion relieved by this sudden confidence. My mother tilted back her head and dropped the coated bread into her open mouth. When she finished chewing, she closed the subject. "His wife should know what her husband is up to. I'm going to tell her one day."

When I was walking down my father's street early last Tuesday morning, it didn't even occur to me that my father would be at his apartment. I was on my way to the subway after leaving the apartment of a man with whom I had just spent the night. This man is a friend of a man at work with whom I have also spent the night. The man at work, call him Jack, is my friend now — he said that working together made things too complicated — and we sometimes go out for a drink at the end of the day. We bumped into his friend at the bar near our office. The friend asked me to dinner and then asked me to come up to his apartment for a drink and then asked if he could make love to me. After each question, I paused before answering, suspicious because of the directness of his invitations, and then when he would look away as if it didn't really matter, I would realize that in fact I had been waiting for these questions all night, and I would say yes.

When we walked into this man's living room, he flicked a row of switches at the entrance, turning on all the lights. He brought me a glass of wine and then excused himself to use the bathroom. I strolled over to the large picture window to admire the view. Looking out from the bright room, it was hard to make out anything on the street. The only movement was darting points of light. "It's like another world up here," I murmured under my breath. I heard the toilet flush and waited at the window. I was thinking how he could walk up behind me and drape his arm over my shoulder and say something about what he has seen out this window, and then he could take my chin and turn it toward him and we could kiss. When I didn't hear any movement behind me, I turned around. He was standing at the entrance of the room. "I'd like to make love to you," he said. "Would that be all right?" There was no music or TV, and it was so silent that I was afraid to speak. I smiled, took a sip of wine. He shifted his gaze from my face to the window behind me. I glanced out the window too, then put my glass down on the sill and nodded yes. "Why don't you take off your coat," he said. I slipped my trenchcoat off my shoulders and held it in front of me. He pointed to a chair in front of the window, and I draped the coat over its back. Then he asked me to take off the rest of my clothes.

Once I was naked, he just stood there staring at me. I wondered if he could see from where he was standing that I needed a bikini wax. I wanted to kiss him, we hadn't even kissed yet, and I took a small step forward and then stopped, one foot slightly in front of the other, unsteady, uncertain what to do next. "Beautiful," he finally whispered. And then he kept whispering beautiful, beautiful, beautiful . . .

I had just reached my father's block, though lost in my thoughts I didn't realize it, when from across the street I heard a woman's voice. "Zachary!" the voice called out, the stress on the last syllable, the word rising in mock annoyance, the way my mother said my father's name when he teased her. All other times, she called him, as everyone else did, just Zach. I looked up, and there was my father pushing a woman up against the side of a building. His building, I realized.

My father's face was buried in her neck, and she was laughing. I recognized from her reaction that he was giving her the ticklish kind of blowing kisses that I hated. I had stopped walking and was staring at them. I caught the woman's eye briefly, and then she looked away and whispered something in my father's ear. His head jerked up and whipped around. I looked down quickly and started walking away, as if I had been caught doing something wrong. If my father had run after me and asked what I was doing in this neighborhood so early in the morning, I wouldn't have known what to tell him. I glanced back, and the woman was walking down the street the other way, and my father was standing at the entrance of his building. He was watching the woman. She was rather dressed up for so early in the morning, wearing a short black skirt, stockings, and high heels. She pulled her long blond hair out from the collar of her jacket and shook it down her back. Her gait looked slightly self-conscious, the way a woman's does when she knows she is being watched. Before I looked away, my father glanced in my

direction. I avoided meeting his eyes and shook my head, a gesture
I hoped he could appreciate from his distance. As I hurried to the
subway, the only thought I had was fleeting: my man had not gotten
up from bed to walk me out the door.

For the next few days I waited for the phone to ring. Neither man
called. I asked Jack, the man at work, if he had heard from his
friend. "Sorry, not a peep," he said. He patted me on the knee and
said that he was sure his friend enjoyed the time we spent together
and that I would probably hear from him soon.

It was unusually warm that day, and I walked home rather than
taking the subway. All the way home, I kept picturing myself back in
the man's apartment. I saw us as someone would have if they had
been floating nine stories high above the busy avenue that night
and had picked out the man's lighted window to peer into: a young
woman, naked, moving slowly across a room to kiss the mouth of
her clothed lover. It seemed that the moment was still continuing,
encapsulated eternally in that bright box of space.

When I walked in the door that afternoon, my phone was ringing. I rushed to answer it before the machine picked it up. It was my
mother. She had already left a message on my machine earlier in
the week to call her about making plans to go home the following
weekend. Whether I should tell her about my father was a question that had been gathering momentum behind me all week. My
mother is a passionate, serious woman. My father met her when she
was performing modern dance in a club in West Berlin. The act
before her was two girls singing popular American show tunes, and
after her, for the finale, there was a topless dancer. She didn't last
there for very long. My father liked to describe how the audience of
German men would look up at her with bemused faces. Her seri-
ousness didn't translate, he would say, and the Germans would be
left wondering if her modern dancing was another French joke that
they didn't get. After the shows, all the women who worked there
had to *faire la salle,* which meant dancing with the male customers.
At this point in the story I would ask questions, hoping that a bit of
scandal in my mother's past would be revealed, or at least to find
out that she had had to resist some indecent propositions at one
time. But my mother always jumped in to say that she had learned
that if you don't invite that kind of behavior, then you won't receive
it. Such things never happen by accident. My father married my

mother, he would explain, because she was one of the last women left who could really believe in marriage. He said she had enough belief for the both of them. I hadn't called my mother back.

"Oh, sweetie, I'm glad I caught you," she said. "You're still going to take the 9:05 train Saturday morning, right?"

"Uh-huh."

"Okay, Daddy will have to pick you up after he drops me off at the hairdresser's. I'm trying to schedule an appointment to get a perm."

"Ahh."

"I feel like it's been forever since I've seen you. Daddy and I were just saying last night how we still can't get used to you not being around all the time."

I tried to picture myself back in my parents' house. I couldn't place myself there again. I couldn't remember where in the house we spent our time, where we talked to each other: around the dining room table, on the couch in the den, in the hallways; I couldn't remember what we talked about.

"Is everything okay, honey? You sound tired."

"Hmmm."

"All right. I can take a hint. I'll let you go."

After we hung up, I said to my empty apartment, "I caught Daddy with another woman." Once these words were out of my mouth, I couldn't get away from them. I went out for a drink.

When I woke up the next morning, I decided to cut off all of my hair. I have brown curly hair like my father's. It's quite long, and when I stood in that man's living room, I pulled it in front of my shoulders so that it covered my breasts. The man liked that, he told me afterward as he held me in his bed. He said that I had looked sweetly indecent. I lost my nerve in the hairdresser's chair and walked out with bangs instead. In the afternoon, I went to a psychic fair with a friend, and a fortuneteller told me that she saw a man betraying me. "Tell me something I don't know," I said, but that would have cost another ten dollars.

I called my father Sunday morning at home. I knew when he answered the phone that he had gotten up from the breakfast table, leaving behind a stack of Sunday papers and my mother sipping coffee.

"We have to talk before I come home next weekend."

"Okay. Where would you like to meet?" He didn't say my name, and his voice was all business.

"Let's have dinner somewhere." He suggested a restaurant, and we agreed to meet the next evening after work.

"Tomorrow, then." I put a hint of warning in my voice.

"Yes. All right," he said, and hung up. I wondered if my mother asked him who had called, and if she did, what he told her.

Next I called up the man in whose living room I had stood naked. The phone rang many times. I was about to hang up, disappointed that there was not even a machine so I could hear his voice again, when a sleepy voice answered. I was caught by surprise and forgot my rehearsed line about meeting at a bakery I knew near his apartment for some sweetly indecent pastries. I hung up without saying anything.

The waiter takes our empty plates away. My father refills my glass. I have drunk two glasses of wine already and am starting to feel sleepy and complaisant. My father has already told me that he is not planning on seeing the woman again, and I am beginning to wonder what it is that I actually want my father to say.

He drums his fingers on the edge of the table. I can see that he is growing tired of being solicitous. He sought my opinion on the wine, he noticed that I had my bangs cut, he remembered the name of my friend at work whom I was dating the last time we got together.

"I'm not with him anymore," I explain. "We thought it was a bad idea to date since we work together." I consider telling my father about the other man, to let him know that I understand more about this world of affairs than he thinks. He would be shocked, outraged. Or would he? I'm not sure of anything anymore.

I let myself float outside the man's window again, move closer to peer inside. But this time I can't quite picture his face. What color are his eyes? They're green, I decide. But then I wonder if I am confusing them with my father's eyes.

"Someday, honey, you'll meet a guy who'll realize what a treasure you are." My father pats my knee.

"Just because he thinks I'm a treasure doesn't mean that he won't take me for granted." I take another sip of wine and watch over the rim of my glass for my father's response. I remember watching him at another table, our dining room table, where he sat across from my mother. She had just made some remark that I couldn't hear from where I perched on our front stairs, spying, as they had a romantic dinner alone with candles and wine. Earlier my father had set up the television and VCR in my room and sent me upstairs to watch a movie. My father put down his glass and got up out of his chair. He knelt at my mother's feet, and though I couldn't hear his words either, I was sure that he was asking her to marry him again.

"Honey. Listen. It was nothing with that woman. It doesn't change the way I feel about your mother. I love your mother very much."

"But it makes everything such a lie," I say, my voice now catching with held-back tears. "What about our family, all the dinners, Sunday mornings around the breakfast table, the walks we love to take . . ." I falter and hold my hands out wide to him.

My father catches them and folds them closed in his own. "No. No. All of that is true. This doesn't change any of that." He is squeezing my hands hard. For the first time during this meal, I can see that I have upset him.

"But it didn't mean what I thought, did it?"

Right then the waiter appears with our check. My father lets go of my hands and reaches for his wallet. Neither of us says anything while we wait for the waiter to return with the credit card slip. I don't repeat my question, because I am afraid that my father will say I'm right.

The next day at work, I ask my friend again about Mr. Sweetly Indecent.

"If you want to talk to him, call him up."

"Do you think I should?"

"It can't hurt."

"If we didn't work together, do you think things could have turned out differently with us?" We are in the photocopying room where, in the midst of our affair, my friend had once lifted my skirt and slid his fingers inside the elastic waist of my pantyhose.

"Oh, hell. You'll meet someone who'll appreciate you. You deserve that. You really do."

I call the man up that night. He doesn't say anything for a moment when I tell him my name. I imagine him reviewing a long line of naked women standing in his living room. "That one," he finally picks me out of the crowd. Or maybe it's just that he's surprised to hear from me.

"I had a really nice time that night," I say. "I thought maybe we could get together again sometime."

"Well, I had a good time too," he says, sounding sincere, "but I think that we should just leave it at that."

"I'm not saying that I want to start dating. I just thought that we could do something again."

"It was the kind of night that's better not repeated. I know. I've tried it before. The second time is always a disappointment."

"But I thought we got along so well." We had talked over dinner about our families; he told me how he was always trying to live up to the kind of man he thought his father wanted him to be. He had talked in faltering sentences, as though this were something that he was saying for the first time.

"We did get along," he says. "God! And you were so beautiful." He pauses, and I know he's remembering that I really was beautiful. "I just want to preserve that memory of you standing in my living room, alone, without any other images cluttering it."

Yes, I want to tell him, I have preserved that image too, but memories need refueling. I need to see you again to make sure that what I remembered is actually true. "Is this because I slept with you on the first night?"

"No. No. Nothing like that. Listen, it was a perfect night. Let's just both remember it that way."

As the train pulls into the station, I spot my father waiting on the platform. I take my time gathering my things so I'm one of the last to exit. He hugs me without hesitation, as though our dinner had never happened. As we separate he tries to take my suitcase from me. It's just a small weekend bag, and I resist, holding on to the shoulder strap. We have a tug of war.

"You're being ridiculous," my father says and yanks the strap from my grip. I trail behind him to the car and look out the window the whole way home.

That afternoon I sit at the kitchen table and watch my mother and father prune the rosebushes dotting the fence that separates our yard from the street. My mother selects a branch and shows my father where to cut. They work down the row quickly, efficient with their confidence in the new growth these efforts will bring. Behind them trails a wake of bald, stunted bushes and their snipped limbs lying crisscross on the ground beneath.

After they have finished cleaning up the debris, my father brings the lawn chairs out of the garage — he brings one for me too, but I have retreated upstairs to my bedroom by this time and watch them from that window — and my mother appears with a pitcher of lemonade and glasses. My mother reclines in her chair, with my father at her side, and admires their handiwork. Her confidence that the world will obey her expectations makes her seem so foolish to me, or perhaps it is because every time I look at her, I think of how she is being fooled.

On Sunday morning my mother heads off to mass, and I am left alone in the house with my father. He sits with me at the kitchen table for a while, both of us flipping through the Sunday papers. I keep turning the pages, unable to find anything that can hold my attention. He's not really reading either. He is too busy waiting on me. He hands me the magazine and style sections without my even asking. He refills my coffee. When Georgie, our Labrador retriever, scratches at the door, he jumps up to let her out. When he sits back down, he gathers all the sections of the paper together, including the parts that I am looking at, and stacks them on one corner of the table. I look at him, breathe out a short note of exasperation.

"Are you ever going to forgive me?" he asks.

"Why aren't you going to see that woman again? Just because I caught you?"

He looks startled and answers slowly, as if he is just testing out this answer. "She didn't mean anything to me. It was like playing a game. It was fun, but now it's over."

"Do you think that she expected to see you again?"

"No. She knew what kind of a thing it was. And I'm sure that she prefers it this way too. She has her own commitments to deal with."

"Maybe she does want to see you again. Maybe she felt like you had something really special together. Maybe she's hoping that you would leave Mom for her."

"Honey, when you get older, you'll understand that there are a lot of different things that you can feel for another person and how it's important not to confuse them. I love your mother, and I'm very devoted to her. Nothing is going to change that."

My father sits with me a few minutes more, and when there doesn't seem to be anything else to say, he stands up and wanders off. I realize that if I had told my father about the man during our dinner, he would have understood what kind of a thing that was before I even did.

When my mother gets back, she joins me at the kitchen table.

"Do you want to talk about something, honey? You seem so sad." I look at my mother, and the tears that have been welling in my eyes all weekend threaten to spill over.

"Daddy says you're having boy trouble."

I shake my head no, unable to speak.

My mother suggests that we take the dog out for a walk, just the two of us, so we can catch up. She gathers our coats, calls Georgie, and we head out the door. "I don't even know what's going on in your life since you've moved out. It's strange," she says. "I used to know what you did every evening, who you were going out with, what clothes you chose to wear each day. Now I have no idea how you spend your time. It was different when you were at college. I could imagine you in class, or at the library, or sitting around your dorm room with your roommate. Sometimes I used to stop whatever I was doing and think about you. She's probably just heading off to the cafeteria for breakfast right now, I would tell myself."

We are walking down our street toward the harbor.

"But you know that I go to work every day. You know what my apartment looks like. It's the same now."

"No, it's not," she says. "It's really all your own life. You support yourself, buy all your own clothes, decide if and when to have breakfast. And somehow I don't feel right imagining what your day is like. It's not really my business anymore."

"I don't mind, Mom, if you want to know what I'm doing." We have reached the harbor, and my mother is bending over the dog to let her off the lead so I'm not sure if she hears me. She pulls a tennis ball out of her pocket, and Georgie begins to dance backward. My mother starts walking to the water. I stay where I am and look off across the harbor. On the opposite shore, some boats have been pulled up onto the beach just above the high-tide mark for the winter. They rest on the side of their hulls and look as if they've been forgotten, as if they will never be put back in the water again.

My mother turns back toward me, holding the tennis ball up

high over her head. Georgie is prancing and barking in front of her. "You know what I love about dogs? It's so easy to make them happy. You just pet them or give them a biscuit or show them a ball, and they always wag their tails." She throws the ball into the water, and Georgie goes racing after it.

My mother's eagerness to oblige surprises me. I think of her dancing with men in that club in West Berlin. I had always imagined her as acting very primly, holding the men away from her with stiff, straight arms. Perhaps she wasn't that way at all. Maybe she leaned into these men, only drawing back to toss her head in laughter at the jokes they whispered in her ear.

"Mom, what made you go out with Dad when you worked in that club? You didn't go out with many of the men that you met there, did you?"

"Your father was the only one I accepted, though I certainly had many offers."

"Did he seem more respectable?"

"Oh, he came on like a playboy as much as the next one."

"Then why did you say yes?"

"Well, somehow he seemed like he didn't quite believe his whole act. Though he wouldn't say that if you asked him. I guess I felt I understood something about him that he didn't even know about himself. So he went about seducing me, all the while feeling like he had the upper hand, and I would go along, knowing that I had a trick up my sleeve too."

She isn't looking at me as she says this. She is turned toward the water, though I know that she is not looking at that either. She is watching herself as a young woman twirling around a room with my young father. They dance together well; I have seen them dance before, and this memory brings such a pleased private smile to her lips that I don't say anything that would contradict her.

I am quiet during dinner. My parents treat me like I am sick or have just suffered some great loss. My mother won't let me help her serve the food. My father pushes seconds on me, saying that I look too skinny. "Maybe I should take you out to dinner more often," he says.

I look up from my heaping plate of food, half expecting him to wink at me.

"That's right. You two met for dinner this week. See, honey, that's just the kind of thing I was talking about. It's nice that you and your father can meet and have dinner together. Like two friends."

My parents tell stories back and forth about me when I was young; many stories I have heard before. Usually I enjoy these conversations. I would listen to them describe this precocious girl and the things she had done that I couldn't even remember, only interrupting to ask in an incredulous and proud tone, "I really did that?" I was always willing to believe anything my parents told me, so curious was I to understand the continuum of how I came to be the woman I was. Tonight, while these memories seem to console my parents, I can only hear them as nostalgic, and they remind me of everything that has been recently forsaken.

After dinner I insist on doing the dishes. I splash around in the kitchen sink, clattering the plates dangerously in their porcelain bed. I pick up a serving platter, one from my mother's set of good china inherited from my grandmother, and consider dropping it to the floor. I have trouble picturing myself actually doing this. I can only imagine it as far as my fingers loosening from the edges of the platter and it sliding down their length, but then in my mind's eye, instead of the platter falling swiftly, it floats and hovers the way a feather would from one of the peacocks pictured on the china's face. I have no trouble picturing the aftermath once it lands: my mother rushing in at the noise with my father a few steps behind, not sure if he must concern himself, and she angry at my carelessness. I imagine yelling back at her. I would tell her that it's no use. Old china, manicured lawns, a happy dog: these things don't offer any guarantee.

I stand there holding the platter high above the kitchen floor, imagining the consequences with trepidation and relief, as if this is what the weekend had been leading up to and with one brief burst of courage I could put it behind me. I stand considering and strain to hear my parents' voices in the dining room, thinking their conversation might offer me some direction. I put the platter down and peek around the open kitchen door. A pantry separates me from the dining room. I can see them: they are talking, but I can't make out their words.

They are both leaning forward. My mother cradles her chin in the palm of her hand. Abruptly she lifts her head, sits up tall, and points at my father. His arms are folded in front of him, and he looks down and shakes his head. I am reminded again of that dinner of my parents that I spied on years ago, but this time what I remember is the righteousness of my mother's posture as she sat across from my father and tossed off remarks, and the guilty urgency of my father's movements as he sank to his knees at her feet, and how there was something slightly orchestrated about their behavior, as though their exchange had a long history to it. And the next thing I remember makes me tiptoe away, as I did when I was a child, aware that I had witnessed a private moment between my parents not meant for my eyes. What I remember now is how many years ago my mother had reached down her hand and pulled my father up and kept pulling him in toward herself so that she could hold him close.

JOHN UPDIKE

My Father on the Verge of Disgrace

FROM THE NEW YORKER

IT FILTERED even into my childhood dreams, the fear. The fear that he would somehow fall from his precarious ledge of respectability, a ledge where we all stood with him. "We all": his dependents — my mother, her parents, myself. The house we lived in was too big for us: my grandfather had bought it in 1922, when he felt prosperous enough to retire. Within the decade, the stock market crash took all his savings. He sat in one corner of the big house, the little "sunroom" that looked toward the front yard, the hedge, and the street with its murmuring traffic. My grandmother, bent over and crippled by arthritis, hobbled about in the kitchen and out into the back yard, where she grew peas and kept chickens. My mother had her nook upstairs, at a little desk with wicker sides, where she did not like to be interrupted, and my father was generally out somewhere in the town. He was a tall, long-legged man who needed to keep moving. The year I was born, he had lost his job, as salesman in the mid-Atlantic territory for a line of quality English china. Only after three years — anxious years for him, but for me just a few smells and radiant visions retained by my infant memory — did he succeed in getting another job, as a high school teacher. It was as a schoolteacher that I always knew him. Wearing a suit, his shirt pocket holding a pack of cigarettes and a mechanical pencil and a fountain pen, he loomed to me as a person of eminence in the town; it was this sense of his height that led, perhaps, to my fear that he would somehow topple.

One of my dreams, borrowing some Depression imagery from the cartoons in the newspaper, had him clad in a barrel and, gray-

faced, being harried down the town hall steps by the barking appa-
ritions of local officialdom. The crowd began to throw things, and
my attempt at explaining, at pleading for him, got caught up in my
throat. In this present day of strip malls and towns that are mere
boundaries on a developer's map, it is hard to imagine the core of
authority that existed then in small towns, at least in the view of a
child — the power of righteousness and enforcement that radiated
from the humorless miens of the central men. They were not necessarily officials — the town was too small to have many of those. And
the police chief was a perky, comically small man who inspired fear
not even in first-graders, as he halted traffic to let them cross the
street to the elementary school. But certain local merchants, a
clergyman or two, the undertaker whose green-awninged mansion
dominated the main intersection, across from a tavern and a drug-
store, not to mention the druggist and the supervising principal of
the school where my father taught, projected an aura of potential
condemnation and banishment.

To have this power, you had to have been born in the town, or at
least in the locality, and my father had not been. His accent, his
stride, were slightly different. This was Pennsylvania, and he was
from New Jersey. My mother came from the area, and she may have
married my father in hopes of escaping it. But the land of six
decades ago was less permeable than it is now; it exerted a grip.
Fate, or defeat, returned my parents to my grandfather's big house,
a house where only I, growing up day by day, felt perfectly at home.

I was proud of my schoolteacher father. If his suit was out of
press and his necktie knotted awry, I was too new to the world to
notice. He combed his hair back and, in the style of his generation,
parted it near the middle. In our kitchen, he would bolt his orange
juice (squeezed on one of those ribbed glass sombreros and then
poured off through a strainer) and his toast (the toaster a simple
tin box, a kind of little hut with slit and slanted sides, that rested
over a gas burner and browned one side of the bread, in stripes, at
a time), and then he would stride, so hurriedly that his necktie flew
back over his shoulder, down through our yard, past the grape-
vines hung with buzzing Japanese beetle traps, to the yellow brick
building, with its tall smokestack and wide playing fields, where
he taught. Though the town had some hosiery and hat factories
tucked around in its blocks of row houses, the high school was the

most impressive building on my horizon. To me, it was the center of
the universe. I enjoyed the gleams of recognition that fell to me
from my father's high visibility. His teaching colleagues greeted me
on the street with a smile; other adults seemed to know me and
included me in a sort of ironical forbearance. He was not a drinker
— his anxious stomach was too tender for that — but he had the
waywardly sociable habits of a drinker. He needed people, believed
in their wisdom and largesse, as none of the rest of us who lived in
the house did: four recluses and an extrovert. Imitating my mother,
I early developed a capacity to entertain myself, with paper and the
images it bore. When school — the elementary school, at the other
end of town, along the main street — took me into its classes, I felt,
in relation to my classmates, slightly timid.

He called me "young America," as if I were more bumptious than
I was. He pushed me about the town with a long stick he had made,
whose fork gripped the back of my red wagon, so that all I had to do
was sit in it and steer. No more births followed mine. My bedroom
was a narrow back room, with a bookshelf and some framed illustrations, by Vernon Grant, of nursery rhymes; it overlooked the back
yard and adjoined my parents' bedroom. I could hear them talk at
night; even when the words were indistinct, the hiss of unhappiness, of obscure hot pressures, came through the walls. "*That son of
a bitch,*" my father would say, of some man whose name I had
missed. "*Out to get me,*" I would hear. Who could this enemy be, I
would wonder, while my mother's higher, more rhythmic voice
would try to seal over the wound, whatever it was, and I would be
lulled into sleep, surrounded by my toys, my Big Little Books, my
stacked drawings crayoned on the rough dun-colored paper supplied at school, the Vernon Grant figures presiding above the bookshelf — a band of cheerful, long-nosed angels who lived in shoes
and tumbled downhill. Paper, I felt, would protect me. Sometimes
in my parents' room there were quarrels, stifled sobs from my
melodious mother and percussive rumbling from my father; these
troubles were like a thunderstorm that whipped and thumped the
house for half an hour and then rolled off into the sky to the east.

One center of trouble, I remember, was a man called Otto
Werner, which Otto pronounced as if the *W* were a *V*. Among the
Pennsylvania Germans, he was exceptionally German, with a tooth-
brush mustache, a malicious twinkle in his eye, and an erect, jerky

way of carrying himself. He too was a schoolteacher, but not in our town's system. He and my father, on weekends and in the summer, traveled to Philadelphia, an hour and a half away, to accumulate credits toward a master's degree. Having a master's would improve my father's salary by a few sorely needed dollars.

The first scandal that attached itself to Otto concerned his standing on the steps of some building at the University of Pennsylvania and shouting, "*Heil, Hitler!*" The United States was not yet in the war, and a pro-German Bund openly met in our local city of Brewer, but still it was an eccentric and dangerous thing to do. Otto was, my father admitted, "a free spirit." But he owned a car, and we did not. We once did — a green Model A that figures in my earliest memories — but somewhere in the thirties it disappeared. In a town so compact one could walk anywhere within twenty minutes, and in a region webbed with trolley tracks and train tracks, the deprivation did not seem radical. Once the war came, even those who owned cars couldn't drive them.

A worse scandal than "*Heil, Hitler!*" had to do with a girl at the high school. My father carried a few notes from Otto to her, and it turned out they were love notes, and he was aiding and abetting the corruption of a minor. The girl's parents got involved, and members of the school board were informed. Not only could my father get fired, I understood; he could go to jail for his part in this scandal. As I lay in my bed at night I could hear my parents talking in a ragged, popping murmur like the noise of something frying; I could feel the heat, and my father twisting in his agony, and the other adults in the house holding their breath. Had there been trysts, and had my father carried the notes that arranged them? It was like him; he was always doing people unnecessary favors. Once he walked out into a snowstorm to go and apologize to a boy in one of his classes with whom he had been impatient, or sarcastic. "I hate sarcasm," he said. "Everybody in this part of the world uses it, but it hurts like hell to be on the receiving end. Poor kid, I thought he stunk the place up to get my goat, but upon sober reflection I believe it was just one more case of honest stupidity." His subject was chemistry, with its many opportunities for spillage, breakage, smells, and small explosions.

The scandal with the girl somehow died away. Perhaps the notes he carried were innocent. Perhaps he persuaded the principal and the school board that he, at least, was innocent. There had been a romance, because within a year or two the girl, graduated now, married Otto. The couple moved to the Southwest but occasionally would visit my parents. When my mother became a widow, living alone in a farmhouse ten miles from the town, the couple would visit her as part of their annual eastern pilgrimage. Though twenty years younger, Mrs. Werner went plump early, and her hair turned white, so the age difference became less and less noticeable. They had bought a Winnebago and would pull up alongside the barn and Otto would limp across the yard to greet my mother merrily, that twinkle still in his eye. My mother would be merry in turn, having forgotten, it seemed, all the woe he once brought us. In trying to recall the heat in the old house, the terror he had caused, I have forgotten the most interesting thing about him: he had only one leg. The other was a beige prosthesis that gave him his jerky walk, a sharp hitch as if he were tossing something with his right hip. Remembering this makes him seem less dangerous: how could the world ever punish a one-legged man for shouting "*Heil, Hitler!*" or for falling in love with a teenager from another school system?

The country ran on dimes and quarters. A hamburger cost ten cents, and I paid ten cents to get into the moviehouse, until a war tax made it eleven. The last year of the war, a month before V-E Day and Hitler's vanishing — *poof!* — from his underground bunker, I turned thirteen, and old Mrs. Naftzinger in the little glass booth somehow knew it. An adult ticket cost twenty-seven cents, and that was too much for me to go twice a week. The economics of my grandfather's house seemed simple: my father brought home his pay every other week in a brown envelope, and the money was dumped in a little red-and-white recipe box that sat on top of the icebox. Anybody who needed money fished it out of the box; each lunchtime I was allowed six cents, a nickel and a penny, to buy a Tastykake on the way back to elementary school. My grandfather did the packaged-food shopping at Tyse Segner's store, a few houses away. Tyse, who lived in the back rooms and upstairs with his wife, was a man of my grandfather's generation — a rather ill-tempered one, I thought, considering all the candy he had behind his counter and could eat for free whenever he wanted. My mother usually bought fresh meat and vegetables at Bud Hoffert's Acme, two blocks away, past the ice plant, up on Second Street. Bud wore rimless glasses and a bloody apron. My grandmother did the cooking but never shopped; nor did my father — he just brought home, as he said, "the bacon." The little tin recipe box never became quite empty; I never had to do without a noontime Tastykake. I moved a kitchen chair next to the icebox to stand on while I fished the nickel and the penny from the box, beneath a clutter of folded dollars and scattered quarters. When the tin bottom began to show, more coins and bills somehow appeared, to tide us over, and these, it slowly dawned on me, were borrowed from the high school sports receipts.

My father had charge of them, as an extracurricular duty: at football games he would sit at a gap in the ropes, selling tickets and making change from a flat green box whose little compartments were curved to let your fingers scoop up the coins. At basketball games he would sit with the box at a little table just inside the school's mighty front portals, across from the glass case of silver trophies and around the corner from the supervising principal's office. The green box would come home with him, many nights, for safekeeping. The tickets fascinated me — the great wheels of them, as wide as dinner plates but thicker. They came in two distinct colors, blue for adults and orange for students, and each ticket was numbered. It was another kind of money. Each rectangle of the thin, tightly coiled cardboard possessed, at the right time, a real value, brought into play by a sports event; money and time and cardboard and people's desire to *see* were magically interwoven. My father was magical, converting into dollars and quarters and dimes the Tuesday and Friday night basketball crowds and the outdoor crowd that straggled out of the town's streets onto the football field on Saturday afternoons. (It was easy to sneak under the ropes, but many grownups didn't bother, and solemnly paid.) The tickets, numbered into the hundreds, were worth nothing until my father presided at his little table. He always made the balance right when he got his paycheck, or so he assured my mother. She had begun to get alarmed, and her alarm spread to me.

My memories of their conversations, the *pressure* of them, have me leaning my face against the grain of the wooden icebox, a zinc-lined cabinet whose dignity dominated our kitchen as it majestically digested, day after day, a succession of heavy ice blocks fetched in a straw-lined truck and carried with tongs into the house by a cheerful man with a leathern apron down his back, to ward off the wet and the chill. I could feel the coldness on my cheek through the zinc and wood as my parents' faces revolved above me and their voices clung to my ears.

"Embezzlement," my mother said, a word I knew only from the radio. "What good will you be to any of us in jail?"

"I make it square, right to the penny. Square on the button, every other week, when I get my envelope."

"Suppose Danny Haas some week decides to deposit the receipts on a Friday instead of a Monday? He'd ask, and you'd be short."

Danny Haas, I knew, taught senior-high math and headed up the school athletics program; a short man who smoked cigars and wore suits with broad stripes, he nevertheless was one of the righteous at the town's core. My tall father and he sometimes clowned together, because of their height discrepancy, but it was clear to me who had the leverage, the connections, the power to bring down.

"He won't, Lucy," my father was saying. Whenever he used my mother's name, it was a sign that he wanted to end the conversation. "Danny's like all these Dutchmen, a slave to habit. Anyway, we're not talking Carnegie-Mellon bucks here, we're talking relative peanuts." How much, indeed? A ten-dollar bill, in those days, looked like a fortune to me; I never saw a twenty, not even when the recipe box was fullest.

"Nobody will think it's peanuts if it's missing."

My father became angry, as much as he ever did. "What can I do, Lucy? We live poor as dump dogs anyway." The phrase "dump dogs" had to be one he had brought from his other life, when he lived in another state and was a boy like me. He went on, venting grievances seldom expressed in my hearing. "We've got a big place here to heat. We can't all go naked. The kid keeps growing. My brown suit is wearing out. Mom does what she can in her garden, but I've got five mouths to feed." He called my grandmother Mom and exempted her, I felt, from the status of pure burden. My mother's work at her wicker desk produced no money, my grandfather in his pride had bought too big a house, and I — I didn't even go out and shovel snow for neighbors in a storm, because I was so susceptible to colds. My father was warming to his subject. "Count 'em — five! *Nihil ex nihilo*, Dad used to say." Dad was his own father, dead before

I was born. "You don't get something for nothing," he translated. "There are no free rides in this life."

My mother feebly used the word *economize,* another radio word, but even I could feel it was hopeless; how could I go without my Tastykake, when nobody else in my class was that poor? My father had to go on stealing from the school, and would someday be chased in his barrel down the town hall steps.

During the war things eased a bit. Men were scarce, and he got summer jobs that did not aggravate his hernia; he was made a timekeeper for a railroad work crew. The tracks were humming and needed to be kept up. In the history books our time in the war looks short: less than four years from Pearl Harbor to V-J Day. Yet it seemed to go on forever, while I inched up through the grades of elementary school. It became impossible to imagine a world without the war, without the big headlines and the ration tokens and coupons and the tin-can drives and Bing Crosby and Dorothy Lamour selling War Bonds at rallies. I reached seventh grade, a junior-high grade, housed in the grand yellow brick building where my father taught.

I was too young for chemistry, but there was no missing his high head and long stride in the halls. Sharing the waxed, locker-lined halls with him all day, being on his work premises, as it were, did not eradicate my anxiety that he would be brought low. The perils surrounding him became realer to me. We students filled the halls with a ruthless, trampling sound. My father was a notoriously poor disciplinarian; he was not German enough, and took too little pleasure in silence and order. Entire classes, rumor reached me from the upper grades, were wasted in monologues in which he tried to impart the lessons that life had taught him — you don't get something for nothing, there are no free rides. These truths were well illustrated in the workings of chemistry, so perhaps he wasn't as far off the point as the students thought. They played a game of getting him going and thus sparing themselves classwork for the day. He would suddenly throw a blackboard eraser up toward the ceiling and with a boyish deftness catch it, saying, "What goes up must come down." He told the momentarily silenced students, "You're on top of Fools' Hill now, but you'll come down the other side." He did not conceal from them his interest in the fruitful possibilities of disorder; so many great chemical discoveries, after all, were accidents. He loved chemistry. "Water is the universal solvent," I often heard him pronounce, as if it were a truly consoling formula, like "This too will pass away." Who is to say his message did not come through all the classroom confusion — the notes being passed, the muttered asides of the class clown, the physical tussles at the rear of the room?

He was the faculty clown, to my discomfort. His remarks in assembly always got the students laughing, and in the spring, in the annual faculty assembly program, he participated in a, to me, horrifying performance of the Pyramus and Thisby episode of *A Midsummer Night's Dream*. Gotten up as a gawky, dirndl-clad, lipsticked Thisby, in a reddish blond wig with pigtails, my father climbed a little stepladder to reach the chink in the wall. The Wall was played by the thickset football coach, Tank Geiger, wearing a football helmet and a sheet painted to resemble masonry.

I had noticed in the privacy of our home how my father's legs, especially where his stockings rubbed, were virtually hairless compared with those of other men. Now the sight of his hairless legs, bare for all to see, as he mounted the ladder — the students around me howling at every mincing step he took upward — made me think his moment to topple had come. Mr. Geiger held up at arm's height a circle-forming thumb and forefinger to represent the chink in the wall; on the opposite side of the wall, little Mr. Haas climbed his ladder a step higher than my father, to put his face on the same level. "O, kiss me," he recited, "through the hole of this vile wall." Mr. Geiger mugged in mock affront, and the auditorium rocked. My father, in his high Thisby voice, answered, "I kiss the wall's hole, not your lips at all," and his and Mr. Haas's faces slowly met through the third teacher's fingers. The screams of disbelieving hilarity around me made my ears burn. This had to be ruinous, I thought. This was worse than any of my dreams.

But the next day my father loped through the halls with his head high, his hair parted in the middle as usual, in his usual shiny suit, and school life continued. "Burning," went another of his chemical slogans, "destroys nothing. It just shuffles the molecules."

At the war's end, we moved from the house that was too big to a small farmhouse ten miles away. It was my mother's idea of economizing. The antique small-town certainties I had grown up among were abruptly left behind. No more wood icebox, no more tin toaster, no more Vernon Grant nursery rhymes framed above my bed, no more simply running down through the yard to the eighth grade. My father and I were thrown together in a state of daily exile, getting into the car — we had to acquire a car — before the frost had left the windshield and returning, many nights, after dusk, our headlights the only ones on the pitted dirt road home. He still took the ticket money at the basketball games and, as another extracurricular duty, coached the swimming team, which, since the school had no pool, practiced at the YMCA in the city of Brewer's dingy and menacing downtown. The ten-year-old car we acquired kept giving us adventures: flat tires, broken axles, fearful struggles to put on tire chains at the base of a hill in the midst of a snowstorm. We sometimes didn't make it home, and walked and hitchhiked to shelter — the homes of fellow teachers, or what my father cheerfully called "fleabag" hotels. We became, during those years of joint commuting, a kind of team — partners in peril, fellow sufferers on the edge of disaster. It was dreadful but somehow authentic to be stuck in a stalled car with only four dollars between us, in the age before ATMs. It was — at least afterward, in the hotel, where my father had successfully begged the clerk to call Danny Haas to vouch for us — bliss, a rub against basic verities, an instance of survival.

I stood in sardonic, exasperated silence during his conversations with hotel clerks, garage mechanics, luncheonette waitresses, strangers on the street, none of whom were accustomed to encountering such a high level of trust. It was no mistake that he had wound up in education; he believed that everyone had something to teach him. His suppliant air humiliated me, but I was fourteen, fifteen; I was at his mercy, and he was at the mercy of the world. I saw him rebuffed and misunderstood. Flecks of foam would appear at the corners of his mouth as he strove to communicate; in my helpless witnessing I was half blinded by impatience and what now seems a mist of love, a pity bulging toward him like some embarrassing warpage of my own face.

He enjoyed human contact even at its least satisfactory, it slowly came to me. "I just wanted to see what he would say," he would explain after some futile tussle with, say, the policeman in charge of the municipal garage to which our nonstarting car had been towed, parked as it had been in a loading zone by the railroad platform; the cop refused to grasp the distinction between my father's good intentions and the car's mechanical misbehavior. "I used to land in the damnedest little towns," he would tell me, of his days selling china. "In upstate New York, West Virginia, wherever, you'd just get off the train with your sample case and go into any store where you saw china and try to talk them into carrying your line, which usually cost a bit more than the lines they had. You never knew what would happen. Some of them, at these dumps in the back of nowhere, would come up with the most surprising orders — tall orders. This was before the Depression hit, of course. I mean, it hit in '29, but there was a grace period before it took hold. And then you were born. Young America. Your mother and I, it knocked us for a loop, we had never figured on ourselves as parents. I don't know why not — it happens all the time. Making babies is the number-one priority for human nature. When I'm standing up there trying to pound the periodic table into their jiggling heads I sometimes think, These poor devils, they just want to be making babies."

My own developing baby-making yen took the form, first, of learning to smoke. You couldn't get anywhere in the high school society of the late forties without smoking. I had bought a pack — Old Golds, I think, because of the doubloons — at the Brewer railroad station, while my father was coaching the swimming team. Though the first drags did, in his phrase, knock me for a loop, I stuck with it; my vagabond life as his satellite left me with a lot of idle time in luncheonette booths. One winter morning when I was fifteen, I asked him if I could light up a cigarette in the car on the way to school. He himself had stopped, on his doctor's advice. But he didn't say no to me, and more than thirty years after I too quit, I still remember those caustic, giddying drags mixed with the first grateful whiffs of warmth from the car heater, while the little crackling radio played its medley of the Ink Spots and farm reports. His tacit permission, coming from a schoolteacher, would have been viewed, we both knew, as something of a disgrace. But it was my way of becoming a human being, and part of being human is being on the verge of disgrace.

Moving to the country had liberated us both, I see now, from the small-town grid and those masters of righteousness. The shopping fell to us, and my father favored a roadside grocery store that was owned and run, it was rumored, by a former Brewer gangster. Like my father, Arty Callahan was tall, melancholy, and slightly deaf; his wife was an overweight, wisecracking woman whose own past, it was said, was none too savory. My father loved them, and loved the fifteen minutes of delay their store gave him on the return home. Both Mr. and Mrs. Callahan took him in the right way, it seemed to me, with not too much of either amusement or gravity; they were, all three, free spirits and understood one another. While he talked to them, acting out, in gestures and phrases that had become somewhat stylized, his sense of daily peril, I would sit at a small Formica-topped table next to the magazine rack and leaf through *Esquire*, looking for Varga girls. I would sneak a look at Arty Callahan's profile, so noncommittally clamped over his terribly false teeth, and wonder how many men he had killed. The only gangsterish thing he did was give me ten dollars — a huge amount for an hour's work — for tutoring his son in algebra on Saturdays, when I was old enough to drive the car there.

We had traded in our car for a slightly newer and more dependable one, though still a prewar model. By the time I went off to college I no longer feared — I no longer dreamed — that my father would be savaged by society. He was fifty by then, a respectable age. Living his life beside him for five years, I had seen that his flirtation with disgrace was only that, not a ruinous infatuation. Nothing but death could topple him, and even that not very far, not in my mind.

MATTHEW CRAIN

Penance

FROM HARPER'S MAGAZINE

WHEN I HAULED the crew back to my shop, there was a little foreign car parked by the front door. It was hot and raining, and as I backed the truck and trailer of mowers and equipment inside, a young woman I didn't know got out and opened the passenger door and tried to coax a young man out of the car. Finally he got out, and as he followed her I saw he wasn't a hunchback but he walked real slow and bent over, swinging his arms out in front of him and bobbing his head back and forth like a chicken. I remembered I had seen him before, pushing an empty grocery basket up the street.

They ducked through the rain pouring across the door in a waterfall.

"Are you Mr. Caleb Andrews?" she said.

I shook her hand. She was tiny and wore sandals and what I call granny glasses. She said her name was Mary Sterne and that she worked for the Washington County Mental Health Association. They were all the talk for turning the old George McKinney house into a home for their patients. She pulled the boy around from behind her and said his name was Dennis Hatchett. I knew by looking at him that he wasn't all there. The boys were knocking around the shop with rakes and gas cans, but he didn't notice them; he kept his head down while she talked. His pants were too short and his shirt was buttoned wrong. She had to nudge him before he'd shake my hand, and when he did he looked up through the black hair stringing down in his face, grunted a high grunt, then looked again at his feet. Lonnie came up and said they had cleaned the mowers and asked me now what should they do, but really he wanted to see the woman's wet blouse. I told him to load up the truck with mulch and the wheelbarrow and get ready to set out some shrubs around the First Federal Bank, but he just stood there. The woman said she had seen my ad in the paper and wanted to know if I still needed a landscaper. I was one man short, and the crew didn't like it because they were on summer vacation from high school and wanted to quit work by five in the afternoon, then clean up and go out. I didn't like it because I hate to feel so behind and like I'm always trying to catch up. The year before, I had hired a man with one arm, so I asked her, "Can he push a lawn mower?"

She said, "Why don't you ask him?"

I asked him, and he nodded his head up and down. It was all I could do not to say, *Say Yes sir or No sir and show me respect.*

I caught Lonnie grinning and whispered in his ear, "I don't pay you to play with your dick."

He walked off in a huff, and I told the woman that the pay was four dollars an hour and each man brought his dinner. I said to him, "Can you be here by six tomorrow morning?"

He kept his head down, and his eyes flittered back and forth. I wanted to take him by the jaw and say, *Look at your elder when he talks to you.*

She nudged him, then said to me, "He'll be here."

I was glad she left. She didn't wear a brassiere, and I can't be responsible for what one of the crew might say.

The next morning when I rolled into the shop at a quarter of six, Dennis was waiting by the door.

That first week Dennis nearly drove me crazy. He didn't know how to mow at all. He wouldn't turn a corner but would come back the way he came, throwing the clippings right back into the grass. He couldn't guide the wheel correctly and not leave skips and streaks. He wasn't strong enough to push the mower. If he got on a sideways bank, he'd push it off to the bottom, and then I'd have to drag it out and start it up again. Dennis wore slick-soled dress shoes, and when it was wet he slid all over the place and made the goddamnedest mess that ever was. If he had slipped backward, he would have pulled that mower over on top of him. I can't afford insurance on these boys, so I told Dennis always to walk over his land and pick up any big limbs or trash. I bought him a pair of safety glasses, but he wouldn't wear them because Lonnie called him "bubble eyes."

He didn't have any patience. Anything that didn't work right, he'd kick it. If the mower choked or ran out of gas, he'd walk off and leave it and sit down in the truck and put his head on the dash and hold his breath. Then when everybody else was through, I'd have to send one of them out to finish his work. The boys didn't like that, and I didn't blame them.

The third day Dennis worked for me we mowed the Lone Oak Cemetery, then right before dinner we drove to Four Corners and started on the lot behind Bunk Devine's grocery. Four Corners is a traffic light hanging over where Old Dixie Highway and Route 88 intersect at Whitey England's Chevron station. Bunk's is on the northwest corner, with a trashy culvert alongside and a rented-out trailer at the back. The trailer's sewer was always backing up and overflowing into that ditch, and it grew up in thick grass and mosquitoes. I hated going there. A slouchy blond-headed woman with three boys lived there, and none of them had the same daddy. She'd stand in the door in her nightgown while we worked, and I told Bunk she had no business looking like that before a gang of men. But Bunk couldn't see past the little rent he got out of her.

Lonnie, Buford, and Tom sprayed themselves with Off, then put the can back in the truck behind the seat so Dennis wouldn't get any. Diesel fuel works better, so I wet a rag and rubbed it over my arms, neck, and head. Dennis sniffed the rag, then gave it back. "It mess up my hair."

I told him that soap and water would wash it out, but he wouldn't take it. "Fine," I said. "Let the mosquitoes eat you up."

I sent the others off Weedwacking around the store. After he'd picked up the trash off the lot, I set him to mowing, watched him make a couple passes, then started toward the store to get my money from Bunk. I turned and saw Dennis smacking at the mosquitoes on his arms and the back of his neck and guiding the mower with one hand — just what I told him never to do. Then the mower hit something and died.

Dennis left it and sat down in the truck. I tipped the mower on its side. A coil of TV cable was wrapped around the blade, locking a $110 engine.

You apologize to me!

Don't hit him! He's a boy!

Stop mothering him! He'll learn not to tear up my tools!

Lonnie walked up, gunning the Weedwacker, and asked what

happened. He had that silly-ass grin on his face like he expected to
see a fight.

I lifted the mower into the back of the truck, then got a spare
from the trailer.

"I'll do it," Lonnie said. "Or we'll never get done."

"Dennis has got to learn to finish his job," I said.

I got Dennis out of the truck, his arms and face covered with
mashed mosquitoes. I wiped his arms with the diesel-fuel rag, then
cranked the mower and said, "Keep your head out of your ass, son.
And hurry up so we can eat."

Friday afternoon of that first week we quit at four-thirty, and as soon
as Lonnie, Tom, and Buford got their pay they went to the bank to
cash their checks. I was driving into town and had just set the
thermos top on the dash and poured the last of my coffee into it
when I saw his green polyester pants and yellow shirt walking along
the highway. I picked him up. All week I hadn't said much to him
because it was enough trying to keep him from mowing over his
own foot. I asked him where his home was, and he started rocking
back and forth and said, "Barren Lake." Barren Lake is a couple
counties west of Sellersville.

Then he began snapping his knees open and shut and said, "Him
hit me."

I thought he meant one of the crew, and looked at him and asked
him who.

He whined like a pup. "Her hit me."

I was reaching for my coffee when Dennis opened the door and
tried to jump out. I pulled him by the arm back across the seat next
to me, stopped the truck, leaned over him, closed the door, and
locked it. All the way into town he hit and kicked at me. I wanted
to hit him and say, *Shut up that goddamned blubbering*. But he wasn't
my son.

When I let him off at his house, he marched across the lawn to
the front porch past Mary Sterne watering the plants. She called
after him as he slammed through the front door, then set her
watering can down and came out to me.

I told her what had happened, and she pushed her glasses up on
her nose and put her hands on her hips. "Dennis had an extremely
traumatic childhood."

"How in hell was I supposed to know?"

She tucked her hair behind her ear. "You do now, Mr. Andrews." She went back in the house.

My father's old double-cab International truck sits three in the front, three in the back, and every morning the boys flipped a coin to decide who had to sit beside Dennis. I brought my lunch every day, but occasionally when we were out by the interstate I stopped at a fast-food place to give us a treat. None of them would sit with Dennis. They ate enough to choke a horse, but Dennis always ate a single hamburger, no pop, no fried potatoes, and he kept his arm around the tray, guarding his food. I never saw him chew. He stuck half the hamburger in his mouth and swallowed it whole, then rocked back and forth at the table. One time when we ate out a couple high school girls came in and the boys were eyeing them, and then Lonnie started whispering around, and they got to giggling at Dennis. We were on our way to the next job when we passed these same girls riding bicycles along the side of the road. Lonnie sat in the back with his arm hanging out the window and yelled, "Can I be your bicycle seat?" Dennis sat beside me. Lonnie nudged Dennis and said, "Was that a boy or girl on that bicycle?"

"Her girl," Dennis said.

Lonnie asked him how he knew, and Buford and Tom started snickering. Dennis grabbed his chest like he had tits and said, "Me see her."

"She said she likes you," Lonnie said, then burst out laughing.

I stopped at Ray Sipe's filling station and sent Dennis in to get a bag of ice for the water jug. I turned around in the seat and told Lonnie, "You know better than to make fun of somebody who can't defend himself."

"What's with you, Mr. Andrews?" he said. "He can't work, and you let him get away with anything. I was just shooting the shit."

I said, "You're fixing to shoot your ass right out of a job."

The next morning we were at the shop ready to go and there was no Lonnie. I called his house and he said that he quit and for me to mail him his check. He didn't have the common courtesy to tell me to my face, and I told him if he wanted his money to come and get it. He never did.

The others still didn't pal around with Dennis, but they didn't tease him either.

*

Dennis seemed to find himself on the Weedwacker. Maybe it was because it made him slow down and be careful, but over the weeks he got so he did a nice job going around things. He learned to put gas and oil in the mowers and clean the grass from under them, and when it was his turn to sweep up the shop, he did a better job than the rest. Dennis imitated everything anybody did around him. If somebody said something funny or a song came over the radio, Dennis mocked it. I smoke, have since I was five. So Dennis started smoking four packs a day. One time Tom and Buford were horsing around and Buford shot Tom the finger, and the rest of the day Dennis went around giving cars, birds, the sun, everything, the finger. He cut his bangs out of his eyes and held his head up and was proud of himself. He told me that ten people lived at that house and each had certain responsibilities. They kept a cat and dog, and somebody had to feed them and clean out their pen. One laundered, and the ones who couldn't cook cleaned the house. It was Dennis's job to mow the yard and get the groceries. They all ate at the table together and had to be in bed by ten o'clock.

On his breaks he would practice adding columns of numbers and would work long-division problems and ask me to check them. He held the pen like it was an ice pick. I could barely read his handwriting.

Buford and Tom snickered, but I told them that at least he was trying to improve himself, that they'd sit around on their asses and let everybody pass them by.

"Me go to school and get a job. Me mow yards," Dennis said.

Buford said, "Shit. You can't even read."

"Me can so read."

Buford took Dennis's cigarettes. He said, "Read that."

"Pall Mall," Dennis said.

"It's Pell Mell, you dumb-ass," Buford said.

I said, "Professor, you'd better give your diploma back."

One Monday morning Dennis came to work and didn't say anything all day. I asked him what was wrong, but he wouldn't talk. That evening after work I stopped at the Greyhound Supermarket and ran into Brother Tupper Harris. He baptized me when I was twelve and preached my parents' funerals. He stopped his basket alongside mine and said that yesterday the Church of Christ had sent a van to where Dennis lived and took Dennis to Sunday school, and that after the sermon when they were singing about the blood of the lamb, Dennis had started crying.

Brother Harris looked up and down the grocery aisle, then said that afterward he had asked Dennis, "Son, what was you crying about?" and the boy had said, "I feel bad for that lamb." Brother Harris stepped back laughing and almost choked on the chew of tobacco in his mouth.

I said, "My Bible says to *help* the afflicted and orphans."

He cleared his throat and here came that righteous look of his, but I'd be damned if I was gonna hear one of *his* sermons. I put my finger right in his face and said, "And don't it say that the angels in heaven rejoice when somebody tries to change himself?"

"You got no business pointing the finger of scorn at *me*, Caleb Andrews," he said. "It's been *years* since you even darkened the door of a church. Why, when was the last time you prayed?"

I said, "I'll step behind a tree and talk to God myself. You nice gentle loving churchgoers with your wagging tongues, your prayers never go any higher than your own ears."

I drove straight to the McKinney place. Bedford Street was quiet except for Ray Sipe mowing his yard. Nobody answered at the front door, so I went around back to the garden. There were giant sunflowers around its fence. Two rows of sweet corn, tomatoes, beans, cabbage, onions, squash, and carrots all growing on raised beds.

Mary Sterne was bent over pulling beets. She was barefoot and wore a tank top and a pair of gym shorts, and when she saw me she walked the row and met me at the gate.

"Did you dig those raised beds by yourself, Miss Sterne?" I asked her.

"Dennis helped," she said. "Call me Mary." She wiped the sweat off her nose, pushed up her granny glasses, then pointed at the nasturtiums planted around the potato vines and said she didn't use insecticide but planted certain kinds of flowers around certain kinds of vegetables. "But I can't get Dennis to pick the potato bugs," she said. Her legs and underarms were as hairy as any man's. I was starting to get a hard-on, so I kept to the other side of the gatepost. I asked her where Dennis was.

"He's inside. You're welcome to stay for dinner, Mr. Andrews."

Ray Sipe drove the riding mower around the corner of his house, not watching where he was going. His tongue would stretch from here to the Gulf of Mexico.

I said, "I've got work to do at the shop."

Three women were in the kitchen fixing supper, and they told me Dennis was upstairs cleaning the TV room. There was a white Siamese cat mewing all upset at the top of the stairs. I walked down the hall, passed a bathroom just as the toilet flushed, and found Dennis in the front room, sitting on the edge of the couch, watching *The Three Stooges*. The vacuum cleaner stood in the middle of the floor, its cord snaking back to the wall outlet. I sat down in a straight chair and was going to tell Dennis not to go back to the Church of Christ when down the hall a door slammed and somebody shouted. Dennis got up and turned the TV to the evening news as this fat-ass pranced into the room and ran Dennis through this long soul-brother routine, shaking hands three different ways, slapping palms. This man wore a tight T-shirt and cut-off sweatpants pulled high in his crotch. His legs were pale, smooth like he'd shaved them, and covered with scabby crab-lice bites. His hair was white blond and wet-combed back in wings that stuck to the sides of his head. I stood up and introduced myself. Just speaking to me seemed to bother him.

He said his name was James Nass. His palm was wet, oily wet.

The three of us stood close together, but Dennis wouldn't look at us. He kept glancing at the TV.

James Nass looked me in the eye. "Dennis said you need somebody." Half his voice was southern, but he'd get three quarters of the way through a word and roll it out in a northern brogue. He wheezed like he had asthma.

"No, I found a man," I said, and he knew I was lying.

He coughed in my face, and his breath stank like cigarettes and cough drops. "Sure." Then he told Dennis to stop by his room.

When James Nass left, Dennis turned the TV off. "Him move here last week."

"Don't fool with him," I said. "In the army we called clowns like him 'screwballs.' They get you in trouble but won't get you out. And don't go back to the Church of Christ; it only drives an enmity between you and everybody else."

Independence Day I took Dennis fishing. Mary answered the door. I gave her a box of my son's books about trains, and she put it in the hall and came back out. She wore hiking shorts, a man's white shirt, and underneath you could see a navy polka-dot bikini top. She shouted into the house to Dennis that I was there, then asked if she could come too.

I said, "Do you know how to fish?"

She brought her hand from behind her back and gave me a plastic tub full of fat night crawlers. "Got them from the garden. Can I come or not?"

I made Dennis wear my life jacket. He sat in the front of the boat, Mary sat in the middle, I sat in the back and rowed. When we came to the shady shallow cove where I always fish, Mary said to go past, to a bank, and I said, "I thought you were fishing."

"Me? Stick a worm on a hook? I'd die. I came to work on my tan." She got out and climbed up the bank, then spread out her towel and began unbuttoning her shirt.

Dennis looked like he was watching a murder. I nudged him with the handle and gave him the oar.

Mary lay down quickly, and all I could see was the bottoms of her feet.

I paddled us back to the cove and got Dennis started. I was determined he was going to catch a fish. I cast the line out next to a tree that had fallen in the water where the fish were likely to be, then gave Dennis the rod and reel and showed him how to crank the line in just quick enough to spin the lure. He lit one cigarette off the butt of another and thumped the butt in the lake.

"For Chrissakes, son," I said. "You'll scare the fish."

I dropped my line off the side and stuck the end of the cane pole under the seat, then unscrewed the top off the thermos, filled it, and set it on the middle bench. It didn't make any difference to her that she was alone in a garage full of strangers: she came into the shop with her blouse soaked and you could see her nipples and tits, she saw the boys looking, she knew I was trying not to, but she wasn't ashamed, didn't try to hide it. That's rare.

A gang of men in a motorboat rounded the bend, the driver steering with one hand, the sun glaring off his beer can as he turned it up and drained it. He stopped where Mary was and let out a howl, and then they all started whooping and hollering. When the waves began rocking us, Dennis began sucking in air and grabbed onto the side of the boat and dropped my rod and reel into the water. I leaned forward to grab him, and when I raised off the seat he tipped the boat and almost threw me into the lake. I can't swim.

"Dennis, you control yourself," I said as that boatload of drunks cut one last circle and left.

An hour or so later the sun was up in the sky and it was too hot for the fish to bite. Mary was squatted down on her heels waiting for us, her shirt draped over her arm. She'd burned her chest. Back at the truck she stepped behind a bush and peed, then we ate dinner on the tailgate: a long loaf of brown tough bread she'd baked, a bowl of German potato salad, coleslaw, baked beans, and chocolate oatmeal cookies, all Mary's.

"You shouldn't have done that," I said. "Laid out where people could see you."

"That's their problem," she said, and took out a bottle of wine.

Something like icewater shot up my nose. I couldn't hear anything; all I knew was not to open my mouth. I felt like I was sinking, falling backward, then crashing against a rock wall.

She cut the foil off the neck with an army knife. The cork popped and she said, "This is good stuff. I had to go to the next county to get it." She took out three plastic cups from the basket and gave a cup to me.

"Oh, come on. A little won't hurt," she said, and began pouring. I held the cup by the rim up to the sun and stared at the light on the wine's squiggly surface. Then Dennis looked at me, and it was like having your eyes held open and somebody packing grit under the lids. Go ahead, I told myself. You can drink the taste from around the liquor. Pain traced every vein in my head, then shot down my throat into my empty lungs. I felt like I was somersaulting. I got off the tailgate and gave the cup back to Mary.

"I can drive back if that's what you're worried about," she said. "You're not a teetotaler, are you?"

"I belong to AA."

"I didn't know," she said and stopped pouring the wine into her cup. "I'm sorry. I hope I haven't ruined today."

I told her she hadn't, but she had.

Every two weeks Mary checked on Dennis, and the next time she came it was dinnertime. The rest of the crew had gone to town to eat; Dennis had brought his lunch and was eating in my truck. Mary and I were in my office. She had her hair pinned up and wore a sleeveless dress and smelled like sweat and magnolia mixed. She told me about James Nass. She said he came out of Florida and had goofed off a couple of years overseas in the army, then came back blown out of his mind on dope. He had worked awhile as a roadie for a rock-and-roll band, then got on the GI Bill and started school to be a physical education teacher, then flunked. One minute he was fine and then the next he thought the enemy were coming after him. She said that she wasn't equipped to handle James Nass's kind of problem, but when I asked her what his problem was, her face got red and she said she didn't feel right talking about it.

"You brought it up," I said. "What does he do?"

Her dress was way up over her knee, but she didn't seem to care.

"Every evening at six when the news comes on, James locks himself and the cat in the TV room and masturbates to Melissa West, one of the Channel Four newscasters. Each time the station breaks, he goes to the bathroom and washes his hands."

I leaned toward her. "Have you caught Dennis doing that?"

"No, but surely you've noticed how he copies everyone around him."

She said Nass had more or less adopted Dennis, all the time borrowing money from him, and when Dennis came in from work, they'd drive around half the night.

"Is James Nass dangerous?"

"The medication he takes is the equivalent of speed. This year he's been in three different homes."

I offered her a cigarette, but she thanked me and said she didn't smoke, and when I lit mine she coughed and got up, came beside the desk, and reached up to open the window, and I saw how hairy her armpits were. "You can't deny him," she said, looking at my son's senior picture on the desk, then at me. She sat down. "How old is he?"

I pressed myself back in my chair and blew the cigarette smoke up at the fluorescent light. I looked at my son's picture. He leans forward and grins like somebody's just said, Let's go get a case of beer! His hair is parted down the middle and comes down over his ears.

But that's the style, Daddy.

Maybe for faggots it is. But not for you!

He wears a green velour shirt. My wife got mad when she saw this picture because Robert pushed up his sleeves to show off his fore-arms.

I looked at Mary Sterne, and we both realized we were alone in the back of the shop. She stood and smoothed down her dress, pulling the top tight across her chest. I saw her out, then when I went back to my dinner and saw the patch of sweat where her legs had stuck to the chair and the dusty back of my son's picture frame, I locked the door and sat down in the truck with Dennis and waited until the others came back.

Dennis had always talked only when he had to, but after a month of running around with James Nass, he'd follow me around and want to tell me where they went the night before and all the smart things James Nass had said. He had always walked to work, but this James Nass had an old '57 Chevy and started driving him, and while we were servicing the mowers, James sat in his car and played his radio or poked around the shop, nosing into everything and boss-ing. Buford and Tom were men, as big as me, but they didn't know what to do with him when he talked real loud and fast in that half-ass northern brogue. I'd hitch the truck to the trailer and pull out of the shop, lock up, and he'd be leaning against his car. I'd stand by the truck door and stare at him until finally he'd creep his car across the lot and out to the street. He'd even follow us from job to job, park in the nearest shade, lean the seat back and doze, and every five or ten minutes motion Dennis over. Then at the end of the day when I came in, he'd be sitting there, radio blasting. Mary said that sometimes when Dennis went to the grocery now he'd make one of his friends push the basket and walked far in front and ignored him like a boss.

Then we mowed Miss Roxie Hardy's yard. Miss Roxie is in her late seventies, lives alone — has ever since her husband died — and still tries to keep up with everything that goes on. It was about eight in the morning, and she came out with her straw hat tied on her head and followed Dennis to the side of her house where she grew a fence of red peonies. I didn't want her to, but she held them up so Dennis could mow under the blossoms. And he ran the front wheel of his mower under the fence. He didn't shut off the engine and then unhang the wheel; he jerked until he broke the bottom strand of fence, then went on mowing like nothing had happened. When we finished, Miss Roxie brought out a box of ice cream and stood on the cistern rock and gave us each an ice cream cone. Dennis's face was dirty. She gave Dennis his and said, "Son, you got something black around your mouth."

Dennis said, "You got something black between your legs," then grinned at Buford and Tom, and they looked at me.

Miss Roxie said, "Boy, somebody should've drowned you in the bathwater."

I apologized to Miss Roxie, then sent Dennis to the truck. When we got away from her house, I threw his ice cream out the window.

The next morning there was no Dennis. We gassed up the mowers and loaded them on the trailer, put new blades on the Weedwackers, and by then it was ten after six and still no Dennis. I was on the phone with Mary when James Nass's car pulled into the lot. Dennis came in the garage door, stumbling drunk. Buford and Tom sat down on the back of the trailer and started giggling. I went out, and James Nass was sitting on his heels in the shop door by the gas cans.

"Get that goddamned cigarette out of your mouth," I said.

He wore a blue muscle shirt, camouflage shorts, and rubber shower sandals. He stood up and flicked his cigarette out the door.

I said, "And haul your sorry ass off my property."

He made big eyes and whistled. Dennis was down on his knees in the gravel, puking hamburgers.

"I'll arrest you for terroristic threatening," James Nass said. He looked at Buford and Tom. "Then you'll have to find some new butt buddies."

They started to jump him, but James Nass backed out to his car and drove off laughing and scooting gravel all the way to the street. I grabbed Dennis up by the arm and set him down in my office and made him drink all my thermos of coffee.

I made him look at me. I said, "You work today and then you're done. I'm not having a drunk work for me."

"Me not drunk."

I gave him a clean T-shirt of mine and said, "Don't back-talk me. Mary is going to bring you over here tomorrow morning to get your check. Now get your ass in that truck and get to work."

We had two jobs that morning, the nursing home and the grounds around Hensley's Ford. I took Dennis off the mower and kept him on the Weedwacker, thinking that the twenty-pound en-

gine on his back and having to stoop and go slow and concentrate
would work the drunk out of him.

The haze and humidity burned off at noon, and it was in the low
nineties. Dennis was pale and white around the mouth and didn't
eat lunch. He sat in the truck with his head on the dash.

The job that afternoon was Lakeside Apartments. There wasn't a
big lawn to mow, only small patches of grass between the buildings.
At the back of the apartments were little concrete patios where the
tenants set out flowers and special shrubs, and that was the tedious
part: edging around the patio while somebody stood there in his
house slippers telling you to be careful.

Buford and Tom were mowing, I sent Dennis to Weedwack. I was
at the truck gassing a mower when a woman in a bathing suit
walked up. "I was lying out on my patio," she said, jabbing her
finger in my face, "when that goon-looking moron that works for
you cut down my yucca." She threw a yucca stalk onto the back of
the trailer.

I went across the parking lot and around the side of the building,
and there was Dennis sitting under a tree. When he saw me, he got
up and ran to where James Nass was Weedwacking around an air-
conditioning unit. It took me five long steps to cross the courtyard
and kick James Nass in the ass. He swung the Weedwacker at me,
and I stepped out of the way and there was Dennis in my place. It
slashed his face from ear to ear. I could see his jawbone exposed
and the sides of his teeth, and then the blood came out of his
mouth in a sheet that stuck to his shirt like a bib.

I kicked James Nass in the nuts, and as he bent over I pulled the
Weedwacker off his shoulder and hit him over the head with the
engine. I got on top of him, pinned his elbows under my knees, and
hit him for every lash my drunken father hit me with a razor strap,
every drink I ever drank, every time I see my dead son's face, eyes
wide and mouth screaming when my truck pins him to his car,
every day of the nine years I spent in the penitentiary, every night I
wake up with my palm flat on the mattress where my ex-wife slept,
every time my father and wife and son jump up out of the ground
and throw their dead arms around my neck and my father bites my
ear, my wife bites my breast, and my son kisses me with the taste of
his clean jeans and aftershave, and my wife's powdery nightgown
and my father's pissy trousers smother me.

*

The first thing I saw when I woke up was the cement ceiling through the empty mattress springs of the top bunk. There was the same toilet with no lid, the same sink that dripped water constantly, the same cuss words and dirty drawings scratched into the walls. I got off the bunk and stood and saw the other drunks in the other cell watching me, and in the aisle outside my cell was my wife and Sheriff Lawler and his deputies. My wife's face was white as a sheet of paper. The sheriff and deputies watched me from under their broad brims. "We found you in the next county," Sheriff Lawler said. "You had drove out in the middle of an apple orchard . . ."

My wife wiped her eyes with a crumpled tissue and said it like she was standing up before her class, reciting them a fact they had to memorize for a test: "You ran over and killed your son."

I sat down on the bunk and stared through the bars at the other empty cell.

Sheriff Lawler came through the door from his office, opened the cell door, and sat down beside me. I didn't move or look him in the face.

I asked him about Dennis.

Sheriff Lawler sighed and scratched his chin whiskers and said that Dennis was laid up in the Sellersville Hospital with four hundred stitches in his face. The Weedwacker had cut off his tongue. He stared at the side of my head until I looked at him. He said James Nass was in the VA Hospital at Fort Buell with a broken nose, a cracked skull, crushed throat, and one eye gouged out. He took off his hat, ran his hand through his hair, then fiddled with his hatband. He said, "The woman at Lakeside Apartments says James Nass took the Weedwacker away from the Hatchett boy and destroyed her property, and when you went out to stop it in the fight the boy got hit. Is that how it happened?"

I said it was, and he said, "So you was taking up for the boy?"

"I was."

"Mary Sterne says that after you called her asking where the boy was, she drove over to your shop but you'd already gone, and then she drove all over looking for you and finally saw your truck at Lakeside Apartments. She saw you nearly kill James Nass. She left."

I looked at him.

"When I went over to get her statement, she'd packed up that little car and was heading back up east wherever she came from.

From what she said, there's another counselor, a man, supposed to arrive later today."

I did not know what to do. "How come she left?"

"I guess you scared her half to death." He stood, hitched up his belt over his gut, and told me to come on, he'd drive me home.

On the way I got him to stop at the hospital. At the nurse's station when we asked where Dennis was, the nurses stopped writing in their files and charts and pretended not to watch, but when I was out of their sight I heard their chair wheels squeak and their chair backs pop as they rolled together. *Oh, you remember. He killed his son.*

Dennis had a private room at the end of the hall. Dr. Hockman stepped out of Dennis's room. So fat that the legs of his stethoscope didn't meet around his neck, thick bifocals that made his eyes fill the entire lens, he dug a pack of cigarettes from the pocket of his white coat, then lit one. "So you saw it happen?"

I stared into his nosy face.

"Caleb wants to see the boy," the sheriff said.

"I put him under sedation," Dr. Hockman said, the smoke coming out of his mouth as he spoke. He puffed again, then took a last look at me, then opened the door.

No flowers, no cards, only a plastic water pitcher turned upside down on a gray steel bedside table. A radiator beneath the window, daylight on the metal trunk of the IV tree, the yellow tube running into the top of his wrist. His feet stuck out from under the sheet, and I covered them with a blue blanket. I leaned over the bed rail. His head was completely bundled and they had cut two holes for his eyes. Stitches crawled down the side of his neck and diagonally across his chest.

"It hit him at an angle," Dr. Hockman said, squinting at the smoke stinging his eyes and tracing his fat finger above the stitches.

I asked him what had happened to Dennis's tongue, and he looked at the sheriff like I was crazy. He said, "The paramedics couldn't find it. No good anyhow. By now it's dead."

My truck was parked in the corner of the yard under the tree I chain the dog to, and she barked and jumped in circles, glad to see me. It didn't make any difference to her what I did; my hand was just as good as any. I fed and watered her, shelled a couple ears of corn for the chickens, and when the phone started ringing I let the

sonofabitch ring and sat down on the back doorstep, a limestone
step, the step where I'd sit after my wife would take Robert and go
to her mother's because I'd be on a crying drunk. On the west side
of the house, it was still cool, and across the field I saw my neighbor's Holstein stringing out from the back of the milk parlor into
the sun, the sun on the tops of the trees around his house, the sun
on the TV antenna, and wondered if what I'd done had made the
news. Just across the field cars and trucks were parked around Ray
Sipe's white gas station, and no doubt they'd seen the sheriff drive
by and were up there now sitting around saying, Well, I heard this,
and another says, Well, one of the boys that works for him says that.
I sat there and looked at the dead grape arbor where I grew grapes
that she made jelly and I made wine, at the tractor tire where she set
out begonias, then at the growed-up half-acre we used to raise a
garden in; then I imagined I heard the Volkswagen's engine down-
shifting, heard it come up the gravel drive, and the dog started
barking and stood woofing and looking out the corner of her eyes
at me, heard the emergency brake pull up, heard the door slam,
and with the engine idling, Mary, in a pink dress and black belt
around her waist, Mary came around the side of the house, and the
instant I stood she put her arms around me, and I let her cry and I
cried, and we stood on the step at the back of the house, pressed
together, and I kept her shoulders in my hands and her itchy braid
between my arms and her back and her cold sticky glasses lenses on
my chest. Then the night is clear, a new-moon black, yet the security
lights around the parking lot and between the buildings override
the stars. The katydids scratch and sing in the culvert beside the
road. A frog hopscotches across the surface of the lake. Hidden
behind shrubs, the air-conditioning units kick on. The lawn rises to
a knoll where the wooden deck overlooks the swimming pool. My
rake lies on the walk leading to the patios where I see the black
shapes of flowers and deck chairs. At a window on the second floor,
a man in a white T-shirt locks his sliding door, then draws the
curtain. The water sprinklers shut off, and mists of water chill my
back. I lie on my stomach. The wet has soaked to the skin, and as I
inch forward on my elbows my boots squeak in the grass. From the
parking lot, both sides of the walk, the strips of lawn between the
patios to this circle of grass in the center of the courtyard. Mary and
I have found a cigarette butt, a marble, a bottle cap, and a Bazooka

Joe comic. Mary crawls on her hands and knees, a pin light in her mouth, sweeps her hands through the grass. I press my forehead to the ground, shut my eyes, then run my fingers through the mower wheel's track. It's here. We've found it and can give it back to him. But the phone is ringing, the dog is at the end of her chain barking and beating her tail in the dirt, Jesus says the dead bury the dead but the dead bury the living: the dead tell me what I should have done nine years ago and act like I can return and do it, and I try to do like they say. I obey, but the instant I do, they say, "But you didn't do it *then*," and I begin the whole cycle again.

LORRIE MOORE

People Like That Are the Only People Here

FROM THE NEW YORKER

A BEGINNING, an end: there seems to be neither. The whole thing is like a cloud that just lands, and everywhere inside it is full of rain. A start: the Mother finds a blood clot in the Baby's diaper. What is the story? Who put this here? It is big and bright, with a broken, khaki-colored vein in it. Over the weekend, the Baby had looked listless and spacy, clayey and grim. But today he looks fine — so what is this thing, startling against the white diaper, like a tiny mouse heart packed in snow? Perhaps it belongs to someone else. Perhaps it is something menstrual, something belonging to the Mother or to the Babysitter, something the Baby has found in a wastebasket and for his own demented baby reasons stowed away here. (Babies — they're crazy! What can you do?) In her mind, the Mother takes this away from his body and attaches it to someone else's. There. Doesn't that make more sense?

Still, she phones the children's hospital clinic. Blood in the diaper, she says, and sounding alarmed and perplexed, the woman on the other end says, "Come in now."

Such pleasingly instant service! Just say "blood." Just say "diaper." Look what you get.

In the examination room, the pediatrician, the nurse, and the head resident all seem less alarmed and perplexed than simply perplexed. At first, stupidly, the Mother is calmed by this. But soon, besides peering and saying "Hmm," the doctor, the nurse, and the head resident are all drawing their mouths in, bluish and tight —

morning glories sensing noon. They fold their arms across their white-coated chests, unfold them again, and jot things down. They order an ultrasound. Bladder and kidneys. Here's the card. Go downstairs, turn left.

In Radiology, the Baby stands anxiously on the table, naked against the Mother, as she holds him still against her legs and waist, the Radiologist's cold scanning disk moving about the Baby's back. The Baby whimpers, looks up at the Mother. *Let's get out of here,* his eyes beg. *Pick me up!* The Radiologist stops, freezes one of the many swirls of oceanic gray, and clicks repeatedly, a single moment within the long, cavernous weather map that is the Baby's insides.

"Are you finding something?" asks the Mother. Last year, her Uncle Larry had a kidney removed for something that turned out to be benign. These imaging machines! They are like dogs, or metal detectors: they find everything but don't know what they've found. That's where the surgeons come in. They're like the owners of the dogs. *Give me that,* they say to the dog. *What the heck is that?*

"The surgeon will speak to you," says the Radiologist.

"Are you finding something?"

"The surgeon will speak to you," the Radiologist says again. "There seems to be something there, but the surgeon will talk to you about it."

"My uncle once had something on his kidney," says the Mother. "So they removed the kidney and it turned out the something was benign."

The Radiologist smiles a broad, ominous smile. "That's always the way it is," he says. "You don't know exactly what it is until it's in the bucket."

"In the bucket," the Mother repeats.

"That's doctor talk," the Radiologist says.

"It's very appealing," says the Mother. "It's a very appealing way to talk." Swirls of bile and blood, mustard and maroon in a pail, the colors of an African flag or some exuberant salad bar: *in the bucket* — she imagines it all.

"The surgeon will see you soon," he says again. He tousles the Baby's ringlety hair. "Cute kid," he says.

"Let's see now," says the Surgeon, in one of his examining rooms. He has stepped in, then stepped out, then come back in again. He has crisp, frowning features, sharp bones, and a tennis-in-Bermuda tan. He crosses his blue-cottoned legs. He is wearing clogs.

The Mother knows her own face is a big white dumpling of worry. She is still wearing her long, dark parka, holding the Baby, who has pulled the hood up over her head because he always thinks it's funny to do that. Though on certain windy mornings she would like to think she could look vaguely romantic like this, like some French Lieutenant's Woman of the Prairie, in all her saner moments she knows she doesn't. She knows she looks ridiculous — like one of those animals made out of twisted party balloons. She lowers the hood and slips one arm out of the sleeve. The Baby wants to get up and play with the light switch. He fidgets, fusses, and points.

"He's big on lights these days," explains the Mother.

"That's okay," says the Surgeon, nodding toward the light switch. "Let him play with it." The Mother goes and stands by it, and the Baby begins turning the lights off and on, off and on.

"What we have here is a Wilms' tumor," says the Surgeon, suddenly plunged into darkness. He says "tumor" as if it were the most normal thing in the world.

"Wilms'?" repeats the Mother. The room is quickly on fire again with light, then wiped dark again. Among the three of them here there is a long silence, as if it were suddenly the middle of the night. "Is that apostrophe *s* or *s* apostrophe?" the Mother says finally. She is a writer and a teacher. Spelling can be important — perhaps even at a time like this, though she has never before been at a time like this, so there are barbarisms she could easily commit without knowing.

The lights come on; the world is doused and exposed.

"*S* apostrophe," says the Surgeon. "I think." The lights go back out, but the Surgeon continues speaking in the dark. "A malignant tumor of the left kidney."

Wait a minute. Hold on here. The Baby is only a baby, fed on organic applesauce and soy milk — a little prince! — and he was standing so close to her during the ultrasound. How could he have this terrible thing? It must have been *her* kidney. A fifties kidney. A DDT kidney. The Mother clears her throat. "Is it possible it was my kidney on the scan? I mean, I've never heard of a baby with a tumor, and frankly, I was standing very close." She would make the blood hers, the tumor hers; it would all be some treacherous, farcical mistake.

"No, that's not possible," says the Surgeon. The light goes back on.

"It's not?" says the Mother. Wait until it's *in the bucket,* she thinks. Don't be so sure. *Do we have to wait until it's in the bucket to find out a mistake has been made?*

"We will start with a radical nephrectomy," says the Surgeon, instantly thrown into darkness again. His voice comes from nowhere and everywhere at once. "And then we'll begin with chemotherapy after that. These tumors usually respond very well to chemo."

"I've never heard of a baby having chemo," the Mother says. Baby and Chemo, she thinks: they should never even appear in the same sentence together, let alone the same life. In her other life, her life before this day, she was a believer in alternative medicine. Chemotherapy? Unthinkable. Now, suddenly, alternative medicine seems the wacko maiden aunt to the Nice Big Daddy of Conventional Treatment. How quickly the old girl faints and gives way, leaves one just standing there. Chemo? Of course: chemo! Why, by all means: chemo. Absolutely! Chemo!

The Baby flicks the switch back on, and the walls reappear, big wedges of light checkered with small framed watercolors of the local lake. The Mother has begun to cry: all of life has led her here, to this moment. After this there is no more life. There is something else, something stumbling and unlivable, something mechanical, something for robots, but not life. Life has been taken and broken, quickly, like a stick. The room goes dark again, so that the Mother can cry more freely. How can a baby's body be stolen so fast? How much can one heaven-sent and unsuspecting child endure? Why has he not been spared this inconceivable fate?

Perhaps, she thinks, she is being punished: too many babysitters too early on. ("Come to Mommy! Come to Mommy-Babysitter!" she used to say. But it was a joke!) Her life, perhaps, bore too openly the marks and wigs of deepest drag. Her unmotherly thoughts had all been noted: the panicky hope that his nap would last just a little longer than it did; her occasional desire to kiss him passionately on the mouth (to make out with her baby!); her ongoing complaints about the very vocabulary of motherhood, how it degraded the speaker ("Is this a poopie onesie? Yes, it's a very poopie onesie!"). She had, moreover, on three occasions used the formula bottle as flower vases. She twice let the Baby's ears get fudgy with wax. A few afternoons last month, at snack time, she placed a bowl of Cheerios on the floor for him to eat, like a dog. She let him play with the Dustbuster. Just once, before he was born, she said, "Healthy? I just want the kid to be rich." A joke, for God's sake. After he was born, she announced that her life had become a daily sequence of mind-wrecking chores, the same ones over and over again, like a novel by Mrs. Camus. Another joke! These jokes will kill you. She had told too often, and with too much enjoyment, the story of how the Baby had said "Hi" to his high chair, waved at the lake waves, shouted "Goody-goody-goody" in what seemed to be a Russian accent, pointed at his eyes and said "Ice." And all that nonsensical baby talk: wasn't it a stitch? *Canonical babbling*, the language experts called it. He recounted whole stories in it, totally made up, she could tell; he embroidered, he fished, he exaggerated. What a card! To friends she spoke of his eating habits (carrots yes, tuna no). She mentioned, too much, his sidesplitting giggle. Did she have to be so boring? Did she have no consideration for others, for the intellectual demands and courtesies of human society? Would she not even attempt to be more interesting? It was a crime against the human mind not even to try.

Now her baby, for all these reasons — lack of motherly gratitude, motherly judgment, motherly proportion — will be taken away.

The room is fluorescently ablaze again. The Mother digs around in her parka pocket and comes up with a Kleenex. It is old and thin, like a mashed flower saved from a dance; she dabs it at her eyes and nose.

"The baby won't suffer as much as you," says the Surgeon.

And who can contradict? Not the Baby, who in his Slavic Betty Boop voice can say only *mama, dada, cheese, ice, bye-bye, outside, boogie-boogie, goody-goody, eddy-eddy,* and *car.* (Who is Eddy? They have no idea.) This will not suffice to express his mortal suffering. Who can say what babies do with their agony and shock? Not they themselves. (Baby talk: isn't it a stitch?) They put it all no place anyone can really see. They are like a different race, a different species: they seem not to experience pain the way we do. Yeah, that's it: their nervous systems are not as fully formed, and *they just don't experience pain the way we do.* A tune to keep one humming through the war. "You'll get through it," the Surgeon says.

"How?" asks the Mother. "How does one get through it?"

"You just put your head down and go," says the Surgeon. He picks up his file folder. He is a skilled manual laborer. The tricky emotional stuff is not to his liking. The babies. The babies! What can be said to console the parents about the babies? "I'll go phone the oncologist on duty to let him know," he says, and leaves the room.

"Come here, sweetie," the Mother says to the Baby, who has toddled off toward a gum wrapper on the floor. "We've got to put your jacket on." She picks him up and he reaches for the light switch again. Light, dark. Peekaboo: Where's baby? Where did baby go?

At home, she leaves a message — Urgent! Call me! — for the Husband on his voice mail. Then she takes the Baby upstairs for his nap, rocks him in the rocker. The Baby waves goodbye to his little bears, then looks toward the window and says, "Bye-bye, outside." He has, lately, the habit of waving goodbye to everything, and now it seems as if he sensed some imminent departure, and it breaks her heart to hear him. *Bye-bye!* She sings low and monotonously, like a small appliance, which is how he likes it. He is drowsy, dozy, drifting off. He has grown so much in the last year he hardly fits in her lap anymore; his limbs dangle off like a Pietà. His head rolls slightly inside the crook of her arm. She can feel him falling backward into sleep, his mouth round and open like the sweetest of poppies. All the lullabies in the world, all the melodies threaded through with maternal melancholy now become for her — abandoned as mothers can be by working men and napping babies — the songs of hard, hard grief. Sitting there, bowed and bobbing, the Mother feels the entirety of her love as worry and heartbreak. A quick and irrevocable alchemy: there is no longer one unworried scrap left for happiness. "If you go," she keens low into his soapy neck, into the ranunculus coil of his ear, "we are going with you. We are nothing without you. Without you, we are a heap of rocks. Without you, we are two stumps, with nothing any longer in our hearts. Wherever this takes you, we are following; we will be there. Don't be scared. We are going too, wherever you go. That is that. That is that."

"Take notes," says the Husband, after coming straight home from work, midafternoon, hearing the news, and saying all the words out loud — *surgery, metastasis, dialysis, transplant* — then collapsing in a chair in tears. "Take notes. We are going to need the money."

"Good God," cries the Mother. Everything inside her suddenly begins to cower and shrink, a thinning of bones. Perhaps this is a soldier's readiness, but it has the whiff of death and defeat. It feels like a heart attack, a failure of will and courage, a power failure: a failure of everything. Her face, when she glimpses it in a mirror, is cold and bloated with shock, her eyes scarlet and shrunk. She has already started to wear sunglasses indoors, like a celebrity widow. From where will her own strength come? From some philosophy? From some frigid little philosophy? She is neither stalwart nor real-istic and has trouble with basic concepts, such as the one that says events move in one direction only and do not jump up, turn around, and take themselves back.

The Husband begins too many of his sentences with "What if." He is trying to piece everything together, like a train wreck. He is trying to get the train to town.

"We'll just take all the steps, move through all the stages. We'll go where we have to go, we'll hunt, we'll find, we'll pay what we have to pay. What if we can't pay?"

"Sounds like shopping."

"I cannot believe this is happening to our little boy," he says, and starts to sob again.

What is to be said? You turn just slightly and there it is: the death of your child. It is part symbol, part devil, and in your blind spot all along, until it is upon you. Then it is a fierce little country abduct-ing you; it holds you squarely inside itself like a cellar room, the best boundaries of you are the boundaries of it. Are there windows? Sometimes aren't there windows?

The Mother is not a shopper. She hates to shop, is generally bad at it, though she does like a good sale. She cannot stroll meaningfully through anger, denial, grief, and acceptance. She goes straight to bargaining and stays there. How much? She calls out to the ceiling, to some makeshift construction of holiness she has desperately though not uncreatively assembled in her mind and prayed to; a doubter, never before given to prayer, she must now reap what she has not sown; she must reassemble an entire altar of worship and begging. She tries for noble abstractions, nothing too anthropo-morphic, just some Higher Morality, though if this particular High-ness looks something like the Manager at Marshall Field's, sucking a Frango mint, so be it. Amen. Just tell me what you want, requests

the Mother. And how do you want it? More charitable acts? A
billion, starting now. Charitable thoughts? Harder, but of course!
Of course! I'll do the cooking, honey, I'll pay the rent. Just tell me.
Excuse me? Well, if not to you, to whom do I speak? Hello? To whom
do I have to speak around here? A higher-up? A superior? Wait? I
can wait. I've got the whole damn day.

The Husband now lies next to her on their bed, sighing. "Poor
little guy could survive all this only to be killed in a car crash at the
age of sixteen," he says.

The Mother, bargaining, considers this. "We'll take the car
crash," she says.

"What?"

"Let's Make a Deal! Sixteen is a full life! We'll take the car crash.
We'll take the car crash in front of which Carol Merrill is now
standing."

Now the Manager of Marshall Field's reappears. "To take the
surprises out is to take the life out of life," he says.

The phone rings. The Husband leaves the room.

"But I don't want these surprises," says the Mother. "Here! You
take these surprises!"

"To know the narrative in advance is to turn yourself into a
machine," the Manager continues. "What makes humans human is
precisely that they do not know the future. That is why they do the
fateful and amusing things they do: who can say how anything will
turn out? Therein lies the only hope for redemption, discovery,
and — let's be frank — fun, fun, fun! There might be things people will get away with. And not just motel towels. There might be
great illicit loves, enduring joy — or faith-shaking accidents with
farm machinery. But you have to not know in order to see what
stories your life's efforts bring you. The mystery is all."

The Mother, though shy, has grown confrontational. "Is this the
kind of bogus, random crap they teach at merchandising school?
We would like fewer surprises, fewer efforts and mysteries, thank
you. K through 8; can we just get K through 8?" It now seems like
the luckiest, most beautiful, most musical phrase she's ever heard:
K through 8 — the very lilt. The very thought.

The Manager continues, trying things out. "I mean, the whole
conception of 'the story,' of cause and effect, the whole idea that
people have a clue as to how the world works, is just a piece of

laughable metaphysical colonialism perpetrated upon the wild country of time."

Did they own a gun? The Mother begins looking through drawers.

The Husband comes back in the room and observes her. "Ha! The Great Havoc That Is the Puzzle of All Life!" he says of the Marshall Field's management policy. He has just gotten off a conference call with the insurance company and the hospital. The surgery will be Friday. "It's all just some dirty capitalist's idea of a philosophy."

"Maybe it's just a fact of narrative, and you really can't politicize it," says the Mother. It is now only the two of them.

"Whose side are you on?"

"I'm on the Baby's side."

"Are you taking notes for this?"

"No."

"You're not?"

"No. I can't. Not this! I write fiction. This isn't fiction."

"Then write nonfiction. Do a piece of journalism. Get two dollars a word."

"Then it has to be true and full of information. I'm not trained. I'm not that skilled. Plus, I have a convenient personal principle about artists' not abandoning art. One should never turn one's back on a vivid imagination. Even the whole memoir thing annoys me."

"Well, make things up but pretend they're real."

"I'm not that insured."

"You're making me nervous."

"Sweetie, darling, I'm not that good. I can't *do this.* I can do — what can I do? I can do quasi-amusing phone dialogue. I can do succinct descriptions of weather. I can do screwball outings with the family pet. Sometimes I can do those. Honey, I only do what I can. I do *the careful ironies of daydream.* I do *the marshy ideas upon which intimate life is built.* But this? Our baby with cancer? I'm sorry. My stop was two stations back. This is irony at its most gaudy and careless. This is a Hieronymus Bosch of facts and figures and blood and graphs. This is a nightmare of narrative slop. This cannot be designed. This cannot even be noted in preparation for a design —"

"We're going to need the money."

"To say nothing of the moral boundaries of pecuniary recompense in a situation such as this —"

"What if the other kidney goes? What if he needs a transplant? Where are the moral boundaries there? What are we going to do, have bake sales?"

"We can sell the house. I hate this house. It makes me crazy."

"And we'll live — where, again?"

"The Ronald McDonald place. I hear it's nice. It's the least McDonald's can do."

"You have a keen sense of justice."

"I try. What can I say?"

The Husband buries his face in his hands: "Our poor baby. How did this happen to him?" He looks over and stares at the bookcase that serves as their nightstand. "And is any one of these baby books a help?" He picks up the Leach, the Spock, the *What to Expect*. "Where in the pages or index of any of these does it say 'chemotherapy' or 'Hickman catheter' or 'renal sarcoma'? Where does it say 'carcinogenesis' or 'metastasis'? You know what these books are obsessed with? *Holding a fucking spoon*." He begins hurling the books off the nightstand and against the far wall.

"Hey," says the Mother, trying to soothe. "Hey, hey, hey." But compared with his stormy roar, her words are those of a backup singer — a Shondell, a Pip — a doo-wop ditty. Books, and now more books, continue to fly.

Take Notes.

Is "fainthearted" one word or two? Student prose has wrecked her spelling.

It's one word. Two words — faint hearted — what would that be? The name of a drag queen.

Take Notes.

In the end you suffer alone. But at the beginning you suffer with a whole lot of others. When your child has cancer you are instantly whisked away to another planet: one of bald-headed little boys. Pediatric Oncology. Peed-Onk. You wash your hands for thirty seconds in antibacterial soap before you are allowed to enter through the swinging doors. You put paper slippers on your shoes. You keep your voice down. "Almost all the children are boys," one of the nurses says. "No one knows why. It's been documented, but a lot of people out there still don't realize it." The little boys are all from sweet-sounding places, Janesville and Appleton — little heartland towns with giant landfills, agricultural runoff, paper factories, Joe McCarthy's grave. (Alone a site of great toxicity, thinks the Mother. The soil should be tested.)

All the bald little boys look like brothers. They wheel their IVs up and down the single corridor of Peed-Onk. Some of the lively ones, feeling good for a day, ride the lower bars of their IVs while their large, cheerful mothers whizz them along the halls. *Wheee!*

The Mother does not feel large and cheerful. In her mind she is scathing, acid-tongued, wraith-thin, and chain-smoking out on a fire escape somewhere. Below her lie the gentle undulations of the Midwest, with all its aspirations to be — to be what? To be Long Island. How it has succeeded! Strip mall upon strip mall. Lurid water, poisoned potatoes. The Mother drags deeply, blowing clouds of smoke out over the disfigured cornfields. When a baby gets cancer, it seems stupid ever to have given up smoking. When a baby gets cancer, you think, Whom are we kidding? Let's all light up. When a baby gets cancer, you think, Who came up with *this* idea? What celestial abandon gave rise to *this*? Pour me a drink, so I can refuse to toast.

The Mother does not know how to be one of these other mothers, with their blond hair and sweatpants and sneakers and determined pleasantness. She does not think that she can be anything similar. She does not feel remotely like them. She knows, for instance, too many people in Greenwich Village. She mail-orders oysters and tiramisù from a shop in SoHo. She is close friends with four actual homosexuals. Her husband is asking her to Take Notes.

Where do these women get their sweatpants? She will find out.

She will start, perhaps, with the costume and work from there.

She will live according to the bromides: Take one day at a time. Take a positive attitude. *Take a hike!* She wishes that there were more interesting things that were useful and true, but it seems now that it's only the boring things that are useful and true. *One day at a time.* And *At least we have our health.* How ordinary. How obvious. One day at a time: you need a brain for that?

*

While the Surgeon is fine-boned, regal, and laconic — they have correctly guessed his game to be doubles — there is a bit of the mad, over-caffeinated scientist to the Oncologist. He speaks quickly. He knows a lot of studies and numbers. He can do the math. Good! Someone should be able to do the math! "It's a fast but wimpy tumor," he explains. "It typically metastasizes to the lung." He rattles off some numbers, time frames, risk statistics. Fast but wimpy: the Mother tries to imagine this combination of traits, tries to think and think, and can only come up with Claudia Osk from the fourth grade, who blushed and almost wept when called on in class but in gym could outrun everyone in the quarter-mile, fire-door-to-fence dash. The Mother thinks now of this tumor as Claudia Osk. They are going to get Claudia Osk, make her sorry. All right! Claudia Osk must die. Though it has never been mentioned before, it now seems clear that Claudia Osk should have died long ago. Who was she, anyway? So conceited, not letting anyone beat her in a race. Well, hey, hey, hey — don't look now, Claudia!

The Husband nudges her. "Are you listening?"

"The chances of this happening even just to one kidney are one in fifteen thousand. Now, given all these other factors, the chances on the second kidney are about one in eight."

"One in eight," says the Husband. "Not bad. As long as it's not one in fifteen thousand."

The Mother studies the trees and fish along the ceiling's edge in the Save the Planet wallpaper border. Save the Planet. Yes! But the windows in this very building don't open, and diesel fumes are leaking into the ventilating system, near which, outside, a delivery truck is parked. The air is nauseous and stale.

"Really," the Oncologist is saying, "of all the cancers he could get, this is probably one of the best."

"We win," says the Mother.

"'Best,' I know, hardly seems the right word. Look, you two probably need to get some rest. We'll see how the surgery and histology go. Then we'll start with chemo the week following. A little light chemo: vincristine and —"

"Vincristine?" interrupts the Mother. "Wine of Christ?"

"The names are strange, I know. The other one we use is acti-nomycin-D. Sometimes called dactinomycin. People move the *D* around to the front."

"They move the *D* around to the front," repeats the Mother.

"Yup," the Oncologist says. "I don't know why, they just do!"

"Christ didn't survive his wine," says the Husband.

"But of course he did," says the Oncologist and nods toward the Baby, who has now found a cupboard full of hospital linens and bandages and is yanking them all out onto the floor. "I'll see you guys tomorrow, after the surgery." And with that the Oncologist leaves.

"Or, rather, Christ was his wine," mumbles the Husband. Everything he knows about the New Testament he has gleaned from the soundtrack of *Godspell.* "His blood was the wine. What a great beverage idea."

"A little light chemo. Don't you like that one?" says the Mother. "*Eine kleine* dactinomycin. I'd like to see Mozart write that one up for a big wad o' cash."

"Come here, honey," the Husband says to the Baby, who has now pulled off both his shoes.

"It's bad enough when they refer to medical science as an inexact science," says the Mother. "But when they start referring to it as an art I get extremely nervous."

"Yeah. If we wanted art, Doc, we'd go to an art museum." The Husband picks up the Baby. "You're an artist," he says to the Mother with the taint of accusation in his voice. "They probably think you find creativity reassuring."

The Mother sighs. "I just find it inevitable. Let's go get something to eat." And so they take the elevator to the cafeteria, where there is a high chair, and where, not noticing, they all eat a lot of apples with the price tags still on them.

Because his surgery is not until tomorrow, the Baby likes the hospital. He likes the long corridors, down which he can run. He likes everything on wheels. The flower carts in the lobby! ("Please keep your boy away from the flowers," says the vender. "We'll buy the whole display," snaps the Mother, adding, "Actual children in a children's hospital — unbelievable, isn't it?") The Baby likes the other little boys. Places to go! People to see! Rooms to wander into! There is Intensive Care. There is the Trauma Unit. The Baby smiles and waves. What a little Cancer Personality! Bandaged citizens smile and wave back. In Peed-Onk there are the bald little boys to play with. Joey, Eric, Tim, Mort, and Tod. (Mort! Tod!) There is the four-year-old, Ned, holding his little deflated rubber ball, the one with the intriguing curling hose. The Baby wants to play with it. "It's mine, leave it alone," says Ned. "Tell the baby to leave it alone."

"Baby, you've got to share," says the Mother from a chair some feet away.

Suddenly, from down near the Tiny Tim Lounge, comes Ned's mother, large and blond and sweatpanted. "Stop that! Stop it!" she cries out, dashing toward the Baby and Ned and pushing the Baby away. "Don't touch that!" she barks at the Baby, who is only a baby and bursts into tears because he has never been yelled at like this before.

Ned's mom glares at everyone. "This is drawing fluid from Neddy's liver!" She pats at the rubber thing and starts to cry a little.

"Oh, my God," says the Mother. She comforts the Baby, who is also crying. She and Ned, the only dry-eyed people, look at each other. "I'm so sorry," she says to Ned and then to his mother. "I'm so stupid. I thought they were squabbling over a toy."

"It does look like a toy," agrees Ned. He smiles. He is an angel. All the little boys are angels. Total, sweet, bald little angels, and now God is trying to get them back for himself. Who are they, mere mortal women, in the face of this, this powerful and overwhelming and inscrutable thing, God's will? They are the mothers, that's who. You can't have him! they shout every day. You dirty old man! *Get out of here! Hands off!*

"I'm so sorry," says the Mother again. "I didn't know."

Ned's mother smiles vaguely. "Of course you didn't know," she says, and walks back to the Tiny Tim Lounge.

The Tiny Tim Lounge is a little sitting area at the end of the Peed-Onk corridor. There are two small sofas, a table, a rocking chair, a television, and a VCR. There are various videos: *Speed, Dune, Star Wars.* On one of the lounge walls there is a gold plaque with the musician Tiny Tim's name on it: years ago, his son was treated at this hospital, and so he donated money for this lounge. It is a cramped little lounge, which one suspects would be larger if Tiny Tim's son had actually lived. Instead, he died here, at this hospital, and now there is this tiny room which is part gratitude, part generosity, part *Fuck you.*

Sifting through the videocassettes, the Mother wonders what science fiction could begin to compete with the science fiction of cancer itself: a tumor, with its differentiated muscle and bone cells, a clump of wild nothing and its mad, ambitious desire to be something — something inside you, instead of you, another organism but with a monster's architecture, a demon's sabotage and chaos. Think of leukemia, a tumor diabolically taking liquid form, the better to swim about incognito in the blood. George Lucas, direct that!

Sitting with the other parents in the Tiny Tim Lounge, the night before the surgery, having put the Baby to bed in his high steel crib two rooms down, the Mother begins to hear the stories: leukemia in kindergarten, sarcomas in Little League, neuroblastomas discovered at summer camp. *Eric slid into third base, but then the scrape didn't heal.* The parents pat one another's forearms and speak of other children's hospitals as if they were resorts. "You were at St. Jude's last winter? So were we. What did you think of it? We loved the staff." Jobs have been quit, marriages hacked up, bank accounts ravaged; the parents have seemingly endured the unendurable. They speak not of the *possibility* of comas brought on by the chemo but of the *number* of them. "He was in his first coma last July," says Ned's mother. "It was a scary time, but we pulled through."

Pulling through is what people do around here. There is a kind of bravery in their lives that isn't bravery at all. It is automatic, unflinching, a mix of man and machine, consuming and unquestionable obligation meeting illness move for move in a giant, even-Steven game of chess: an unending round of something that looks like shadowboxing — though between love and death, which is the shadow? "Everyone admires us for our courage," says one man. "They have no idea what they're talking about."

I could get out of here, thinks the Mother. I could just get on a bus and go, never come back. Change my name. A kind of witness relocation thing.

"Courage requires options," the man adds.

The Baby might be better off.

"There are options," says a woman with a thick suede headband. "You could give up. You could fall apart."

"No, you can't. Nobody does. I've never seen it," says the man. "Well, not *really* fall apart." Then the lounge is quiet. Over the VCR someone has taped the fortune from a fortune cookie. *Optimism,* it says, *is what allows a teakettle to sing though up to its neck in hot water.* Underneath, someone else has taped a clipping from a summer horoscope. *Cancer rules!* it says. Who would tape this up? Somebody's twelve-year-old brother. One of the fathers — Joey's father — gets up and tears them both off, makes a small wad in his fist.

There is some rustling of magazine pages.

The Mother clears her throat. "Tiny Tim forgot the wet bar," she says.

Ned, who is still up, comes out of his room and down the corridor, whose lights dim at nine. Standing next to the Mother's chair, he says to her, "Where are you from? What is wrong with your baby?"

In the little room that is theirs, she sleeps fitfully in her sweatpants, occasionally leaping up to check on the Baby. This is what the sweatpants are for: leaping. In case of fire. In case of anything. In case the difference between day and night starts to dissolve and there is no difference at all so why pretend. In the cot beside her the Husband, who has taken a sleeping pill, is snoring loudly, his arms folded about his head in a kind of origami. How could either of them have stayed back at the house, with its empty high chair and empty crib? Occasionally the Baby wakes and cries out, and she bolts up, goes to him, rubs his back, rearranges the linens. The clock on the metal dresser shows that it is five after three. Then twenty to five. And then it is really morning, the beginning of this day, Nephrectomy Day. Will she be glad when it's over, or barely alive, or both? Each day of this week has arrived huge, empty, and unknown, like a spaceship, and this one especially is lit an incandescent gray.

"He'll need to put this on," says John, one of the nurses, bright and early, handing the Mother a thin greenish garment with roses and teddy bears printed on it. A wave of nausea hits her: this smock, she thinks, will soon be splattered with — with what?

The Baby is awake but drowsy. She lifts off his pajamas. "Don't forget, *bubeleh,*" she whispers, undressing and dressing him. "We will be with you every moment, every step. When you think you are asleep and floating off far away from everybody, Mommy will still be there." If she hasn't fled on a bus. "Mommy will take care of you. And Daddy too." She hopes the Baby does not detect her own fear and uncertainty, which she must hide from him, like a limp. He is hungry, not having been allowed to eat, and he is no longer amused by this new place but worried about its hardships. Oh, my baby, she thinks. And the room starts to swim a little. The Husband comes in to take over. "Take a break," he says to her. "I'll walk him around for five minutes."

She leaves but doesn't know where to go. In the hallway she is approached by a kind of social worker, a customer relations person, who had given them a video to watch about the anesthesia: how the parent accompanies the child into the operating room, and how gently, nicely the drugs are administered.

"Did you watch the video?"

"Yes," says the Mother.

"Wasn't it helpful?"

"I don't know," says the Mother.

"Do you have any questions?" asks the video woman. *Do you have any questions?* asked of someone who has recently landed in this fearful, alien place seems to the Mother an absurd and amazing little courtesy. The very specificity of a question would give the lie to the overwhelming strangeness of everything around her.

"Not right now," says the Mother. "Right now I think I'm just going to go to the bathroom."

When she comes back to the Baby's room, everyone is there: the Surgeon, the Anesthesiologist, all the nurses, the social worker. In their blue caps and scrubs they look like a clutch of forget-me-nots, and forget them who could? The Baby, in his little teddy-bear smock, seems cold and scared. He reaches out and the Mother lifts him from the Husband's arms, rubs his back to warm him.

"Well, it's time!" says the Surgeon, forcing a smile.

"Shall we go?" says the Anesthesiologist.

What follows is a blur of obedience and bright lights. They take an elevator down to a big concrete room, the anteroom, the green-room, the backstage of the operating room. Lining the walls are long shelves full of blue surgical outfits. "Children often become afraid of the color blue," one of the nurses says. But of course. Of course! "Now, which one of you would like to come into the operating room for the anesthesia?"

"I will," says the Mother.

"Are you sure?" says the Husband.

"Yup." She kisses the Baby's hair. Mr. Curlyhead people keep calling him here, and it seems both rude and nice. Women look admiringly at his long lashes and exclaim, "Always the boys! Always the boys!"

Two surgical nurses put a blue smock and a blue cotton cap on the Mother. The Baby finds this funny and keeps pulling at the cap. "This way," says another nurse, and the Mother follows. "Just put the Baby down on the table."

In the video, the mother holds the baby and fumes from the mask are gently waved under the baby's nose until he falls asleep. Now, out of view of camera or social worker, the Anesthesiologist is anxious to get this under way and not let too much gas leak out into the room generally. The occupational hazard of this, his chosen profession, is gas exposure and nerve damage, and it has started to worry him. No doubt he frets about it to his wife every night. Now he turns the gas on and quickly clamps the plastic mouthpiece over the Baby's cheeks and lips.

The Baby is startled. The Mother is startled. The Baby starts to scream and redden behind the plastic, but he cannot be heard. He thrashes. "Tell him it's okay," says the nurse to the Mother.

Okay? "It's okay," repeats the Mother, holding his hand, but she knows he can tell it's not okay, because he can see that not only is she still wearing that stupid paper cap but her words are mechanical and swallowed, and she is biting her lips to keep them from trembling. Panicked, he attempts to sit, he cannot breathe, his arms reach up. *Bye-bye, outside.* And then, quite quickly, his eyes shut, he untenses and has fallen not into sleep but aside to sleep, an odd, kidnapping kind of sleep, his terror now hidden someplace deep inside him.

"How did it go?" asks the social worker, waiting in the concrete outer room. The Mother is hysterical. A nurse has ushered her out.

"It wasn't at all like the filmstrip!" she cries. "It wasn't like the filmstrip at all!"

"The filmstrip? You mean the video?" asks the social worker.

"It wasn't like that at all! It was brutal and unforgivable."

"Why, that's terrible," she says, her role now no longer misinformational but janitorial, and she touches the Mother's arm. The Mother shakes her off and goes to find the Husband.

She finds him in the large mulberry Surgery Lounge, where he has been taken and where there is free hot chocolate in small plastic-foam cups. Red cellophane garlands festoon the doorways. She has totally forgotten it is as close to Christmas as this. A pianist in the corner is playing "Carol of the Bells," and it sounds not only unfestive but scary, like the theme from *The Exorcist.*

There is a giant clock on the far wall. It is a kind of porthole into the operating room, a way of assessing the Baby's ordeal: forty-five minutes for the Hickman implant; two and a half hours for the nephrectomy. And then, after that, three months of chemotherapy. The magazine on her lap stays open at a ruby-hued perfume ad.

"Still not taking notes," says the Husband.

"Nope."

"You know, in a way, this is the kind of thing you've *always* written about."

"You are really something, you know that? This is life. This isn't a 'kind of thing.'"

"But this is the kind of thing that fiction is: it's the unlivable life, the strange room tacked on to the house, the extra moon that is circling the earth unbeknownst to science."

"I told you that."

"I'm quoting you."

She looks at her watch, thinking of the Baby. "How long has it been?"

"Not long. Too long. In the end, those're the same things."

"What do you suppose is happening to him right this second?"

Infection? Slipping knives? "I don't know. But you know what? I've gotta go. I've gotta just walk a bit." The Husband gets up, walks around the lounge, then comes back and sits down.

The synapses between the minutes are unswimmable. An hour is thick as fudge. The Mother feels depleted; she is a string of empty tin cans attached by wire, something a goat would sniff and chew, something now and then enlivened by a jolt of electricity.

She hears their names being called over the intercom. "Yes? Yes?" She stands up quickly. Her voice has flown out before her, an exhalation of birds. The piano music has stopped. The pianist is gone. She and the Husband approach the main desk, where a man looks up at them and smiles. Before him is a Xeroxed list of patients' names. "That's our little boy right there," says the Mother, seeing the Baby's name on the list and pointing at it. "Is there some word? Is everything okay?"

"Yes," says the man. "Your boy is doing fine. They've just finished with the catheter and they are moving on to the kidney."

"But it's been two hours already! Oh, my God, did something go wrong, what happened, what went wrong?"

"Did something go wrong?" The Husband tugs at his collar.

"Not really. It just took longer than they expected. I'm told everything is fine. They wanted you to know."

"Thank you," says the Husband. They turn and walk back toward where they were sitting.

"I'm not going to make it," sighs the Mother, sinking into a fake leather chair shaped somewhat like a baseball mitt. "But before I go I'm taking half this hospital out with me."

"Do you want some coffee?" asks the Husband.

"I don't know," says the Mother. "No, I guess not. No. Do you?"

"Nah, I don't either, I guess," he says.

"Would you like part of an orange?"

"Oh, maybe, I guess, if you're having one." She takes a temple orange from her purse and just sits there peeling its difficult skin, the flesh rupturing beneath her fingers, the juice trickling down her hands, stinging the hangnails. She and the Husband chew and swallow, discreetly spit the seeds into Kleenex, and read from photocopies of the latest medical research which they begged from the intern. They read, and underline, and sigh and close their eyes, and after some time the surgery is over. A nurse from Peed-Onk comes down to tell them.

"Your little boy's in recovery right now. He's doing well. You can see him in about fifteen minutes."

How can it be described? How can any of it be described? The trip and the story of the trip are always two different things. The narrator is the one who has stayed home but then, afterward, presses her mouth upon the traveler's mouth, in order to make the mouth work, to make the mouth say, say, say. One cannot go to a place and speak of it, one cannot both see and say, not really. One can go, and upon returning make a lot of hand motions and indications with the arms. The mouth itself, working at the speed of light, at the eye's instructions, is necessarily struck still; so fast, so much to report, it hangs open and dumb as a gutted bell. All that unsayable life! That's where the narrator comes in. The narrator comes with her kisses and mimicry and tidying up. The narrator comes and makes a slow, fake song of the mouth's eager devastation.

It is a horror and a miracle to see him. He is lying in his crib in his room, tubed up, splayed like a boy on a cross, his arms stiffened into cardboard "no-no"s so that he cannot yank out the tubes. There is the bladder catheter, the nasal-gastric tube, and the Hickman, which, beneath the skin, is plugged into his jugular, then popped out his chest wall and capped with a long plastic cap. There is a large bandage taped over his abdomen. Groggy, on a morphine drip, still he is able to look at her when, maneuvering through all the vinyl wiring, she leans to hold him, and when she does he begins to cry, but cry silently, without motion or noise. She has never seen a baby cry without motion or noise. It is the crying of an old person: silent, beyond opinion, shattered. In someone so tiny, it is frightening and unnatural. She wants to pick up the Baby and run — out of there, out of there. She wants to whip out a gun: *No-nos, eh? This whole thing is what I call a no-no.* "Don't you touch him!" she wants to shout at the surgeons and the needle nurses. "Not anymore! No more! No more!" She would crawl up and lie beside him in the crib if she could. But instead, because of all his intricate wiring, she must lean and cuddle, sing to him, songs of peril and flight: "We gotta get out of this place, if it's the last thing we ever do. We gotta get out of this place. Baby, there's a better life for me and for you."

Very 1967. She was eleven then, and impressionable.

The Baby looks at her, pleadingly, his arms outstretched in surrender. To where? Where is there to go? Take me! Take me!

That night, post-op night, the Mother and the Husband lie afloat in their cots. A fluorescent lamp near the crib is kept on in the dark. The Baby breathes evenly but thinly in his drugged sleep. The morphine in its first flooding doses apparently makes him feel as if he were falling backward — or so the Mother has been told — and it causes the Baby to jerk, to catch himself over and over, as if he were being dropped from a tree. "Is this right? Isn't there something that should be done?" The nurses come in hourly, different ones — the night shifts seem strangely short and frequent. If the

Baby stirs or frets, the nurses give him more morphine through the Hickman catheter, then leave to tend to other patients. The Mother rises to check on him herself in the low light. There is gurgling from the clear plastic suction tube coming out of his mouth. Brownish clumps have collected in the tube. What is going on? The Mother rings for the nurse. Is it Renee or Sarah or Darcy? She's forgotten.

"What, what is it?" murmurs the Husband, waking up.

"Something is wrong," says the Mother. "It looks like blood in his N-G tube."

"What?" The Husband gets out of bed. He too is wearing sweat-pants.

The nurse — Valerie — pushes open the heavy door to the room and enters quickly. "Everything okay?"

"There's something wrong here. The tube is sucking blood out of his stomach. It looks like it may have perforated his stomach and now he's bleeding internally. Look!"

Valerie is a saint, but her voice is the standard hospital saint voice: an infuriating, pharmaceutical calm. It says, *Everything is normal here. Death is normal. Pain is normal. Nothing is abnormal. So there is nothing to get excited about.* "Well, now, let's see." She holds up the plastic tube and tries to see inside it. "Hmm," she says. "I'll call the attending physician."

Because this is a research and teaching hospital, all the regular doctors are at home sleeping in their Mission-style beds. Tonight, as is apparently the case every weekend night, the attending physician is a medical student. He looks fifteen. The authority he attempts to convey he cannot remotely inhabit. He is not even in the same building with it. He shakes everyone's hand, then strokes his chin, a gesture no doubt gleaned from some piece of dinner theater his parents took him to once. As if there were an actual beard on that chin! As if beard growth on that chin were even possible! *Our Town! Kiss Me Kate! Barefoot in the Park!* He is attempting to convince if not to impress.

"We're in trouble," the Mother whispers to the Husband. She is tired, tired of young people grubbing for grades. "We've got Dr. Kiss Me Kate here."

The Husband looks at her blankly, a mixture of disorientation and divorce.

The medical student holds the tubing in his hands. "I don't really see anything," he says.

He flunks! "You don't?" The Mother shoves her way in, holds the clear tubing in both hands. "That," she says. "Right here and here." Just this past semester she said to one of her own students, "If you don't see how this essay is better than that one, then I want you to just go out into the hallway and stand there until you do." Is it important to keep one's voice down? The Baby stays asleep. He is drugged and dreaming, far away.

"Hmm," says the medical student. "Perhaps there's a little irritation in the stomach."

"A little irritation?" The Mother grows furious. "This is blood. These are clumps and clots. This stupid thing is sucking the life right out of him!" Life! She is starting to cry.

They turn off the suction and bring in antacids, which they feed into the Baby through the tube. Then they turn the suction on again. This time on low.

"What was it on before?" asks the Husband.

"High," says Valerie. "Doctor's orders, though I don't know why. I don't know why these doctors do a lot of the things they do."

"Maybe they're — not all that bright?" suggests the Mother. She is feeling relief and rage simultaneously: there is a feeling of prayer and litigation in the air. Yet essentially she is grateful. Isn't she? She thinks she is. And still, and still: look at all the things you have to do to protect a child, a hospital merely an intensification of life's cruel obstacle course.

The Surgeon comes to visit on Saturday morning. He steps in and nods at the Baby, who is awake but glazed from the morphine, his eyes two dark, unseeing grapes. "The boy looks fine," he announces. He peeks under the Baby's bandage. "The stitches look good," he says. The Baby's abdomen is stitched all the way across, like a baseball. "And the other kidney, when we looked at it yesterday face to face, looked fine. We'll try to wean him off the morphine a little, and see how he's doing on Monday."

"Is he going to be okay?"

"The boy? The boy is going to be fine," he says, then taps her stiffly on the shoulder. "Now, you take care. It's Saturday. Drink a little wine."

*

Over the weekend, while the Baby sleeps, the Mother and the Husband sit together in the Tiny Tim Lounge. The Husband is restless and makes cafeteria and sundry runs, running errands for everyone. In his absence, the other parents regale her further with their sagas. Pediatric cancer and chemo stories: the children's amputations, blood poisoning, teeth flaking like shale, the learning delays and disabilities caused by chemo frying the young, budding brain. But strangely optimistic codas are tacked on: endings as stiff and loopy as carpenter's lace, crisp and empty as lettuce, reticulate as a net — ah, words. "After all that business with the tutor, he's better now, and fitted with new incisors by my wife's cousin's husband, who did dental school in two and a half years, if you can believe that. We hope for the best. We take things as they come. Life is hard."

"Life's a big problem," agrees the Mother. Part of her welcomes and invites all their tales. In the few long days since this nightmare began, part of her has become addicted to disaster and war stories. She only wants to hear about the sadness and emergencies of others. They are the only situations that can join hands with her own; everything else bounces off her shiny shield of resentment and unsympathy. Nothing else can even stay in her brain. From this, no doubt, the philistine world is made, or should one say recruited? Together the parents huddle all day in the Tiny Tim Lounge — no need to watch *Oprah*. They leave *Oprah* in the dust. *Oprah* has nothing on them. They chat matter-of-factly, then fall silent and watch *Dune* or *Star Wars,* in which there are bright and shiny robots, whom the Mother now sees not as robots at all but as human beings who have had terrible things happen to them.

Some of their friends visit with stuffed animals and soft "Looking good"s for the dozing baby, though the room is way past the stuffed animal limit. The Mother arranges, once more, a plateful of Mint Milano cookies and cups of takeout coffee for guests. All her nutso pals stop by — the two on Prozac, the one obsessed with the word "penis" in the word "happiness," the one who recently had her hair foiled green. "Your friends put the *de* in *fin de siècle*," says the Husband. Overheard, or recorded, all marital conversation sounds as if someone must be joking, though usually no one is.

She loves her friends, especially loves them for coming, since there are times they all fight and don't speak for weeks. Is this friendship? For now and here, it must do and is, and is, she swears it is. For one, they never offer impromptu spiritual lectures about death, how it is part of life, its natural ebb and flow, how we all must accept that, or other such utterances that make her want to scratch out somebody's eyes. Like true friends, they take no hardy or elegant stance loosely choreographed from some broad perspective. They get right in there and mutter "Jesus Christ!" and shake their heads. Plus, they are the only people who will not only laugh at her stupid jokes but offer up stupid ones of their own. *What do you get when you cross Tiny Tim with a pit bull?* A child's illness is a strain on the mind. They know how to laugh in a flutey, desperate way — unlike the people who are more her husband's friends and who seem just to deepen their sorrowful gazes, nodding their heads in Sympathy. How Exiling and Estranging are everybody's Sympathetic Expressions! When anyone laughs, she thinks, Okay. Hooray! A buddy. In disaster as in show business.

Nurses come and go; their chirpy voices both startle and soothe. Some of the other Peed-Onk parents stick their heads in to see how the Baby is and offer encouragement.

Green Hair scratches her head: "Everyone's so friendly here. Is there someone in this place who isn't doing all this airy, scripted optimism — or are people like that the only people here?"

"It's Modern Middle Medicine meets the Modern Middle Family," says the Husband. "In the Modern Middle West."

Someone has brought in takeout lo mein, and they all eat it out in the hall by the elevators.

Parents are allowed use of the Courtesy Line.

"You've got to have a second child," says a friend on the phone, a friend from out of town. "An heir and a spare. That's what we did. We had another child to insure we wouldn't off ourselves if we lost our first."

"Really?"

"I'm serious."

"A formal suicide? Wouldn't you just drink yourself into a life-long stupor and let it go at that?"

"Nope. I knew how I would do it even. For a while, until our second came along, I had it all planned."

"You did? What did you plan?"

"I can't go into too much detail, because — hi, honey! — the kids are here now in the room. But I'll spell out the general idea: R-O-P-E."

Sunday evening she goes and sinks down on the sofa in the Tiny Tim Lounge next to Frank, Joey's father. He is a short, stocky man with the currentless, flat-lined look behind the eyes that all the parents eventually get here. He has shaved his head bald in solidarity with his son. His little boy has been battling cancer for five years. It is now in the liver, and the rumor around the corridor is that Joey has three weeks to live. She knows that Joey's mother, Roseanne, left Frank years ago, two years into the cancer, and has remarried and had another child, a girl named Brittany. The Mother sees Roseanne here sometimes with her new life — the cute little girl and the new full-haired husband, who will never be so maniacally and debilitatingly obsessed with Joey's illness as Frank, her first husband, is. Roseanne comes to visit Joey, to say hello and now goodbye, but she is not Joey's main man. Frank is.

Frank is full of stories — about the doctors, about the food, about the nurses, about Joey. Joey, affectless from his meds, sometimes leaves his room and comes out to watch TV in his bathrobe. He is jaundiced and bald, and though he is nine he looks no older than six. Frank has devoted the last four and a half years to saving Joey's life. When the cancer was first diagnosed, the doctors gave Joey a 20 percent chance of living six more months. Now here it is almost five years later, and Joey's still here. It is all due to Frank, who early on quit his job as vice president of a consulting firm in order to commit himself totally to his son. He is proud of everything he's given up and done, but he is tired. Part of him now really believes that things are coming to a close, that this is the end. He says this without tears. There are no more tears.

"You have probably been through more than anyone else on this corridor," says the Mother.

"I could tell you stories," he says. There is a sour odor between them, and she realizes that neither of them has bathed for days.

"Tell me one. Tell me the worst one." She knows he hates his ex-wife and hates her new husband even more.

"The worst? They're all the worst. Here's one: one morning I went out for breakfast with my buddy — it was the only time I'd left

Joey alone ever, left him for two hours is all — and when I came back his N-G tube was full of blood. They had the suction on too high, and it was sucking the guts right out of him."

"Oh, my God. That just happened to us," said the Mother.

"It did?"

"Friday night."

"You're kidding. They let that happen again? I gave them such a chewing-out about that!"

"I guess our luck is not so good. We get your very worst story on the second night we're here."

"It's not a bad place, though."

"It's not?"

"Naw. I've seen worse. I've taken Joey everywhere."

"He seems very strong." Truth is, at this point Joey seems like a zombie and frightens her.

"Joey's a fucking genius. A biological genius. They'd given him six months, remember."

The Mother nods.

"Six months is not very long," says Frank. "Six months is nothing. He was four and a half years old."

All the words are like blows. She feels flooded with affection and mourning for this man. She looks away, out the window, out past the hospital parking lot, up toward the black marbled sky and the electric eyelash of the moon. "And now he's nine," she says. "You're his hero."

"And he's mine," says Frank, though the fatigue in his voice seems to overwhelm him. "He'll be that forever. Excuse me," he says. "I've got to go check. His breathing hasn't been good. Excuse me."

"Good news and bad," says the Oncologist on Monday. He has knocked, entered the room, and now stands there. Their cots are unmade. One wastebasket is overflowing with coffee cups. "We've got the pathologist's report. The bad news is that the kidney they removed had certain lesions, called 'rests,' which are associated with a higher risk for disease in the other kidney. The good news is that the tumor is Stage I, regular cell structure, and under five hundred grams, which qualifies you for a national experiment in which chemotherapy isn't done but your boy is simply monitored with ultrasound. It's not all that risky, given that the patient's watched closely, but here is the literature on it. There are forms to sign, if you decide to do that. Read all this and we can discuss it further. You have to decide within four days."

Lesions? Rests? They dry up and scatter like M&Ms on the floor. All she hears is the part about no chemo. Another sigh of relief rises up in her and spills out. In a life where there is only the bearable and the unbearable, a sigh of relief is an ecstasy.

"No chemo?" says the husband. "Do you recommend that?"

The Oncologist shrugs. What casual gestures these doctors are permitted! "I know chemo. I like chemo," says the Oncologist. "But this is for you to decide. It depends how you feel."

The Husband leans forward. "But don't you think that now that we have the upper hand with this thing we should keep going? Shouldn't we stomp on it, beat it, smash it to death with the chemo?"

The Mother swats him angrily and hard. "Honey, you're delirious!" She whispers, but it comes out as a hiss. "This is our lucky break." Then she adds gently, "We don't want the Baby to have chemo."

The Husband turns back to the Oncologist. "What do you think?"

"It could be," he says, shrugging. "It could be that this is your lucky break. But you won't know for sure for five years."

The Husband turns back to the Mother. "Okay," he says. "Okay."

The Baby grows happier and strong. He begins to move and sit and eat. Wednesday morning they are allowed to leave, and to leave without chemo. The Oncologist looks a little nervous. "Are you nervous about this?" asks the Mother.

"Of course I'm nervous." But he shrugs and doesn't look that nervous. "See you in six weeks for the ultrasound," he says, then he waves and leaves, looking at his big black shoes.

The Baby smiles, even toddles around a little, the sun bursting through the clouds, an angel chorus crescendoing. Nurses arrive. The Hickman is taken out of the Baby's neck and chest, antibiotic lotion is dispensed. The Mother packs up their bags. The baby sucks on a bottle of juice and does not cry.

"No chemo?" says one of the nurses. "Not even a little chemo?"

"We're doing watch-and-wait," says the Mother.

The other parents look envious but concerned. They have never seen any child get out of there with his hair and white blood cells intact.

"Will you be okay?" says Ned's mother.

"The worry's going to kill us," says the Husband.

"But if all we have to do is worry," chides the Mother, "every day for a hundred years, it'll be easy. It'll be nothing. I'll take all the worry in the world if it wards off the thing itself."

"That's right," says Ned's mother. "Compared to everything else, compared to all the actual events, the worry is nothing."

The Husband shakes his head. "I'm such an amateur," he moans.

"You're both doing admirably," says the other mother. "Your baby's lucky, and I wish you all the best."

The Husband shakes her hand warmly. "Thank you," he says. "You've been wonderful."

Another mother, the mother of Eric, comes up to them. "It's all very hard," she says, her head cocked to one side. "But there's a lot of collateral beauty along the way."

Collateral beauty? Who is entitled to such a thing? A child is ill. No one is entitled to any collateral beauty.

"Thank you," says the Husband.

Joey's father, Frank, comes up and embraces them both. "It's a journey," he says. He chucks the Baby on the chin. "Good luck, little man."

"Yes, thank you so much," says the Mother. "We hope things go well with Joey." She knows that Joey had a hard, terrible night.

Frank shrugs and steps back. "Gotta go," he says. "Goodbye!"

"Bye," she says, and then he is gone. She bites the inside of her lip, a bit tearily, then bends down to pick up the diaper bag, which is now stuffed with little animals; helium balloons are tied to its zipper. Shouldering the thing, the Mother feels she has just won a prize. All the parents have now vanished down the hall in the opposite direction. The Husband moves close. With one arm he takes the Baby from her; with the other he rubs her back. He can see she is starting to get weepy.

"Aren't these people nice? Don't you feel better hearing about their lives?" he asks.

Why does he do this, form clubs all the time — why does even this society of suffering soothe him? When it comes to death and dying, perhaps someone in this family ought to be more of a snob.

"All these nice people with their brave stories," he continues as they make their way toward the elevator bank, waving goodbye to the nursing staff as they go, even the Baby waving shyly. *Bye-bye! Bye-bye!* "Don't you feel consoled, knowing we're all in the same boat, that we're all in this together?"

But who on earth would want to be in this boat? the Mother thinks. This boat is a nightmare boat. Look where it goes: to a silver-and-white room, where, just before your eyesight and hearing and your ability to touch or be touched disappear entirely, you must watch your child die.

Rope! Bring on the rope!

"Let's make our own way," says the Mother, "and not in this boat."

Woman Overboard! She takes the Baby back from the Husband, cups the Baby's cheek in her hand, kisses his brow and then, quickly, his flowery mouth. The Baby's heart — she can hear it — drums with life. "For as long as I live," says the Mother, pressing the elevator button — up or down, everyone in the end has to leave this way — "I never want to see any of these people again."

There are the notes.

Now, where is the money?

MEG WOLITZER

Tea at the House

FROM PLOUGHSHARES

I WAS BORN on the grounds of the Mount Mohonk Hospital for the Insane, where my father was chief of psychiatry, and because of this I grew accustomed to the sounds of misery before I went to sleep at night. I would lie in bed upstairs in my family's house, which was situated one hundred yards from the main building, and after lights out I would hear shrieking and weeping as though animals were being slaughtered. No, no, it was nothing like that, my father assured me, coming into the bedroom. These patients were in psychic anguish, he said, and no one was laying a hand on them.

Now it has been nearly fifty years since I lived there, and while the hospital still exists, its nurses now wear street clothes, the bars have been sandblasted off all its windows, and "Insane" has long been extinguished from its name. But back when I lived on the grounds of the hospital with my father and mother, the gates were pad-locked at dusk by an aging groundskeeper, and those nighttime shrieks echoed through the surrounding hills, frightening the lo-cals and waking the deer.

"Is anyone being beaten?" I asked my father before bed.

"No one is being beaten," he answered.

"Is anyone being whipped?"

"No one is being whipped."

"Slapped?"

"No one is being slapped."

"Throttled?"

"Where did you learn *that* word?" asked my father. And so it went, this bedtime ritual, and though many of the patients stayed up weeping and howling throughout the long night, I was able to sleep the fluent sleep of children. To the patients, this place was a hospital, a prison, but to me it was home.

It was my father who decided that I would become a doctor. He had read in one of his medical journals that an unprecedented number of girls were entering the field of medicine, and there were even photographs accompanying the article, as if anyone needed proof: a fleet of bulky young women in white coats and harlequin glasses, standing behind an autoclave. The idea of me, a seven-year-old girl who pasted pictures of iceboxes and hairstyles into scrapbooks, eventually transforming into one of these women seemed a reach. But my mother had been told she could bear no more children. This meant that there would never be a son, so one morning my father walked into my room, sighed, then stretched the jaws of a stethoscope around my neck. For a brief moment, thinking it was jewelry, I picked up the silver disk at the bottom and held it between my fingers like a religious medal. My father tried to smile encouragingly, for this was clearly a big moment for him, a rite of passage. His stethoscope and his trays of equipment and his vast library with titles such as *The Hysterical Female* and *Sexual Normality and Abnormality: Twelve Case Studies* — all of this would be turned over to me at some appropriate point in my life.

By the time I grew up, most of the authors were long dead, as were their tormented patients. Even the publishing houses — with names like Pingry & Seagrove, Burroway Bros., Smollett and Sons — no longer existed. The entire world as I knew it then no longer existed, but seemed to have been snuffed out like some ancient star. Back when my father decided I would become a doctor, the Depression had settled in over the whole country. Nurses had been "let go," as my father said, and I pictured packs of women in white scattering across the lawn, their fluted cupcake-paper nurses' caps sent sailing. Week after week, families yanked seriously ill patients out of the hospital. A schizophrenic man might be shipped off to distant cousins in Iowa or Nebraska, doomed to spend his days with an American Gothic couple who had agreed, for a fee, to take in this peculiar relative who never spoke. The farm couple would stare in perplexity at their boarder and wonder what in the world to do with him: sit him down on a thresher and put him to work? Wrap his hands around the swollen udder of a cow? Or just let him sit on the porch and rock? Other patients were pulled out of the hospital and deposited on the streets of New York City, which swallowed them effortlessly. Many of these men and women drank themselves sick or froze during the long winter.

A small, elite population remained at Mount Mohonk throughout the Depression, and these patients were my father's bread and butter. They were an unlikely assortment of men and women whose families had secret, inexplicable reservoirs of money, and who seemed untouched by dark times. Here was the nucleus of unassailably rich America: shrewd bankers who could afford to keep unbalanced, yammering wives confined to the mountaintop for as long as it took. And sometimes it took forever.

Over the years, seeing the same faces in the windows of the hospital, the same figures in soft robes lumbering down the gravel footpath, I became comforted by how little anything changed. The faces were as familiar as those of relatives seen year after year at holiday dinners. There was Harry Beeman, a financier who had jumped from his fifteenth-floor office in the Bankers' Equity Building, only to bounce twice on the striped tarp of the building's awning, crushing several ribs and both legs. Now he limped through the halls of Mount Mohonk with a copy of the *Financial Times* in front of his face, muttering about figures as though any of it still mattered to him. There was Mildred Vell, a society matron with milky cataracts and a delusion about being Eleanor Roosevelt, which none of the nurses really minded, because it made Mildred a great help on the ward, always volunteering for some project or other. The core group of patients never grew worse, never seemed to get better, and never asked when they could leave. The world wasn't going to open up for these people; it stayed stubbornly shut, an aperture that let in no outside light.

The same was true, in a way, for my family. We seemed separated from the world, at least the world as it revealed itself through the large rosewood radio that sat in the living room. The Depression touched the edges of our lives, fraying them, certainly, but leaving everyone intact. What I did learn about the world came largely from a source that had been available to me for years, but which I had never thought to consult. One morning, when I was twelve years old, with my mother in the kitchen downstairs and my father at the hospital across the lawn, I entered my father's study, mounted a rolling ladder that was attached to the floor-to-ceiling bookshelves, and brought down the copy of *Sexual Normality and Abnormality: Twelve Case Studies.*

What did I know about these matters? All morning I sat with the book heavy in my lap, struggling to make out the tiny typeface. I sat with legs crossed, chewing a piece of hair, shocked but caught up in the tide of words and their meanings. All winter my father kept the thermostat in his study at a constant fifty-eight degrees, and I imagined that the temperature had to be kept so low or else the books might self-destruct. It was as though I were holding the original Gutenberg Bible in my hands, and this room served as some special emergency vacuum in case of fire or apocalypse. But even if there was an apocalypse, these words would float over the wreckage of the world, so deep were they embedded in me, so deep already at twelve.

And all my father had done was drape a stethoscope around my neck. But somehow he had crowned me some twisted version of Miss America: Miss Toilet Mouth, Miss Disgusting Secrets, *Little* Miss Disgusting Secrets. I could hardly get through the week without dipping into my new fund of knowledge. Images scrolled by in pornographic frescoes, and I realized that I could have become rich in the playground of my day school had I sold my classified information. Any single page torn from *Sexual Normality and Abnormality: Twelve Case Studies* would have fetched a good price at school, and since the volume was over five hundred pages long, my father would have never known the difference. But I couldn't tear anything out of that book; it would have been like ripping "Letters to the Romans" out of the Gutenberg Bible. Entire sections stayed in my mind, eventually memorized as thoroughly as the Pledge of Allegiance.

"Miss H.," began the case study on p. 348, "was born in a rural home in Norway to illiterate farming parents. Because she did not attend school, but instead worked the fields alongside her brothers, she had no official medical records. It was not until many years later, when she was working as a cook in the village of S— and was subsequently hospitalized for acute appendicitis at the regional clinic in that village, that physicians discovered the truth about Miss H. She was a rarity, a true hermaphrodite, equipped with both phallus and vagina, the former being no bigger than a pea pod, the latter equally undeveloped. The doctors at the clinic in S—— allowed a small group of visiting medical students to view their patient's deformity, and she was thusly paid a wage to appear regularly at lectures at the medical college in nearby O——. Miss H.'s life, while spent alone, proved far more satisfying than the lives of other such individuals, many of whom attempt to join in sexual relations, and who find their advances rebuffed, often by a horrified individual who has just realized the True Nature of this creature. Sometimes, the hermaphrodite can find a peaceful home among the denizens of a carny troupe or travelling sideshow."*

The story of Miss H. was as riveting as it was appalling; I could imagine the woman's wide Nordic face, and even, if I tried hard enough, her collision of sex organs. Sometimes I would forgo the text entirely and just read the index, my finger skittering along the stunning list of words. Every body part was in this list, and every perverse activity; nothing was excluded. All the shameful words from the school bathroom walls were here, printed neatly on heavy bond paper, not gouged into plaster by a twelve-year-old's erratic penknife. No janitor had tried to paint over them, to refinish the surface with some virginal gloss. No, these words were *actually meant to be understood.*

So this was my future, this world where people with contorted minds and bodies coupled blindly in assorted ways. I couldn't bear to believe it, yet I knew it was true. I knew it because of my parents, could see it in their eyes and their easy posture when they were together. My father was always touching my mother; there was rarely a moment when they were in the same room and their limbs did not lightly connect. Since my mother could not conceive, what they did in their bedroom was done for the pleasure of it. They were a good fit, my father with his red mustache and rimless glasses and thick arms, my mother with her black hair swept off her neck with a silver comb.

They had met and fallen in love one summer when both of their families were staying at a bungalow colony in the Catskills called Lustig's. My father, David Welner, was a young medical student at the time, which gave him a certain clout. Whenever anyone ap-

*Dr. Lucian Hargreaves, *Sexual Normality and Abnormality: Twelve Case Studies* (New York: Eppler and Keeney, 1919).

proached him that summer, he would cheerfully agree to listen to a litany of complaints, to inspect what someone called, under his breath, a "suspicious" mole. In reality, he had no clinical experience yet; at City College's medical school, his class was still enmeshed in the fundamentals of biology and chemistry, spending afternoons drawing diagrams of the Krebs Cycle, or becoming familiar with the respiratory systems of fish. When he lifted the ribbed undershirt of a sixty-year-old man on vacation and peered at a dark brown disk the size of a quarter, he was simply using a combination of common sense and bits of knowledge he had gathered from the weekly "Ask Dr. Colin Sylvester" column in the *New York Herald*. But he charmed everyone, and no one was worse off for his diagnosis.

"Avoid the sun like the plague, Mrs. Kimmel," he told a woman with parchment skin. "Get some rest," he told a nervous young newlywed husband. All around the colony, men and women followed David Welner's instructions, lying in the shade for naps, swigging plenty of fresh water, eating roughage. Everyone was happy, mosquitoes dotted the surface of the lake, the summer slowly unrolled.

Toward the end of the season, my parents became engaged. My father had been chosen to judge the bungalow colony's annual beauty pageant. Of the twelve Brooklyn and Bronx girls who paraded along the dock, making their way across the scarred planks in their stiletto heels, my mother was the one he chose, hands down. At eighteen, Justine Fogel was tall, with a head of jet hair and high, impressive breasts. She was planning on studying voice in Manhattan in September. A neighbor knew of a vocal coach named Oskar Mennen who would instruct her once a week for a low fee. His slogan was "If *you've* got a sliding scale, I've got one too."

But my mother never went to see Oskar Mennen. Instead, she married David Welner shortly after Labor Day, and the couple moved to a tenement apartment on Chrystie Street in Lower Manhattan. During the day, my father went to classes and my mother sat at home practicing scales; at night they cooked a plain dinner on their stove and went to bed. Sometimes in the middle of the night, he woke up and sat in the living room studying; she could see a tiny yellow bulb burning in the living room, and his silhouette curved in concentration under the light.

Slowly, my father became noticed in his classes. One day he attracted the attention of a visiting professor of psychiatry named Fox Mendelson, and over the years the two men kept up a correspondence. Later, when my father was looking for a position, Mendelson recommended him to the board of trustees at a private hospital called Mount Mohonk. The job paid poorly, but my father was willing. He was a Jew, and had noticed a distinct strain of anti-Semitism among psychiatrists, despite the fact that their god was a Jew himself. In the hospitals and clinics of New York City, he encountered psychiatrists with names like Warner Graves and Loren St. John, men with silver-threaded hair and deep, uninflected voices and degrees from Amherst and Harvard. What my father had going for himself was wit, dexterity, and the ability to leap from bed at four in the morning to subdue a schizophrenic who was smacking a nurse over the head with a cast-iron bedpan. He was handsome and didn't seem too ambitious, and he raised interesting points during grand rounds. At age thirty-two, he became the youngest chief psychiatrist in the brief and undistinguished history of the Mount Mohonk Hospital for the Insane.

He and my mother inhabited the large house across the lawn from the hospital, taking as their bedroom the room that overlooked the road out front. It was almost possible for them to lie in their four-poster and imagine that they lived in a normal home, on a real street, like any other young couple. But at night, when the howling started, they remembered.

My father was a hit with the nurses and orderlies. He strode the shining halls of the hospital as though he had been running the place since birth. Even his memos were praised. ("Re: hospital gowns. It has come to my attention that the dung-colored gowns worn by our patients are perhaps no good for morale. Might we find something with a bit more dash — perhaps peach or sky-blue?")

My mother fell quickly, but less gracefully, into her role as the chief psychiatrist's wife. Before the Depression, her job largely entailed standing in the middle of her kitchen, conferring with a mute Negro hospital cook about upcoming dinner parties at the house. She would wave her pale hands vaguely, opening drawers and pointing to spoons and knives, saying, "Now, there are the spoons. Oh, and the knives." She was hesitant in this role; no one had ever waited on her before except her grandmother, who used to section her grapefruit for her with a serrated knife. But that was different. That was family. This was help. *Help;* the word itself was so strong, something you would call out when you were drowning. Her whole life was becoming unrecognizable.

They were aimless, both of my parents, rolling around in this huge house together, anxious to populate the rooms with children. By the time I was born, they were ready, tired of seeing only mentally ill people, eager for an infant's simple and understandable cry. But when the obstetrician told my mother that she could bear no more children, my father let his only daughter into his life in a way that no one, not even his wife, had been allowed.

Every few months he took me on a whirlwind tour of the hospital: the dining room, which smelled perennially of fried flounder, the occupational therapy room, where dead-eyed patients pressed images of dogs and presidents onto copper sheeting, the solarium, the visitors' lounge. We breezed past doors with doctors' names stenciled onto the grain, and past doors with signs that read WARN-ING: ELECTRICITY IN USE. These doors were always shut, and I longed to see what electricity looked like when it was "in use." And I also longed to see where the patients actually lived, where they showered and dressed and bathed. But the wards themselves, with their heavy doors with chicken wire laced into the glass, were off-limits. I was allowed to see hospital life only from a distance, watching as patients slogged through the halls in their dung-colored gowns and flannel robes. I often stood staring at them, and once I made prolonged eye contact with an obese man whose face was blue with stubble, until I was whisked off into the nurses' lounge, where big band music emanated from the radio, and I was given a handful of sourballs by a trio of fussing women. And then the tour was over.

Although I was allowed into the hospital only at my father's invitation, I was free to explore the grounds whenever I liked. With the sun sinking and the air aromatic with pine and earth and Salisbury steak, the whole place smelled like a summer camp. One day, at the rear entrance of the building, I saw delivery men unloading drums of institutional disinfectant. As they rolled them up a ramp and into the service entrance, I could read the words "Whispering Pines," and even though the name referred to nothing more than a rancid fluid that would be swabbed across the floors and walls at dawn, it sounded like the perfect alias for the hospital, the ideal name for a splendid summer camp.

Whispering Pines, I whispered to myself as I stepped into the thicket that continued until the edges of the grounds, where it was held back by the iron fence. Vines flourished along that fence, wound around the spokes like a cat winding around a human leg. Just as the patients often seemed to want out, so did the vegetation. Everything grew frantically at the farthest reaches of the property. The most tangible signs of the times could be found there, at the edges of the land, where nobody had bothered to prune or clip or chop away at the excess. Sometimes a group of patients would sit on Adirondack chairs on the lawn, taking in a chilly hour of sun, and sometimes a nurse would take a patient on a supervised stroll, but only along the circular path closest to the hospital, and never into the woods. The woods were mine, at least for a while.

The summer I turned fourteen, my father implemented a program he called "Tea at the House." This involved inviting a promising patient to join him and my mother for afternoon tea in our living room. The patient was always someone at least a little bit appealing, someone who wouldn't make any sudden moves. Someone very close to health, who needed a bit of encouragement to topple him or her completely onto the other side.

The first person invited to Tea at the House was a woman named Grace Allenby, a young mother who had had a nervous breakdown and was unable to complete any action, even dressing herself in the morning, without dissolving into hysterical, gulping sobs. At the hospital she had made a slow but admirable recovery. She came to tea on the Friday before her husband was to take her home, and I sat watching at the top of the stairs. Both Mrs. Allenby and my mother were lovely-looking and uncertain, like the deer that occasionally made a wrong turn in the woods and wound up stunned and confused and frightened on the hospital lawn. The women shyly traded recipes, while my father sat between them, nodding with benevolence.

"What you want to do is *this,*" Mrs. Allenby kept saying, and as she spoke she blinked rapidly, as if to remove a speck from her eye. "You take an egg and you beat it very hard in a bowl with a whisk. Then what you want to do is *this . . .*" The living room smelled strongly of Oolong tea, my father's favorite. He liked it because it was the closest thing to drinking pipe tobacco.

I eavesdropped on several Teas at the House over the year, and I came to understand that mental patients could be divided into two groups: those who wore their affliction outright like a bold political stance, and those who hid it so actively that that became their trademark, grinning until their teeth might splinter, wanting so badly to hold themselves together.

Warren Keyes was of the second variety. He was a nineteen-year-old Harvard undergraduate who had tried to kill himself in his dormitory room eight months earlier, and who was close to leaving Mount Mohonk to return to school. Over dinner, my parents discussed this boy, who would be coming to Tea at the House the following day. "He's young," my father said, "and good-looking, in that Harvard way."

Warren Keyes registered in my mind in that moment, was locked into place even before I had met him. Here was a Harvard man. That went over well with my father, who often fantasized about a privileged upbringing, complete with long walks along the Charles River and various racquet sports. And it went over well with me too, for even before I met Warren Keyes, I had sculpted his features and his limbs into some crude rendering of attractiveness.

The next afternoon at four o'clock, Warren sat in the living room gripping the fragile handle of a teacup. He had trooped across the lawn with a squat nurse, who now sat in the foyer, dully knitting like Madame Defarge. I knew that he had been invited to the house as a reward for getting well, but casting a critical, fourteen-year-old eye on him from the top of the stairs, even I could see that he was not well.

"Warren plans on returning to Harvard next semester," my father said. My mother hummed a response. "Leverett House, isn't it?" my father went on, he who had studied at City College, yet who knew the names of all the houses at Harvard. He, who had ascended to chief of psychiatry at Mount Mohonk and yet who was, irrevocably, a Jew.

"No, Adams House," said Warren. His voice was relaxed, although his cup jitterbugged in its saucer.

Conversation pushed on about Harvard in general, football season, and New England weather. My mother didn't add much, and my father kept plying Warren with questions, which he politely, if wearily, answered. At the end of the hour, Warren Keyes looked exhausted. I imagined that he would go back to his hospital bed and sleep for thirty-six hours straight, regaining his strength.

Breaking his own tradition but questioned by no one, Dr. Welner invited Warren Keyes back for a second Tea at the House, and then a third. On his fourth tea, he was unaccompanied by the dour-faced nurse. Instead, he made a solo flight across the lawn, his coattails floating out behind him. That afternoon, I had been strategically sitting on the porch doing my homework before taking a walk in the woods. My hair was sloppily bound up behind my head with elastic, and there was ink on my fingers, for I had not yet mastered the fountain pen. But even so, Warren Keyes climbed onto the porch and gave me a good hard look. Although it was not the first time I had seen Warren Keyes, it was the first time he saw me.

"I'm the daughter," I said. He nodded. "They're inside," I told him, inclining my head toward the screen door. Deep in the house, the teakettle shrilled.

"Do you like tea?" Warren asked. It was the kind of question that my father's colleagues often asked me when they came to dinner: well-meaning and uninteresting probings from people who had no idea of what to say to children, yet somehow, maddeningly, meant to be answered.

"I like it okay," I said.

"Your mother makes good tea," Warren said. "It's Chinese, you know."

I slid off the railing. "I have to go," I said.

His eyes widened slightly. "Where are you going?" he asked.

And for some reason, I told him. I told him where I went every afternoon; I practically drew him a treasure map with an X. Later, I sat in the woods reading *The Red Badge of Courage,* and suddenly there was a parting of branches. Warren Keyes came through, stooped and stumbling in. He had in his hand a familiar folded linen napkin with scalloped edges. He squatted down beside me, this handsome, ruined Harvard sophomore, and he opened the napkin, which contained three golden circles: my mother's Belgian butter cookies. I took them silently, and ate them just as silently, while Warren watched.

"So what's it like to live here?" he asked.

What it was like, I thought, was like anything else. Like going to the day school seven miles away. Like owning arms. I shrugged. How I wanted to ask him a similar question: What was it like to live *there*, inside a hospital for the insane? What was it like to be insane? Was it like a long and particularly vivid nightmare? Did you know you were insane? Did you long to crawl out of your body? Did you actually see things — shapes and animals and flames dancing across the walls of your room at night? But I couldn't bring myself to ask him anything at all. Light was draining from the patch of woods, and suddenly Warren said, "May I ask you something?"

"Yes," I said.

"Could I maybe touch you?" the boy asked.

I nodded solemnly, really believing, in that moment, that he was referring to my hand, or my arm. He wanted to touch me to see if I was real, the way, years earlier, I myself had surreptitiously touched the bloodless face of my cousin's beloved china doll. He wanted to touch me in order to have the experience of touching someone who wasn't insane — someone who had a normal life and lived with her parents in a real house without bars on the windows. He wanted to touch me to see what I was like.

Warren came closer, sliding across the dirt floor to where I sat with my book. "I won't hurt you," he said.

"I know," I said. When his hand came down on one of my breasts, those recent arrivals, I could not have been more shocked. I did not know how to stop this, and I felt at once hurled out of my own realm and into his. "Now wait," I said, but his hands were already moving freely above my clothes. He seemed not to have heard me. He sat in front of me, touching my breasts, my neck, my shoulders, and in fact he wasn't hurting me. So what was I upset about? I didn't know what to call it, this thing he was doing, this casual exploration. It was his face that frightened me — the intense and worshipful expression on his features, as though he were kneeling and lighting candles. His mouth hung open, his eyes were focused.

"I'm not hurting you," he kept repeating. "I'm not hurting you."

And all I could answer was, "No. You're not."

I closed my eyes so I wouldn't have to see his face. I closed them as if to block out a strong sunlight. I felt myself grow dizzy, but I thought it would be worse if I fainted, because who knew what would happen then? When I came to, I could never be sure of what had taken place. So I made myself stay conscious, and I felt each motion he made, the starfish movements of his fingers as they slipped beneath my blouse and headed downward. I knew the names of all the parts he was touching, and in my panic I recited them under my breath. His hands toured a living index from the back of my father's book, and as they did, I summoned up all the words I knew. But what good did it do me to know these things, to know what they meant when I couldn't even *manage* them?

He moved against me as if in a trance, and I felt like a wall, something for others to rub against; I was a cat scratching post, a solid block. I felt his large hand inside my underwear, so out of place, so wrong. The elastic waistband with its row of rosettes was pulled taut against his knuckles. Just that morning I had chosen the underwear from a drawer, where it lay with the others, ironed, white, floral, and touched only by me and by Estella, who did our family's laundry. No one else was meant to touch it. Warren's hand was trapped inside it, like an animal that had run into a tent and was now caught. It seemed there against its will, if that were possible, if hands had a will of their own.

Now one of Warren's fingers was separating itself from the other fingers and pushing into me, sliding up into my body. I felt a shiver of pain, and then something that wasn't pain at all, but surprise. I sat straight up and started to cry. His big finger, which had held on to my mother's teacup, which probably wore a Harvard ring sometimes, which had a flat fingernail that he trimmed in his cubicle in the hospital for the insane, if they let him have nail scissors, was deeply embedded in me, like something drilled into the ground to test for water or crude oil. Like a machine, a spike, testing the earth for vibrations or for moisture. The finger felt all these things, but I felt nothing.

After some endless time, Warren Keyes made a small sound like a lamb bleating or a hinge groaning open, and I knew that it was over. I sank back onto the surface of leaves, my body returning to itself: small, flexible, a skater's body, while Warren turned away from me, wiping his face and the front of his trousers with my mother's napkin.

In a gentle, quaking voice, he told me it was better if we left the woods separately and, of course, if I told no one about what had happened. "There's nothing to tell, anyway," he added. "I didn't hurt you." And it was true; he hadn't hurt me.

I left first, walking slowly with book in hand as though nothing had happened, like a dreamy teenaged girl leaving an afternoon of reading, but when I reached the edge of the woods, where the lawn began, I broke into a run toward the lights of my parents' house. Inside, I walked straight up the stairs, claiming I was ill and didn't want dinner. My mother pressed a cool hand to my forehead, but I shrugged it off. There would be no more touching today; even the back of a familiar hand, prospecting for fever, was too much.

That night, before going to sleep, I pushed up the window by the bed and poked my head out. From the hospital across the lawn, I heard the familiar crying and baying, and without thinking, I opened my mouth and softly joined the chorus. The sound came naturally, and I hung out that window in the warm spring night, howling quietly in a low, effortless voice, as though I had been doing it since I was born, as though it was natural to my species.

Weeks passed, and I noticed my own shift in feeling almost as though I were charting the progress of a bruise, watching it go from black to blue to brown to yellow, until finally it was only a smudge, a small trace memory. I didn't understand whether what had happened was something that Warren Keyes had actually wanted to have happen, or whether he had been unable to stop himself because he was, as the name of the hospital announced, insane. Should I have felt furious, or should I have felt compassion, as my father would have? I was lost, not knowing, and after a while it became too late to ask anyone. Time separated me from the memory, and other things rose to replace it — real things, much more important than a young man touching a girl in the woods of a mental hospital somewhere in the mountains of New York State.

Arching over everything was the war in Europe. It had come into our lives through the large rosewood cabinet that my father kept in the living room beneath a Winslow Homer print, and now during dinner parties, when the meal was through, my father and his colleagues gathered around it. The maid moved through the rooms emptying ashtrays, while the doctors' wives sat quietly, sipping brandy and looking concerned, and the men outshouted the broadcast with a running commentary of their own. They argued about invasions and strategies, and I was confused. How much would the war in Europe affect any of us? After all, the Depression had touched only the edges of our lives. The hospital had far fewer patients and a much smaller staff than it once had, but still it stayed intact, a neutral duchy in the middle of a rapidly dividing world. I decided that a war on another continent could not really touch anybody here, not these psychiatrists with their identical little mustaches, or these wives who sat listening to the barbershop quartet of male voices around them, or even me. For a while I was actually able to sustain this feeling; for a while I hung suspended in it.

But then eventually we were in the war too; *we,* my father had said, and the word referred to some of the hospital's staff. Dr. Rogovin, Dr. Sammler, young Dr. Herd, and several of the orderlies had all enlisted. Nurses too left that winter to work for the Red Cross. Whispering Pines had actually gone to war.

Then one night at dinner late that January, my father slipped a letter from his breast pocket. It was written on Harvard stationery. "You remember Warren Keyes," my father said to my mother. "That Harvard boy." When I heard this, my hand sent a butter knife involuntarily crashing against a glass. After the chime subsided, my father began to read the letter aloud:

Dear Dr. Welner,

  I hope you still remember me. You helped me a great deal not too long ago, and after leaving the hospital I returned to school where I gave my attention to Classics and found great pleasure in my work. Last year I took first prize here for my translations of Catullus. I wanted to let you know that I have enlisted in the Navy, and, despite my psychiatric record, have been accepted. Before I go overseas, I thought I should write you a short note to thank you for everything you have done. My regards to your wife.

Respectfully,
Warren Keyes

I sat very still at the table while my father finished reading. As he held the page up toward the light, I could see the silhouette of a small, perfect crimson seal shining through.

ANTONYA NELSON

Unified Front

FROM THE MIDWESTERNER

JACOB'S WIFE liked to blame his hair, which had gone white as Santa's just after he turned forty. Now it was six years later.

"You're too old-looking to be anybody's dad," she said. He knew Cece intended no unkindness; she was trying to keep her chin up. After all, she had wanted a baby her whole life. She used to pretend to breast-feed her dolls, lifting her shirt to smack a hard plastic head against her own flat chest. She had been the champion of younger, rejected neighbor children, had held the plump hand of her little sister, then her cousins, then a nephew, then godchildren, now great-nieces. When was her turn? Where was her baby?

Jacob held her hand on the 737 bound for that big theme park in Florida, the oasis in the orange groves with the giant golf ball and the mouse. Cece needed a holiday; she'd picked the unlikeliest place on the planet. "Did she think we can't do math?" Cece demanded of him before takeoff, apropos of nothing. He knew which "she" was meant; there was another "she" they didn't discuss. "Did she think we couldn't add up for ourselves how old we'd be when the child was sixteen?"

Jacob lifted the armrest between them and scooted closer to his wife, who lurched away to look him up and down: Was he feeling sorry for her? In the aisle a flight attendant mimed pleasure as she demonstrated the use of the oxygen mask without mussing her makeup. One of the other flight attendants was pregnant, and behind them sat a mother and toddler, evidence of the cruel way life rubbed one's nose in one's misery. And, Jacob thought as he recalled his and Cece's destination, the foolish way one rubbed one's own nose in it.

"We're being punished," Cece said, seeming to decide that Jacob's sympathy was bearable.

"We did nothing wrong," he said. "You buckled up?"

"Like a seat belt would do any good in an airplane crash." She might scoff, but she buckled, pulling the excess tight. She was forty-one years old and no larger than a young girl, optimistically wearing shorts, in Chicago, in mid-November, as a gesture of belief in the balmy reputation of Florida. Since she hadn't had a baby, her lap lay flat as it had fifteen years ago, when they'd married. Jacob had told her then, whenever she worried before the mirror, that he would welcome stretch marks, those scars like the scales of fish, the pearly opalescence of nearly torn flesh, those private hieroglyphs between them. Jacob kissed her cheek. He closed his eyes and let himself imagine the face of the woman who'd told them they couldn't adopt a baby, that they were too old. This offense hardly registered with him, but on Cece's behalf a dark rage bloomed deep inside him. He wanted to take cartoonish revenge against Adoptive Services: hit the woman — who was pregnant, smug fertile creature! — and tip her desk on its side, scatter her files and forms like confetti, bash together the heads of her assistants like coconuts, toss a brick or sizzling stick of dynamite through the plate glass window, write huffy letters, and make obscene anonymous phone calls.

"Kill the messenger," Cece sardonically encouraged him. He was fuming, but she accepted the news calmly; she'd learned to expect precisely the worst. There were a few reasons she believed she deserved no baby: she'd kept the faith for too long, been too confident of her own reproductive fitness. She'd not come on her knees to the threshold of Adoptive Services, had in fact steadfastly shunned them, and now she was to suffer her own arrogance: where once those ministers of babies might have welcomed her, they now cavalierly closed the door.

And then there was Crystal, of course. Crystal's child — the baby who'd been most clearly their destiny — would have been three years old now. Crystal had jumped from Jacob and Cece's fourth-floor balcony in her eighth month, surviving but killing the baby. She'd tried to reach Jacob and Cece — had come to their apartment to wait for them, used her key to let herself in, drunk a full bottle of gin, eaten whatever food she could find, then opened the sliding glass balcony door. Jacob and Cece had been in the Ozarks. That was the last vacation they'd taken, and they'd taken it to escape Crystal. Jacob could not think of that part of his life without wondering what would have changed had he done something differently, just a minor yet crucial contingency in the events. A little gesture the size of a note or a phone call might have safeguarded their child, and Jacob sometimes feared that he'd brought on the disaster by not wanting that child enough. He'd known Crystal better than Cece had; he should have predicted her reaction. And perhaps he *had* predicted it, perhaps he'd even taken advantage of it — he literally squirmed to think so. If the baby had lived, it would have now been approximately the age of the one sitting behind Jacob on the plane, the one kicking unceasingly into the region of Jacob's kidneys.

Cece tugged at his sleeve and said, "Remember that kid I told you about, the girl on the trip home from Germany?" This was an old story, one Cece did not realize she had told far too many times. Jacob imagined that she thought of it more often than she actually admitted, that she sometimes suppressed the urge to tell him. Years earlier, before the airlines got technical about it — before some parent sued, Jacob assumed — Cece had been given the charge of an eight-year-old girl for the duration of a flight from Frankfurt to Chicago. "The mother picked me because she thought I was the most reliable-looking person in the waiting area," Cece said now. (She had some good stories she'd told Jacob only once; on occasion she surprised him with a brand-new one, an incident from her past plucked like a fruit, handed him to delight him, fresh and delicious. But he'd heard about the German girl a dozen times.) Cece loved having been chosen; she'd loved the little girl, who spent the flight explaining her family troubles — the divorce, the new step- and half-siblings, the intercontinental visits. Cece always concluded the story wondering whether the girl, Hannelore, would remember her, that and the fact that the child's father, in America, hadn't bothered to thank Cece for her transatlantic pampering.

"She was such a sweet child," Cece said now, sentimentally. "I always wanted my daughter to be just like her, smart and funny."

Jacob grunted.

Later, when their 737 hit a pocket of rough weather, the cabin's interior rattled as if to shake itself from its exoskeleton, and Cece grabbed Jacob's hand. He'd been dozing, dreaming of children, great swarms of them, their faces hissing up at him like a cave full of bats caught in a sudden light.

"As if this might help," Cece said, squeezing the blood from his flesh, not letting go of him until the air smoothed once more.

"I've never seen so many fat white thighs," Jacob commented twenty-four hours later. "People are ugly animals, aren't they? I'd give away my three-day pass to see just one alligator." Jacob talked because Cece wouldn't; someone had to fill the silence.

Not too long after, they sat on a ride through Neverland. "There's your gator," Cece told him.

What was she looking for? Jacob wondered. Clearly she had something in mind, the way she moved from ride to ride, choosing long lines, buying popcorn and then throwing half of it away, sitting listlessly on the tram and monorail, then hustling as fast as possible to the gift shop to purchase a bag of presents, leaving Jacob trailing behind. At the end of the first day they soaked in the (not so) hot tub at their hotel and listened to children playing in the swimming pool.

"We could adopt an older girl," Jacob said, so physically relieved to be sitting rather than walking, so comforted by the darkening night sky and the dull images behind his own eyelids in place of the garish ones he'd been blitzed by all day long, he said whatever came floating through his mind, his lazy familiar thoughts leaking from his mouth. "Plenty of older children need parents."

"I'm a good person," Cece responded with her own weary refrain, "but I'm not a saint. I could only love a teenager when I remembered it as an infant. Besides, we don't want to inherit problems."

Their next step was to adopt a child from another country. Jacob knew this was coming, an inevitability mushrooming on the horizon. They would find their baby far south of here, a doe-eyed brown child. He was not unhappy with that scenario; he preferred not knowing the parents, the language, or the shaky lawfulness of it all. But it exhausted him, the anticipation of the work involved. "You like Florida?" he asked.

She sighed. "Do you?"

"I do." He did; the weather was his friend, gentle and humane, utterly unlike the weather of his homeland. "I may discover I hate winter if we stay here much longer."

"Is my bathing suit frumpy?" Cece asked. Jacob opened his eyes to look at her. She was so small only her head showed, and Jacob couldn't recall what her suit looked like, under the bubbling water. She said, "I feel a funk coming on. There are about a thousand different ways to hate this place. I thought everybody would be happy, but nobody's happy, everybody's miserable."

"Not me," he told her. "I like the palm trees. Palm trees make it an official vacation."

"All the crying children," Cece said, "they make me sad. And all the angry moms and dads, so mean to their children. Plus, now my hair's all rank from this chlorine, and my bathing suit is so cruddy it could stand up without me."

But this was part of Cece's personality, to choose Florida and read a guidebook about it and make the trip and then complain. She complained so that Jacob would play the other role, the promoter, the endorser. She would summon the black cloud so that he could paint the silver lining; she would hate it so that he could enjoy it. He remembered there were fireworks. "Let's go back to the park," he said, though he had no real interest in making the trek again. "We'll watch the fireworks."

Jacob didn't need a baby. Since the horrific year when Cece had befriended Crystal and convinced her not to have an abortion, the idea of a baby always brought with it a queasy dread. Besides, he had Cece, although he knew that wasn't a fitting substitute to broadcast to the world. Marriages ought to be between equals, but Jacob hadn't ever known an equal in love. It was always somebody feeling more than the other, somebody protecting, somebody requiring safe harbor or permission or simple compliance. He loved Cece in the sheltering way of a parent; he wanted to cover her eyes and ears from the unkind news of the world. He loved her the other way too, the way that made him want to bite her on the thigh, hold her naked body. She was everything to him, a little person who bought her clothing in the boys' section of J. C. Penney, flannel shirts and Wrangler jeans, her fingertips reaching only as far as her hips. Something in her genetic composition made her thumbs stumpy like the heads of turtles and her arms abbreviated — simian, it was called, the tell-tale crease cutting straight across her palm so she could fold her hand in half like the mouth of a puppet. Traits left over from the apes, traits found in 5 percent of the normal population. "Five percent of the *normal* population," Cece would always emphasize. He loved that.

In front of the hotel bathroom mirror Cece shedded her dreadful suit and studied her naked body in the unforgiving light. "My breasts are shrinking and I'm sprouting facial hair. Maybe I'm turning into a man."

"I don't think so," Jacob said, standing behind her, patting her clammy rear end.

"Okay then — a neuter. Give me that, will you?"

"Let's go to the fireworks."

"Why do I like those things, anyway?"

"They remind you of sex," he said.

Jacob dreamed about Crystal. Of course. Crystal Lake, the girl with the preposterous name, the psychopath who'd detonated in their lives. She'd been his student in the required senior class, "Peer Leadership," a mediocre student held back a year, an indolent girl with a bad reputation and a sly smile. This was no excuse; he'd betrayed the central edict of his profession by sleeping with her. He'd had sex with her and she'd become pregnant, though it wasn't quite as elementary as it sounded. In the first place, she'd slept with so many boys that the odds of the baby being Jacob's were low. Second, she'd blackmailed him, stoically refusing to tell whose the baby was, so that neither her parents nor Cece had ever discovered the affair, let alone his infidelity. This left Jacob open to whatever impulse might seize her. He'd settled for halfhearted gratitude, wholehearted hatred. Cece pitied her and Crystal soaked it up like a sponge. She had not told the grownups, but Jacob had read the knowledge in his other students' eyes, and as an enduring murmur in succeeding classes, a rumor just wild enough to be true.

In Florida, in his dream, Crystal was throwing a party in Jacob and Cece's hotel room. The cookies she'd made in the microwave were delicious. Jacob kissed her, then maneuvered himself between her legs. By then he'd figured out it was a dream, that there wasn't any harm in having sex. And it felt good to slam against her, to hurt her this way because there wasn't any other way to do so. At home there was that punishing patch of ground where she'd fallen, a place Jacob's eye strayed to when he rounded their building for the underground garage. He did not love her, he did not desire her — he wanted honest release.

When he woke, Cece was already up, strategizing with her pamphlets and a pencil, devising a game plan. The sun shone through gaps where the hotel room curtains didn't meet, beneath the door, in a piercing ray of white from the peephole in the door. It was aggressive, this sunlight. Outside on the balcony, the season could easily have been summer — palm trees, green grass, people in shorts and shades, the soothing sound of lawn mowers. In the bathroom, Cece had left her discreet monthly sanitary wrappers: not pregnant, again. Her gynecologist had explained that Cece's eggs were tough-skinned things, impenetrable. At the fertility clinic the doctor had injected Jacob's sperm, hoping to boost infiltration of the resistant, fickle egg. Jacob sat in a chair beside Cece during this procedure, tempted to make jokes, loathing the man whose head and shoulders disappeared under the tent created by the sheet over Cece's raised legs.

Cece claimed not to blame Jacob for the one child they'd conceived, long before they were married, before they knew they would marry, before they knew even the easiest secrets about each other. But Jacob had been the one to suggest the abortion, and then he hadn't been able to go with her. He'd just begun a job and didn't feel he could ask for time off. At the clinic they'd let her sleep afterward. When Jacob picked her up, she was still too muddled by anesthesia for her grief to show. Then her younger sister had come to town with her baby, and Cece had had to pretend there'd never been a pregnancy; otherwise, wouldn't everyone feel awkward and squeamish? And Jacob stood by like a gawking stranger, only beginning to comprehend the tenderness Cece could bring forth in him, while Cece held her nephew in her short arms and grew misty-eyed. When she'd bled, later, Jacob was at work — a job he'd left after only three months, a job that amounted, in the end, to nothing — so her sister took her to the hospital, bringing along the baby nephew, who slept in his cloth bag on his mother's chest, and though Cece lost a lot of blood, she was fine, but after that there simply were no more babies, as if Jacob and Cece had been given their chance and squandered it.

"If we hurry," Cece told him from the made bed as he flopped over like a fish in the messy one, "we can see the parade." She tapped the metal cylinder of the pencil eraser on her teeth, which made Jacob's tonsils wobble. He thought about Crystal, about the phone messages she'd left on their answering machine, about the mess she'd made when she finally came over the evening she'd leapt from the ledge. There was drinking, smoking, crying, phone calls to anyone whose number she could remember; she even cut up Cece's dresses with pinking shears — a sick party with only one guest. She'd been an unreliable caretaker of their child, a deranged babysitter from a bad movie; a child in a grown-up suit of whom real grownups had made grown-up demands.

"Parade," Cece said, pulling Jacob's toes.

Jacob stared straight up. Above him, the fan looked like a giant starfish glommed on to the ceiling.

Cece ate mouse-ear–shaped ice cream and mouse-ear–shaped pancakes. She bought a mouse hat and a mouse shirt for herself, and a pair of mouse pajamas for her youngest niece. She sat on benches in her mouse clothes like a ten-year-old, dangling her legs and letting the sun turn her pale skin a bright pink. Most of what she saw she absorbed in silence, though in the darkened cars as they passed by Indians or mobsters or spacemen, she held on to Jacob's arm. Jacob felt like Gulliver in the Lilliputian theme parks; they had not been designed for tall men, and he kept cracking his head against roofs and doorways.

On the fourth day Cece pointed out a double stroller carrying twins. The girls sucked pacifiers and wore mouse bonnets on their big heads. "Cute," Cece said.

Jacob followed Cece, who followed the twins, whose parents had three other children. There were two more girls and a teenage boy whose head had recently been half shaved — for reasons of fashion, evidently — leaving scabs. The mother leaned on the stroller as if to prop herself up; she had a disposition to go with her stout body, and she never quit talking, a flowing litany of instructions to keep the family machine functioning.

"She's a breeder," Cece said, and Jacob realized the woman was pregnant on top of everything else.

Originally, Cece and Jacob had held three-day passes, but Cece had wanted more and Jacob had made this fourth day a gift to her.

Jacob, utterly depleted, exhausted, had to keep remembering his selflessness. His nose had been sunburned and his feet had blistered; he was weary of the sunshine, having discovered he could not entirely trust it when it shone so singlemindedly, and the music that surrounded them made him long for the common noise of his dark, gray city. Though he had tried, he could not find the dirty underworkings of the park. The bathrooms were spotless, the trash cans always almost empty; a whole fleet of men in jumpsuits scurried around with scoops and brooms, whisking away the waste. You presented your passport and they let you in; they kept all the unpleasantness on the other side of the gate. It was a bright, seamless world, as insidiously seductive as a drug trip. What if he began to prefer it?

"Cece, do you remember hearing about some sort of accident here once? Some horse that bolted?" Jacob recalled that a bystander had happened to videotape the event, and that his camera had been confiscated, his footage destroyed, his teenager's college education guaranteed as part of the coverup. Or something like that. "A scandal," Jacob said. "Remember?"

Cece listened impassively; people in line frowned at him. They shuffled forward and she leaned close to his ear as if to kiss it, saying, "You don't care about having a baby, do you?" Although they knew each other well, it sometimes became necessary to ask questions to which they already knew the answers.

"Only because you do," he said, it being impossible for him to lie to her.

She stepped away. "Is that because you're a man? Is that why? If that's why, then I'm glad I'm not a man. I wouldn't be a man for a million bucks." Her eyes were suddenly wet, and the people in line frowned once more. What had Jacob said to upset his wife so?

Jacob was thinking he wouldn't be a woman either, at least not one like Cece. Maybe some other woman, but he couldn't have suffered the longing she endured, the consuming desire to give birth. He wondered if he shouldn't be wounded, that he wasn't enough for her. She, after all, was enough for him, a fact he'd discovered during his affair with Crystal.

They boarded their boat and began floating through a long maze of animated figures, all singing the same song, a song that proclaimed harmony in the world, happiness, equity. In the boat ahead of them rode the family with twins. Their parents held them up as if to push them even closer to the spectacle, and the babies' arms waved, their heads turned to look from one side of the canal to the other at all those blinking, dancing, spinning, smiling dolls. Jacob was reminded of a horror film, but the children seemed pleased.

From the boats they followed to the skyway gondola, where the canned yodeling and the wait in line gave Jacob a headache. A wasp circled the crowd, making people bat their hands and duck their heads. It was the only piece of ungoverned nature Jacob had seen here, and as a result he cheered it on, hoping it would sting somebody. Cece stared at the family, whose sullen son had dashed away to a more dangerous ride. The older girls begged for trinkets — the same souvenirs Cece had been buying for days — and the mother threatened them that if they didn't stop complaining they were never going anywhere again. The father thought the girls could have one prize each. The mother argued that simply coming here should be prize enough and, furthermore, that her husband should back her up, regardless of the issue, when they were with the kids. "Unified front," she said, as if nothing but blind compliance would be tolerated; whether he disagreed was irrelevant. One twin fussed, thrashing her arms, tossing her pacifier to the ground, while the other watched placidly, pacifier bobbing between her lips. The wasp circled.

"Which one of those babies would you want?" Cece whispered to Jacob.

Neither, he thought. "The calm one," he said. This baby sat blinking, sucking. Jacob believed that he himself might appear contented — overwhelmed, in fact, stunned — to be pushed around in a stroller among the life-size stuffed animals and bright whirling gadgetry.

Of course, Cece would prefer the unhappy baby. "That one will take no crap," she proclaimed.

Way up in the gondola, Jacob rested his sore heels on the opposite seat where Cece faced him to watch the car bearing the family, ahead of them. Jacob looked out over the park, hoping to catch a glimpse of something beyond it. As a child he'd been taken annually to a small amusement park on his midwestern city's outskirts, and one of the pleasures there was the high ride into the sky on the Ferris wheel. You could spin downward into the clownish chaos of Joyland — organ music, sickening cotton candy, black-toothed carnies — then up for a serene vista of the surrounding farmland, the slow, fat river shining gold in the sunset, the distant orange earthmovers riding over the lumpy jumble of the city dump.

But here there was nothing but park as far as the eye could see, beyond the rides the lakes and highways and mouse-eared traffic signs, a country unto itself, manicured as a golf course, pristine as idealism, perfect as plastic. It was undeniably grand and attractive, but it did not, finally, appeal to Jacob. The swinging basket he sat in suddenly made him aware of being off the ground, that he could fall. Again he thought of Crystal.

Crystal probably believed he'd escaped feeling guilt. There wasn't any way he could convince her otherwise, he knew. Cece had insisted she not have an abortion — despite her immaturity, despite her ostracized life — and then Cece and Jacob had both promised to be available, to be pregnant with her. True, she'd taken advantage — borrowing money, spending all her time on their couch, blackmailing Jacob for favors and attention — but that was no excuse. When they left without telling her where they were going — escaping to Missouri, to a little cabin near the water, just for two nights — she'd behaved like any neglected child. They'd reneged; so would she.

He could not imagine what her life was, now. He'd heard that she finished high school and went on to college out west. She had never revealed her affair with Jacob to Cece, and perhaps the whole horrible ordeal had made her a better person. Jacob wondered if he was a better person than he'd been then. His seduction of Crystal, his single infidelity, had taught him that he would never betray Cece again. Humans erred; this was central to Jacob's knowledge of the world. He'd erred, and Cece would have forgiven him had she ever discovered his offense. And he'd not been entirely unhappy to have Crystal's baby disappear from their lives, no matter how much it meant to Cece. *This* infidelity, he knew, Cece would not have forgiven.

The gondola ride ended after no more than four minutes. "The time ratio, waiting to riding, is not good," Jacob told Cece, shaken by his trip through the air. "Roughly ten to one, as I figure it. And this is the off-season. Imagine this place in July." He saw the whole compound in his mind's eye as a melting structure, a magnificent birthday cake left too long in the sun, a whim of the tyrannical rodent with his pinched, shrill voice.

Cece trailed after the twins, whose father carried both girls down from the landing while their mother led, angrily bouncing the stroller on each step. Outside again, they stopped to get their bearings, then headed toward the long line winding around the enclosed roller coaster. The building was supposed to resemble a space station. Their gloomy, ugly, half-bald son was already in the middle of the line, staring dispassionately as his parents and sisters approached.

Cece, following, said to Jacob, "Watch the people standing behind him in that line."

Sure enough, there was grumbling when the family cut in. But the big mother ignored it, preempting with conviction, busy reconfiguring the double-wide stroller and ordering her son to seek out hot dogs for them all while they held his place. Cece occupied herself with her purse, locating sunglasses and a map of the park, standing alongside the line without actually being in it.

"That mother's going to go on the roller coaster," she predicted, "even though she's pregnant." A sign outside this ride warned various types to beware: people with back or neck injuries, small children, pregnant women. "She's so hardy she doesn't think twice about it," Cece added. Had the woman wanted to, she could have heard the remark, but she was haughty with bottles and powdered formula — motherhood made her oblivious. One of the older daughters was sent to a drinking fountain for water. The husband was given the task of smearing sunscreen on everyone's face. When the son returned, they ate their hot dogs quickly, the mother sucking mustard off her fingers.

The two older daughters were left with the babies while mom and dad and brother stepped into the cool dark of the building. The girls each took a handle of the fat stroller — the kind designed for jogging moms, bicycle-wheeled and expensive — and steered it toward the shaded exit ramp on the far side of the roller coaster. They sat on a curb and ignored their sisters, one of whom cried and the other of whom sat looking around like a sated toad. Jacob thought his feet had never felt so fatigued in all his life.

And then Cece was gone, on her way over to the children, striding fast on her short legs, leaving Jacob alone to watch. She waved at the big girls, exclaimed over the little ones. She asked to hold the noisy one, reaching out without waiting for permission.

Jacob steeled himself. If Cece took that baby, he would not only have to hire a lawyer and come up with bail money, but first he would have to pluck the child from her arms. He'd have to streak after her through the crowds, dashing among the rides and costumed characters — all this nonsense that his wife wanted so badly to claim a share of — and bring her to the ground. Security here, he was sure, would be exemplary — quick and efficient, sovereign. It would be of no interest to anyone but Jacob that she had waited for a twin to kidnap, waited to steal a baby who wouldn't be as missed.

It was hot and Jacob's head felt cooked. The setting was surreal, and thoughts of Crystal Lake had made him feel crazy. Sense was abandoning him. He focused on his wife, who was rocking the squirming, unhappy child. She had a way with babies, a rhythm in her hips, a friendly smile. Babies had been stolen from her and she'd had no recourse. Her desire was larger than his. She alone understood its power, the force it had to make her behave less like a saint and more like a mortal. Watching her now, dizzy with sun and loyalty, Jacob pledged himself to her anew: if she ran, he would not stop her. When she ran, he would follow.

Wayne in Love

FROM NEW ENGLAND REVIEW

WHEN WAYNE got back from not going to California, the HoJo in Scottsdale still leaking, he hoped, but didn't see how, since if it rained in the desert it wouldn't be much, he drove over to his and Felicia's house, which was now Felicia's and the kids', and walked in as if it were still his too. Felicia was standing on what looked like a miniature walker for old folks. It had four chrome legs about a foot high and a pink vinyl pad on the top and was slanted backwards just like a walker. Only Felicia was standing on it and looking at herself in the mirror over the sofa. Wayne reached under the cushions of the sofa and withdrew his army WWI bayonet, which he had kept there against intruders when he lived there.

"What the hell you doing?" he asked Felicia.

"This," Felicia said, turning one way and another to look at her hips, which were in pink shorts the exact color of the vinyl pad she stood on, "is a Exer-Step."

"A what?"

"You step on it."

"I see that. Any beer?"

"No."

Wayne looked at his bayonet: it was the narrow kind, very heavy, with the most prodigious blood groove he had ever seen on a knife of any kind. It was not imaginable to him that a bayonet like this one could kill someone better, or more efficiently or quickly, or let you get it out of the victim easier or whatever the hell a blood groove actually did or was supposed to do. *Blood groove.* It sounded like a joke, or something to tell a recruit and laugh at him if he believed it. It was probably a way to save steel.

Felicia stepped off the Exer-Step and back up, and stepped back off and back on and looked at her hips some more. Wayne pressed his crotch to her leg, at about her knee.

"Hey, Ugly."

"Don't say that to me, Wayne."

"Okay. How about a knobber?"

"Not now. Later."

"Sounds like a weenie."

Wayne struck an elaborate, stylized martial-arts pose and said, "I'm a burnin, burnin hunk of love," and threw the bayonet at the back of the front door, which it struck not with the blade but with the short, heavy, fat, machined handle, making a deep, dull contusion in the door and falling to the floor with a thick twang. Two boys ran into the room at the sound and saw immediately the bayonet and the fresh wound in the door and Wayne and said, in unison and looking at Felicia to gauge her approval, *"Cool!"* Felicia was expressionless, so the boys leapt on the bayonet and fought over it until Wayne took it from them and put it through his belt pirate-style.

"Git."

The boys did.

"There *is* some beer, I think, Wayne," Felicia said.

"Who brought it?"

"Nobody."

"Nobody, shit."

"Nobody, Wayne."

"*I* didn't leave it."

"Wayne, *you left.*"

"Okay. Okay. Don't give me the Fifth Amendment or third-degree burns or —" He stopped speaking, overcome by the sight of Felicia's pale thigh going into the Exer-Step-pink nylon so loosely a hand could easily glide up there, meeting no restriction.

"Our Lady of Prompt Succor," he declared, brandishing the bayonet and trying to kiss her.

"Don't. I'm sweaty."

"Okay."

Felicia went to shower and Wayne went to the kitchen, where he parted items in the refrigerator with the bayonet until he found the beer. These he would have stabbed to extract if it wouldn't have wasted a beer. He felt good, suddenly, very good. He almost took a

beer into the back yard and punctured it with the bayonet to test
out the blood groove, but did not. Yet. "Goddamn *beer groove*," he
said aloud, holding a beer in one hand and the bayonet in the
other. He regarded the bayonet and its groove a moment, put it on
top of the refrigerator, and walked back into the living room holding his crotch, with certain fingers extended and certain folded as
he'd seen black rappers do. The fingering was the same as the
Texas Longhorn Hook 'em Horns sign.

What do they call it — fragrant dereliction?
   What?
   Romans. Somebody. Napoleons.
   Be quiet.
   I'm about to pop.
   Don't.
   I could come back, do this to you all the time.
   No, you couldn't!
   Come back, do it sometimes.
   Not come back. Sometimes, maybe.
   Whatever. *Changkaichek!*
   Oh, Wayne.
   Hey. That mudpuppy'll be back hard in ten minutes.
   I don't have ten minutes.
   What?
   Work.
   Sounds like a personal problem.
   Actually, it *is*, Wayne. I have to have two jobs now.
   Oh.
   And . . .
   And what?
   Don't be here when I get back, if you want *sometimes*.
   Shee*yit*.
   That's right.

Wayne left without showering, wondering where Felicia's second
job was, where she . . . how she kept care of the kids. It was a vague,
troubling haze of guilt that felt like a huge ball of tangled monofilament filling the back seat of the car. A ball of monofilament that
size could not be dealt with with less than a flamethrower. It would
ensnare birds, it would hook something, it would trip you, you'd see

a piece of good tackle in it and never cut your way in, it would foul your next cast, it would williefy your entire life. If his life was a happy, larky fishing trip, he had a ball of monofilament half the size of the boat beside him. And it didn't have anything to do with him anymore. Felicia had had it. She wouldn't *let* him untangle it. Which he didn't want to, couldn't do anyway. How did marriage and kids look like such a hot idea before you had it and like such a clusterfuck after you got it? It was like praying for rain and getting struck by lightning. "I feel like going to Italy," Wayne said aloud in the Impala. He pictured wearing rather pointy, thin-soled shoes and yelling at people without having to fight them and drinking things he'd never heard of (and *liking* them) and mountains, maybe, and fountains and marble and beautiful women who would talk to you whether you understood them or not and whether they understood you or not, a problem that sign language would solve anyway, and what it would be like sleeping with dark world-famous-loving women who did not wear pink shorts the same pink as a miniature geezer walker, stepping on it about once an hour. He was ready for a beer. He was not ready for the want ads, but it looked like time.

After securing his position at Ponderosa Roofing and Sheet Metal, which also manufactured, it turned out, serious roofing equipment, for which Wayne thought he could be a sales representative, particularly for the gas-powered gravel scarifier, as it was properly called, or power spudder, as it was known by those who used it, Wayne went on a date. There was a woman in the office named Pamela Forktine and Wayne could not resist asking her every morning for plastic spoons for the coffee-stirring operations, which were prodigious operations at Ponderosa or any other roofing company at six in the morning among troops as hungover and blear — their brogans flared open at the untied ankles and sticking to the floor, their flannel shirts not altogether tucked in, their hair wet-combed — as the troops at Ponderosa or any roofing company.

Wayne said, "Spoons, Ms. Forktine. Ms. Forktine, spoons." Pamela Forktine was older than Wayne. She had put up with the advances of every description of loser-testosterone-hardcase it was conceivable to put up with, until Wayne. Wayne was to her mind so far gone on rancid testosterone he was sweet. That her fifteen or so years on him did not seem to bother him — a direct result, as she saw it, of the hormonal dementia these boys suffered — made her certain he was sweet.

The fifteen or so years she had on him did *not* bother Wayne, until they went out and Pamela Forktine took the bull by the horns and said, while they were going counterclockwise in their cowboy boots and she was looking for Wayne's chest hair between the pearl snaps of his shirt with her finger, "You want to do the bone dance?"

"Do *what?*" Wayne said, stopping their counterclockwise drift among the stream and creating eddies of resentment on the floor around them. "I mean, *sure,*" he said, and they got going again.

"It's what kids say," Pamela Forktine said. "Bone in, bone out."

Wayne sort of bent over at the waist, blowing his nose at this. He turned a red far deeper than the yoke on his shirt. He had a piece of ass, it was a lock, but this kind of talk embarrassed him to a dangerous point. If Pamela Forktine wanted to do the bone dance, then Pamela Forktine had best not say any more about it.

They went to her house. There she scared Wayne by looking in another room and announcing, "It's okay. He's out."

"Who?"

"Rafe."

"Rafe?"

"Oh. Raphael."

"Who's Raphael?"

"My son."

"How old is he?"

"Nineteen." Pamela Forktine had led Wayne into the living room and was making them a drink in the kitchen. Wayne pondered getting beat up by a nineteen-year-old kid named Raphael. His original concern had been that Pamela Forktine was married and that he might be shot by a Mr. Forktine. That was, now, preferable to this other. Raphael Forktine was either going to be a homosexual of some sort or some kind of terminator. *Rafe Forktine* sounded like death row.

When he looked back on it, picturing Pamela Forktine's death-row-candidate son beating the everliving shit out of him might have been the high point in the travail of his and Pamela Forktine's imminent time together. But Rafe Forktine did not burst in and rescue Wayne from what was about to happen. No one did, including God.

Before God and everybody else, Pamela Forktine walked in the room with two drinks and her blouse open, no bra. This required of Wayne a careful, very casual double-take. Her breasts were not altogether visible because they seemed to point down and away from each other, like a cartoon hound dog's eyes. It was the end of subtlety on Pamela Forktine's part. "Where's that bone, Wayne?"

Wayne turned red and made a splitting noise.

"In here?" Pamela Forktine made one stroking pass, one unzipping pass, and scared Wayne with an immediate and vigorous program of what he would later term gobbling. It included a gobbling noise. Wayne would have laughed but was too frightened. The gobbling worked, though, and Pamela Forktine got up very cuddly in his neck, her knees facing him on the sofa, and said, "Oh, sweetie. I hope I'm okay."

"You're okay, *sure* you're okay —"

"No, I mean. Well, I've been . . ."

This scared Wayne again. "You've been . . . what?"

"Dry."

"What?"

"I've been, well, *dry.*"

There they were in a brightly lit living room waiting for a nineteen-year-old son to avenge his mother, who said things like *bone in bone out,* gobbled you, was dry. Wayne was about to lose it. Why did pussy have to be this way? Why could it not be like a magazine? Like a book? Like at least a *story,* something that went smooth and *worked.*

But Pamela Forktine was not giving up. She gobbled, she got Wayne into the bedroom, she got on Wayne, and Wayne had a passing fancy that her hair felt like hemp and her skin like party balloons three days after the party. But this felt good, this harsh rope and loose satin, and made its opposite number, fine hair and young tight flesh, seem like tomatoes and eggplants, and Wayne began if not gobbling back at least nibbling this satiny crinkly Pamela Forktine, and Pamela Forktine when that didn't tickle too much seemed to like it and kept saying "Oh, sweetie" and was not dry. It worked. Wayne gasped up on her like a shipwrecked man on his found island. "Oh sweetie, sweetie, sweetie," Pamela Forktine said, patting his head in rhythm.

This was a very sad and silly business, Wayne thought, this woman calling him this for not doing any more than not losing his desire and spooing in her in five minutes, but she was calling him this *sweetie* nonsense without any joke, she was serious, and that made Wayne feel, despite himself, good. She could by God call him whatever she wanted to. What had she ever done to him? She had *fucked* him, that's what, and that was what he'd asked for. He was going to be man enough to take what he got if he was man enough to ask for it.

And he was asking for it, man or not. *Man.* God, or whoever, put you here, and you have to ask for it. He puts water here and it *has* to run downhill. You get up there in fucking hundred-and-twenty-degree heat and *have* to stop its running. You fix the fucking leak.

"I sprung a leak in you, Pamela Forktine," Wayne said.

"You sure did."

"Was it too soon?"

"No, sweetie. It was just fine."

Just fine, Wayne knew, meant too soon. So what? Was that his fault? No, it was not. Water runs downhill. It has to.

It was not a new beginning, but it was, Wayne thought, new enough. He was half asleep and inadvertently said, aloud, "New enough," and Pamela Forktine said, "Hmmm? Did you say nude enough?"

"Sounds like a wiener," Wayne said.

They nestled and snuggled together. Pamela Forktine said, "Do you like cereal? Rafe likes cereal. You can stay. There's enough."

"There's nude enough?"

"Nude enough."

It was their first joke together. Wayne said, "I had a twin brother no one knows about. Sparky. Sparky died and Wayne lived."

"I'm sorry, sweetie. How old was he?"

"Sparky was three. Minutes."

"Mmmm."

"Nude enough."

"I'm nude enough, Wayne."

"What? More?"

"Sounds like a wiener, sweetie."

Wayne liked women who said what they wanted. Up to a point. This was the point. This was precisely the point. He liked Pamela Forktine.

Wayne took, as he puts it, a dump. This came out of him loose and burning. It made him step more highly than usual for a few minutes

afterward and wish for some kind of soothing salve. "Is there any
beer?" he asked Pamela Forktine. This was probably a mistake, at
nine in the morning with a new woman with a teenage *(underage)*
son possibly already in the kitchen eating cereal. Next he would be
watching cartoons. Wayne gave this some thought. Maybe this was
not the place to be.

Pamela Forktine had not heard him, apparently, and he heard
no noise in the kitchen, so he tiptoed in there and looked, and
there was no beer. He went back in the bathroom and closed the
door and looked at himself in the mirror. His hair was dirty and it
had the kind of control to it that suggested someone had jerked
large chunks of it out. Except it was so greasy, how could anyone get
a *grip* on it? Wayne did this himself — grabbed a chunk of hair —
and felt it slipping in his hand well before it hurt to pull it. He
thought about a shower. That might constitute a moving-in gesture
— he did not want that. And he did not want this Rafe character,
convict or cartoon-watcher cereal-eater, to find him in the shower
the first time they met.

He looked at himself again. His face was, as all faces are to their
owners, inscrutable. It was "normal" up to a point. It had high,
glossy, rather boyish cheeks and a freckled nose, not too veined,
and the always slightly burned forehead was plain. Then the
trouble started. That wild skyline of hair, and, when he smiled,
something that gave Wayne the willies, like mold on cheese gave
him the willies, because you never knew, once you got away from
outright yellow cheese into cheese that was white, or nearly white, it
could be bluish or greenish, and soft, you never knew *how* soft until
you touched it — once you got away from yellow cheese you did not
know if the mold was mold or part of the cheese itself. That was the
feeling he had, looking at his teeth in Pamela Forktine's mirror on
a Saturday morning. He looked around the bathroom: it was good
old tile, black and white, and she had knickknack shelves everywhere and all the towels and face towels neatly hung, and the toilet
was covered in carpet that matched the rug on the floor. He smiled
at himself quickly and got the blue-cheese willies and got in the
shower anyway.

He soaped up very, very well and took two or three kinds of
shampoo from a rack of them, whether they said Conditioner or
not or Oily or Dry or Normal, and washed everything hard and got
a boner. All right. He was back. The killer was back.

TIM GAUTREAUX

Welding with Children

FROM THE ATLANTIC MONTHLY

TUESDAY WAS about typical. My four daughters — not one of them married, you understand — brought over their kids, one each, and explained to my wife how much fun she was going to have looking after them again. But Tuesday was her day to go to the casino, so guess who got to tend the four babies. My oldest daughter also brought over a bed rail that the end broke off of. She wanted me to weld it. Now, what the hell you can do in a bed that'll cause the end of a iron rail to break off is beyond me, but she can't afford another one on her burger-flipping salary, she said, so I got to fix it with four little kids hanging on my coveralls. Her boy is seven months, nicknamed Nu-Nu, a big-headed baby with a bubbling tongue always hanging out of his mouth. My second oldest, a flight attendant on some propeller airline out of Alexandria, has a little six-year-old girl named Moonbean, and that ain't no nickname. My third daughter, who is still dating, dropped off Tammynette, also six. Last to come was Freddie — my favorite, because he looks like those old photographs of me when I was seven. He has a round head with copper bristle for hair, cut about as short as Velcro. He's got that kind of papery skin, like me, but it's splashed with a handful of freckles.

When everybody was on deck, I put the three oldest in front of the TV and rocked Nu-Nu to sleep before dropping him in the port-a-crib. Then I dragged the bed rail and the three awake kids out through the trees, back to my tin workshop. I tried to get something done, but Tammynette got the big grinder turned on and jammed a file against the stone just to laugh at the sparks. I got the thing unplugged and then started to work, but when I was setting the bed rail in the vise and clamping on the ground wire from the welding machine, I leaned against the iron and Moonbean picked the electric rod holder off the cracker box and struck a blue arc on the zipper of my coveralls, low. I jumped back like I was hit with religion and tore those coveralls off and shook the sparks out of my drawers. Moonbean opened her goat eyes wide and sang, "Whoo. Grendaddy can bust a move." I decided I better hold off trying to weld with little kids around.

I herded them into the yard to play, but even though I got three acres, there ain't much for them to do at my place, so I sat down and watched Freddie climb on a Oldsmobile engine I got hanging from a willow oak on a long chain. Tammynette and Moonbean pushed him like he was on a swing, and I yelled at them to stop, but they wouldn't listen. It was a sad sight, I guess. I shouldn't have had that greasy old engine hanging from a K-mart chain in my side yard. I knew better. Even in this central Louisiana town of Gumwood, which is just like any other red-dirt place in the South, trash in the yard is trash in the yard. I make decent money as a now-and-then welder.

I think sometimes about how I even went to college once. I went a whole semester to LSU. Worked overtime at a sawmill for a year to afford the tuition and showed up in my work boots to be taught English 101 by a black guy from Pakistan who couldn't understand one word we said, much less us him. He didn't teach me a damn thing and would sit on the desk with his legs crossed and tell us to write nonstop in what he called our portfolios, which he never read. For all I know, he sent our papers back to Pakistan for his relatives to use as stove fuel.

The algebra teacher talked to us with his eyes rolled up like his lecture was printed out on the ceiling. Most of the time he didn't even know we were in the room, and for a month I thought the poor bastard was stone blind. I never once solved for x.

The chemistry professor was a fat drunk who heated Campbell's soup on one of those little burners and ate it out of the can while he talked. There was about a thousand of us in that classroom, and I couldn't figure out what he wanted us to do with the numbers and names. I sat way in the back, next to some fraternity boys who called me Uncle Jed. Time or two, when I could see the blackboard off on the horizon, I almost got the hang of something, and I was glad of that.

I kind of liked the history professor, and learned to write down a lot of what he said, but he dropped dead one hot afternoon in the middle of the pyramids and was replaced by a little porch lizard that looked down his nose at me where I sat in the front row. He bit on me pretty good, I guess because I didn't look like nobody else in that class, with my short red hair and blue jeans that were blue. I flunked out that semester, but I got my money's worth learning about people that don't have hearts no bigger than birdshot.

Tammynette and Moonbean gave the engine a long shove and then got distracted by a yellow butterfly playing in a clump of pigweed, and that nine-hundred-pound V-8 kind of ironed them out on the backswing. So I picked up the squalling girls and got everybody inside, where I cleaned them good with Go-Jo.

"I want a Icee!" Tammynette yelled while I was getting the motor oil from between her fingers. "I ain't had a Icee all day."

"You don't need one every day, little miss," I told her.

"Don't you got some money?" She pulled a hand away and flipped her hair with it like a model on TV.

"Those things cost most of a dollar. When I was a kid, I used to get a nickel for candy, and that only twice a week."

"Icee!" she yelled in my face. Moonbean took up the cry and called out from the kitchen in her dull little voice. She wasn't dull in the head, she just talked low, like a bad cowboy actor. Nu-Nu sat up in the port-a-crib and gargled something, so I gathered everyone up, put them in the Caprice, and drove them down to the Gumwood Pak-a-Sak. The baby was in my lap when I pulled up, and Freddie was tuning in some rock music that sounded like hail on a tin roof. Two guys I know, older than me, watched us roll to the curb. When I turned the engine off, I heard one of them say, "Here comes Bruton and his bastardmobile." I grabbed the steering wheel hard and looked down on the top of Nu-Nu's head, feeling like someone just told me my house burned down. I'm always sun-burned, so the old men couldn't see the shame rising in my face. I got out, pretending I didn't hear anything, Nu-Nu in the crook of my arm like a loaf of bread. I wanted to punch the guy who said it and break his upper plate, but I could imagine the article in the local paper. I could see the memories the kids would have of their grandfather whaling away at two snuff-dripping geezers. I looked them in the eye and smiled, surprising myself. Bastardmobile. Man.

"Hey, Bruton," said the younger one, a Mr. Fordlyson, maybe sixty-five. "All them kids yours? You start over?"

"Grandkids," I said, holding Nu-Nu over Fordlyson's shoes, so maybe he'd drool on them.

The older one wore a straw fedora and was nicked up in twenty places with skin-cancer operations. He snorted. "Maybe you can do better with this batch," he told me. He was also a Mr. Fordlyson, the other guy's uncle. He used to run the hardwood sawmill north of town, was a deacon in the Baptist Church, and owned about one percent of the pissant bank down next to the gin. He thought he was king of Gumwood, but then every old man in town who had five dollars in his pocket and an opinion on the tip of his tongue thought the same.

I pushed past him and went into the Pak-a-Sak. The kids saw the candy rack and cried out for Mars Bars and Zeros. Even Nu-Nu put out a slobbery hand toward the Gummy Worms, but I ignored their whining and drew them each a small Coke Icee. Tammynette and Moonbean grabbed theirs and headed for the door. Freddie took his carefully when I offered it. Nu-Nu might be kind of wobble-headed and as plain as a melon, but he sure knew what an Icee was and how to go after a straw. And what a smile when that Coke syrup hit those bald gums of his.

Right then Freddie looked up at me with his green eyes in that speckled face and said, "What's a bastardmobile?"

I guess my mouth dropped open. "I don't know what you're talking about."

"I thought we was in a Chevrolet," he said.

"We are."

"Well, that man said we was in a —"

"Never mind what he said. You must have misheard him." I nudged him toward the door and we went out. The older Mr. Fordlyson was watching us like we were a parade. I tried to look straight ahead. In my mind the newspaper bore the headline "LOCAL MAN ARRESTED WITH GRANDCHILDREN FOR AS-SAULT." I got into the car with the kids and looked back out at the Fordlysons where they sat on a bumper rail, sweating through their white shirts and staring at us. Their kids owned sawmills, ran fast-food franchises, were on the school board. They were all married. I guess the young Fordlysons were smart, though looking at that pair you'd never know where they got their brains. I backed out onto the highway, trying not to think, but to me the word was spelled out in chrome script on my fenders: *Bastardmobile*.

On the way home Tammynette stole a suck on Freddie's straw, and he jerked it away and called her a word I'd heard only from the younger workers at the plywood mill. The word hit me in the back of the head like a brick, and I pulled off the road onto the gravel shoulder. "What'd you say, boy?"

"Nothing." But he reddened. I saw he cared what I thought.

"Kids your age don't use language like that."

Tammynette flipped her hair and raised her chin. "How old you got to be?"

I gave her a look. "Don't you care what he said to you?"

"It's what they say on the comedy program," Freddie said. "Everybody says that."

"What comedy program?"

"It comes on after the nighttime news."

"What you doing up late at night?"

He just stared at me, and I saw that he had no idea of what *late* was. Glendine, his mama, probably lets him fall asleep in front of the set every night. I pictured him crumpled up on that smelly shag rug she keeps in front of the TV to catch the spills and crumbs.

When I got home, I took them all onto our covered side porch. The girls began to struggle with jacks, their little ball bouncing crooked on the slanted floor. Freddie played tunes on his Icee straw, and Nu-Nu fell asleep in my lap. I stared at my car and wondered if its name had spread throughout the community, if everywhere I drove people would call out, "Here comes the bastardmobile!" Gumwood is one of those towns where everybody looks at everything that moves. I do it myself. If my neighbor, Miss Hanchy, pulls out of her lane, I wonder, Now where is the old bat off to? It's two-thirty, so her soap opera must be over. I figure her route to the store, and then somebody different drives by and catches my attention, and I think after them. This is not all bad. It makes you watch how you behave, and besides, what's the alternative? Nobody giving a flip about whether you live or die? I've heard those stories from the big cities about how people will sit in an apartment window six stories up, watch somebody take ten minutes to kill you with a stick, and not even reach for the phone.

I started thinking about my four daughters. None of them has any religion to speak of. I thought they'd pick it up from their mama, like I did from mine, but LaNelle always worked so much that she just had time to cook, clean, transport, and fuss. The girls grew up watching cable and videos every night, and that's where they got their view of the world, and that's why four dirty blondes with weak chins from St. Helena Parish thought they lived in a Hollywood soap opera. They also thought the married pulpwood-truck drivers and garage mechanics they dated were movie stars. I guess a lot of what's wrong with my girls is my fault, but I don't know what I could've done different.

Moonbean raked in a gaggle of jacks, and a splinter from the porch floor ran up under her nail. "Shit dog," she said, wagging her hand like it was on fire and coming to me on her knees.

"Don't say that."

"My finger hurts. Fix it, Paw-Paw."

"I will if you stop talking like white trash."

Tammynette bounced her jacks ball and picked up on fivesies. "Melvin says 'shit dog.'"

"Would you do everything your mama's boyfriend does?"

"Melvin can drive," Tammynette said. "I'd like to drive."

I got out my penknife and worked the splinter from under Moonbean's nail while she jabbered to Tammynette about how her mama's Toyota cost more than Melvin's teeny Dodge truck. I swear I don't know how these kids got so complicated. When I was their age, all I wanted to do was make mud pies or play in the creek. I didn't want anything but a twice-a-week nickel to take to the store. These kids ain't eight years old and already know enough to run a casino. When I finished, I looked down at Moonbean's brown eyes, at Nu-Nu's pulsing head. "Does your mamas ever talk to y'all about, you know, God?"

"My mama says 'God' when she's cussing Melvin," Tammynette said.

"That's not what I mean. Do they read Bible stories to y'all at bedtime?"

Freddie's face brightened. "She rented *Conan the Barbarian* for us once. That movie kicked ass."

"That's not a Bible movie," I told him.

"It ain't? It's got swords and snakes in it."

"What's that got to do with anything?"

Tammynette came close and grabbed Nu-Nu's hand and played the fingers like they were piano keys. "Ain't the Bible full of swords and snakes?"

Nu-Nu woke up and peed on himself, so I had to go for a plastic diaper. On the way back from the bathroom I saw our little book-rack out the corner of my eye. I found my old Bible-stories hard-back and took it out on the porch. It was time somebody taught them something about something.

They gathered round, sitting on the floor, and I got down amongst them. I started into Genesis and how God made the earth, and how he made us and gave us a soul that would live forever. Moonbean reached into the book and put her hand on God's beard. "If he shaved, he'd look just like that old man down at the Pak-a-Sak," she said.

My mouth dropped a bit. "You mean Mr. Fordlyson? That man don't look like God."

Tammynette yawned. "You just said God made us to look like him."

"Never mind," I told them, going on into Adam and Eve and the garden. Soon as I turned the page, they saw the snake and began to squeal.

"Look at the size of that sucker," Freddie said.

Tammynette wiggled closer. "I knew they was a snake in this book."

"He's a bad one," I told them. "He lied to Adam and Eve and said to not do what God told them to do."

Moonbean looked up at me slow. "This snake can talk?"

"Yes."

"How about that. Just like in cartoons. I thought they was making that up."

"Well, a real snake can't talk nowadays," I explained.

"Ain't this garden snake a real snake?" Freddie asked.

"It's the devil in disguise," I told them.

Tammynette flipped her hair. "Aw, that's just a old song. I heard it on the reddio."

"That Elvis Presley tune's got nothing to do with the devil making himself into a snake in the Garden of Eden."

"Who's Elvis Presley?" Moonbean sat back in the dust by the weatherboard wall and stared out at my overgrown lawn.

"He's some old singer died a million years ago," Tammynette told her.

"Was he in the Bible too?"

I beat the book on the floor. "No, he ain't. Now pay attention. This is important." I read the section about Adam and Eve disobeying God, turned the page, and all hell broke loose. An angel was holding a long sword over Adam and Eve's downturned heads as he ran them out of the garden. Even Nu-Nu got excited and pointed a finger at the angel.

"What's that guy doing?" Tammynette asked.

"Chasing them out of Paradise. Adam and Eve did a bad thing, and when you do bad, you get punished for it." I looked down at their faces, and it seemed that they were all thinking about something at the same time. It was scary, the little sparks I saw flying in their eyes. Whatever you tell them at this age stays forever. You got to be careful. Freddie looked up at me and asked, "Did they ever get to go back?"

"Nope. Eve started worrying about everything, and Adam had to work every day like a beaver just to get by."

"Was that angel really gonna stick Adam with that sword?" Moonbean asked.

"Forget about that darned sword, will you?"

"Well, that's just mean," is what she said.

"No, it ain't," I said. "They got what was coming to them." Then I went into Noah and the Flood, and in the middle of things Freddie piped up.

"You mean all the bad people got drownded at once? All *right*."

I looked down at him hard and saw that the Bible was turning into one big adventure film for him. Freddie had already watched so many movies that any religion he heard about would nest in his brain on top of *Tanga the Cave Woman* and *Bikini Death Squad*. I got everybody a cold drink and a jelly sandwich, and after that I turned on a window unit and handed out Popsicles. We sat inside, on the couch, because the heat had waked up the yellow flies outside. I tore into how Abraham almost stabbed Isaac, and the kids' eyes got big when they saw the knife. I hoped that they got a sense of obedience to God out of it, but when I asked Freddie what the point of the story was, he just shrugged and looked glum. Tammynette, however, had an opinion. "He's just like O. J. Simpson!"

Freddie shook his head. "Naw. God told Abraham to do it just as a test."

"Maybe God told O. J. to do what he did," Tammynette sang.

"Naw. O. J. did it on his own," Freddie told her. "He didn't like his wife no more."

"Well, maybe Abraham didn't like his son no more neither, so he was gonna kill him dead, and God stopped him." Tammynette's voice was starting to rise the way her mother's did when she'd been drinking.

"Daddies don't kill their sons when they don't like them," Freddie told her. "They just pack up and leave." He broke apart the two halves of his Popsicle and bit one and then the other.

Real quick I started in on Sodom and Gomorrah and the burning of the towns full of wicked people. Moonbean was struck by Lot's wife. "I saw this movie once where Martians shot a gun at you and turned you into a statue. You reckon it was Martians burnt down those towns?"

"The Bible is not a movie," I told her.

"I think I seen it down at Blockbuster," Tammynette said.

I didn't stop to argue but pushed on through Moses and the Ten Commandments, spending a lot of time on No. 6, since that one give their mamas so much trouble. Then Nu-Nu began to rub his nose with the backs of his hands and started to tune up, so I knew it was time to put the book down and wash faces and get snacks and play crawl-around. I was determined not to turn on the TV again, but Freddie hit the button when I was in the kitchen. When Nu-Nu and I came into the living room, they were in a half-circle around a talk show. On the set were several overweight, tattooed, frowning, slouching individuals who, the announcer told us, had tricked their parents into signing over ownership of their houses and then evicted them. The kids watched like they were looking at cartoons — which is to say, they gobbled it all up. At a commercial I asked Moonbean, who has the softest heart, what she thought of kids that threw their parents into the street. She put a finger in one ear and said through a long yawn that if the parents did mean things, then the kids could do what they wanted to them. I shook my head, went in the kitchen, found the Christmas vodka, and poured myself a long drink over some ice cubes. I stared out in the yard to where my last pickup truck lay dead and rusting in a pile of wisteria at the edge of the lot. I formed a little fantasy about gathering all these kids into my Caprice and heading out northwest to start over, away from their mamas, TVs, mildew, their casino-mad grandmother, and Louisiana in general. I could get a job, raise them right, send them to college so that they could own sawmills and run car dealerships.

A drop of sweat rolled off the glass and hit my right shoe, and I looked down at it. The leather lace-ups I was wearing were paint-spattered and twenty years old. They told me I hadn't held a steady job in a long time, that whatever bad was gonna happen was partly my fault. I wondered then if my wife had had the same fantasy: leaving her scruffy, sunburned, failed-welder husband home and moving away with these kids, maybe taking a course in clerical skills and getting a job in Utah, raising them right, sending them off to college. Maybe even each of their mamas had the same fantasy, pulling their kids out of their parents' gassy-smelling old house and heading away from the heat and humidity. I took another long swallow and wondered why one of us didn't do it. I looked out to my Caprice, sitting in the shade of a pecan tree, shadows of leaves moving on it, making it quiver like a dark-green flame, and I realized we couldn't drive away from ourselves. We couldn't escape in the bastardmobile.

In the pantry I opened the house's circuit panel and rotated out a fuse until I heard a cry from the living room. I went in and pulled down a storybook, something about a dog saving a train. My wife bought it twenty years ago for one of our daughters but never read it to her. I sat in front of the dark television.

"What's wrong with the TV, Paw-Paw?" Moonbean rasped.

"It died," I said, opening the book. They squirmed and complained, but after a few pages they were hooked. It was a good book, one I'd read myself one afternoon during a thunderstorm. But while I was reading, this blue feeling got me. I began to think, What's the use? I'm just one old man with a little brown book of Bible stories and a doggie-hero tale. How can that compete with daily MTV, kids' programs that make big people look like fools, the Playboy Channel, the shiny magazines their mamas and their boy-friends leave around the house, magazines like *Me*, and *Self*, and *Love Guides*, and rental movies where people kill each other with no more thought than it would take to swat a fly — nothing at all like what Abraham suffered before he raised that knife? But I read on for a half-hour, and when that dog stopped the locomotive before it pulled the passenger train over the collapsed bridge, even Tammynette clapped her sticky hands.

The next day I didn't have much on the welding schedule, so after one or two little jobs, including the bed rail that my daughter began to rag me about, I went out to pick up a window grate the town marshal wanted me to fix. It was hot right after lunch, and Gumwood was quivering with heat. Across from the cypress railroad station was our little red-brick city hall with a green copper dome on it, and on the grass in front of that was a pecan tree and a wooden bench under it. Old men sometimes gathered there under the cool branches and told each other how to fix tractors that hadn't been made in fifty years, or how to make grits out of a strain of corn that didn't exist anymore. Locals called that pecan the Tree of Knowledge. When I walked by, going to the marshal's office, I saw the older Mr. Fordlyson seated in the middle of the long bench, blinking at the street like a chicken. He called out to me.

"Bruton," he said. "Too hot to weld?"

I didn't think it was a friendly comment, though he waved for me to come over. "Something like that." I was tempted to walk on, but he motioned for me to sit next to him, which I did. I looked across the street for a long time. "Yesterday at the store," I began, "you said my car was a bastardmobile."

Fordlyson blinked twice but didn't change his expression. Most local men would be embarrassed at being caught in rudeness, but he sat there with his face as hard as a plowshare. "Isn't that what it is?" he said at last.

I should have been mad, and I was mad, but I kept on. "It was a mean thing to let me hear." I looked down and wagged my head. "I need help with those kids, not your meanness."

He looked at me with his little nickel-colored eyes glinting under that straw fedora with the black-silk hatband. "What kind of help you need?"

I picked up a pecan that was still in its green pod. "I'd like to fix it so those grandkids do right. I'm thinking of talking to their mamas and —"

"Too late for their mamas." He put up a hand and let it fall like an ax. "They'll have to decide to straighten out on their own.

Nothing you can tell those girls now will change them a whit." He said this in a tone that hinted I was stupid for not seeing this. Dumb as a post. He looked off to the left for half a second and then back. "You got to deal directly with those kids."

"I'm trying." I cracked the nut open on the edge of the bench.

"Tryin' won't do shit. You got to take them to Sunday school every week. You go to church?"

"Yeah."

"Don't eat that green pecan — it'll make you sick. Which church you go to?"

"Bonner Straight Gospel."

He flew back as though he'd just fired a twelve-gauge at the dog sleeping under the station platform across the street. "Bruton, your wild-man preacher is one step away from taking up serpents. I've heard he lets the kids come to the main service and yells at them about frying in hell like chicken parts. You got to keep them away from that man. Why don't you come to First Baptist?"

I looked at the ground. "I don't know."

The old man bobbed his head once. "I know damned well why not. You won't tithe."

That hurt deep. "Hey, I don't have a lot of extra money. I know the Baptists got good Sunday school programs, but . . ."

Fordlyson waved a finger in the air like a little sword. "Well, join the Methodists. The Presbyterians." He pointed up the street. "Join those Catholics. Some of them don't put more than a dollar a week in the plate, but there are so many of them, and the church has so many services a weekend, that the priests can run the place on volume, like Wal-Mart."

I knew several good mechanics who were Methodists. "How's their children's programs?"

The old man spoke out of the side of his mouth. "Better'n you got now."

"I'll think about it," I told him.

"Yeah, bullshit. You'll go home and weld together a log truck, and tomorrow you'll go fishing, and you'll never do nothing for them kids, and they'll all wind up serving time in Angola or on their backs in New Orleans."

It got me hot the way he thought he had all the answers, and I turned on him quick. "Okay, wise man. I came to the Tree of Knowledge. Tell me what to do."

He pulled down one finger on his right hand with the forefinger of the left. "Go join the Methodists." Another finger went down, and he told me, "Every Sunday take them children to church." A third finger, and he said, "And keep 'em with you as much as you can."

I shook my head. "I already raised my kids."

Fordlyson looked at me hard and didn't have to say what he was thinking. He glanced down at the ground between his smooth-toe lace-ups. "And clean up your yard."

"What's that got to do with anything?"

"It's got everything to do with everything."

"Why?"

"If you don't know, I can't tell you." Here he stood up, and I saw his daughter at the curb in her Lincoln. One leg wouldn't straighten all the way out, and I could see the pain in his face. I grabbed his arm, and he smiled a mean little smile and leaned in to me for a second and said, "Bruton, everything worth doing hurts like hell." He toddled off and left me with his sour breath on my face and a thought forming in my head like a raincloud.

After a session with the Methodist preacher I went home and stared at the yard and then stared at the telephone until I got up the strength to call Famous Amos Salvage. The next morning a wrecker and a gondola came down my road, and before noon Amos loaded up four derelict cars, six engines, four washing machines, ten broken lawn mowers, and two and a quarter tons of scrap iron. I begged and borrowed Miss Hanchy's Super-A and bush-hogged the three acres I own and then some. I cut the grass and picked up around the workshop. With the money I got from the scrap, I bought some aluminum paint for the shop and some first-class stuff for the outside of the house. The next morning I was up at seven replacing screen on the little porch. On the big porch on the side I put down a heavy coat of glossy green deck enamel. At lunch my wife stuck her head through the porch door. "The kids are coming over again. How you gonna keep 'em off of all that wet paint?"

My knees were killing me, and I couldn't figure how to keep Nu-Nu from crawling out here. "I don't know."

She looked around at the wet glare. "What's got into you, changing our religion and all?"

"Time for a change, I guess." I loaded up my brush.

She thought about this a moment and then pointed. "Careful you don't paint yourself in a corner."

"I'm doing the best I can."

"It's about time," she said under her breath, walking away.

I backed off the porch and down the steps and then stood in the pinestraw next to the house, painting the ends of the porch boards. I heard a car come down the road and watched my oldest daughter drive up and get out with Nu-Nu over her shoulder. When she came close, I looked at her dyed hair, which was the color and texture of fiberglass insulation, the dark mascara, and the olive skin under her eyes. She smelled of cigarette smoke, stale smoke, like she hadn't had a bath in three days. Her tan blouse was tight and tied in a knot above her navel, which was a lardy hole. She passed Nu-Nu to me like he was a ham. "Can he stay the night?" she asked. "I want to go hear some music."

"Why not?"

She looked around slowly. "Looks like a bomb hit this place and blew everything away." The door to her dusty compact creaked open, and a freckled hand came out. "I forgot to mention that I picked up Freddie on the way in. Hope you don't mind." She didn't look at me as she mumbled this, hands on her hips. Freddie, who had been sleeping, I guess, sat on the edge of the car seat and rubbed his eyes like a drunk.

"He'll be all right here," I said.

She took in a deep, slow breath, so deathly bored that I felt sorry for her. "Well, guess I better be heading on down the road." She turned and then whipped around on me. "Hey, guess what."

"What?"

"Nu-Nu finally said his first word yesterday." She was biting the inside of her cheek, I could tell.

I looked at the baby, who was going after my shirt buttons. "What'd he say?"

"Da-da." And her eyes started to get red, so she broke and ran for her car.

"Wait," I called, but it was too late. In a flash she was gone in a cloud of gravel dust, racing toward the most cigarette smoke, music, and beer she could find in one place.

I took Freddie and the baby around to the back steps by the little

screen porch and sat down. We tickled and goo-gooed at Nu-Nu
until finally he let out a "Da-da" — real loud, like a call.

Freddie looked back toward the woods, at the nice trees in the
yard, which looked like what they were now that the trash had been
carried off. "What happened to all the stuff?"

"Gone," I said. "We gonna put a tire swing on that tall willow oak
there, first off."

"All right. Can you cut a drain hole in the bottom so the rain-
water won't stay in it?" He came close and put a hand on top of the
baby's head.

"Yep."

"A big steel-belt tire?"

"Sounds like a plan." Nu-Nu looked at me and yelled, "Da-da,"
and I thought how he'd be saying that in one way or another for the
rest of his life and never be able to face the fact that Da-da had
skipped town, whoever Da-da was. The baby brought me into focus,
somebody's blue eyes looking at me hard. He blew spit over his
tongue and cried out, "Da-da," and I put him on my knee, facing
away toward the cool green branches of my biggest willow oak.

"Even Nu-Nu can ride the tire," Freddie said.

"He can fit the circle in the middle," I told him.

HESTER KAPLAN

Would You Know It Wasn't Love

FROM GULF COAST

WHEN WALT thinks about his daughter Rosie and her disintegrating marriage, he can't help thinking about himself too. He's not
moved to pity, either for his own sick self or for Rosie and Tim; what
he feels instead is the misery and waste of this breaking-up of lives.
He's edgy now when he's always been patient, but he's a man with a
disease, out of control sometimes, sometimes hateful, he knows,
but forgiven. His wife Helen, well ahead of him into Rosie's mess
already, has bags under her eyes, and a penchant for salty things
which she eats until her mouth swells up. After dinner, Walt caught
her gulping glass after glass of water at the kitchen sink. He felt as
though he'd walked in on something he shouldn't have seen, but
he couldn't look away. Recently Helen has stopped acknowledging
his private moments — the time his swollen fingers refused to hold
a glass so that it fell and shattered on the floor, when his morning
stiffness had him groping at the wall for something to lean against.
He knows she's witnessed them. He's seen her worried shadow pass
by, heard her gasp.

   On the downstairs extension in his study off the kitchen, and
Helen upstairs on the bedroom phone, they talk to Rosie. Walt
wants to understand what's going on, but she sniffles more than she
speaks a full sentence, so that again he isn't sure what the problem
is. After Rosie says goodbye to her parents, Walt and Helen stay on
the line. Tim is brooding and inscrutable, Walt says to Helen — has
she ever met a man who wasn't? — but did that mean Rosie should
walk away from her marriage? It's an old theme he's brought up:
the fear that they've babied their youngest daughter to the point of
hobbling her.

Walt thinks it's strange — but also a little easier — to talk to Helen tonight over the phone so they don't have to look at each other. He can imagine that she's not quite as familiar to him, nor he so familiar to her, that they might come up with something they haven't said before.

The operator interrupts before Helen can answer, so Walt walks upstairs to finish the conversation. Helen turns to him as he enters the bedroom, and in the light of her reading lamp, he sees the chapping around her thin mouth, like cheap lipstick. He wonders, too tired for passion, how long it has been since they've really kissed, tongues and all, with his hands on her solid body; certainly since the start of Rosie's crisis.

"Why are you telling me this about Tim?" Helen asks him angrily, and her face blushes red. Her eyes are a cold blue. "Inscrutable? Brooding? Those are ridiculous words. What am I supposed to do with them? Are they going to help the situation somehow?"

Walt has no answer for his wife. He hadn't intended to sound so cold-hearted, only firm. Helen returns to the student papers she's correcting for tomorrow, and Walt goes downstairs to his study again. When he kneels slowly in front of the closet, he almost expects to find that the rheumatoid arthritis has reached his knees, as his doctor has warned that it might one of these days. But he is relieved to be spared so far, and digs around in the back where he keeps all his cassette tapes: of his lectures, the babies' chatter, of his girls' clumsy and beautiful recitals and plays, of school speeches and dinner parties, Helen singing tipsy at his forty-seventh birthday party. He's sentimental about these sounds the way others are about photographs.

The sharp plastic boxes are a comfort to him. Walt is aware that he's a technological oddity these days, preferring his inoffensive, nonobtrusive tape recorder and cassettes, when he could get sound and picture with a camcorder the size of his palm, the minor heft of a small melon. One day he intends to do something with all of the tapes he's collected, turn them into some kind of a history of his family he might listen to when he's finally crippled. Through old corduroy pants, Walt's bones begin to grind against the floor, and it takes him a while to locate the cassette he's after. He finds it near the back finally, and stands up.

Walt pushes the play button on his recorder, sits in his armchair the cat has scratched bare, and listens. His study needs repainting, he sees. The bad light plays up how much they've let slide in the past two years since he's been sick, as though the only thing to focus on is the mysterious course his body is taking. He remembers four years before deciding to leave the tape running even as his favorite dog vomited under the kitchen table, as Helen dropped an empty pan on the floor, and the dishwasher started with its splash of water. It was the noise behind the negotiations he'd wanted to record as much as the discussion itself of the wedding's guest list and the meaning of an open bar. Helen and Rosie had hardly protested against the taping and what their own words might hold them to later on, and then only because they understood it was expected of them, just as the taping was expected of him.

But Walt hears now, very clearly with nothing to distract him in his quiet house, that Tim was not so sure about being recorded, collected. The boy clears his throat too often and says almost nothing, as though it weren't his wedding they were planning but someone else's entirely. Again and again, over side A and B of the cassette, Walt hears Tim clear his thick throat. He swears it sounds like thunder rumbling behind Rosie's voice full of premarriage optimism. If ambivalence makes a noise, this is it, Walt thinks, and turns off the tape recorder with a jab of his thumb.

"You motherfucker," he mumbles, though he is not quite sure who he is naming.

Walt knows the tape isn't going to tell him what to do about his daughter's problems. After all, it didn't tell him that his adored dog was going to die two weeks after the tape was made, choked to death on a splintered pork chop bone dug out of the kitchen garbage. It didn't tell Walt that the reason he sometimes winced from pain as he held a pencil, or answered his wife irritably when he didn't mean to, was the onset of arthritis that wasn't going to go away.

As he puts the cassette back in its box, he knows that there's nothing really to do but let Rosie come back home for a while, as she wants. Helen has said yes, of course, immediately, come to us, we're here, but Walt already feels the burden of having her home again. He sees in the wrinkles of his face, his thinning hair, his thickening joints, a man who has no room for this sort of thing at the moment, a man who has no idea how much room is left at all.

But Rosie is still his daughter, and he adores her, even if he doesn't feel like being anyone's father right now.

The following Tuesday, it is close to eight as Walt nears the Greyhound bus station, but the expressway is crowded even for a weekday in early December, and the traffic has stopped moving. Helen, on her way out to her reading group earlier, told him to take Cambridge Street downtown, but he's ignored her advice. Walt knows he'll be late meeting Rosie's bus from New York, and he worries about her in a familiar way. Rosie is twenty-five years old, has a job as a paralegal, an apartment on 73rd Street, a husband — is he still that? — someday she'll have kids. She's an independent person, he'd like to believe, but will she know enough to come and look outside for her father instead of expecting that he'll find her?

Walt remembers asking Rosie the same about Tim once: does he know to meet us in your office? Meaning, is this man you're in love with, the one your mother is sure you'll marry just by the tone of your voice when you talk about him, capable of thinking of others? Walt had been in Manhattan for a conference at NYU. After lunch, he took a bus uptown to meet Rosie at work; Tim was supposed to meet them there too. As he watched the city through the sooty window, Walt found it hard to believe that his daughter lived in a place where there were so many things to do, to go wrong, and so many people to choose from. He carried in his briefcase a glass paperweight he'd bought for her in a store off Washington Square that morning.

Rosie's office was a small room off a hallway of other small rooms inhabited by women bent over papers or keyboards, fingering their earrings. She had a picture of her parents on her desk, which made Walt feel a little weak, and she put the paperweight next to it. When Tim didn't show up, and Walt and Rosie ran out of things to say after a while — easy without the clutter of the family — Rosie began to look miserable, her dark eyes watered, and she pulled hair loose from her ponytail. It was a habit she and her sister shared, as they shared their mother's thin face and high forehead.

"I don't know, honey," Walt said gently, and looked at his watch, "maybe he thought we were going to meet him downstairs. Do you remember what you told him?" He hated when his daughter acted stupid, and here she was stupid about love, the worst of all things. It made him feel sorry for both of them.

Tim was on a bench in the building's courtyard, reclining long-legged and reading a book, when Walt and Rosie came out. He'd picked a spot shaded by a cherry tree in bloom, too beautiful for the city. Tim seemed content, so why should he think others wouldn't be, that they might be waiting for him?

"He doesn't have a watch!" Rosie whispered to her father. She was clearly charmed by this, Walt saw, by her prince in a garden. Tim unfolded slowly to meet them. Rosie bounced on her tiptoes, her heels lifted out of her blue pumps, and Walt noticed that she smelled a bit sweaty. She should be wearing red, rubber-tipped sneakers, he thought to himself, and approached Tim.

"Thought we were going to miss you," Walt said, and raised his eyebrows. It was a voice he often used with his students, a gentle challenge. The boy would not look at him. Tim's surprisingly handsome face was darkened by a two-day-old beard.

"No way," Tim said, and picked at the leaves of the cherry tree. "Where do you want to go now?"

As if, Walt thought, this alone isn't enough for one father for one day, not to mention your dirty fingernails, your lack of a sense of time and expectations, your hold on my baby daughter. You'll take her away from me; I suppose I'll always dislike you for that. But he put his arm across Tim's shoulders, the way he had with his other daughter's boyfriend, because he knew it would make Rosie happy.

"Wherever you two would like to go," Walt said, "is fine by me."

Later, when Walt told Helen about Tim, she laughed. "Pure jealousy," she'd said. "Fathers and their daughters. Rosie's a grownup, let her go. You're the one who always says we baby her too much."

Mothers, Walt thinks now, looking for his daughter in the crowd bulging at the bus station entrance, accept when they have to, let go when they must, but watch out: they'll also turn their back on whoever hurts their child so quickly you'll feel the wind cut your face. Fathers, though, are rigid in the end; they suffer for their hearts that have been won so easily. Or is it my episodes of pain, Walt wonders, that have made my chest feel so tight lately.

He circles the station again but doesn't see Rosie in front. Now he'll be damned if he's going to look around for a parking place when it's cold and dark and he's in prime mugging territory. If Rosie really wants to come home so badly, she'll look outside for him. Walt pops one of his books on tape into the player and drives around and around the block — the traffic pattern is oval, with a light at each end. He's so engrossed by the true-life story of a baseball player (his other daughter gave it to him last birthday) that it takes him a second to realize that the person in the green parka trotting alongside the car and tapping at the window when he stops at a red light is Rosie and not someone trying to take his car. She looks so much like his little girl, like both his little girls at the point when their faces took their final beautiful shapes, her eyes bright with lack of understanding and the red Greyhound sign, that he wonders what year it is, and what year he'd like it to be.

When Walt unlocks the door, Rosie throws her duffle bag in the back seat. He can't help but be dismayed by the size of it, the amount of stuff she's packed for what he thinks is going to be a short visit home. She slips into the front seat and is slightly out of breath when Walt leans over and pulls her face to his lips. Her skin smells of diesel fumes and Jergens, Helen's lotion, so familiar he doesn't want to let her go. Walt notices that Rosie hasn't worn a hat, and that the tips of her ears are flaming cold, and he wants to touch them. Rosie seems lighthearted for the moment as they drive back to Cambridge, chatting about the bus ride, looking all around at the familiar sights, avoiding any mention of Tim or why she has come home. Walt again feels a touch of dismay at this, at how easily she can leave one thing and fall into another, like an experienced traveler crossing time zones.

He remembers driving four hours one July when she was thirteen to pick her up at camp mid-session. She was miserable, she'd said in her letters, she felt like she was in jail. The blackflies by the lake were torture. Walt had glared at the camp director, his daughter's warden in khaki shorts, while Rosie had skipped — skipped! — off to her cabin to get her things, which naturally were not ready, as though this were a game. On the way home they'd stopped for lunch at a diner, and over grilled cheese and thick chocolate milk Rosie told her father about all the wonderful things she'd done for the past few weeks. He couldn't understand her changing from misery to delight so quickly. He felt his solitude shattered — the prospect of both girls away at the same time, just he and Helen alone — but also his loneliness abating.

"Got a couple of days off from work?" Walt asks. They are almost home, and he wants to know how long she'll be staying.

"Until Monday," she sighs, "but I may quit anyway. I'm not crazy about the job." Walt knows by the way she's caught her breath that she's looking at his twisted hands on the steering wheel. When he looks down too, he sees rocks under his skin.

"Well, being crazy about something isn't always the standard to measure things by, Rosie. In fact, the older you get, the less good a standard it becomes." When he realizes how sad and defeated this sounds, he pats her on the knee and tells her that he's looking forward to spending time with her. "I'm really glad you're visiting."

During his standard end-of-the-semester lecture, Walt is aware of the wheels of the tape recorder that he's placed on the lectern going round and round, a tiny hiss that only he can hear. He thinks of the letting out and taking up of the tape, and looks at Diana Lux's long legs in their black leggings. She is in his sociology course on community structures, a small, bright head in the first row. Walt is not really listening to what he's saying — he can always rewind later to make sure he hasn't lost his rhythm, just his breath — but wondering if Diana still calls her parents Mommy and Daddy.

Rosie, who has been installed in her old room for a week now, the Monday to return to work come and gone, has taken to calling her parents Walt and Helen, has taken to phoning her older sister long-distance every night. She emerges from her room after a conversation with Tim looking sleepy and red-eyed. Walt would like to call his daughter selfish and spoiled for the way she's descended upon them, but he calls her Rosita and Rosebud instead, and when she needs some money, or she asks him to get her a soda while he's up, he gives it to her. He sits with her at the kitchen table and they talk, they play Scrabble at night. She visited him at his office and they went to the Museum of Fine Arts, and afterwards, at the gift shop, he bought her a silk scarf with a Matisse print on it.

The day after, when he woke in the morning, he felt as though his upper body were encased in cement. He called for his daughter down the hall — Helen had already left for work. Rosie drove him into Boston to the doctor's, dropped him off and parked the car so he wouldn't be late for the appointment. She was there when he was finished, went with him to the pharmacy, and asked how he felt.

Her voice was wobbly with concern, so he showed her his new prescription for Auranofin. "These pills are made from gold extract," he told her. The doctor said they would slow the progression, a word Walt found particularly menacing. "If I take enough of them," he added, not to worry his daughter, "maybe you can melt me down into a pair of earrings."

Meanwhile, Helen has gone from salt to sugar, Walt notices, and hovers over Rosie's problems. Her mouth has stopped swelling; now she has pimples as tiny as grains of sand and grease on the sides of her nose, and she talks a lot.

Diana Lux's face is so bright Walt can hardly stand it, and he looks down at his hands on the oak lectern. He would like Diana to tell him that he doesn't look old enough to have two grown women children, or that he's too old to have one tear at his heart, but he knows that she's unlikely to be thinking anything so complex.

Rosie has found a therapist in Cambridge, and tells her parents when she joins them for dinner in the kitchen.

"I need a safe place right now," she says. Walt thinks she's looking thin and exotic, dressed in black with her hair loose. Her earrings, though, are like something his secretary would wear, big gold globs, panic buttons. "She thinks I didn't feel safe with Tim."

"He didn't beat you up," Helen says, half stating, half asking. They both hold their breath for her answer.

"No, of course not," Rosie says. All she's eaten is a breadstick, Walt notices, and he wonders why this detail takes up so much space in his head.

"Of course not? Is that so obvious?" he asks. His mouth is full of chicken and he swallows. "The way you ran out of there, I thought maybe he did hit you or something, maybe you're afraid to go back. That at least I can make sense of." He is very angry now, and both women at the table look a little scared of what's happening to him.

"It doesn't have to be physical abuse, Dad," she says. Helen nods. "There are other kinds." He wonders at her authority now as she talks with someone else's words.

He is Dad again suddenly. He remembers a time when his daughters came to him with stomachaches, and he could soothe them with a story. Later it was cramps that bothered them; they soothed each other and stayed far away from him. It was like being fenced off from a place you used to live. He wanted to break back in.

"Please. In my day," he starts, and spews a fleck of food onto the table, "you didn't just leave because you didn't feel 'safe.' What is this shit anyway about safety? This has always been your problem,

Rosie, you never feel you have to stick with anything, you can run home anytime you like. Your mother and I are to blame for that too, I'll admit. You come, we take you in."

The women tilt their heads at similar angles.

"She's your daughter, for Godsake," Helen says. "Of course we take her in."

Walt sees that Rosie is close to tears. He puts his napkin on his plate — something he knows Helen hates — and leaves the table. In his study, he hears Helen and Rosie talking in the kitchen and thinks how easily Helen has become a complete mother again, how little she fights this return. Walt feels bad for what he's said but justified in saying it. In a while, he puts in the cassette from that afternoon's lecture.

He can't believe that the voice he hears is his own, and he adjusts the tone on the machine. He sounds flat — dated is how he really thinks of it — the voice of a half-asleep man. From time to time, a staccato cough punctuates his drone, and he imagines that it's Diana Lux trying to rouse him and get his attention, even at this moment in the privacy of his own home, calling him to imagine her in her dorm room in her flannel pajamas. He pictures her tumbling like a gymnast over futons and beanbag chairs, like a doll with string joints.

The light from the kitchen blinds him momentarily. "What are you doing?" Helen asks. It's not accusatory, just curious.

"Listening to today's lecture," he says. "Do you think my voice sounds funny?"

She puts her fingers to her lips. Being married to him for so many years has made her a good listener. "Not really — a little nasal, maybe. Why, do you?"

"I thought it sounded flat. Old."

Helen sits on the arm of his chair. She smells like dish soap and chocolate. "Maybe you need new batteries."

He pats her leg in wool pants. "Maybe you need new batteries," he jokes.

Helen smiles and gets up to straighten a picture on the wall. It happens, by chance, to be one of Rosie at twelve, knocked slightly askew by the swiveling arm of his desk lamp.

"In my day . . ." Helen starts, doing her imitation of Walt, putting her head down on her chest so that a double chin appears and her eyebrows meet, "in my day . . ." She stops, looks at him, and talks in her own voice. "In your day, Walt? My day and your day are the same, remember? You didn't have that day — and what day was it, anyway? — without me." Walt shrugs apologetically.

"Rosie's talking to Tim," Helen adds, matter-of-factly. How easily we pass these things by, Walt thinks, and feels affection for his wife and his long marriage. They've never talked about what will happen if one day he can't move anymore.

"Yes? And what's this about her finding a shrink here? That has the ring of long-term," Walt says. "Doesn't she have to go home at some point? What about her job? And what the hell is she doing about her marriage? Isn't that the problem at hand, as they say?"

Now Helen shrugs, and Walt knows that she too would really like to be done with this — after all, for several years now they've been living a different kind of life — but can't bring herself to say so, won't allow herself. Rosie has always been trouble in one way or another, a baby is always — lovely, painful — trouble.

"And since we're talking about marriage, how's ours?" he says, and holds his arms open to her. It's as close as he can come to apologizing at the moment.

"I'm not really thinking about it," Helen says, which doesn't surprise or hurt him. She holds his hands, and can't help but massage them a little. "I'm thinking about Rosie now, what she's going to do." Before she leaves the room, Helen kisses his forehead and reminds him to take his gold pills.

Tim, Walt has been told by Helen, is coming up from New York Tuesday evening, but on that day Walt pretends he's forgotten and stays at work and eats dinner at the Faculty Club. He hopes Diana Lux will appear at his late office hours. When she doesn't, he thinks spitefully about giving her a C for the semester — she is mediocre, at best. When he gets home just after nine, Helen's car is gone, and he remembers that it's her reading group night, which she aggressively never misses. This means that now he'll actually have to talk to Tim, instead of letting Helen buffer for him, excuse her husband's behavior. The house is warm and dark and smells like tomato soup, and in fact, when he goes into the kitchen, that's just what the smell is. Two empty bowls, skimmed with red, bisected by spoons, are on the table, uncleared. Walt smells Tim too, salty and male, and thinks how much fathers really are like dogs.

By the time Walt reaches the top of the stairs, he can hear that his daughter and her husband are at it — he can't bring himself to think "making love" or even "fucking" at that moment — and the sounds are so easy for him to make out, he's at first delighted by his acuity and then horrified by it. Has he ever listened to other people — Jesus, his daughter! — making love except in the movies? She giggles, he groans, long breaths are let out and grabbed back in. The duet has the most incredible, indescribable fluid life, and he can't bear it.

He reaches into his blazer pocket for the recorder he always carries in case he wants to record random thoughts or reminders, or just the noise of what happens. If you didn't know who or what was making the sounds behind the door, would you know what it was? he wonders. He thinks of a radio contest he used to listen to as a boy where you tried to identify certain sounds — a sewing machine whirring, crackers breaking, a cat licking herself. Can I pretend this is not my daughter, he thinks now, but just noise too? Would you know it wasn't love?

Walt turns the recorder on and lays it on the rug outside the door. He sits in his bedroom in the dark, sliding toward the floor on the slippery bedspread, and waits until it is quiet. Then he retrieves the machine, its red *on* light like a rat's eye in the dark hall.

"Dad?" Rosie says from inside as he picks it up. He is frozen in a painful crouch, and wonders if he'll be able to rise again. Her voice sounds full, as though her throat has been opened.

"Oh, hi," Walt says, straining, not to be defeated. He can just imagine Tim, arms behind his big head, bare-chested, hairy armpits, staring at the ceiling. "It's late, sweetheart. I'll see you in the morning." He makes a point of shutting his bedroom door loudly, just as he's made a point not to acknowledge Tim.

When Helen comes home and upstairs, Walt says he has a surprise for her. A small smile crosses her face — at fifty-three, she does want to believe in good surprises still, miracle cures. When he plays the tape for her, her eyes widen as though she's spotted something across the room and she leans toward it. She is holding the book from her group against her chest.

"Guess," Walt says. "Guess what it is."

"What is this? Jesus Christ," she says, and rushes for the recorder, but she can't immediately find the button to turn it off and for a second turns up the volume. "This is sick, really crazy," she says, but hands the machine back to Walt and sits down on the bed next to him. "What are you doing?" she pleads.

"I don't want them fucking in my house," he says firmly. "If she doesn't love him, she shouldn't be fucking him either. Should I have to listen to this?"

"Oh, Walt," Helen moans. "You sound like an old man." Her eyes narrow. "Rosie doesn't know what she wants. They're married, they're adults, they're allowed not to know. No one made you listen."

"They should go home."

Helen shakes her head at him. "Why are you doing this?" She is disappointed and crying when she says, "Don't make us hate you."

The next morning Helen leaves early to teach a class, and when Walt goes downstairs for coffee, Rosie and Tim are at the kitchen table, posed over empty bowls again, their dark heads together. He sees that Tim's bare feet are resting on top of Rosie's under the table. Walt cannot bring himself to talk directly to them, but says a general hello to the room and touches his daughter on the shoulder as he makes his way to the stove. Tim says hi; Rosie, still in her bathrobe, doesn't say anything. She is not capable of hurting her father. Walt wonders if Helen has told them something, warned them about him, and the shame of what he's done, what he's listened to, makes him back away quickly.

"I'm going to be working here today," he announces, and moves into his study. "So . . . I guess I'll see you." An hour later his other daughter calls, but she wants to talk to Rosie and not to him, and he wonders how far his poison has spread. By midafternoon, Walt can't stand the whispering between Tim and Rosie, both the hissing and the caressing that's gone on for hours, and he goes to his office.

Several days later, Diana Lux comes to Walt's office hours to discuss why her term paper is going to be late. He admires her for not lying to him but simply telling him that it's late because she didn't start it early enough. He commends her parents for teaching her honesty and self-reliance, although at the moment he finds it extremely unappealing. He makes his hands into a pyramid on top of his desk. She doesn't appear to notice the almost purple hue to his skin that day.

"Fine," Walt says. Diana's sweatshirt says *University of Wisconsin* on it. They are nowhere near Wisconsin, and Walt suspects it's where her boyfriend goes to school, a big-chested blond sort of guy. "Drop it off in my box when you're done."

"That's okay?" She's done something strange to her hair, so that her bangs point to the ceiling. She sits, like a ballerina, with only her pointed toes touching the floor. He doesn't answer her. "Really?"

I'm not your father, Walt thinks, furious, and damned if I'm going to have to say it twice to reassure you and make you feel good about yourself, good about screwing up but being honest about it.

"It's up to you," he says coldly. "It's your decision, your grade."

Walt knows that she thinks she's been pardoned, when he's done nothing of the sort for her.

Later, when he straightens the papers on his desk before going home, Walt sees that Diana has left her pen. It's a fake fat tortoise-shell thing, with bite marks on the cap. He can't help thinking that her father must have given it to her as he sent her away, and that now she feels she's really lost something important to her, all her good luck and love in that cheap pen. Walt doesn't understand how the pen got on his desk unless she put it there, and he can't remember her moving toward him.

When Walt gets home, he knows that Tim has gone. He also knows that Rosie is still in the house; she has not gone with him. He can't understand why people act like this, so inconclusive with their own lives, so dependent on other people to hold them up, but if anyone's to blame for Rosie being like that, he supposes that he is — he is her father. He sees that Helen is home too, early, that life in his house is taking place without him.

When he calls for Helen and Rosie, ready to be forgiven — he's sick, he's scared, he'll tell them, he's hateful and he hates his body — they don't answer him. He feels a terrible need to be included.

Upstairs, he hears voices again behind a closed door, this time in the bathroom. The water is running into the clawfoot tub, and he listens to Helen and Rosie talking quietly to each other. When Walt puts his hand out to touch the door, he swears he can feel the steam that clouds the bathroom, then Rosie's little sobs and sniffs, and Helen's comfort that finally shakes the house.

He pushes the door open the smallest bit — he wants to witness

as well as hear for once — and sees Helen sitting on a stool next to
the tub. Rosie's head is resting against her mother's thigh, while
her knees poke out of the water, and one hand trails along the
edge, her fingers dripping water onto the floor. They don't notice
him there, and he doesn't want to be seen.

Walt suddenly remembers a photograph he saw in *Life* years before, black-and-white, of a Japanese mother bathing her deformed
and half-grown child in a wooden tub. There was no pleasure on
either of their faces, but it wasn't displeasure or pain either, which
had surprised him. The girl's hands were stiff claws, unable to hold
the cloth, and her mother had to keep the hair back from her
child's eyes. He had stared and stared at the picture without understanding why. Now he admits to himself — back then he had simply
shut the magazine and put it away — what he had been thinking
about: that if the child had died, or if her mother had chosen not to
care for her, to keep her, then there would be no bath, there would
be no moment.

Walt is crying as he shuts the door and goes downstairs into his
study. In a while he hears that the water has been turned off in the
bathroom and the drain opened to let it out. In a gush, it rushes
down from the second floor, down through the pipes that run
through the wall of his study, splashing toward the sewer below him.
It's a warm sound, warm as Helen wrapping a towel around Rosie,
warm as he wrapped his last baby in a blanket and held her to his
chest, warm as though the water's running over him. It sounds too
much like life being washed out of his house, and he can't imagine
there ever being a time when he'd want to hear it again.

Contributors' Notes

CHRIS ADRIAN lives in Virginia, where he is a medical student. His fiction has appeared in *Story, The Paris Review,* and *The New Yorker.* He has a novel forthcoming from Broadway Books in the spring of 1998.

▪ This story started with the title. In the back of my school library hang a bunch of illustrated vignettes from the history of medicine. Some are very dramatic (Semmelweis, Defender of Motherhood!), some are creepy (a picture of Rhazes — the father of Arabic medicine — apparently getting ready to pluck out the eye of a bemeasled child), and some are rather morbid (sailors in a dank-looking ship's hold, prone and moaning with scurvy, who seem to be offering up their sores to the viewer.) Among the creepy pictures is a depiction of a temple of Aesclepius, which shows a lot of tan, swollen-looking ancients reclining in a great hall lit with oil lamps. The patients are being tended by similarly tan and swollen-looking priests, in the shadow of a gigantic statue of Aesclepius. There are various limbs and appendages hanging from the wall, and the way the picture is drawn makes it difficult to figure if they are prosthetic or real. Hence the creepiness. But creepy or not, I used to study under that picture in the hope of receiving whatever small blessing can be obtained from a mass-produced, drug-company–sponsored representation of an antique god of healing, and passing where I was otherwise doomed to fail.

There's a caption beneath the picture: "Every night for a thousand years sick and afflicted pilgrims flocked to the Grecian Temples of Aesclepius." I read it over and over again while I was studying, and over the course of a semester the first six words began somehow to haunt me. I started a few different stories using them as a title. The stories were generally about hospitals (except one about a Greek lady whose hair talks to her), and they all had in common the fact that the picture pops up somewhere, usually incongruously, often hideously so.

Later I stumbled across Whitman's letter to Erastus Haskell's parents (Hank Smith in the story) while reading about the life of Whitman's brother. Whitman's stint as a "nurse" in D.C. during the war was a complete surprise to me. I had learned about it in high school, but I forget every last thing I learned in high school. The letter was heartbreaking and I felt an overwhelming urge to steal it, which I did. And then, somehow, a story grew up around the letter. Most of the characters really existed, but I've taken gross and indecent liberties with their lives. I hope they will forgive me, especially Mary Walker, who, though she may very well have been somebody's lover, was never Canning Woodhull's.

CAROL ANSHAW is the author of the novels *Seven Moves* and *Aquamarine* and is currently at work on a new novel, *Almost There*. This is her second appearance in this series; her story "Hammam" was selected for *The Best American Short Stories 1994*. She teaches at Vermont College and the School of the Art Institute of Chicago.

▪ I worked on this story over a period of three or four years. The impulse to write it came from having been on both sides of this emotional equation — listening to friends through their obsessions and broken hearts, as well as dragging them along through mine. Which got me thinking about the pull — the gruesome centrifugal force — exerted by these (soap) operatic events, romance gone awry but romantic nonetheless.

Also, I first came to Chicago during the 1968 Democratic convention, which means thirty years now of observing myself and friends as we all passed through the seventies, eighties, and nineties. I'm curious at the way some have changed their coloration, like chameleons, to match the backdrop of the moment better, and fascinated by the others who — like Jean and Alice and Tom, the romantic figures in this story — have hung tough with their original versions of self, their belief systems as permanent as tattoos.

I mostly write novels, and I suspect this shows in the compressed quality of the short fiction I've attempted. With "Elvis Has Left the Building," I'm operating on the same principle as the clown car in the circus. I want you to open up the story and have more fun tumble out than you might have expected.

POE BALLANTINE writes: "I am forty-two. College dropout. Live in a motel room. I generally move every year, but I am tired of moving and I like this room so I think I will stay another year. I have had lots of odd jobs, mostly cooking. I worked at the radio antenna factory just across the tracks for a while, then sold a couple of stories, so I quit March 5, and if I live on $400 a month and this wisdom tooth coming in doesn't knock the rest of my teeth sideways, I will be able to write until August."

▪ I thought this would be the simplest story in the world to write. It was merely about being born into a lucky house and the children across the street being born into an unlucky house, a mood-theme piece rich with droll details and seemingly profound ideas which I thought I could substitute for a plot. However, a story without a plot is often like a mammal without a spine, so the thing went through vast circus and jelly-roll contortions before ever finding a place to stand and lean its elbow up on the china hutch. I wrote the first draft severely and suicidally depressed and working as a cook at the Olde Main Street Inn in Chadron, Nebraska, in 1994. I was pushing for a longer piece, but it ended on its own with the line, "I was simply too lucky to be forgiven." For a while it was something like a mininovel with paragraph-length chapters; then, as I continued to excise irrelevant parts, it became a *New Yorker*-style deli-slicer with numbered vignette paragraphs (I sent it to them, by the way, and they wrote on the rejection slip, "Good Story. Try us again?"). Gradually it evolved into a story called "1024 Theories of Evil," which was repeatedly turned down by publications of merit (but usually with some positive comment), largely, I imagine, because it still had no plot. Stubbornly and plotlessly, I continued to revise, and finally I submitted a highly polished version to *The Sun,* who said, "Cut out all this Theories of Evil stuff" (The Self-Centered Ego, The Fallen Angel, The Untamed Beast, The Misdirected Ghost, The Psychopath, Genius, The Unknown, Society, Anger, Duality, Evolution, Laziness, Destruction, Untruth, Desire, Ignorance, Knowledge, Illusion, Material Existence Within Time, Mary Baker Eddy's Nonevil, Saint Augustine's Absence of Good, Shakespeare's Divine Drama, Tolstoy's Resistance, Leibniz's Presupposition of Virtue, Klee's Primal Ground, *Die Hard II*). The Theories of Evil stuff was what held the story together, I thought, but I took it out, and it slid away like an oily gray stomach tumor down the drain; then I put in a plot and realigned the frame to subordinate. About three versions later I came up with what you see. I owe a great debt to both editors at *The Sun,* Sy Safransky and Andrew Snee, for their patience and perspicacity. And I also must credit my own God-given dimwitted persistence (and luck). We work in the dark. We do what we can. The rest is the madness of art. Still, most reasonable human beings would've abandoned the project long ago.

BLISS BROYARD grew up in Connecticut and attended the University of Vermont and the writing program at the University of Virginia. Her fiction and essays have appeared in *Grand Street, The Pushcart Prize, Ploughshares,* and the anthology *Personals: Dreams and Nightmares from the Lives of 20 Young*

Writers. Knopf will publish her first collection of short stories, *My Father, Dancing,* in 1999. She lives in Brooklyn, New York.

▪ "Mr. Sweetly Indecent" was written virtually in one sitting, while I was traveling from Ann Arbor, Michigan, to Boston, Massachusetts. I was in the airport waiting for my plane to board, idly watching the greetings and partings taking place around me, when I caught eyes with a young woman as she embraced an older man. There was something hungry and guilty in her expression that made me think that the couple was not supposed to be together. I wondered who she was worried might spot them. Since the man was old enough to be my father, I decided it was his daughter who had caught them. I opened my notebook and began writing a scene where the daughter confronts her father about what she has seen.

The daughter's own affair was woven in, I suppose, because of my interest in the experience of a child crossing over into the adult world only to bump into her parents there. There's something unnerving about realizing that your parents have already mapped out much of this terrain you're desperately trying to claim as your own, especially when the confidence you've mustered in order to burst into this world has you believing that you're the only authority around.

I worked on the story while I waited for my plane, for the entire three-hour flight, and then kept writing in the terminal in Boston until I'd finished. I had never before and have never since written a story in one rush like this. And when I think about how the story came to be, it is the circumstances under which it was written that loom largest in my mind. The anonymous, unanchored feeling of being in an airport terminal and flying high above the earth liberated me from some of my normal writing anxieties. I followed the story where it took me, without thinking ahead about plot, character development, or really any thematic concerns. In retrospect, I see that some aspects of where the story was written found their way into it: eavesdropping and voyeurism, a sense of traveling between separate worlds, and the feeling I often have while flying of a temporary suspension of my belief in how things are supposed to work.

EMILY CARTER is a freelance writer who makes her living doing restaurant guides and film reviews and teaching short fiction. Her work has appeared in *The New Yorker, Story, Open City,* and *Great River Review.* She lives in Minneapolis with her cat, Biberkopf, and her pit bull, Betty, who is the sweetest and most gentle of canine companions.

▪ At one point it was suggested to me that a series of short fictions dealing with AIDS, and specifically women with AIDS, might be a grant-worthy project. Being HIV-positive, I thought, might after all have its advantages. No one was rushing to publish my fiction, but I could at least make them feel a vague sense of moral unease about their continued rejection of my work.

My pecuniary and manipulative agenda was the motivation for a lot of stories that seemed to have nothing whatsoever to do with the epidemic, but in which the AIDS virus would crop up unannounced and depart just as quickly. I would describe the hero or heroine and add what amounted to the coda: "By the way, she had AIDS. As a woman, this was terribly difficult for her to deal with."

Then I'd get on with what I really wanted to write about, which was usually something about historical train wrecks, crows, and grain elevators. This story is actually about being HIV-positive, and while I've never put an ad in the personals, yet it does reflect my own experience. More than that, it's supposed to be a lighthearted take on the different kinds of attitudes I've encountered toward the disease, and toward female sexuality in general. I've written things in anger that I hoped would repulse the reader and make the hair on the back of her neck stand up. This one, however, was written to make her smile.

KATHRYN CHETKOVICH's short story collection, *Friendly Fire,* won the 1998 John Simmons Short Fiction Award and will be published this fall by the University of Iowa Press. Chetkovich lives in Boulder Creek, California.

▪ I wrote the first version of this story fifteen years ago, when I was halfway through a creative writing program and my critical understanding of what constitutes a story had begun to interfere with my capacity to actually write one. My doubts, by this time well informed and well articulated, were looming large, and in an effort to get something, anything, down on paper, I began this story, with no real idea of where it was going. A couple of years before, I had lived for a while in a house with two other women, some mice, and a baby grand piano that was never played, and I started there.

I worked on the story off and on for the next several years, periodically sending it out, getting it back, and then — a little compulsively, maybe — rewriting it, often with the unnerving suspicion that I was making it different but not necessarily better. I enjoyed fooling around with the various elements, but at some point the story itself always seemed to slip away from me — I couldn't figure out what it was "about." But the last time I went to work on it, a couple of things seemed to have worked their way to the surface. I knew the narrator had to have a secret, and the story picked up some energy when I figured out what that secret was. And then I realized that the mice, who had been recklessly killed, maimed, and poisoned in various earlier drafts, should be spared. When I wrote my way to that new ending, the story, although still a mystery to me in some ways, seemed to work.

My thanks to Howard Junker, at *ZYZZYVA,* who rejected an early version with the advice "Trust the mice." When he took the story this time around, he lopped off some of the throat-clearing at the beginning and tightened some loose screws at the end; after I got over my injured resistance to his intrusions, I saw that he was right.

MATTHEW CRAIN lives in California.

▪ I worked on a college grounds crew, and at our morning breaks there was a retarded teenage boy overseeing the doughnuts. We loved to tease and pull pranks on him. This was a Jesuit school and the priests *ate,* let me tell you, and we'd put him up to stealing their goodies; somebody was always passing him a dirty magazine just to see what he'd say. I was the best at mocking how he talked.

Well, two years later, on a hot afternoon in a room with just one window even with the ground, when I was writing but no words were sparking, right in the window at my head came a Weedwacker digging down in the dirt, hitting the frame and spitting gravel through the screen. I jumped away and shouted up to the dumbass running it, You trying to cut my head off? Then I remembered the day we let the retarded boy run a Weed-wacker and he cut off the tip of his shoe; I said, Let's pretend I'm him and see what trouble I get into. I began talking like him, and suddenly scene after scene unfolded across my mind like a fan with pictures painted on it, each picture holding itself clear until I could write it out, each containing a new person, and then came the man he worked for, and every time he was the subject of a sentence he'd want the next sentence too. This happened again and again and I hated it, hated as he'd pull the words to him and I'd have to start all over again. But if I didn't turn it over to him, I knew I wouldn't be true to what he squeezed inside me. I'd see him in my mind, not his face all the time, mostly my mouth near his neck, and he gave off a heat much like a man I admire and have always enjoyed quoting. So I began writing down his sayings, just letting him talk, when suddenly the fan snapped open again and I was off to the side as a truck crashed into the back of a car, crushing the boy bent over in the truck, then in a shed watching that truck back in a trailer loaded with lawnmowers, the doors open and sweaty, tired men getting out, and there is the man, and all at the same time I was outside and inside him: I was him and what I'd done was repeating itself inside me as here come a young woman with a retarded boy wanting work.

TIM GAUTREAUX is the author of a collection of stories, *Same Place, Same Things* (1996), and a novel, *The Next Step in the Dance* (1998). His stories have appeared in *The Atlantic Monthly, Harper's Magazine, GQ, Story, New Stories from the South,* and *The Best American Short Stories.* He has a doctorate in English from the University of South Carolina. He was born and raised in southern Louisiana and presently lives with his wife and two sons in Hammond, where he is writer in residence at Southeastern Louisiana University.

▪ I still enjoy teaching an American literature survey course, but I've noticed over the past fifteen years or so an increase in the numbers of very young women who have one or two children. Sometimes they bring the kids to lecture with them, and that's fine with me. Some of these women have husbands who work, I guess, or have no husbands, or still live with their parents. School's the right place for them.

I was in Wal-Mart one day, in the compressed-air-driven tools, sandpaper, Bondo, and auto paint aisle, when I heard a phlegm-filled smoker's voice float over the racks from the motor oil section. It was a middle-aged man talking to a friend he'd bumped into. He was complaining about his three daughters, who kept having children out of wedlock and then bringing them over to his house for him and his wife to take care of. The old guy had a great voice, southern, smart, and full of humor. But it was full of hurt too. His blue-collar salary was being eaten up by Cokes and diapers, and his blue-collar heart was smashed flat by children who were running their lives like a drunk runs a truck with bald tires downhill in a rainstorm. He was typical of grandparents all over who are raising their grandchildren, maybe because they didn't raise their children right to begin with. Most of them try to do better the second time around.

Pretty soon I started the story, writing in first person in the old guy's voice. I put in something out of the ordinary to get the ball rolling; you can't get a story going unless some conflict at least slightly out of the ordinary happens, something that precipitates the rest of the story, like that little electric spark that starts your backyard grill on a summer afternoon when the relatives and friends are coming over for a picnic.

That day at Wal-Mart I could have crossed over and looked at the complaining grandfather; I could have pretended to look at cans of Motor Honey and Smoke-No-Mo' and done some writerly spying. But I didn't want to see him. I had his voice, and that was enough for a start.

HESTER KAPLAN's short stories have appeared in *Story, Agni Review, Ploughshares, Glimmer Train, Press,* and elsewhere. Kaplan has recently finished a collection of stories and a novel. She lives in Providence, R.I., with her husband, the writer Michael Stein, and their two children.

▪ I know a man who tape-records everything. It is possible he has spy aspirations, but I suspect he simply likes to *listen* to the past — and add the rest himself. What is interesting about recorded noise is how it exists only in the context the listener creates for it. Are those singing birds in a cage or are they in a tree? What may sound like the gentle crackle and hiss of logs in the fireplace may actually be the last smoldering bits of a burned-down house. And who hasn't asked when they hear themselves on a tape, "Is that really the way I sound?"

Walt, the father in "Would You Know It Wasn't Love," wants to hold off the future and grab just a little more of the past. Children, like nothing else, can make you feel this way. With his tape recorder, Walt has extracted the sounds of life and love from their surroundings for so long, it is hard for him to put them back in place.

I come from a family of obsessive radio listeners, and am one myself. When I was a kid, there was a radio contest in which listeners were asked to identify sounds. Usually they were impossible noises like a turning screw or a sheet billowing on a clothesline, and I don't think I ever heard anybody guess correctly. Still, I dreamed that someday I would grow up and win the contest.

DORAN LARSON is a novelist whose first stories appeared in *The Iowa Review.* That journal will publish a novella, *Syzygy,* in December 1998. He has recently completed the first volume of a five-volume novel chronicling an American family from 1877 to 2007. A sequel to "Morphine," "Asbestos," appeared in *Boulevard,* and is dedicated to Jon and Zachary Edwards Larson and to the memory of Sandra Larson.

▪ Writing fiction this late in western capitalism is not gestation or gardening; those metaphors became obtuse in the seventeenth century; they are defaced coin, says the Frenchman (and we love Shakespeare so, not only for speaking them best but for speaking them *last* with exchange, even use value). Writing fiction today is editorial work — an act of collage: memory, movies, anecdote, magazine photos, pop discourses, books, obsessions, TV, ads, radio, memory, experience . . . boiled up in the genetic crockpot of mood.

(This perhaps should be qualified: If you are straight, white, male, middle-class, American, you can choose not to create self-consciously postmodern texts. But because the culture is the theme park built to *your* specifications, it is nearly impossible to escape postmodern methods.)

In 1993 my sister-in-law died of breast cancer. I understood her suffering, and then my brother's grief, only from visits and imagination. My partner reworked her loss, brilliantly, in an essay on Matuschka, mastectomy, and heroic iconography, bringing to my attention Lacquer's *Making Sex.* I regularly flip through art books. I'd just seen the movie *Quiz Show,* with those soundproof booths. My partner's grandfather was a refinisher of fine furniture, French. My initial interest in art was in sculpture, but I lacked other than technical skill. I've spent time under the knife, caught in X-rays, under antiseptic hands. A friend sent a postcard of Donatello's David . . . Grief started it. A need to recoup loss. This stuff, organized, reorganized, gave the need meaning. I sincerely believe every word of a piece of fiction can, in theory, be traced to a source.

We live today amid ritualized antihumanisms. Among those intelligent enough to feel despair, some seek a shaman in the literary artist. Artists love flattery; and the scam doesn't work without mystifying process.

The weather is unpredictable, but it is not mysterious.

Wall Street is unpredictable, but it is not mysterious.

Writing is unpredictable (like street and sky, there are too many variables). Its mystery vanishes, like a shadow, the moment the light aimed at your characters turns back upon yourself.

LORRIE MOORE is the author of two novels and three collections of stories, the most recent of which is *Birds of America*. She lives in Madison, Wisconsin.

▪ This story has a relationship to real life like that of a coin to a head. It is dedicated to my son.

ANTONYA NELSON is the author of three collections of short stories and the novels *Talking in Bed* and *Nobody's Girl*. She teaches creative writing at New Mexico State University and in the Warren Wilson M.F.A. program.

▪ In January of 1991 my son Noah was born in the local Las Cruces hospital. Not long after we had brought him home, a baby was stolen from the same hospital. The Gulf War was in action, but I was busy with my boy, and the only news that stuck with me, that made any kind of lasting imprint during that newborn month, was the abduction of the baby from our hospital. A nurse came into the nursery to which I had just entrusted my own baby and took somebody else's. The detail that seduced me was the one that turned the kidnapper from creature into character: she had stolen a twin. As a nurse, she had had plenty of access to babies; I like the idea that she waited until there were two, that in some region of her soul a small voice was arguing that at least these parents would be *less* bereft. And while I identified with her desire to have a baby, my own entry into the story was as stricken witness rather than as desperate kidnapper — Jacob rather than Cece.

There are a thousand things to hear about, informationally, daily, but the thing that doesn't go away is the one to pay attention to.

When Noah was old enough to appreciate the hubbub, we decided to visit a famous theme park wherein I expected to find nothing redeemable. Before we went, I kept hearing stories about the nasty business going on beneath the pristine surface of the place, mishaps and coverups, accidents and conspiracies. Hence: characters, setting, premise.

The real kidnapped baby, FYI, traveled across the country in a car with his abductor and then was finally found, restored to his parents and brother, apparently none the worse for wear. Someday he will no doubt sit or play alongside Noah in some class or other.

Vaquita, a collection of EDITH PEARLMAN's stories published by the Pittsburgh University Press, won the 1996 Drue Heinz Prize for Literature. Her recent work has appeared or will soon appear in the journals *Ascent, Antioch Review, Alaska Quarterly Review, Kalliope,* and *Witness;* in the magazines *Smithsonian* and *Hope;* on the editorial pages of the *Boston Globe;* on the travel pages of the *New York Times;* and in the anthology *An Intricate Weave.*

▪ I had heard of a playful Torah study group similar to the one in "Chance," and I had been a participant when a local synagogue embraced a salvaged Torah. I wanted to write about both things, but several years of daydreaming had to pass until I realized that the lighthearted luck of the draw and the fateful luck of geography could be twined into one tale. So I had theme and plot. Now I needed to develop characters through draft after draft, using (among other things) recollections of adolescence, voodoo doings I'd been told about, reports from the shtetl. At last the characters' particulars began to bulge from the page. But it wasn't until the final several drafts that I appreciated the importance of Margie: always trying to catch your attention by a combination of work, patience, imagination, and guile; always hoping for luck. Like a poker player, to be sure. Like a writer as well, I couldn't help thinking.

PADGETT POWELL's first novel, *Edisto* (1984), was nominated for the National Book Award. He has since written four more books of fiction: *A Woman Named Drown* (1987), *Typical* (1991), *Edisto Revisited* (1996) and, most recently, *Aliens of Affection* (1998), in which "Wayne in Love" appears. He teaches at the University of Florida.

▪ "Wayne in Love" is a distillation of some of the more spirited adventures of a career I had in industrial roofing. Some of Wayne's moments are infected with some of my own, as usual. I am drawn to the idea that a man can be so frightened that he isn't, can have so little that he doesn't have so little. It's a fun kind of piece for me, and I trust for readers also.

ANNIE PROULX lives and writes in Wyoming.

▪ "The Half-Skinned Steer" was written specifically for the Nature Conservancy's unusual benefit anthology of short stories, *Off the Beaten Path: Stories of Place* (1998). The idea was interesting — it was to be a collection of stories inspired by writer visits to Nature Conservancy sites. The stories were to emerge from impressions and observations of the specific site, and could take form freely. I agreed to the project on the condition I could visit a site in Wyoming. There were three, and originally I planned to spend time at all of them, blending them into a single story, but bad weather and brief time trimmed that plan to a single three-day visit to the extraordinary 10,000-acre Ten Sleep Preserve on the south slope of the Big Horns.

The focal point of the preserve was a spectacular river-cut canyon, fine country for mountain lions and raptors. Several extremely rare plant species found only in the Big Horns grew there. There were brilliant Native American pictographs on limestone walls sheltered by overhangs, their meanings and functions still little understood. Billy Creek ran through a narrow gorge, the trail above it still deep in snow at the end of May.

The story that emerged does not realistically depict the Ten Sleep Preserve but is fiction loosely attached to a certain place. The substructure of the story is based on an old Icelandic folktale, "Porgeir's Bull," which I have heard in Canada in several versions over the years. In these tales the bull haunts Porgeir's descendants for nine generations.

The story was published in November 1997 in *The Atlantic Monthly* and the payment donated to the Wyoming chapter of the Nature Conservancy. On a personal note, "The Half-Skinned Steer" became the starting point for a collection of short fiction set in Wyoming, a project that has absorbed all my interest for the last year.

DIANE SCHOEMPERLEN lives in Kingston, Ontario, with her son and two cats. She has published four collections of short fiction in Canada, including *The Man of My Dreams* (1990), which was shortlisted for the Governor-General's Award, Canada's highest literary prize. Her first novel, *In the Language of Love,* was published in Canada by HarperCollins in 1994 and in the United States by Viking Penguin in 1996. "Body Language" appears in her collection of illustrated stories, *Forms of Devotion,* which was published in the spring of 1998 by HarperCollins (Canada) and Viking Penguin (U.S.).

▪ The main character of my novel, *In the Language of Love,* is a collage artist. While researching collage techniques for that book, I became more and more interested in this form of visual art and began creating some collages myself. Toward this end, I accumulated a series of volumes of historical wood engravings and line drawings which were copyright-free. Soon my living room walls were full and I began to think about incorporating some of the illustrations into my writing. I had long been interested in the idea of illustrated fiction and was especially inspired by *The Book of Embraces* by Eduardo Galeano, *The Art Lover* by Carole Maso, and two stories by Donald Barthelme called "At the Tolstoy Museum" and "The Flight of Pigeons from the Palace."

I tossed ideas for illustrated stories around in my mind for some time, and my decision to give it a try was probably cemented by my young son's saying one day that it was too bad my books didn't have pictures in them. I thought he had a good point. For so many people, picture books are one of the great joys of childhood. Why should we as grownups have to give them up?

"Body Language" is the second story I wrote in the series of eleven that became the collection *Forms of Devotion*. The illustrations in it come from a large weighty volume called *Images of Medicine*. Although in some of the other stories I made collages with the illustrations, in "Body Language" I used them just as they originally appeared in early anatomical textbooks. By showing various body parts in isolation, the pictures are meant to function as a graphic (somewhat absurd, possibly disturbing) counterpoint to the text.

The first line that came to me was "His spine is stiff with offense." I remember the moment well. I had just informed a man who was being belligerently persistent in his romantic pursuit of me that I was definitely not interested. He finally got the message. He said it didn't matter. He said he thought that any woman of my age (I was thirty-eight at the time) who was still single would be grateful that a man still wanted her. From my kitchen window I watched him walk away, visibly wounded and angry. His spine was indeed stiff with offense. Just when I might have been feeling sorry for having hurt him or angry at his insulting arrogance, instead I stood there thinking about how a person's true frame of mind can be so vividly revealed by the body. No matter how desperately we may try to hide our feelings, still the body can always give us away.

AKHIL SHARMA is a recent graduate of Harvard Law School. Before law school he was a screenwriter at Universal Studios, where the vast hopelessness of trying to write ridiculous things ("Devices," a wife-swapping murder mystery) and bumbling even these made him grind his teeth until they became as delicate as Murano glass.

▪ All that happens when I get something wonderful like this award is that my neuroses move into a bigger house.

Part of this is because success appears random. When *Playboy* rejected "Cosmopolitan," they said it was too sad for them. *The New Yorker* explained that the story felt familiar (which for all I know is true and may mean that the *New Yorker* editor is better read than I am).

Part of my sense of luck comes from having been helped by so many people. "Cosmopolitan" would have been written without Russell Banks, but it would have been relatively shapeless and tedious (the first draft had some wife-beating thrown in to make a point whose purpose I cannot remember). Russell Banks (as wonderful a teacher as he is a writer) many times raised his baffled eyes at me and offered gently phrased bits of common sense. ("In fiction, epiphanies that occur in dreams don't have that much power," he once said, referring to one of the climaxes that, thank God, I got rid of in my revisions.)

There have been other very generous teachers. Paul Auster gave me lists of books to read and spent hours talking about what I read. Tony Kushner inspired me to see how many wild combustible elements can be brought into one room. John McPhee taught me the necessity of structure, of keeping the soufflé from collapsing. Toni Morrison, who speaks prose (gorgeous suspended sentences that you want to sketch as she says them), would watch me babbling and boasting and then, when I was exhausted, she tried showing me the importance of candor. Joyce Carol Oates (wry, gentle, incredibly honest) appeared to work as hard on my stories as she did on her own. There is also, of course, Nancy Packer (a much neglected writer whose *In My Father's House* is so good that it makes your hair stand on end), my dear friend for many years.

All these people are part of my good fortune.

MAXINE SWANN has been living in Paris since 1991. In 1997 she received a master's degree in literature from the Sorbonne for a thesis on Proust's style. She is currently spending eight months in Punjab, Pakistan, where she is collaborating on a screenplay with Juan Pablo Domenech and writing her first novel. "Flower Children" was her first publication.

▪ This is a story I'd been trying to write since I'd begun writing, but I couldn't for years find the way to say it. I remember feeling desperate one afternoon. It was in my mother's house, years ago. In the next few hours I found the refrain, a simple list of sentences that read like a song:

They (the children) don't understand how the tree frogs sing . . .
They don't understand how the dew falls or when . . .
Although they kill things themselves, they don't understand why
    anything dies or where the dead go . . . etc.

After that, the rest of the story came quite easily. The last part, the end, came in a rush, one night late. It was summer, I remember, and I was alone. I felt a delicious sensation of lightness and slept that night very hard.

JOHN UPDIKE was born in 1932, in Shillington, Pennsylvania, and graduated from Harvard College in 1954. After a year at an English art school and a two-year stint as a "Talk of the Town" reporter for *The New Yorker,* he moved to Massachusetts in 1957, and has lived there ever since. His most recent novel is *Toward the End of Time.* Updike made his first appearance in *The Best American Short Stories* in 1959; "My Father on the Verge of Disgrace" is his ninth contribution to these pages.

▪ No doubt about it, this story has something to do with my real father. It took me back into the mythic territory of memory out of which I wrote my novel *The Centaur* over thirty-five years ago. As I have aged, my boy-hood has become so far away, so strangely furnished — the icebox, the tin toaster, the recipe box holding all our money — as to be fabulous. And boyhood's buried shames — a child's sense of peril, of his and his family's inferiority within the perceived social system — can at last come out into the open. The detail about stealing the ticket money to pay the grocer still pains and frightens me to divulge, as if some surviving members of the school board in the 1930s might demand from me the long-due reckon-ing. To give myself confessional room there is a small but necessary re-move of invention: my real father taught algebra and not chemistry, and he never sold china. It was another man, in another stage of my life, who told me about the joys of descending on a strange town and coming away with a tall order. In truth I scarcely know what in this story is made up or not; it delves into a layer of my earthly duration so ancient and fraught that truth and fiction are interchangeably marvelous. Life, you could say, is a tall order.

MEG WOLITZER is a novelist whose new book, *Surrender, Dorothy,* will be published in the spring. She has taught at the University of Iowa Writer's Workshop and Skidmore College, among others, and is a recipient of a grant from the National Endowment for the Arts. She lives in New York City with her husband and two sons.

▪ When I was a teenager I spent two summers at a wonderful perform-ing arts camp in the Berkshires called Indian Hill. The camp is now de-funct, but it meant a great deal to me, and the image of its main building — a slightly crumbling mansion set on a stately lawn — has often returned to me both in dreams and when I am writing fiction. In "Tea at the House," the psychiatric hospital I've invented is pretty much a stand-in for the mansion at Indian Hill. This has an emotional logic about it, because the story is, in a sense, about adolescence, a territory I've been returning to since my first novel, *Sleepwalking.*

In this short story I wanted to write about the muteness of adolescent girls — the mix of quiet humiliation and pride that seems to be a requisite part of becoming sexual, of becoming an adult. Added to this is a slightly playful interest I've had in those old-fashioned psychiatric hospitals — probably spawned by repeated readings in ninth grade of *I Never Promised You a Rose Garden* and repeated viewings of *David and Lisa.* I wanted to create a small world that doesn't exist anymore, and within that a world of adolescence that doesn't exist within *me* anymore but that I think about a great deal.

100 Other Distinguished Stories of 1997

SELECTED BY KATRINA KENISON

KLIMASEWISKI, MARSHALL
The Last Time I Saw Richard.
Missouri Review, Vol. 19, No. 3.
KOBIN, JOANN
Rain. *New England Review,* Vol. 18,
No. 2.

LASDUN, JAMES
Lime Pickle. *Yale Review,* Vol. 85,
No. 2.
LEE, REBECCA
The Banks of the Vistula. *Atlantic
Monthly,* November.
LEVIANT, CURT
Consolation. *Zoetrope,* Vol. 1, No. 2.
LOPEZ, BARRY
The Letters of Heaven. *Georgia
Review,* Vol. 51, No. 3.

MARTIN, LEE
Bad Family. *Nebraska Review,* Vol. 25,
No. 2.
MATTISON, ALICE
Sebastian Squirrel. *Glimmer Train,* 22.
Selfishness. *The New Yorker,* April 7.
MCCANN, COLUM
As Kingfishers Catch Fire. *Story,*
Spring.
MCKNIGHT, REGINALD
Boot. *Story,* Spring.
MEHTA, SUKETA
Gare du Nord. *Harper's Magazine,*
August.
MILLHAUSER, STEVEN
The Knife Thrower. *Harper's
Magazine,* March.
MOJTABAI, A. G.
Isolation. *Antioch Review,* Vol. 55,
No. 4.
MOODY, RICK
Whosoever. *The New Yorker,* March
17.
MUKHERJEE, BHARATI
Happiness. *DoubleTake,* Vol. 3, No. 3.
MUNRO, ALICE
The Children Stay. *The New Yorker,*
December 22 and 29.

NATTEL, LILIAN
The Stranger in the Woods.
Fiddlehead, 193.
NEVAI, LUCIA
Stepmen. *Zoetrope,* Vol. 1, No. 2.
NOEL, KATHARINE
Visits. *Gulf Coast,* Vol. 9, No. 1.
NOVAKOVICH, JOSIP
Bruno. *Kenyon Review.* Vol. 20, No. 1.
Crimson. *Manoa,* Vol. 9, No. 2.

OATES, JOYCE CAROL
Faithless. *Kenyon Review,* Vol. 19,
No. 1.
Ugly Girl. *Paris Review,* 143.
OFFUTT, CHRIS
Barred Owl. *DoubleTake,* Winter.

PHILLIPS, JAYNE ANNE
Age of Wonders. *DoubleTake,* Winter.
POWELL, PADGETT
Two Boys. *Harper's Magazine,* April.
PROULX, ANNIE
Brokeback Mountain. *The New
Yorker,* October 1.
PULLINGER, KATE
The Visits Room. *Gargoyle,* 39–40.

RAWLEY, DONALD
Dark Hands. *American Short Fiction,*
28.
RICHARD, MARK
Memorial Day. *Oxford American,* 18.
RICHARD, NANCY
The Order of Things. *Shenandoah,*
Vol. 47, No. 2.
ROBINSON, J. JILL
Who Says Love Isn't Love?
Fiddlehead, 190.

SCOTT, JOANNA
Worry. *Salmagundi,* 112.
SCHWARZCHILD, EDWARD L.
Open Heart. *River Styx,* 48.
SECREAST, DONALD
The Sins of Summer. *Oxford
American,* 17.

Editorial Addresses of American and Canadian Magazines Publishing Short Stories

When available, the annual subscription rate and the name of the editor follow the address.

African American Review
Stalker Hall 212
Indiana State University
Terre Haute, IN 47809
$24, Joe Weixlmann

Agni Review
Creative Writing Department
Boston University
236 Bay State Road
Boston, MA 02115
$12, Askold Melnyczuk

Alaska Quarterly Review
Department of English
University of Alaska
3211 Providence Drive
Anchorage, AK 99508
$8, Ronald Spatz

Alfred Hitchcock's Mystery Magazine
1540 Broadway
New York, NY 10036
$34.97, Cathleen Jordan

American Letters and Commentary
Suite 56

850 Park Avenue
New York, NY 10021
$5, Jeanne Beaumont, Anna Rabinowitz

American Literary Review
University of North Texas
P.O. Box 13615
Denton, TX 76203
$15, Lee Martin

American Short Fiction
Parlin 108
Department of English
University of Texas at Austin
Austin, TX 78712-1164
$24, Joseph Krupa

American Voice
332 West Broadway
Louisville, KY 40202
$15, Sallie Bingham, Frederick Smock

Analog Science Fiction/Science Fact
1540 Broadway
New York, NY 10036
$34.95, Stanley Schmidt

Another Chicago Magazine
Left Field Press
3709 North Kenmore
Chicago, IL 60613
$8, Sharon Solwitz

Antietam Review
82 West Washington Street
Hagerstown, MD 21740
$5, Suzanne Kass

Antioch Review
P.O. Box 148
Yellow Springs, OH 45387
$35, Robert S. Fogarty

Apalachee Quarterly
P.O. Box 20106
Tallahassee, FL 32316
$15, Barbara Hamby

Appalachian Heritage
Berea College
Berea, KY 40404
$18, Sidney Saylor Farr

Arkansas Review
Dept. of English and Philosophy
P.O. Box 1890
Arkansas State University
Stae University, AR 72467
$20, Norman Lavers

Ascent
English Dept.
901 8th St.
Moorehead, MN 56562
$9, W. Scott Olsen

Atlantic Monthly
77 N. Washington Street
Boston, MA 02114
$15.94, C. Michael Curtis

Baltimore Review
P.O. Box 410
Riderwood, MD 21139
Barbara Westwood Diehl

Bananafish
P.O. Box 381332

Cambridge, MA 02238-1332
Robin Lippincott

Bellingham Review
MS 9053
Western Washington University
Bellingham, WA 98225
$10, Robin Hemly

Baffler
P.O. Box 378293
Chicago, IL 60637
$20, Thomas Frank, Keith White

Bellowing Ark
P.O. Box 45637
Seattle, WA 98145
$15, Robert R. Ward

Beloit Fiction Journal
Beloit College
P.O. Box 11
Beloit, WI 53511
$9, Fred Burwell

Big Sky Journal
P.O. Box 1069
Bozeman, MT 59771-1069
$22, Allen Jones, Brian Baise

Black Warrior Review
P.O. Box 2936
Tuscaloosa, AL 35487-2936
$14, Christopher Chambers

Blood & Aphorisms
P.O. Box 702
Toronto, Ontario
M5S ZY4 Canada
$18, Michelle Alfano, Dennis Black

BOMB
New Art Publications
10th floor
594 Broadway
New York, NY 10012
$18, Betsy Sussler

Border Crossings
Y300-393 Portage Avenue
Winnipeg, Manitoba

R3B 3H6 Canada
$23, *Meeka Walsh*

Boston Book Review
30 Brattle Street
Cambridge, MA 02138
$24, *Theoharis Constantine*

Boston Review
Building E53
Room 407
Cambridge, MA 02139
$15, *editorial board*

Bottomfish
DeAnza College
21250 Stevens Creek Blvd.
Cupertino, CA 95014
$5, *David Denny*

Boulevard
4579 Laclede Avenue #332
St. Louis, MO 63108
$12, *Richard Burgin*

Briar Cliff Review
3303 Rebecca Street
P.O. Box 2100
Sioux City, IA 51104-2100
$4, *Phil Hey*

Bridges
P.O. Box 24839
Eugene, OR 97402
$15, *Clare Kinberg*

The Bridge
14050 Vernon Street
Oak Park, MI 48237
$8, *Helen Zucker*

BUZZ
11835 West Olympic Blvd.
Suite 450
Los Angeles, CA 90064
$14.95, *Renee Vogel*

Callaloo
Dept. of English
Wilson Hall
University of Virginia

Charlottesville, VA 22903
$35, *Charles H. Rowell*

Calyx
P.O. Box B
Corvallis, OR 97339
$18, *Margarita Donnelly*

Canadian Fiction
Box 946, Station F
Toronto, Ontario
M4Y 2N9 Canada
$34.24, *Geoffrey Hancock*

Capilano Review
Capilano College
2055 Purcell Way
North Vancouver,
British Columbia
V7J 3H5 Canada
$25, *Robert Sherrin*

Carolina Quarterly
Greenlaw Hall 066A
University of North Carolina
Chapel Hill, NC 27514
$10, *Shannon Wooden*

Century
P.O. Box 150510
Brooklyn, NY 11215-0510
$33, *Robert J. Killheffer*

Chariton Review
Division of Language & Literature
Northeast Missouri State University
Kirksville, MO 63501
$9, *Jim Barnes*

Chattahoochee Review
DeKalb Community College
2101 Womack Road
Dunwoody, GA 30338-4497
$15, *Lamar York*

Chelsea
P.O. Box 773
Cooper Station
New York, NY 10276
$13, *Richard Foerster*

Chicago Review
5801 South Kenwood
University of Chicago
Chicago, IL 60637
$18, Andrew Rathman

Cimarron Review
205 Morrill Hall
Oklahoma State University
Stillwater, OK 74078-0135
$12, Gordon Weaver

Cities and Roads
P.O. Box 10886
Greensboro, NC 27404
$15.75, Tom Kealey

Clackamas Literary Review
196 South Molalla Ave.
Oregon City, OR 97045
$6, Jeff Knorr and Tim Schell

Colorado Review
Department of English
Colorado State University
Fort Collins, CO 80523
$18, David Milofsky

Columbia
415 Dodge
Columbia University
New York, NY 10027
$13, Gregory Cowles

Commentary
165 East 56th Street
New York, NY 10022
$39, Neal Kozodoy

Confrontation
English Department
C. W. Post College of Long Island
    University
Greenvale, NY 11548
$8, Martin Tucker

Conjunctions
21 East 10th St.
#3E
New York, NY 10003
$18, Bradford Morrow

Cream City Review
University of Wisconsin, Milwaukee
P.O. Box 413
Milwaukee, WI 53201
$12, Andrew Rivera

Crescent Review
P.O. Box 15069
Chevy Chase, MD 20825-5069
$21, J. Timothy Holland

Crucible
Barton College
College Station
Wilson, NC 27893
Terence Grimes

Cut Bank
Department of English
University of Montana
Missoula, MT 59812
$12, Marcus Hersh and Amanda E. Ward

Denver Quarterly
University of Denver
Denver, CO 80208
$25, Bin Ramke

Descant
P.O. Box 314, Station P
Toronto, Ontario
M5S 2S8 Canada
$25, Karen Mulhallen

Descant
Department of English
Texas Christian University
Box 32872
Fort Worth, TX 76129
$12, Neal Easterbrook

DoubleTake
Center for Documentary Studies
1317 West Pettigrew Street
Durham, NC 27705
$32, Robert Coles, Alex Harris

Eagle's Flight
P.O. Box 832
Granite, OK 73547
$5, Rekha Kulkarni

Elle
1633 Broadway
New York, NY 10019
$24, Patricia Towers

Epoch
251 Goldwin Smith Hall
Cornell University
Ithaca, NY 14853-3201
$11, Michael Koch

Esquire
250 West 55th Street
New York, NY 10019
$17.94, Rust Hills,
   Erika Mansourian

Eureka Literary Magazine
Eureka College
P.O. Box 280
Eureka, IL 61530
$10, Loren Logsdon

event
c/o Douglas College
P.O. Box 2503
New Westminster, British Columbia
V3L 5B2 Canada
$15, Christine Dewar

Farmer's Market
Elgin Community College
1700 Spartan Drive
Elgin, IL 60123
$10, Rachael Tecza

Fiction
Fiction, Inc.
Department of English
The City College of New York
New York, NY
$7, Mark Mirsky

Fiction International
Department of English and
   Comparative Literature
San Diego State University
San Diego, CA 92182
$14, Harold Jaffe, Larry McCaffery

Fiddlehead
UNB Box 4400
University of New Brunswick
Fredericton, New Brunswick
E3B 5A3 Canada
$16, Don McKay, Bill Gaston

Fish Stories
5412 N. Clark, South Suite
Chicago, IL 60640
$10.95, Amy G. Davis

Five Points
Department of English
Georgia State University
University Plaza
Atlanta, GA 30303-3083
$15, Pam Durban

Florida Review
Department of English
University of Central Florida
P.O. Box 25000
Orlando, FL 32816
$7, Russell Kesler

Folio
Department of Literature
The American University
Washington, D.C. 20016
$10, Cynthia Lollar

Fourteen Hills
Department of Creative Writing
San Francisco State University
1600 Holloway Avenue
San Francisco, CA 94132
$12, Amanda Kim

Gargoyle
Paycock Press
c/o Atticus Books and Music
1508 U Street, NW
Washington, DC 20009
$20, Richard Peabody and Lucinda
   Ebersole

Geist
1062 Homer Street #100
Vancouver, Canada

V6B 2W9
$20, Stephen Osborne

Genre
7080 Hollywood Blvd.
Suite 1104
Hollywood, CA 90028
$19.95, Ronald Mark Kraft

Georgetown Review
400 East College Street, Box 227
Georgetown, KY 40324
$10, John Fulmer

Georgia Review
University of Georgia
Athens, GA 30602
$18, Stanley W. Lindberg

Gettysburg Review
Gettysburg College
Gettysburg, PA 17325
$24, Peter Stitt

Glimmer Train Stories
812 SW Washington Street
Suite 1205
Portland, OR 97205
$29, Susan Burmeister, Linda Davies

Good Housekeeping
959 Eighth Avenue
New York, NY 10019
$17.97, Arleen L. Quarfoot

GQ
350 Madison Avenue
New York, NY 10017
$19.97, Ilena Silverman

Grain
Box 1154
Regina, Saskatchewan
S4P 3B4 Canada
$23.95, Connie Gault

Grand Street
131 Varick Street
New York, NY 10013
$40, Jean Stein

Granta
2-3 Hanover Yard

Noel Road Islington
London, England N1 8BE
$32, Ian Jack

Great River Review
211 West 7th Street
Winona, MN 55987
$12, Pamela Davies

Green Hills Literary Lantern
North Central Missouri College
Box 375
Trenton, MO 64683
$5.95, Jack Smith

Green Mountain Review
Box A 58
Johnson State College
Johnson, VT 05656
$12, Tony Whedon

Greensboro Review
Department of English
University of North Carolina
Greensboro, NC 27412
$8, Jim Clark

Gulf Coast
Department of English
University of Houston
4800 Calhoun Road
Houston, TX 77204-3012
$22, Derrick Burleson

Gulf Stream
English Department
Florida International University
North Miami Campus
North Miami, FL 33181
$4, Lynne Barrett, John Dufresne

G.W. Review
Box 20B, The Marvin Center
800 21st Street
Washington, DC 20052
$9, Jane A. Roh

Habersham Review
Piedmont College
Demorest, GA 30535-0010
$12, Frank Gannon

Harper's Magazine
666 Broadway
New York, NY 10012
$18, Lewis H. Lapham

Harvard Review
Poetry Room
Harvard College Library
Cambridge, MA 02138
$12, Stratis Haviaris

Hawaii Review
University of Hawaii
Department of English
1733 Donagho Road
Honolulu, HI 96822
$25, Lisa Chang

Hayden's Ferry Review
Box 871502
Arizona State University
Tempe, AZ 85287-1502
$10, Melissa Olson, Verania White

High Plains Literary Review
180 Adams Street, Suite 250
Denver, CO 80206
$20, Robert O. Greer, Jr.

HR
1733 Donagho Road
University of Hawaii, Manoa
Honolulu, HI 96822
$25, Robert Sean Macbeth, S. Gonzalez

Hudson Review
684 Park Avenue
New York, NY 10021
$24, Paula Deitz, Frederick Morgan

Image
323 S. Broad Street
P.O. Box 674
Kendall Square, PA 19348
$30, Gregory Wolfe

Ink
P.O. Box 52558
St. George Postal Outlet
264 Bloor Street
Toronto, Ontario

M5S 1Vo Canada
$8, John Degan

International Quarterly
P.O. Box 10521
Tallahassee, FL 32302
$22, Catherine Reid, Virgil Suarez

Iowa Review
Department of English
University of Iowa
308 EPB
Iowa City, IA 52242
$18, David Hamilton

Iris
Box 323 HSC
University of Virginia
Charlottesville, VA 22908
$17, Kristen Staby Rembold

Italian Americana
University of Rhode Island
College of Continuing Education
199 Promenade Street
Providence, RI 02908
$15, Carol Bonomo Albright

Jewish Currents
22 East 17th Street, Suite 601
New York, NY 10003-3272
$20, editorial board

Journal
Department of English
Ohio State University
164 West 17th Avenue
Columbus, OH 43210
$8, Kathy Fagan, Michelle Herman

Kairos
Dundurn P.O. Box 33553
Hamilton, Ontario
L8P 4X4
Canada
$12.95, R.W. Megens

Kalliope
Florida Community College
3939 Roosevelt Blvd.
Jacksonville, FL 32205
$12.50, Mary Sue Koeppel

Karamu
English Department
Eastern Illinois University
Charleston, IL 61920
$6.50, Peggy L. Brayfield

Kenyon Review
Kenyon College
Gambier, OH 43022
$22, Marilyn Hacker

Kiosk
English Department
306 Clemens Hall
SUNY
Buffalo, NY 14260
$6, Lia Vella

Laurel Review
Department of English
Northwest Missouri State University
Maryville, MO 64468
*$8, Craig Goad, David Slater, William
    Trowbridge*

Lilith
250 West 57th Street
New York, NY 10107
$16, Susan Weidman

Literal Latté
Suite 240
61 East 8th Street
New York, NY 10003
$25, Jenine Gordon

Literary Review
Fairleigh Dickinson University
285 Madison Avenue
Madison, NJ 07940
$18, Walter Cummins

Louisiana Literature
Box 792
Southeastern Louisiana University
Hammond, LA 70402
$10, David Hanson

Lynx Eye
1880 Hill Drive
Los Angeles, CA 90041
$20, Pam McCully, Kathryn Morrison

Madison Review
University of Wisconsin
Department of English
H. C. White Hall
600 North Park Street
Madison, WI 53706
$15, Joley Wood

Malahat Review
University of Victoria
P.O. Box 1700
Victoria, British Columbia
V8W 2Y2 Canada
$15, Derk Wynand

Manoa
English Department
University of Hawaii
Honolulu, HI 96822
$18, Ian MacMillan

Many Mountains Moving
2525 Arapahoe Road
Suite E4-309
Boulder, CO 80302
$18, Naomi Horii, Marilyn Krysl

Massachusetts Review
Memorial Hall
University of Massachusetts
Amherst, MA 01003
*$15, Jules Chametsky, Mary Heath, Paul
    Jenkins*

Matrix
1455 de Paisonneuve Blvd. West
Suite LB-514-8
Montreal, Quebec
H3G IM8 Canada
$15, Terence Byrnes

Michigan Quarterly Review
3032 Rackham Building
University of Michigan
Ann Arbor, MI 48109
$18, Laurence Goldstein

Mid-American Review
Department of English
Bowling Green State University

Bowling Green, OH 43403
$12, Rebecca Meacham

Midstream
110 East 59th Street
New York, NY 10022
$21, Joel Carmichael

Midwesterner
Big Shoulders Publishing
343 S. Dearborn Street
Suite 610
Chicago, IL 60604
(has ceased publication)

Minnesota Review
Department of English
State University of New York
Stony Brook, NY 11794-5350
$12, Jeffrey Williams

Mississippi Review
University of Southern Mississippi
Southern Station, P.O. Box 5144
Hattiesburg, MS 39406-5144
$15, Frederick Barthelme

Missouri Review
1507 Hillcrest Hall
University of Missouri
Columbia, MO 65211
$19, Speer Morgan

Modern Words
350 Bay Street #100
San Francisco, CA 94133
$20, Garland Richard Kyle

Ms.
230 Park Avenue
New York, NY 10169
$45, Marcia Ann Gillespie

Nassau Review
English Department
Nassau Community College
One Education Drive
Garden City, NY 11530-6793
Paul A. Doyle

Nebraska Review
Writer's Workshop, ASH 212

University of Nebraska
Omaha, NE 68182-0324
$10, Art Homer, Richard Duggin

New Delta Review
Creative Writing Program
English Department
Louisiana State University
Baton Rouge, LA 70803
$7, Mindy Meek

New England Review
Middlebury College
Middlebury, VT 05753
$23, Stephen Donadio

New Letters
University of Missouri
4216 Rockhill Road
Kansas City, MO 64110
$17, James McKinley

New Orleans Review
P.O. Box 195
Loyola University
New Orleans, LA 70118
$18, Ralph Adamo

New Quarterly
English Language Proficiency
 Programme
University of Waterloo
Waterloo, Ontario
N2L 3G1 Canada
*$11.50, Peter Hinchcliffe,
 Kim Jernigan, Mary Merikle,
 Linda Kenyon*

New Renaissance
9 Heath Road
Arlington, MA 02174
$11.50, Louise T. Reynolds

New Yorker
25 West 43rd Street
New York, NY 10036
$32, Tina Brown

Nightsun
School of Arts and Humanities
Dept. of English
Frostburg State University

Frostburg, MD 21532-1099
$5, Brad Barkley

Nimrod
Arts and Humanities Council
  of Tulsa
2210 South Main Street
Tulsa, OK 74114
$15, Francine Ringold

North American Review
University of Northern Iowa
1222 West 27th Street
Cedar Falls, IA 50614
$18, Robley Wilson, Jr.

North Dakota Quarterly
University of North Dakota
P.O. Box 8237
Grand Forks, ND 58202
$25, William Borden

Northeast Corridor
Department of English
Beaver College
450 S. Easton Road
Glenside, PA 19038-3295
$10, Susan Balee

Northwest Review
369 PLC
University of Oregon
Eugene, OR 97403
$20, John Witte

Notre Dame Review
Department of English
University of Notre Dame
Notre Dame, IN 46556
$15, Valerie Sayers

Oasis
P.O. Box 626
Largo, FL 34649-0626
$22, Neal Storrs

Ohio Review
Ellis Hall
Ohio University
Athens, OH 45701-2979
$16, Wayne Dodd

Ontario Review
9 Honey Brook Drive
Princeton, NJ 08540
$12, Raymond J. Smith

Onthebus
Bombshelter Press
6684 Colgate Avenue
Los Angeles, CA 90048
$28, Jack Grapes

Open City
225 Lafayette Street
Suite 1114
New York, NY 10012
$24, Thomas Beller, Daniel Pinchbeck

Other Voices
University of Illinois at Chicago
Department of English
(M/C 162) 601 South Morgan Street
Chicago, IL 60680
$20, Lois Hauselman

Oxford American
115½ South Lamar
Oxford, MS 38655
$16, Marc Smirnoff

Oyster Boy Review
103B Hanna Street
Carrboro, NC 27510
$12, Chad Driscoll, Damon Suave

Paris Review
541 East 72nd Street
New York, NY 10021
$34, George Plimpton

Parting Gifts
3413 Wilshire Dr.
Greensboro, NC 27408-2923
Robert Bixby

Partisan Review
236 Bay State Road
Boston, MA 02215
$22, William Phillips

Playboy
Playboy Building

919 North Michigan Avenue
Chicago, IL 60611
$24, Alice K. Turner

Pleiades
Department of English
Central Missouri State University
P.O. Box 800
Warrensburg, MO 64093
$10, R. M. Kinder

Ploughshares
Emerson College
100 Beacon Street
Boston, MA 02116
$21, Don Lee

Porcupine
P.O. Box 259
Cedarburg, WI 53012
$13.95, group editorship

Potpourri
P.O. Box 8278
Prairie Village, KS 66208
$12, Polly W. Swafford

Pottersfield Portfolio
The Gatsby Press
5280 Green Street, P.O. Box 27094
Halifax, Nova Scotia
B3H 4M8 Canada
$18, Ian Colford

Prairie Fire
423-100 Arthur Street
Winnipeg, Manitoba
R3B 1H3 Canada
$24, Andris Taskans

Prairie Schooner
201 Andrews Hall
University of Nebraska
Lincoln, NE 68588-0334
$22, Hilda Raz

Press
125 West 72nd Street
Suite 3-M
New York, NY 10023
$24, Daniel Roberts

Prism International
Department of Creative Writing
University of British Columbia
Vancouver, British Columbia
V6T 1W5 Canada
$16, Ian Cockfield

Provincetown Arts
650 Commercial Street
Provincetown MA 02657
$10, Christopher Busa

Puerto del Sol
P.O. Box 3E
Department of English
New Mexico State University
Las Cruces, NM 88003
$10, Kevin McIlvoy

Quarry Magazine
P.O. Box 1061
Kingston, Ontario
K7L 4Y5 Canada
$22, Mary Cameron

Quarterly West
312 Olpin Union
University of Utah
Salt Lake City, UT 84112
$12, Margot Schilpp

RE:AL
School of Liberal Arts
Stephen F. Austin State University
P.O. Box 13007
SFA Station
Nacogdoches, TX 75962
$15, Dale Hearell

Redbook
959 Eighth Avenue
New York, NY 10017
$11.97, Dawn Raffel

Riversedge
Dept. of English
University of Texas, Pan-American
1201 West University Drive, CAS 266
Edinburg, TX 78539-2999
$12, Dorey Schmidt

River Styx
Big River Association
14 South Euclid
St. Louis, MO 63108
$20, Richard Newman

Room of One's Own
P.O. Box 46160
Station D
Vancouver, British Columbia
V6J 5G5 Canada
$22, collective

Salamander
48 Ackers Avenue
Brookline, MA 02146
$12, Jennifer Barber

Salmagundi
Skidmore College
Saratoga Springs, NY 12866
$18, Robert Boyers

San Jose Studies
c/o English Department
San Jose State University
One Washington Square
San Jose, CA 95192
$12, John Engell, D. Mesher

Santa Monica Review
Center for the Humanities
Santa Monica College
1900 Pico Boulevard
Santa Monica, CA 90405
$12, Lee Montgomery

Saturday Night
Suite 400
184 Front Street E
Toronto, Ontario
M5V 2Z4 Canada
$26.45, Robert Weaver

Seattle Review
Padelford Hall, GN-30
University of Washington
Seattle, WA 98195
$9, Charles Johnson

Seventeen
850 Third Avenue

New York, NY 10022
$14.95, Susan Brenna

Sewanee Review
University of the South
Sewanee, TN 37375-4009
$18, George Core

Shenandoah
Washington and Lee University
P.O. Box 722
Lexington, VA 24450
$15, R. T. Smith

The Slate
Box 58119
Minneapolis, MN 55458
*$15, Chris Dall, Rachel Fulkerson,
   Jessica Morris*

Sonora Review
Department of English
University of Arizona
Tucson, AZ 85721
$12, Hannah Hass

So to Speak
4400 University Drive
George Mason University
Fairfax, VA 22030-444
$7, Nolde Alexius

South Carolina Review
Department of English
Clemson University
Clemson, SC 29634-1503
$10, Frank Day, Carol Johnston

South Dakota Review
University of South Dakota
P.O. Box 111 University Exchange
Vermillion, SD 57069
$15, Brian Bedard

Southern Exposure
P.O. Box 531
Durham, NC 27702
$24, Jordan Green

Southern Humanities Review
9088 Haley Center
Auburn University

Auburn, AL 36849
$15, Dan R. Latimer, Virginia M.
Kouidis

Southern Review
43 Allen Hall
Louisiana State University
Baton Rouge, LA 70803
$20, James Olney, Dave Smith

Southwest Review
Southern Methodist University
P.O. Box 4374
Dallas, TX 75275
$20, Willard Spiegelman

Spec-lit
Columbia College Chicago
600 South Michigan Ave.
Chicago, IL 60605
$6.95, Phyllis Eisenstein

Story
1507 Dana Avenue
Cincinnati, OH 45207
$22, Lois Rosenthal

Story Head
1340 W. Granville
Chicago, IL 60660
$16, Mike Brehn, Joe Peterson

Story Quarterly
P.O. Box 1416
Northbrook, IL 60065
$12, Margaret Barrett, Anne Brashler,
Diane Williams

Sun
107 North Roberson Street
Chapel Hill, NC 27516
$30, Sy Safransky

Sun Dog
The Southeast Review
406 Williams Building
Florida State University
Tallahassee, FL 32306-1036
$8, Russ Franklin

Sycamore Review
Department of English

Heavilon Hall
Purdue University
West Lafayette, IN 47907
$10, Jon Briner

Talking River Review
Division of Literature
Lewis-Clark State College
500 8th Avenue
Lewiston, ID 83501
$10, group editorship

Teacup
P.O. Box 8665
Hellgate Station
Missoula, MT 59807
$9, group editorship

Thema
Box 74109
Metairie, LA 70053-4109
$16, Virginia Howard

Thin Air
P.O. Box 23549
Flagstaff, AZ 86002
$9, Jeff Huebner,
Rob Morrill

Third Coast
Dept. of English
Western Michigan University
Kalamazoo, MI 49008-5092
$11, Heidi Bell, Kellie Wells

13th Moon
Department of English
SUNY at Albany
Albany, NY 12222
$18, Judith Emlyn Johnson

32 Pages
Rain Crow Publishing
101-308 Andrew Place
West Lafayette, IN 47906-3932
$10, Michael S. Manley

Threepenny Review
P.O. Box 9131
Berkeley, CA 94709
$16, Wendy Lesser

Tikkun
5100 Leona Street
Oakland, CA 94619
$36, Michael Lerner

Trafika
P.O. Box 250822
New York, NY 10025-1536
$35, Scott Lewis, Krister Swartz, Jeffrey
Young

Treasure House
Suite 3A
1106 Oak Hill Avenue
Hagerstown, MD 21742
$9, J. G. Wolfensberger

TriQuarterly
2020 Ridge Avenue
Northwestern University
Evanston, IL 60208
$24, Susan Firestone Hahn

University of Windsor Review
Department of English
University of Windsor
Windsor, Ontario
N9B 3P4 Canada
$19.95, Alistair MacLeod

Unmuzzled Ox
105 Hudson Street
New York, NY 10013
$8.95, Michael Andre

Urbanus
P.O. Box 192561
San Francisco, CA 94119
$8, Peter Drizhal

Vignette
4150-G Riverside Drive
Toluca Lake, CA 91505
$29, Dawn Baille, Deborah Clark

Virginia Quarterly Review
One West Range
Charlottesville, VA 22903
$18, Staige D. Blackford

Wascana Review
English Department

University of Regina
Regina, Saskatchewan
S4S 0A2 Canada
$10, J. Shami

Washington Square
Creative Writing Program
New York University
19 University Place, 2nd floor
New York, NY 10003-4556
$6, Helen Ellis

Weber Studies
Weber State College
Ogden, UT 84408
$10, Neila Seshachari

Wellspring
770 Tonkawa Road
Long Lake, MN 55356
$8, Meg Miller

West Branch
Department of English
Bucknell University
Lewisburg, PA 17837
$7, Robert Love Taylor,
Karl Patten

Western Humanities Review
University of Utah
Salt Lake City, UT 84112
$20, Barry Weller

What?
P.O. Box 1669
Hollywood, CA 90078
$12, collective

Whetstone
Barrington Area Arts Council
P.O. Box 1266
Barrington, IL 60011
$7.25, Sandra Berris, Marsha Portnoy,
Jean Tolle

Wind
RFD Route 1
P.O. Box 809K
Pikeville, KY 41501
$7, Quentin R. Howard

Windsor Review
Department of English
University of Windsor
Windsor, Ontario
N9B 3P4 Canada
$19.95, Alistair MacLeod

Witness
Oakland Community College
Orchard Ridge Campus
27055 Orchard Lake Road
Farmington Hills, MI 48334
$12, Peter Stine

Worcester Review
6 Chatham Street
Worcester, MA 01690
$10, Rodger Martin

Wordwrights
Argonne Hotel
1620 Argonne Place NW
Washington, DC 20009
$10, collective

Xavier Review
Xavier University
Box 110C
New Orleans, LA 70125
$10, Thomas Bonner, Jr.

Yale Review
1902A Yale Station
New Haven, CT 06520
$27, J. D. McClatchy

Yalobusha Review
P.O. Box 186
University, MS 38677-0186
$6, Jill E. Grogg

Yankee
Yankee Publishing, Inc.
Dublin, NH 03444
$22, Judson D. Hale, Sr.

Yemassee
Department of English
University of South Carolina
Columbia, SC 29208
$15, Stephen Owen

Zoetrope
AZX Publications
126 Fifth Avenue, Suite 300
New York, NY 10011
Adrienne Brodeur

ZYZZYVA
41 Sutter Street, Suite 1400
San Francisco, CA 94104
$28, Howard Junker